NEW ATLANTIS
FLAT EARTH BOOK TWO
BY
BRENT GOLEMBIEWSKI

Edited by: JLMG
Cover Design: Tom Edwards Design
Ailerons Font Design: Adilson Gonzales

ISBN: 978-1-7348875-5-6 (eBook)
ISBN: 978-1-7348875-4-9 (Paperback)
ISBN: 978-1-7348875-7-0 (Hardcover)
ISBN: 978-1-7348875-6-3 (Audiobook)

1st Edition

For more information, e-mail: babajagapublishing@gmail.com

For my two boys and loving wife, thanks for the inspiration everyday

"We are going to the moon, that is not very far. Man has so much farther to go within himself."

—Anaïs Ni

PROLOGUE

In the starry darkness of space, she watched the ship drift out of sight as it headed toward the sun. Oxygen levels read 20%. Her body tumbled end over end as the stars zipped by; the sun came and went. She tapped a button in her glove.

"Thruster boots depleted," the suit replied.

Her eyes tried to focus, exploring through the glass shell in front of her. For a moment, she thought to swing her arms to stop the endless spinning, but knew better and tossed it out of her mind. Her body was trained for such stress, yet she was beginning to feel dizzy. She tried to focus on the glass screen; it didn't help.

"Oxygen 15%" displayed on her visor. She saw the sun come into view once more, the ship was all but a speck in the distance. She hoped it would hit its mark, she hoped Earth would survive, she hoped her love would survive. She took a deep breath, the oxygen count went down 2%. It was inevitable, she would soon be out of air. She contemplated taking her helmet off, it would be quicker...freezing that was...maybe less pain. *No. Soldiers don't quit, soldiers fight to the end, soldiers return with honor.* She closed her eyes, thinking of the warm bed at the resort. His chest rising and falling under her cheek, his heart pounding in her ear.

"Oxygen 5%."

Time was running out for a miracle, she began to accept the inevitable.

I

"Oxygen critical! Critical! Critical!" the suit screamed.

She ignored it a moment. "Suppress alerts," she commanded, wanting peace in her final moments.

She opened her eyes, demanding the suit switch off all internal visuals. The world...the universe, kept spinning. She manipulated her head, scanning for the Earth; it was still there, as alive as ever. It was in good hands, he would take care of it. The gentle hiss of the oxygen system tapered off, silence.

"Bless it!" Just because she accepted the inevitable, didn't mean she welcomed it.

Her eyes, frozen, focused on the Earth. Her tongue felt warm, eyes gritty. Closing them, sleep overtook her. She opened her eyes to a beautiful sunrise, an ocean sprawled out in front of her, the warm sand covered her feet. She noticed a gentle breeze blowing some granules over her ankles, tickling them a bit. She smiled and looked back at the sunrise, the glowing ball climbing above the horizon, its red hue flickering on the blue water. Waves broke gently into the shore, washing the sand back and forth. She raised her hands and watched them, rotating them from front to back. *Where was she? How did she get there?* A blaster was strapped to each thigh. She slid each out, lifting them for examination. The wind began to pick up, more sand blew over her. She glanced up, movement caught her attention. Something was stirring in the water. The sun shone back at her, obscuring her view. She squinted, trying to see. It wasn't just one thing moving, but multiple objects emerging from the sea. The shadowy figures grew from the water, their shapes resembled people. She covered her face from the wind which continued its attack on her skin, now growing in intensity. Light came from one of the figures, a sound hit her ear. She remembered that sound. Instinctively, she raised the blasters, aiming at the objects. A flash of light hit her chest, she gasped for air crumbling into a heap.

Beep, beep, beep. A white ceiling stared back at her. She drew in a breath as if she hadn't breathed in ages. Her vision was fuzzy, she tried to focus on the ceiling, the details once indistinguishable now became apparent. She felt a warm small hand touch hers.

"How are you feeling?"

The voice, it was familiar, but how...how did she get there? Where was she? She turned her head toward the voice. A small brunette stood there holding a tablet, she tried to focus.

"V?" she asked, as if not fully awake.

V stood there smiling. Ariel studied her for a moment, attempting to figure out what had transpired after she closed her eyes. She rubbed her forehead and sat up.

"What happened?" she finally let out.

"You were clinically dead for approximately nine minutes, much longer and we wouldn't have been able to bring you back."

Ariel examined her hands. "We?"

"Zane's here, I picked him up first."

The room rocked, alarms went off. The sound was familiar to her. *We must be on a medical barge.* The sound rattled the room again. V blinked as she stumbled back, catching the wall with her hand. Ariel slipped off the table, her space suit partially still on, the top cut off exposing the elastic undershirt.

She reached for V. "Where are we? What's going on?"

"We're heading to Atlantis, found some data there you might want. Seems TK left behind some presents for us. That's what Zane called them."

Ariel stumbled to the door, still woozy from the near death experience. The shaking didn't help. V slung Ariel's arm around her shoulders and helped her out the door. The ship continued to rock from what felt like cannon blasts. *Only Atlantis has that kind of firepower.* V continued helping her through the ship to the bridge. The door hissed open, the whole front of the ship opened up. The screens wrapped around all four sides, even the floor was lined with them, giving passengers the appearance they were walking out in space. In front was the Moon, Atlantis. Flashes appeared on the surface, blasts trailing up toward them. Ariel stumbled to one of the seats and fixated on the controls.

"It's alive! Glad you're not dead, kid. Any suggestions?"

Ariel grinned. Punching a few keys on the control panel, Zane pulled up the shield percentage for her.

"Yeah, I see it. Not helping right now, just give me

a minute."

She continued pecking away. "This is why you need a hacker on the team," she said under her breath, "Preferably one not on the take with TK."

The shield read 50% and dwindling, Ariel pushed it down out of the way.

"Anything I can do?" Zane asked.

"Can you tell me why they're firing on us?"

Zane pulled a screen up and sent it over to Ariel. It read, "Defense protocol Ares initiated, secure lockdown commencing." Ariel tried to figure out what was going on, she wasn't aware of such a protocol. Must have been something TK left behind to ensure no one did what they were trying to do. The shields kept flashing as the cannons hit, the ship rocked back and forth.

"Ha!" Ariel exclaimed.

Two strokes of the keys and a door in one of the craters opened, the incoming ordinance continued.

"Accelerate, Zane. Take us to that docking bay."

Zane wasted no time pushing the thrusters to full open. The ship accelerated and descended down to the surface of the Moon. V had taken a seat during the whole ordeal and was gripping tightly to the seat, she didn't really like space travel. Ariel glanced over at her, giving her a reassuring smile hoping to calm her nerves. V sent a pursed smile back, clenching her jaw. The ship reached the opening, the shaking of the ship ceased; they were too close for the cannons to lock onto anymore. Zane slowed the ship down as they entered the tunnel, then began the landing sequence.

He stood up and tossed a rifle at Ariel.

She caught it, checked the fusion cell, then quirked an eyebrow at him. "Expecting a welcoming party?"

"Already had one."

Zane was right, the Moon's defense cannons had given them a nice welcome. She was hoping there would be less effort needed to move around inside Atlantis. There wasn't a soul or mediator to be seen on the approach, but TK was crafty, they needed to keep their guard up.

The ramp opened. Zane and Ariel waited in tactical positions, knees bent, rifles aimed ready to fire. V was safely well behind them. They needed her in more ways than one. As the ramp hit the floor, they shuffled their way out, scanning from side to side. Ariel's foot hit the tarmac, she paused focusing on Zane. She slung the rifle onto her back, slipped the blaster from the holster placed on her thigh. *The smaller blaster would be better for tight quarters.*

"Looks clear to me."

Ariel was about to say the same thing. It was eerily silent, no sign of movement or enemy activity. She stepped forward gingerly, Zane mirroring her movements, scanning their surroundings. Nothing.

"Looks like we're good, but keep your guard up," Ariel said.

Zane nodded. She didn't need to tell him his job, but in moments like these he always let her take point.

She waved for V to follow, the tiny doctor trotted

down the ramp and moved in close. Ariel looked back hearing her footsteps.

"You said you had something for me?"

"Yes, it's back in my lab. I stumbled across it while I was searching for my mother's research on the machine we used on J."

Ariel leaned toward her, "What is it?"

"Better if you see it for yourself."

Ariel placed her hands on her hips squinting at Zane, her eyes drifted turning to continue into the city. Zane had landed the ship only a few blocks from V's lab making ground travel time short. Ariel and Zane were on their toes, still taking precautions, heads swiveling from side to side as they entered the building and eventually her lab. Inside, V took the lead, guiding them through a labyrinth of hallways to finally reach an old storage facility. She opened the door using a DNA scan. Ariel stepped in expecting a normal sized room, but what she found was on a much larger scale. What seemed like endless rows of airtight ten foot by ten foot boxes lined the walls. A conveyor type system seemed to stack and rotate the boxes on demand. Ariel had never been in here before. V manipulated a control panel near the entrance to the room, the boxes slid along the wall until the one she'd chosen stopped in front of them and opened. The box was lined with screens embedded to look like the wall, they flickered to life as the three of them entered.

"Data recall," V directed.

On screen, V's mother appeared, standing proud

and proper.

"Mother, explain experiment 5528ME."

V's mother paused a moment on screen then began, "Experiment 5528ME was commissioned by Dr. Arcturus. The requested prototype was to extract actual memories from one subject then place them into another. The first successful trial of extraction was patient number 248. We were able to extract memories intact and pass them on to patient 255. Dr. Arcturus classified the project and limited the production to the prototype. All records were to be destroyed. This is the only remaining copy."

Ariel's head whipped over to V, about to speak.

V lifted a finger and smiled. "Mother, was the prototype used after testing?"

"On record only once. The prototype went missing the day Dr. Arcturus went missing."

"Mother, what is the location of the prototype?"

"Unknown, though the last location was tracked to Sector 7, along with DNA from Dr. Arcturus."

CHAPTER ONE

Light reflected back into his eyes, causing him to squint. He twisted the cold steel back and forth, admiring its beauty and craftsmanship. The blade, flawless as glimmering steel, raced down to a small round hilt; his hand wrapped around a handle covered in a black fabric

J set the blade back on its stand. "Why are we here again?"

People moved about behind him, occasionally bumping his back, he was much taller than all of them. He felt more like an alien here than he ever did in Atlantis. The people spoke in strange sounds he had never heard before, the smell of fried grease filled the air.

"Arigato," Ariel said, taking a basket of fried dumplings from the shopkeeper.

"I told you. We need to meet Professor Ohmura, he knows this sector better than anyone."

"How do you know he's here?"

J had his doubts. They'd been in this sector for the past week, moving from town to town, searching for various Atlantis born professors. He was beginning to notice a pattern. To his surprise, there was a large contingent of Atlanteans who preferred Earth over their regimented moon prison. That's what J had begun to call it himself. Each person they met passed them onto another, it seemed like a veritable wild goose chase.

"Professor Akasaki was a good friend of his. He's sure to have what we need."

1

She handed him the dumpling basket, he raised it up to his nostrils and took a big whiff. He may have felt out of place, but the food almost made it worth it. He took a big bite and chewed it, savoring every second as the flavors rolled around on his tongue. J peered past his food to see a small child staring up at him.

"Konjin," the boy pointed at him.

He had no clue what that meant so he just smiled back, drool slipped out of his mouth as he hadn't finished swallowing the dumpling. The child's eyes grew large, he let out a little gasp, then spun around and ran. J felt a hand grab his, he knew it was Ariel's without looking. Her hand fit perfectly in his.

"Scaring children, I see."

"What? I just smiled at him."

"Next time just say, "Fee Fi Fo Fum"," she said in a deep voice, then snickered.

"What?"

"He called you a giant. You kill me. Never mind, this way."

She led him down an alley, away from the market and commotion. He was relieved to be away from all the people. The sound of chatter trailed off as they continued between two wooden buildings with clay tiles lining the roof. He had never seen buildings like them before. He would have loved to stop and admire them a bit more, but they had a task and, while it was a lot of travel, he just felt fortunate that mediators weren't pouring out of the walls at them. The smaller buildings morphed into larger ones as they walked. Based on the amount of windows he counted, the tallest was about 15 stories high.

"This is it."

Ariel touched her Datacle, it switched off. They stood at the base of one of the tallest buildings in the ally. J peeked past Ariel, the street wasn't much further. Two kids ran by giggling then a woman, presumably their mother, who was screaming in a high-pitched series of tones.

"Why don't I have a translator again?"

"That was your choice, remember? We could've gone to Atlantis and grabbed another one, but you opted to get going. Something about an urge to find your father."

His father. That's what they were doing in this strange place. It seemed silly to him that he'd momentarily forgotten. It was so important, yet the new sector almost completely took all of his attention. This place was such a departure from his home town, yet closer in some ways than Atlantis. He and Ariel studied the door; it was made of wood, but well-weathered and could've used a good sanding and another coat of blue paint. Ariel approached it and gave a hearty knock. J half expected her to come back with a splinter. The door opened and there stood a little old lady in a light blue robe. She was wearing glasses and fiddling with something in her hands. J peered closer. She was shuffling two small tiles with images on them.

The woman spoke to them, but he had no clue what

she was saying. He was beginning to regret his hasty decision to skip the supply run to the moon. Ariel replied. The woman's eyebrows rose up over her frames, she rocked back slightly, then paused, studying them. She spun around and headed into the shadowy building.

"Kuru, kuru," she waved her hand over her head and disappeared into the darkness.

Ariel stepped in. J stared up at the building, it seemed enormous; he hadn't seen anything that large on Earth before. He felt his arm yanked, then went blind. His eyes struggled to adapt to the dim lighting, but began to adjust, absorbing the little bit of light from the hallway he found himself in. Ariel held his hand and pulled him along. He passed multiple open doors; a few were empty, others had people in them playing with tiles. He felt Ariel stop and he glanced past her. The old woman was pointing at a staircase.

"Juugo, juugo."

Ariel thanked her with a bow, J followed suit. This he had picked up from their previous encounters. She started up the stairwell, J right behind her.

"What did she say?"

"15th floor. Hope you're ready for a workout."

It was a far departure from the fast elevators in the futuristic moon city he'd come to know, the most flights he'd ever climbed at once was four. His legs began burning after about the 5th floor, but he pushed through. *At least they weren't running.* They finally exited at the 15th floor, by which point his legs had gone numb. Exploring the hall, he found it was drastically different than the bottom floor. It was brightly lit, the floor was hardwood and glowed as if it had just been buffed, the walls were covered in wood paneling and each door adorned with frosted glass, some letting sunlight in from the room behind them. Ariel headed left.

"How do you know where you're going?"

"I don't," she replied, her eyes flashing back at him. "Gotta start somewhere."

They continued down the hall, peering into each room as they passed. They had no luck with the first couple, a storage closet, an office, but then they came to the third. The door was nearly all glass with a wooden frame, in the top center were symbols written in the foreign language. J wished he could translate them. Ariel pushed it open and walked in.

"Dr. Ohmura?" she asked into the open doorway.

J stepped in after her, he paused as he was met by a large two story room. On one side was a brick wall, the other held floor to ceiling bookcases and the back wall floor to ceiling glass-paned windows. The space had to have stretched 50 feet in both directions. Next to the brick wall sat a wooden desk much too small for the space. The floor was covered in a multitude of decorative rugs, J stepped forward his eyes feasting on the patterns. Ariel continued further into the space, still calling for the professor.

"American?" they heard come from the door behind them.

Ariel and J turned to see a man in his mid-40s wearing a grey suit and coat. He was round and much shorter than even Ariel. His head held a few patches of dark hair, his eyes seemed to be in a constant squint. He held a pipe in one hand and a book in another.

"American, correct?"

His speech was nearly perfect English, J's head pressed back at the question.

"Yes," J dragged out the word.

"Dr. Ohmura?" Ariel queried.

The man raised his pipe and took a long draw on it, his eyes studying the two of them as they stood there returning the gaze. He approached them, head tilted slightly. Ariel and J didn't move, but J examined the book. It was covered in light tan leather, the spine had a symbol stamped on it, one his body shuddered at the sight of.

"What can I help you with?"

J was close enough to nudge Ariel as he attempted to secretly point at the book. Ariel just raised her eyebrows at him, trying to figure out what he was doing. She opened her mouth to question, but was interrupted.

"I don't think you are here on vacation, so what can I help you with Miss...?"

"Ariel. And this is J, son of Arcturus."

J glared at her under his eyebrows, it sounded so formal when she introduced him that way. The man studied them, his bottom lip pressed firmly to the top. He took another draw on his pipe, letting out a cloud of smoke. It hit J in the face, he tried to move but it was too late, the smoke filled his nostrils. J coughed, trying to hold it back, no luck. It made him think back to the cigarette Will gave him. He laughed to himself, thinking of the small paper tube catching on fire. Ariel was further away and fanned her hand in front of her face, deflecting the smoke.

"We're looking for Dr. Ohmura. Is that you?" She was still fanning the smoke.

J nudged her again, this time not so subtly pointing to the book. The man held it up in front of him, the emblem revealed. Ariel's eyes grew large, her mouth opened slightly.

"You like my book?" he asked, still holding it up. The letters "TK" embedded in a circle on the cover clear as day. J regained his composure, the smoke dissipating over his head. The man walked over and placed it on the small desk. Ariel followed, again asking if he was Dr. Ohmura.

"Yes. Now be quick about it. What do you want?"

J couldn't figure out exactly why the man was so snippy, they had only posed a simple question. Ariel approached the desk as the man sat in the chair behind it. He placed the pipe on a holder near the edge then fixed his eyes on them.

"Where's Dr. Arcturus?" she stared at his smug little face.

His reaction to them wasn't what she'd hoped for and he seemed to be on edge after the introduction. Ohmura studied her, head tilted, mouth in an aggressive frown.

He placed his hands on the desk, his fingers interlocked.

"Somewhere," the little man replied, twisting his head to gaze out the window, then slightly shaking it.

"What does that mean?" Ariel held her composure even though her body wanted to do otherwise. J saw her rubbing her fingers together. She stepped closer to the doctor and stood at the edge of the desk. He tilted his head back up at her, feeling her presence. She could sense that he was hiding something and was purposely being difficult. He knew more than he was saying and she was determined to find out what.

"Maybe he's dead." Dr. Ohmura leaned back, crossing his arms. He gave her his back again to stare out the window. J knew that was a possibility, but didn't feel it to be the truth. *Why not just say that in the first place?* He walked closer to the desk, the soft rug giving way under his feet, cushioning every step. He reached out and grabbed Ariel's hand, she shook it off.

"Where's Arcturus? You know something. Why won't you tell us?"

She reached for the book. Instantly the doctor yanked it toward him before she could touch it. Her hand hit the wooden table, empty.

"What's in that book?"

J stood back, unsure of what to do, feeling the tension building in the room. The doctor held the book tightly to his chest, J saw beads of sweat begin to form on his forehead. His face was scrunched up as he glared back at her.

"What's in the book?" she demanded, leaning over the table, both hands firmly planted on top.

Ohmura's head was sweating more, his shoulders tightened. His glassy eyes darted around searching for something. He quickly shot upright and kicked the chair away from him, attempting to run. Ariel was too quick, she'd anticipated it and jumped over the table to grab his collar. The doctor's legs kicked out in front of him from the sudden jerk, their bodies hit the ground. Ariel hopped up and dragged him over to the wall. His back hit, causing him to almost lose the book he so desperately clung to.

"Shut the door," Ariel directed, staring down at Ohmura.

J stared at the doctor in silence, his eyes flipped up to Ariel who was giving him a death stare. He pointed to himself realizing she was talking to him then ran to the door and peeked out into the hallway. Finding it empty, he closed and locked the door before heading back to Ariel's side. The doctor continued to clutch the book tightly between his arms and chest. She stared down at him then lifted the bottom of her flower print dress, exposing a blaster mounted on her thigh. She clicked a switch with her thumb, it began to hum as she raised it to his head. Ohmura tossed the book at her feet raising his hands, Ariel waved J over.

"Open the book. Let's see what the good doctor here is so protective of."

Her gaze never faltered, the blaster still focused on his

head. The sweat was continuing to build and began dripping down Ohmura's neck onto his collar. J moved over and picked up the leather-bound book, carefully opening it. His eyes widened, his ears kicked back, his mouth was loose. Ariel, detecting the silence, glanced over to see J's face glowing, illuminated by the book. Ariel's curiosity pulled her away from her current task and her arm slackened. She felt a sharp strike to her hand, her arm kicked back. Whipping her head back around to her assailant, she saw the doctor run toward the large windows on the adjacent wall. Ariel hesitated a second then swung her blaster, aiming at the man. He crashed into the glass at full speed. Ariel didn't fire, more out of shock than anything else. J witnessed the commotion and froze, disbelieving. They locked eyes for a brief moment before J dropped the book, sprinting to the window. Ariel ran up behind him as they both slid to a stop inches away from the window and gazed down. Ohmura was peeling himself off the roof of the adjacent building a couple of stories below.

"Do we chase him?" J lightly hopped on his toes, he'd never been on this side of the equation. He thought it might feel nice to be doing the hunting for a change. But his aggression was short-lived; he remembered how that worked out for the mediators during their last adventure.

Ariel looked at J, his eyes swept to the book lying open on the ground. "No, I think we have what we came for."

CHAPTER TWO

They stood over the book, their faces bathed in light. Ariel bent down and picked it up. She held it out to J. "You should try it. You seem to have the magic touch."

J glanced down. It wasn't an actual book, not in the physical sense of having a cover and pages. It was a shell holding an electronic tablet of some kind. A spinning TK emblem flipped in a three dimensional space on screen, in the bottom right corner was a picture of a thumb print, on the bottom left the words displayed read "Dr. Arcturus, Experiment Journal." J looked wide-eyed back at Ariel who gave a small nod as she smiled at him. The door rattled as a fist hit it several times. Ariel's eyes flicked about, hunting the room for a possible exit. J admired her a second, she was so strong and beautiful. *Now's not the time.* He scanned the room.

A loud voice called from behind the door, the only word J could pick up was "Ohmura". He shut the book, still searching for a possible escape. He spotted a door tucked in between the bookcases on the far wall. Ariel saw it at the same time and they took off running. J reached the door first, threw it open. It was some sort of storage room. Ariel shoved him in, closing the door behind them, locking it as they went. She slid down on one side of the door amongst a bucket and mops, J did the same on the opposite side, leaning against a few dusty brooms. J's eyes flicked over to Ariel, even in the dimly lit closet her eyes seemed to glow. The people in the hallway began to shout, then J heard a loud crash as the door to the larger room burst open. Ariel snickered, but regained her composure. Whatever it was it would have to wait. Silence was now the name of the game.

They heard footsteps move into the room then screaming even more frantic than the before. J heard crushing glass under heavy pressure, they must be at the window. He kept quiet, almost covering his own mouth, his chest rose and fell heavy, rubbed his cold fingers together. The uproar tapered off, it sounded like a few had left, but the heavy footsteps became louder. The sound of the crunching glass faded and was exchanged with the intermittent squeak of the wooden floor. The footsteps approached the door. J drew his blaster one inch at a time from his waist, he'd been hiding a smaller one under his coat. He glanced at Ariel. Her lips were pinched tight, her eyes darting around. He could tell she was thinking about plan B. The door handle rattled as a hand grabbed it and tried to gain access. The knob stopped its dance, but from the light coming in under the door, both of them could see that the threat hadn't left. Time seemed to stop. After a few moments, the person walked away, heavy footsteps fading into nothing. A few voices tapered off as the hinges on the door to the main room squeaked, but they didn't hear it close.

They shared a glance. J opened his eyes wide and nodded his head toward the door. Ariel shook her head. She lifted her wrist, inspecting the Datacle while she inched to her feet, sliding her back up the wall. J didn't move, he just watched her steady arm reach for the door knob. She twisted it.

"Come on. We need to get out of here," she whispered.

J gained his feet and followed her into the room. Empty.

"Where to now?" James asked, his voice low, eyes fixated on the gaping hole in the window.

She knew he was terrified of heights and they had no fancy boots to walk on walls here. Ariel didn't answer, she just headed over to the window peering down. Hearing footsteps approaching, J's head swung to the door. Instincts took over as he charged toward the window. It seemed like the only option. Ariel lunged toward him, her hand out, planting it into his chest. He bounced back. She grabbed his arm while placing a finger on her lips. She dragged him to the far wall, slapping his back against the wall next to the door. She let go of him and swung to the other side. The door sat slightly ajar, Ariel could see out the crack. A man was coming down the hallway. She moved out of view as he neared the door. J stood there holding the book in one hand against his hip. The other was free, clenching into a fist. The door swung open, J lifted his arm to block it from hitting his face.

The older man walked in carrying a broom. Ariel reached over and grabbed him by the neck as he tried to cry out. Her hands were too quick as she covered his mouth. The man's eyes were huge, frantically flipping around, he was shaking. Ariel whispered something into his ear, he seemed to nod in agreement. She grabbed the tiny purse she was wearing and pulled out a couple coins as she released him from her grip. The man backed away still holding the broom tightly with both hands. Ariel displayed the coins in her open hand and waved him to come closer, handing them to him. She turned to J then pointed her chin at the door, it was enough to get him moving. He peeked out, the hall was clear. He stepped through the doorway and started walking the way they'd come. A hand grabbed his shoulder, he snapped his head back. Ariel was pointing in the other direction, he nodded, following her. They made their way down the stairwell; he was relieved it was down.

On the 8th floor, they heard some chatter and ducked into the hallway. The threat passed and they continued down the stairwell, this time at a quicker pace. Ariel was the first to find the exterior door opening out into the sunlight. J stepped out into a narrow alleyway, the walls so close two people couldn't pass side by side.

"We need to find somewhere to stay for the night," Ariel announced, surveying both directions.

She checked her Datacle. "Still have the book?"

J almost didn't respond, she was staring right at it. "Yep"

She glanced down at her wrist again and tapped a few more commands. "This way."

He followed Ariel at a slow jog, she kept looking back. He did the same, feeling that any minute something was going to start chasing them. His time in Atlantis had taught him to never let down his guard. They finally reached the end of the alley and slowed to a walk. Ariel reached her hand back waiting for J to catch up, he grabbed hold with his free hand. They turned away from the building down the sidewalk. Familiar cars drove by, a Studebaker, a few Chryslers. He even saw a pickup similar to his, but in much better condition. At the next street, Ariel stopped them from going any further. They stood there a moment, J took in the city. It was the biggest, well on Earth the biggest, he had ever seen. Peering down the street, the buildings stretched as far as he could see, nothing was shorter than four stories. In the middle of the road were large metal rails, once he noticed them he couldn't stop noticing them. *Why would train tracks go down the middle of the street?* He shifted to ask Ariel, but at the same time, a trolley car pulled up. He jumped back, figuring out what it was. Ariel snickered, guiding him up the stairs as they climbed aboard. She took a seat near the front, J sat down as quick as he could wanting to get out of sight. His height was proving to be a factor in their ability to keep a low profile. Ariel placed her hand on his thigh as the trolley took off.

"Two stops then we'll get off."

"Where are we heading?'

"The Imperial Hotel. It's one of the larger hotels here, should have plenty of room. Figure it's far enough away from Dr. Ohmura's that we can get some rest and figure out that book."

J glanced down, he hadn't realized he was holding

it so tightly; his knuckles were white, his finger joints stiff. *It had his father's name on it. Could it really be his journal?* He hoped it was and that they'd be able to open it and finally get some answers. He laid it onto his lap and flexed his fingers, then ran his hand over the cover, bowing his head. The letters "TK" stared back at him, his teeth clenched, eyes tightened.

"You okay?" Ariel lowered her head and twisted it to get a good look at him.

"Yeah, just ...this book..."

He ran his fingers over the cover again. Ariel slipped her hand on top of his and gently squeezed.

"We'll figure it out."

The trolley came to a stop, a few new passengers climbed aboard, the last two dressed like police officers. They wore black military style jackets with white collared shirts and ties underneath. A leather strap crossed over one shoulder and down to a belt housing a pistol holster. J tightened his lips and instinctively inched closer to Ariel, she didn't complain. Ariel watched as they headed to some seats further back, J kept his head down, tightly gripping the book. The trolley started again. *One more stop.* He was more than ready to be away from any type of law enforcement, especially since he assumed they were replicants.

After a few more blocks, the trolley again came to a stop. J practically pushed her off the trolley in his haste to get away from the police. She gave him a look and he responded by shrugging his shoulders. Then his eyes shifted to the sight in front of him. He was completely caught off guard by the grandeur of the building. He gawked as he stood there mesmerized by the grand scale of the Imperial hotel. A large rectangular red brick pool stood in the center, running for what seemed like 100 yards to the main entrance. White block statues of samurai adorned each side halfway to the entrance. The main entrance housed multiple brick columns and wooden beams. The building was amazingly symmetrical with two large wings running alongside both sides of the pool, like arms stretched out to greet its guests.

"You coming? Or do you want to get your own room?" Ariel grinned, snapping him out of his trance.

"Yeah," he responded automatically. Then realizing what he'd said, " No! I don't want my own room. Yes, I'm coming. This building is just so beautiful. What did you call it? The impe..."

"Imperial Hotel. For all the faults of TK, they did have some excellent taste when it came to rebuilding Earth."

J agreed. He wished she wouldn't have put it that way, it almost killed his enjoyment of the splendor. Almost. They walked hand in hand up to the main lobby. J was even more impressed when he stepped inside. Bell hops were gathering people's luggage, attendants in white jackets were standing behind the marble counters checking in guests. The ceiling was three stories high with balconies overhanging the main floor. Leather seats were positioned for those who needed a rest from travelling and the carpeting had an intricate woven pattern designed to draw the eye. Ariel walked up to the clerk and slid some coins across the table. The clerk's eyes lit up and he started shouting orders at other employees, then turned back to Ariel and smiled toothily. A few more words that J didn't understand and they found themselves following a bell hop to their room. After three long hallways and a short elevator ride, the bell hop opened their door. J was just as impressed as when he walked into the lobby. Just inside to the right stood a bathroom entirely made of tan marble with gold fixtures. They walked through two more sets of doors into a bedroom. The room was adorned with straight legged furniture of white; covered chairs, a bed with red and gold threads intertwined in an elaborate pattern on the duvet, the walls a light tan brick with perfectly laid mortar in between them.

Ariel walked in and sat down on the bed, J was still gripping the book tightly in his hands. She slipped off her shoes and gave a slight moan, enjoying the fact that her feet were free. She firmly believed that toes should have room to wiggle. Her head flipped toward J who was still standing just inside the door, oblivious to what just happened, still admiring the room.

Ariel smiled up at him. "We're here to work, J."

He gazed at her as she patted the bed. His heart skipped a beat and he smiled back, nearly dropping the book. He composed himself then strolled over.

"Let me see that book."

J sat down next to her and handed it over.

Ariel opened it up, the screen came to life, the emblem glowed back at them. "Let me see your hand," she said, taking it gently before she was done talking. She placed his thumb on the thumbprint icon. "Access Granted" appeared on the screen. J's eyes widened. He and Ariel leaned closer as if the next screen would appear quicker.

The TK emblem dissolved away, a list popped onto the screen. J didn't understand any of it, but began reading them out loud, "Reactor core, Phantom dual accelerator, 5528ME, Gravity Bomb MK3, Project AfterGlow, 988BWG replicator, Single pole era—"

Ariel slapped a hand over his mouth then tapped the screen. J tightened his eyebrows and eyeballed her. Her lips quirked and eyes sparkled impishly.

"Thanks for the commentary, Madden." She glanced down at the screen, "I think this is what we're looking for."

J scanned the book as Ariel removed her hand. The screen was filled with text that made him feel like he was reading a history book from school; single spaced, no pictures, no indents.

"Who writes like that?" Ariel exclaimed. Even she had trouble reading it. Her smile morphed, intensified as she tried to decipher what she was viewing. She reached down after a moment and swiped her finger left.

J studied her. "You can read that fast?"

"I'm getting most of it. Quiet, so I can concentrate."

J attempted to read the next page, but it was more

technical jargon. He had no clue what it was talking about. She swiped again, he tried again but more of the same.

"I—"

Ariel raised her hand, index finger slightly pointed, she flicked the next screen open. J didn't even try this time, he sat back, pressing his elbows into the soft comforter of the bed and let his eyes unfocus, pondering. *How did that strange little old man acquire his father's book? Father.* He never even met the man, at least in person. He still didn't know what to think of him. His mind drifted. *He was the last remaining heir to TK. What did that mean? The Earth was his to rule, like some ancient king inheriting the kingdom?* Lately he'd been trying to forget that aspect, he just wanted to find this man, his father, Arcturus.

"Aha!" Ariel exclaimed, rocking back a bit.

J quickly sat up, hoping to see something miraculous. His eyes explored the screen.

-Project name: Dream Weaver
-Equipment Designation: 5528ME
-Project lead: Dr. Akinosuke
-location: Sector 7
-Commissioned by: Unknown

He stared at Ariel, confused. "What does...how does this help us?"

Ariel pointed at the screen. J bent down closer to see

what she thought was so important. Her finger rested just under the name Dr. Akinosuke. She tapped it, a profile of the doctor glowed as Ariel moved her hand, now pointing at an address.

J rocketed himself backward hitting the comforter with all his force, arms stretched out wide, the bed jumped slightly. He lay there staring at the ceiling. He took a deep breath, "I thought you said you knew where my father was?"

Ariel paused a moment then fell back next to him, staring at the ceiling. "You realize where that is, right?"

J pinched his lips together. Still staring at the ceiling, he began to shake his head slowly side to side then a little quicker. He blurted out, "No," then snapped his head to Ariel.

"It's about 30 minutes by trolley."

She was smiling, expecting a face of delight from J. His mind went to the last trolley ride and the police officers that had boarded.

"Were those officers..."

"What, on the trolley? Yep. You should know that. We've had this discussion before. All the cops on Earth are."

"How can you distinguish them from everyone else?"

"You can't. That's why TK got rid of them, remember?"

He recalled the conversation. He still had trouble believing, they looked so real. Yet he would never forget all of the sparks flying out of various body parts after their previous encounters. He'd hoped to never have another run-in with them, but the way things were going, he felt it inevitable.

"Should we get some dinner? I'm hungry."

J wanted to get his mind off the replicants, in some small way he was trying to convince himself they didn't exist. "Ignorance is bliss," he mumbled to himself, Ariel didn't catch it. Maybe the food would keep his mind off of it. He was hungry, it had been a bit since those dumplings. His mouth watered at the thought.

"Are you sure?" Ariel positioned her head on his chest and laid half of her body over his, her hand on his heart.

He lay there a moment, taking in the feel of her toned body next to his. "I suppose we could lie here a few more minutes."

He closed his eyes, Ariel's body rose and fell on his chest as he took a deep breath. She tightened her hug in response.

CHAPTER THREE

The door rattled, a loud voice called out quickly behind it. J opened his eyes, a hazy ceiling in front of him. More knocking. J bolted upright as if there was a raid on the room. Ariel slid off him and landed softly on the bed, she eked open one eyelid and glared up at him. Closing it again she mumbled, "It's just housekeeping."

He was always amazed at how she could be completely un-phased by things, especially when it came to sleep. He again wished he had agreed to go back to Atlantis. He made a deal with himself, at the next opportunity, they'd go. The door rattled again, the door knob began to turn.

"Puraibashī o onegaishimasu," Ariel grumbled, still not moving.

The knob continued to turn. Ariel repeated the request again, louder and more aggressive. The door began to open, the hinges squeaked slightly.

"Seriously?" Ariel growled. "Īe, kekkōdesu!" she shouted, sitting up.

J rolled off the bed and stood up, scanning the desk in front of him. A clock shined back, the arms read 9:00. He glanced at Ariel, her hair a mess, flowing around her upper body, half of it in her face. Her eyes were focused on the door, eyebrows tightened, her bottom lip pressed tight to the top. J hoped the door would close, he didn't want to see the rage that was about to spew from her. Light shined on the carpet coming from the hallway as the door continued to open. Two shadows stretched along the ground, growing larger, almost blotting out the light. Ariel vaulted off the bed. J watched as her fists tightened, her face never changed. He'd seen this before, it meant chaos was about to ensue. J adjusted his body into a fighting stance, highly doubting it was room service. He didn't need to ask, he was positive. The shadows continued on the floor, Ariel studied her opponents. J still didn't have a good view, but could feel the floor shake as the intruders neared.

"What do you want?"

J raised an eyebrow. *English?*

"The book," a deep voice rumbled as it stepped closer.

Ariel stood her ground. "No," she didn't move a muscle.

J slid forward getting closer to the wall. Around the corner was the entrance and the threat blocked it. He was still a few feet away when the monstrosity came into view. A man, at least he thought it was a man, took one final step in front of Ariel, rattling the ground. He was enormous! J swore he must have had to duck to get into the room. His muscles rippled and tightened as he moved, his suit was a few sizes too small and J thought it might tear open at any minute. His head, proportionally, was too small for his enormous body, as if the wrong-sized head from a doll was place on an alternate body. His belt held a holster. J couldn't see what was inside, but it was larger than anything he'd seen on Earth. The man's tight, small slanted eyes peered down at Ariel's tiny body, nearly within arm's reach.

"The book," he repeated, raising his enormous open hand.

Ariel still didn't move, she didn't even acknowledge that the giant had spoken. Another man stepped in behind him. J knew this man, Dr. Ohmura. He glanced at Ariel, the book sat on the edge of the bed, waiting to be claimed, or stolen. Almost out of instinct, he bolted toward the bed diving headfirst, arms outstretched. Home plate was in front of him and he wouldn't miss. He grabbed it with both hands and tumbled onto the ground behind Ariel. The motion distracted the giant just enough for Ariel to engage. She struck him in the chest with a heel strike, her kick taller than her. It bounced off. The giant didn't move, didn't speak. He simply stood there. Ariel's foot landed on the floor.

"Run, J!" Ariel hastily scrambled for her blaster. The behemoth grabbed her shoulder with one enormous hand, the other a fist sinking into her the stomach. The giant tossed her toward the bed like a throw pillow, her side crashed into the headrest, her breath nonexistent. J hesitated, he couldn't leave her. She lay motionless on the bed, zealously attempting to regain her air. The giant took two steps toward him.

"The book," he growled.

J knew he wasn't going to stop until he had what he came for. He was clutching the book arm over arm and looked down at it. His eyes flicked over to Ariel, she was moving now, crawling over the sheets toward the edge of the bed. His eyes snapped to the giant still stepping

toward him, he inched back bumping into a table. The
table rocked and drew his attention, his head swung back
and down at the table. A low growl came from in front of
him, the gigantic man charged. The man's shoulder was
hit by a blast, knocking him slightly off balance. J dove
out of the way, he watched as the enormous wrecking
ball crashed through the window and wall. Glass fractur-
ing into bits, a high pitched sound filled the room as the
pieces bounced and danced on the table and floor. Bricks
and mortar were strewn outside onto the ground, cement
powder filled the air. The man was gone. J glanced up at
Ariel. He was lying on the floor next to her, book still in
hand. Ariel's arm still outstretched aiming the weapon
out the window as if he would return at any moment.

"Dr...Dr. Ohmura," Ariel remembered, her eyes fixed
on J.

J, realizing he was still there, rocketed to his feet,
exploring the doorway. The doctor stood, still as a stat-
ute, eyes wide staring at the hole where the window once
was. J slipped a hand away from the book, reaching for
his blaster and swinging it up to aim at the small man.
The sound of the demolition was clear and, hearing the
silence, Dr. Ohmura gasped and ran out of the room.

"He's gone," J dropped the weapon to his side.

"The giant?" Ariel questioned. "Check the window."

She was still fumbling off of the bed. J slid over to
the hole, as he would have called it, the window was gone.
Searching, he saw rubble, bits of glass, a curtain rod, bricks.

"He's gone, too!" J panicked. "What do we do?"

Ariel was standing now, clutching her side, her face twisted. Stumbling toward him, she slipped her blaster back in its holster, holding her dress up with the other hand. J wished she'd been doing that under better circumstances. He rushed over to her, grabbing her around the waist.

"I'm fine, J. 'Tis but a flesh wound," she managed a cracked smile.

"We need to get you medical attention."

His eyebrows were raised, lips pursed. He was scrambling to think what to do.

"I'm fine. We need to get out of here before that... thing comes back," she gritted her teeth.

She wasn't sure what the giant was. *Was he a modified E-Rat, if so she had never seen one so big. It didn't feel like flesh when she kicked him. Maybe he was something new.* All she knew was that their only option was to run, simply run. J was of the same opinion and didn't utter another word. Ariel was able to stand on her own now and pointed at the window.

"Are you crazy?" J questioned emphatically. "I wouldn't want you to jump out that window healthy, let alone in the state you're in."

Ariel, standing up straight, still gritting her teeth, retorted, "I appreciate the sympathy, but there's no time. Go."

J glanced over at the gaping void in the structure. As he turned back toward Ariel, she zipped by him, flying out the window. He bolted to the hole, watching her tumble forward and back onto her feet. He stood up and shook his hands, stretching out his arms to full length. "I can do this," he whispered, giving himself a pep talk. He whirled around, still trying to psych himself up. He was greeted by the sight of the giant standing in the doorway again. He didn't have time to think, his body responded instinctively. He pivoted and jumped out initially closing his eyes, but during the fall opening them. He braced for impact bending his knees slightly. His childhood came back to him. Jumping from trees on the farm had always been more enjoyable when he kept his legs bent and tumbled as he hit the ground. Today, for at brief second, he was that child. He came out of the forward tumble in a run.

Ariel was already ahead of him. He glanced back. The giant of a man stood in the hole above, watching. J hoped he would stay there. He soon caught up to Ariel. Looking down, he just realized that somehow, through that whole ordeal, he'd managed to keep the book secure. Ariel pulled up a map on her Datacle then pointed J toward a street up ahead. *How was she still moving, and at that speed?* They rounded the corner and saw a trolley car heading toward them. Ariel clutched the rail as it passed, pulling herself up onto it. J stumbled, but managed to get a hold himself. The two leaned on the seats exhausted. Ariel stumbled, crumpling into a seat. J plopped down next to her.

"This the right way?"

"Yep," she managed in between breaths.

J could see she was still in pain, but doing her best to hide it. He reached for her hand, she welcomed it and squeezed his as they met.

"Should be there in about 20 minutes or so." She glanced back at her Datacle, "Four stops."

Ariel leaned into him, resting her head on his shoulder. He held her hand tight, massaging the base of her thumb. His gaze drifted to the buildings as they went by. He saw a fish market, vegetable stands, intricate paper lanterns hung from many of the building overhangs, large signs with fascinating characters stretched vertically on many of the tall structures. He was caught up, astounded by all he'd seen in the past month. It was more than he'd seen in a lifetime, he still felt unready for it all. The next few stops came and went, he counted in his head to be sure. Ariel could have been asleep for all he knew and he didn't want to wake her too early. She'd been silent the whole ride. The trolley stopped, J nudged Ariel. She roused herself and they climbed down the stairs onto the crumbling road.

"How are you doing?"

"I'm good," she answered gravely.

J's eyebrows climbed his forehead. "What's the address again?"

Ariel rattled it off. He was always astonished that she could remember such details, especially when it came to numbers. He hunted for signs. He wasn't really sure what he was searching for, everything was so different, so foreign.

"There," Ariel pointed to a building across the street.

It was a five story building on the corner of an intersection. The two sides facing the streets held windows, one had a vertical pattern, while the other a horizontal pattern. In between them were large tan panels. The street level was constructed differently than the rest of the building, it was made of hefty stone, cut jagged like he'd seen in history books of castles abroad. A large sign adorned the building, jutting out between two rows of windows. Big, bold characters in white on a red backdrop. Ariel took the time to translate for him. It read, "The Ogino Ginko School of Medicine". She took his hand and they made their way to the entrance.

Upon entering, they were met with a large reception area. Young men and women entered and exited wearing school uniforms. J guessed, judging by their appearance, they had to be around his age. Postal workers were moving boxes on oversized dollies while others sat around. There was an open staircase that ended on the second level balcony overlooking the first floor. Ariel approached the reception desk and asked for Dr. Akinosuke. J didn't understand any of the conversation, but Ariel translated.

"They said he's in class all day. We'll have to wait until school lets out."

"How are we going to do that? What if that thing tracks us down?"

Ariel ignored the question.

"Ariel?" J had been staring at the staircase as he

spoke, but adjusted his focus back on her. She was studying the room, occasionally clutching her side with a
slight wince as she flexed her torso, moving about. She
appeared to be concentrating on the far wall. J opened
his mouth and was about to ask again, but instead squinted his eyes to focus on what Ariel was examining. On the
wall, he spotted a sign. He could actually read it, or at
least they were letters he recognized. They stepped closer
and the letters became more visible. It was a directory
and each name had a room number next to it. Ariel ran
her finger along it stopping at room 225. J peeked at the
name; Dr. Akinosuke.

"We need to find room 225. Do you see any signs?"

J and Ariel scanned the interior. He swung his head
back toward her and shook it as her eyes drifted back,
focusing on him.

"Second floor. Let's start there," she responded to his
lack of discovery.

She hobbled up the stairs, clutching the guard rail as
she went. J noticed that her face tightened at every step.

"Can I help? We really need to get you to a hospital."

"I'll be fine," she grumbled.

J decided it best to keep his mouth shut. He crept
closer to her as they ascended the stairs and slipped his
arm around her waist trying to help support her. He felt
some of her weight slide onto him. At the top, J noticed
a sign listing "RM 200-255" and pointed it out to Ariel.
They continued down a long hallway bracketed by doors
on either side. All were wood, triple-hinged except for

one labeled "Lab" halfway down the hall which appeared to be made of a solid sturdy metal, almost resembling a vault door.

"221, 223, aha 225. Here it is," J exclaimed as they reached the room.

The bell rang, students flooded into the halls. J grabbed Ariel and pulled her to the wall, shielding her with his body, while student after student stormed by as if they were invisible. The chaos lasted a few minutes. J watched for an opening to get them in, but it proved to be harder than he expected. Then, as the last student tucked into the classroom, J found his opening. Supporting most of Ariel's body, they slipped in after. The room was laid out auditorium style, eight rows of seats oriented to face the instructor below. Behind him was a large chalkboard full of writing and images, like some sort of formula. The instructor was a smaller man in his 40's, dark hair, slender build with small almond-shaped eyes. A lone student stepped in after them and shut the door. As he passed, his shoulder bumped Ariel in the side. She winced in pain, falling, then hit the ground with a loud thump. Now on her hands and knees, she coughed up blood. J reached down to grab her. A girl in the top row heard the commotion and shouted, her words indistinguishable to J, her eyes large, eyebrows near the top of her head. The other students, necks like rubber, watched as J huddled next to her on the floor. Another girl let out a gasp, others started murmuring. The instructor stopped and glanced up at them. After a moment of hesitation, he began running up the steps toward them. He spoke very loud and fast, not quite a yell, just authoritative. The students all stood up and backed away. The instructor reached Ariel and knelt down to check on her, she struggled to see him.

"Dr. Akinosuke?" she mumbled over a mouthful of blood.

The man stared back at her, "Atlantean?"

CHAPTER FOUR

He jiggled the key in the lock, the large metal door creaked open as the hinges moved, in need of lubricant. The metal plate was nearly a foot thick and the small doctor struggled to push it open. J bounced as he held Ariel in his arms. She'd put up a fuss, but could do little in her condition.

"So, you're Arcturus' son?" the doctor asked, his voice was sharp and quick.

J didn't know if it was the current situation, his culture or his normal rhythm. The doctor was quick to act and hadn't asked a single question until the steel door was opened. J's head pulled slightly backward at his question, his English was very good.

"Yes," he replied as if it was being forced out.

"This way."

J followed him into an elevator, the doctor closing the door and locking it behind them. Once in the elevator, he slipped a key into a slit and upon twisting it, a panel fell down. It was a scanner. J watched as he placed his hand on it.

"Dr. Akinosuke DNA recognized. What floor?" the elevator asked.

"Level B8, password pizza."

J almost laughed, the doctor sensed it.

"Wouldn't think of that now would you?" he smiled conspiratorially, then examined Ariel again.

The doctor felt her stomach and sides, she flinched

away from it with a shallow moan. J's leg was bouncing, he tried to place all his pressure on the other. Ariel closed her eyes and was taking deep breaths.

"Is she going to be alright?"

"Broken ribs, some internal bleeding. I'll know more when we get to my lab."

The elevator ride seemed like an eternity. J was ready to get her medical attention now, the trip couldn't go fast enough. He only could guess what she was feeling through all of this. J's heart was beating fast as the elevator came to a stop, the doors gliding open.

"When we get in the lab, there is a table. Lay her down on it. She's in a lot of pain, I'd like to get her into surgery as quickly as possible."

The doctor showed genuine concern as V had done for him before. He must be from a doctor line just as she had been. They entered the lab and, just as the doctor said, there was a table near the middle. The room was well lit, a light shade of blue. Lights descended from the ceiling like snakes, he counted five before turning his attention again to the table. He laid Ariel down, her head rolled over to him.

He slipped his hand into hers. "You're good, I mean, you'll be good."

She opened her mouth, but her eyes became heavy and closed. The doctor grabbed his arm and pulled him away into another room. J fought it at first but relented, Ariel needed attention and not necessarily from him in that moment. In the next room, there was a window overlooking the table. Dr. Akinosuke pulled up a display which immediately scanned Ariel's body. J watched as it went through the layers, tissue, muscle, organs, bone. Most of it made no sense to J, he stood there, worthless. *You're good? What a dumb thing to say. Here Ariel was, potentially inches from death, and that's the best he could come up with?*

"She's got a fractured rib, punctured lung, Hemothorax, and multiple bruises. What did this? Was she in a car crash?"

J watched the screen, then focused over on Ariel lying on the table motionless as the scanner retracted. He didn't answer the question, he simply responded with his own, "Is she going to survive?"

Survive. Live. He didn't know what word sounded worse. Maybe he should have said, "Be okay."

Dr. Akinosuke moved his attention back to the screen and typed in a few more commands.

"She'll be fine," he responded absentmindedly, still typing. "But she will need some rest. Do you have a place to stay?"

J's eyes focused on Ariel as the mechanical arms flipped around her, he saw tiny laser blasts more than once. He didn't reply, still focused on Ariel.

"Do you have a place to stay?"

J felt a hand on his shoulder and snapped out of his haze, "No...no we don't, and..."

"I have room here for the night. You can stay if you wish."

J didn't see any other option, they were on the run. Ariel was in no condition to move farther than necessary. He just nodded and continued watching, swallowing hard. The procedure ended and Dr. Akinosuke walked him into the room. Ariel lay there, seemingly asleep, her dress burned from the laser cuts used during the procedure. V had operated on him and Zane before, but he had never witnessed it. No marks were visible on his skin and the same was true with Ariel.

"She's going to be okay?" J asked, after standing by her side a few minutes.

The doctor had given him some time. He nodded with a smile. "She'll be good as new, but it will take some time for the magic to work."

"Magic? Is that real, too?"

A chuckle came from the doctor. "The magic of science. There are no wizards here, only science."

J took a deep breath and gathered himself.

"So, should I carry her?"

Dr. Akinosuke walked over and showed J a small glass display which extended from the table. He took a finger and dragged it in a direction away from J, the table moved. He released his touch and the table stopped.

"You try it."

J hovered his finger above the pad.

"Slowly," the doctor advised.

He pushed his finger forward, moving the bed forward, then released and tried again. It was simple enough and kind of fun. He was escorted to another room, this one was less cold, the walls were lined with painted drywall, the floor covered in carpet, pictures of Mt. Fuji and other locations hung on the wall.

"We should let her get some rest." The doctor stepped out of the room, clicking the light off as he went.

J stood there in the near darkness a moment, he gently ran his hand along her arm then turned to follow their savior out. He soon found himself in another room, similar to the one he had left Ariel in, only this one had two large leather sofas facing each other with a hand painted black coffee table in between displaying an intricate tree and pagoda with two people in long flowing robes sitting as if at a picnic. The doctor motioned for J to have a seat.

"Tea?"

J's mind went back to the last time he had been offered tea, it didn't end so well for his host. He hoped this time would be different.

"Yes, sir," he replied, more out of politeness than actually wanting any. Though, the last cup he had was rather delicious, the sugars bounced on his tongue and the flavor was quite refreshing.

His host opened a cupboard and pulled out a small tea kettle, it was already steaming. J stared at it with wonder. *Was there a stove top in the cupboard?*

"This is loose leaf. I think you'll enjoy it immensely."

The doctor had no accent, yet speaking to his students he'd sounded fluent. His timing had slowed down like an older, privileged gentleman would speak, in no rush to get anywhere, but quick enough not to leave you waiting.

"So, you're Arcturus' son?" he probed, sitting down across from J after pouring tea into a cute little ceramic cup with tiny ornate flowers surrounding the rim.

"Yes. I'm sorry I didn't answer you earlier. I had a lot on my mind," he answered, staring into his cup.

"That's quite alright. With a girlfriend that gorgeous, I would have been anxious myself."

J's face flushed, he continued staring at the tea.

"Try it, it's good. Don't worry, plenty of sugar. Real cane sugar might I add, not that synthetic stuff you find on Atlantis."

He studied J, his eyes even more squinted than usual.

"But you aren't from Atlantis are you? Where are you from?"

"Sector 11, sir."

"Oh stop with the formalities, J. I know that's how you've been raised, but you do know you're the heir, what with TK gone."

J took a deep breath and exhaled bit by bit. He was trying to keep that as far out of his mind as he could. His heart beat quickened slightly and a shiver ran through him. He admired the table while trying to cage his mind elsewhere. The doctor sensed it.

"So, Sector 11. I think I've been there twice. Though, it's been years. Can't really recall why I was there. Probably for one of our annual Atlantean Professors Meetings, those things are always so drear."

"Did you know Mr. MacDunna?" J queried, still

examining the tea.

"Yes I did, good man. Go ahead and drink some."

J swirled the cup then pressed it to his lips sipping a mouthful. His eyes began watering, his taste buds disintegrated, his lips burned, it was too hot. He tried to play it off, to no avail.

"Ha! Sorry, should have warned you. I like my tea hot."

The doctor got up and rummaged through a drawer then threw a small roll of what seemed to be breath mints to him.

"What's this?"

"Take one, suck on it. It will heal your mouth. This is one of my inventions."

J popped one into his mouth, he could feel it beginning to tingle. He raised his hand and touched his lips then licked his finger. The burns had subsided, his taste buds were back, but he wished he hadn't licked his finger, it tasted like dust and dirt.

J gathered himself. "Inventions like the 5528ME?"

Dr. Akinosuke sat back and took a sip of his tea, his eyes were heavy, weighing what was just said.

"Where did you hear that?" his head tilted and one eyebrow lifted.

J sat there a moment contemplating what he should say. *The doctor did help Ariel. Could he be trusted? Should he show him the book? The book, crap! Where was it?* Sweat beaded on his forehead, his hands trembled. That book was what they needed, it was what would lead them to his father, now it was gone. J stared down at his hands, clutching the air. He couldn't hold it in anymore.

"A book. We had a book that...I had it in my hands when we arrived at your classroom."

"This book?"

The doctor lifted up the book, the TK emblem plain as day on the cover. *How did he get it? Could he open it? Was he going to give it back?* J looked down quickly after seeing it displayed in the doctor's hand, his eyes flicked back and forth as if trying to find something to lock onto, but nothing would do.

"Yes," he finally replied, raising his eyes. Sweat started to roll down his temple.

"Here," the doctor tossed it to J. "I can't get into it anyway. But by the sounds of it, you can."

He was right, but should he divulge that? Should he make that known? His run-ins with TK made him think it best to keep that knowledge close to his chest, yet the doctor may have the answers he needed. J opened the book and placed his thumb in the corner, unlocking it. Dr. Akinosuke stood up and walked to the cupboard where he had exposed the tea. He had a hop in his step, almost giddy. His hand stroked his chin, then he wheeled around and paced back toward J. He sat down, taking his hand off his chin only to put it back, his mouth opened as if to speak multiple times, but was speechless. Finally words left his lips.

"Do you realize what you have there?" his fervor evident.

J didn't have a chance to respond.

"That is all of your father's journals and notes, including my research, which I no longer possess. It was destroyed, it's gone." He paused, then continued. "May I download a copy of my research?"

J wanted to say "yes", but saw how eager Dr. Akinosuke was to get access to it. *Was it just his research or did he want his father's, too?*

"I'd like to consult with Ariel when she wakes up, if that's fine by you?" He closed the book and placed it on his lap.

The doctor regarded him, his eyes dimmed slightly as if Christmas would have to wait another day.

"I understand," he said softly.

"So what is 5528ME?" J tried to move the conversation down a slightly different path.

The doctor perked up once more.

"It was my dream machine, well I guess that's what you could call it. It extracts dreams then places them in someone else. Got it working too, but then Arcturus took it and all of my notes." He sank into the couch.

"I promise I'll get you your research back. I just want to make sure Ariel's okay first."

Dr. Akinosuke sat back up.

"So what did Arcturus need it for?"

"I don't know, it was classified. I was commissioned to build a prototype then hand it and all of its data over to him. He was a friend and I accepted. I had hoped he'd change his mind and let me keep my data, but I guess he did what he thought was best. He was always planning, ten steps ahead of everyone, a magnificent chess player."

"What was he like?" J beseeched, leaning in toward the Doctor

"Who? Oh, your father? Arcturus, well, he was very calculating, very smart and clever, which are not always the same thing. He was almost always in conflict with TK council, felt they were glorified slave owners."

J had heard most of this before. He wanted more; he wanted to see the other side.

"What about as a friend? You mentioned that he was your friend."

The doctor paused a moment, tightening his eyes. His jaw slid from one side to the other.

"I guess I would say, loyal. Yes, that's the best word. Loyal. He loved everyone and nearly everyone loved him, even Cyrellia at one time."

Cyrellia? Did he know? J couldn't get the next question out of his mouth quick enough.

"What about Arcturus and Cyrellia? Did they... date?"

Dr. Akinosuke began laughing. He leaned back into the chair, then popped right back up.

"No...no they never dated, but there were a few interactions I saw that indicated that something could have been there. Cyrellia is a difficult woman, to say the least. Downright evil are the words others have used. Your father, on the other hand, was loved by nearly all."

J himself sank down into the couch, his shoulders

which had tightened, were now loose, sagging down to his sides. The doctor glanced at his watch.

"It's getting late. I have a wife I need to get home to. You want to sleep with your girlfriend?"

"Yes," J answered quickly, not even thinking, then looked away from the doctor, straightening his arms.

"Come on then. I'll get you set up."

J felt relieved that he wasn't harassed for his slip. The episode with Zane and Sonya popped in his head. *Ariel would be okay.* His whole body relaxed at the thought. Tomorrow would be a better day. He just knew it

CHAPTER FIVE

Ariel awoke slowly, her dreams had been beautiful and peaceful and she didn't want to lose them. She felt her left hand enclosed in warmth. She opened her eyes to see J clasping her hand between both of his, his eyes intent on her face. Her blue eyes glowed back vibrant and full of life.

"You doin' okay?

Ariel's eyes widened then closed again, opening and shutting as she roused herself. She sat up, her head swung back to J. She was unfamiliar with her surroundings or how she got there. Her head snapped around, eyes darting about.

"Where are we?"

"Dr. Akinosuke's lab. You collapsed on his classroom floor. Do you remember?" he gently released her hand sensing that she needed some space to figure things out. J watched her, intently waiting. She took her thumb and index finger and rubbed her forehead, her other hand touching her exposed side.

"I'm sorry. In all the commotion, I forgot to have J dress you."

J and Ariel's eyes moved to the doorway, Dr. Akinosuke was standing just inside, fabric hanging over one arm and a food tray in the other.

"I brought you something to wear. It's one of my wife's, she is very traditional. It will be a little big, but it was the best I could do. The stores don't open for another hour and the nearest Atlantis port is an hour away."

He strolled over to them. His face glowing, he handed the dress to Ariel.

"How's the patient today? I don't believe I caught your name last night? You know mine, Dr. Akinosuke." He held out a hand to shake Ariel's, she accepted. He quickly stretched it out to J as well.

"And, J. Last night in all the chaos, I didn't officially introduce myself. It is a pleasure to meet you."

J took his hand and shook it. It was small compared to his, the grip firm, but not terribly strong.

"So how are you this morning, miss..."

"Ariel. I'm guessing I have you to thank for patching me up?"

He nodded.

She finished inspecting her ribcage. All the damage was healed and the pain was gone. "Thanks."

"Yes, you took quite a blow. I never did get a response as to what exactly happened."

His attention flipped to J. J shifted his eyes to Ariel, biting his bottom lip slightly.

"Car accident," Ariel offered.

"I see," the Doctor traveled around the table, his eyebrow raised, lips sporting a tight line of a smile. "How is it that J didn't receive any injuries? I assume he was traveling with you."

J clutched Ariel's hand and slightly squeezed, her eyes moved to his. "We talked last night. He knew my father. I think we can trust him."

J thought about the conversation, the doctor's reaction to the book, the excitement he showed at it. Yet, he didn't try to take it. The book was still with him, he glanced over at the TK emblem staring back at him near Ariel's feet.

"I showed him the book." J didn't feel like he needed to mention the fact that he had completely forgotten about the book the moment she collapsed and that Dr. Akinosuke had brought it to him.

Ariel's hardened gaze relaxed, her attention back on the doctor.

"Had a run in with a giant. Know any around here?"

That was Ariel, straight to the point. She never seemed to waste words. J had seen it plenty of times and it was becoming less jarring, to say the least. She tilted her head down, studying the doctor's reaction. It didn't disappoint.

His head whipped toward the book, his eyes expanded as he pointed to it. "He wanted the book didn't he?" his voice shaky.

She didn't respond initially. She wanted to see if he would continue. The doctor moved around, pacing as he crossed his arms. Finally, he spoke again.

"Riku. His name is Riku and he works for Takamori. He will not stop until he gets that book."

J and Ariel turned to each other then back to Dr. Akinosuke.

"Takamori?" Ariel leaned toward the doctor.

Dr. Akinosuke continued his pacing, tapping his

fingers on his bicep, arms still crossed. He stopped and inspected them.

"Takamori is a power-hungry overlord who was banished from Atlantis and sent to Earth to run Sector 7. That man is cunning and crafty, has played the game and kept his mouth shut trying to appease the council and get back into their good graces. With TK gone, who knows what he's planning."

Ariel hopped off the table and slipped off the remains of her dress, it hit the floor without a sound. J gawked, there wasn't a scratch on her. His mind drifted. Tight curves, shapely legs, smooth flawless skin. The perfect female form in his eyes. It made him want to savor the moment, but his conscience took over. He snapped his attention to the doctor.

"So, who's this Riku? He seemed superhuman. He threw Ariel around like a toy, which is normally pretty difficult."

The doctor rummaged through a drawer in the table that stood near the edge of the room, then produced a small device and headed over to J. Ariel was busy putting on the new clothes, a traditional Kimono.

"He is human, though pumped full of so many steroids and enhancements I would say barely so. If you encounter him again, I would run," the doctor's voice trembled.

Ariel let out a slight growl, she was struggling with the sash. The doctor changed direction, heading toward her.

"Here, let me help." Dr. Akinosuke undid the mess she'd made. She'd never worn a Kimono before and struggled to figure out what she was doing, but her stubbornness had stopped her from asking for help. She gritted her teeth while he slipped the sash around her body from the back to the front as he explained the steps. Ariel listened intently, her jaw loosening. She didn't think she'd ever wear one again, but realized it was better not to fight it.

"I have a daughter about your age. I used to tie hers when she was young," he explained as he finished the bow and slid it around to her back.

He reached for her hand. "You will need this where you are going." He placed a small metal device the size and shape of a throwing star in it.

"Would it be possible to get my notes from the book now?"

Ariel glanced over at J, eyebrows tight. His raised in response.

"I told him we would give them to him. It was his dream machine that helped me."

He recalled the planet floating in front of him, the flight in the ship running from TK, it was a glimpse of his father. He wanted more, but was thankful that he had even that much. He hoped there was more in his head, and that the dream machine could help him find it. Ariel's eyebrows dropped slightly seeing J's commitment.

"Do you have a data chip?" she turned to the doctor.

Without hesitation, almost anticipating this moment,

he pulled a cigarette-sized device from his lab coat pocket.

"The book," Ariel waved to J to bring it to her.

J picked up the leather-bound tablet and brought it over. She opened it and invited J to unlock it. Then tapped a few menu options, both on the doctor's device and the book, and handed the device back to the doctor.

"Now, where are we going and where is Arcturus? The book said your dream machine was here."

The doctor starred at Ariel and J a moment, then shook his head.

"No, it hasn't been here in years, and Arcturus... I haven't seen him since he went missing. God knows where he is. He could be..." the doctor's voice trailed off, not wanting to finish his thought.

Ariel tilted her head back and closed her eyes.

"I do know where the machine is, though. You might find some answers there. That's what the star is for, it's a key. In the foothills of Mt. Fuji, there is a storage facility full of equipment. My dream machine was last seen there. I have been unable to gain access as there is a DNA check-point along with the key. J's DNA most certainly would open it. With Riku after you, time will be of the essence. You must go quickly. There is a train that leaves every four hours. If you leave now, you will be able to catch the next one."

"Will you come with us?"

"I am afraid not. I have a family to care for and a run-in with Riku would not end well. I'm a doctor not a fighter."

Ariel snickered. She continued a moment, closing her eyes, holding back the laughter. *Would he ever understand her little inside jokes?*

J still had more questions, but sensed they would have to wait. The doctor escorted them up to the floor they'd entered. He thanked them, once again, for the invaluable data they'd given him back. Ariel was still unsure that it was the right thing to have done; it was classified, by Arcturus no less. J thought it couldn't hurt. In his mind, had the doctor spent enough time on it, he would have been able to replicate it regardless of his notes.

The two hit the street. Ariel was pulling and tugging on her Kimono, she longed for the pants and jacket she was accustomed to. All the Earth clothes seemed too difficult and tiresome to wear. She opened her Datacle and searched for the train station the doctor mentioned. She found it only a few blocks away. J's stomach rumbled, the doctor had given him some food after the tea, but his body needed fuel.

"Can we grab something? I'm starving," J almost sounded like a little kid.

Ariel was taken aback a second then realized he was teasing her. Truth was, she was hungry as well. It had been a long night for both of them and she was running on empty. They headed toward the train station. Finding a small restaurant on the way, they sat down and ordered. J was beaming waiting for the food.

"So what else did the doctor have to say last night?" Ariel broke the silence.

J recalled the conversation and decided to come clean.

"I accidently left the book in the classroom, but he gave it back to me."

"What?" Ariel's voice was elevated. "How could you do that? You know how important that book is." She would have been yelling had they not been in a public restaurant.

J could sense her frustration, but in defense blurted out, "You collapsed! Do you know what that did to me? You were all that mattered at that moment. You're all that matters most moments." He paused and spoke lower, "I was worried I might lose you."

Ariel who had been leaning forward, scolding him, slipped back in her seat. He could see her take a slow relaxing breath as her chest rose and fell.

She reached out to take his hand across the table. "I get it. I do. But you need to be more careful with that book. We know Riku and that guy...Takamori want it. Who knows who else does?"

She was right, it was an important book, their Rosetta Stone for finding his father. Yet to him, it felt more like the Voynich Manuscript. The food arrived. Steamed rice, a bowl of miso soup and some fish. J wasn't accustomed to fish, beef was the typical protein growing up in Eggerton. He was enjoying this newfound taste.

They sat, quietly eating, taking in the beautiful day as the sun shined. The sound of cars and the occasional trolley echoed in from the street just outside their window. J peeked out, watching this strange new land.

People in very different outfits walked by. Many of the women wore dresses, kimonos, like Ariel's, some wore American looking outfits. Men in suits and ties, others in buttoned shirts and shorts. The hustle and bustle of the city was a lot for J and he began daydreaming of his days on the farm. Ariel snapped him back to reality.

"You ready? We have about 30 minutes to catch that train."

They quickly found themselves at the train station. It was a large, four-story, brick building with two wings jutting out from each side. The wings were only two stories tall, but still spectacular. Stone coins marked every corner of the building in a distinct white, a stark contrast to the red brick of the rest of the building. The roof was blue and the central peak held a small fence on top. Windows were interlaced between the white columns stretching vertically every six feet. J slowed his walk as they arrived, marveling at the sight. Inside was no less grand. Ariel left him to his thoughts and stood in line to purchase the tickets. J took it all in, his eyes flicking about from one place to the next. People sat in rows of chairs awaiting the next train. Past them, multiple trains lined up, some leaving, some arriving. People walked everywhere. He noticed a man near the far wall holding a newspaper, peering over it. He was tall and lanky, his dress similar to back home; loafers, pleated brown pants and a button down shirt, solid blue in color. As J's gaze fell upon him, he kicked up the paper over his face. J only saw the dark hair above it.

Ariel walked up next to him and handed him a ticket. "Platform one."

J didn't take his eyes off the peculiar man and snatched the ticket.

"What are you looking at?"

"Nothing. Just admiring the building."

He spun around, eyes to the sky, the tall arched rafters and large clock hanging above.

"It's just so big."

Ariel grinned, but held back a comment, then her eyes explored with him. It was fantastic, yet nothing compared to Atlantis. Though to him, it felt more spectacular for the time period it represented. Like the ancient Egyptians building the pyramids, the archaic technology used to construct the train station was centuries behind what Atlantis used.

Ariel took his arm and led him over to the platform, she was still tugging at her sash.

"We could have stopped and bought you a new outfit" he said offhand, watching her struggle.

"No time."

He was kind of glad she hadn't changed, it was a good look on her. But then again, he thought every look was a good one on her. They boarded the train and found two seats near the rear of the car. As J sat down, he saw a man in brown pants and a blue shirt gawking at him. He quickly ducked into a seat four rows ahead of them. *Is that the same guy? What was so interesting about him?* He was much taller and stuck out, maybe the man thought

him an oddity. Ariel leaned into J as the train departed
the station. He took a deep breath and leaned the seat
back. The man in the blue shirt walked by, glancing
at him as he did. J moved to glance behind him in the
aisle. The man peeked back at him as he continued away
from them. Ariel grumbled a bit, she'd nearly fallen
asleep. She had seemed a little subdued and lethargic all
morning, J thought it must have been the recovery. He
settled into his seat again. Ariel, after looking up at him,
nuzzled his shoulder again.

"Neil Johnston?" J heard nearly as soon as he closed
his eyes. His eyes flicked up into the aisle. The man in
the blue shirt stood with a Cheshire cat grin on his face.

"Neil Johnston?" he asked again as he put his hands
above his head, mimicking shooting a basketball.

Ariel, hearing the hubbub, woke up and conversed
with the man. J didn't understand any of it. Again he
wished he had a stinking translator. Ariel responded to
the man's inquiry, he smiled, then bowed and ran back up
the aisle.

"What was that about?"

"He thinks you're Neil Johnston, a famous basketball
player."

"What did you tell him?" J knew the answer by her
grin.

"That you were."

"What?!" J whisper-shouted.

Ariel shrugged her shoulders still sporting a devious
grin. The man came back with a menu from the diner car

and handed J a pen. J took it and frowned at Ariel.

"Sign it. Don't forget you're Neil Johnston."

He exhaled loudly, hoping that would make this all go away. He could forge one signature, though he felt extremely guilty and it took him a minute to sign, pushing the pen to the paper and retracting it several times. After accomplishing the task, he handed it back to the man who bowed and headed toward the front of the car. J glanced over at Ariel who just started laughing. He spun around to see another man standing there doing the same as the first, pen and menu in hand. J stood up, his eyes exploring the back of the train. At least twenty others were lined up behind him all holding menus and pens. He glowered down at Ariel who tucked her smile down into her chest leaning away from him, biting her bottom lip. J took a deep breath and signed the next man's menu. After twenty people or so, including a few children, one who had five menus to sign, J sat back down heavily into the seat.

"You enjoyed that didn't you," he said, glaring at Ariel's glowing blue eyes

"Immensely," she snickered.

J peered past her out the window, a huge mountain rose up from the surrounding terrain like it didn't belong.

"Is that Mt. F..."

Ariel spun her head around to get a good view.

"Yes, used to be a volcano. Just a shell of itself now, it will never erupt again."

J watched it as it gradually drifted out of view, only

the foothills still in sight.

"I'm going to go get something from the diner car, want anything?" J stood up and stretched.

"A cup of green tea would be nice."

He made his way back to the diner car, passing many of the people he had signed menus for. They nodded as he passed, he returned the gesture desiring to be invisible. He entered the dining car and requested tea and dumplings, they were the only words he'd asked Ariel to teach him. He felt the floor shake behind him as he leaned on the tabletop awaiting his order then felt a presence behind him, it was large and looming. He closed his eyes momentarily. "Please don't be him," he softly pleaded, then slowly turned around.

"The book" Riku said as he towered over J.

CHAPTER SIX

J was frozen, he couldn't move. Riku held out his hand.

"The book," his voice was low and it rumbled like thunder.

J's first thought was to ask if those were the only words he knew. Riku didn't seem all there in the head, and literally those were the only words he had heard come out of his mouth. He thought better of it and decided tact and the truth was better.

"I don't have it," he raised his hands up palms facing the monstrosity of a man.

Riku's eyes grew large, his eyebrows tightened down over them, ripples formed under his lip as he scowled at J. His hands clenched into fists. J saw what was coming next and planned his next move. The giant was big but not that fast, not if he moved first. They stared at each other a moment, a mental battle began, one in which J thought he had the advantage. Riku made the first move, swinging a huge right hook. J tumbled out of the way at his feet then took off running down the aisle.

"Ariel!" he shouted at the top of his lungs, sprinting faster than he'd ever run before. Car by car flew by, they seemed endless. The trip to the diner car had seemed so short. In the next cabin J sighted Ariel standing up gazing back at him. Her eyes widened, her face changed, tightening, her jaw clenched. She slid out into the path, her knuckles white as they tightened into balls. J didn't know what to do, he kept running toward her never looking back. Riku could have been one step behind him for all he knew. Ariel flipped up her Kimono and spun a blaster into her hand spinning it up and backward out of its holster. If he was going to have to continue fighting, she'd have to teach him that. Her legs spanned the two sides of the aisle as she hopped onto the chairs on each side of her.

"Slide!" she called out as he approached.

J dropped down, sliding under her. He flipped over and watched her fire shot after shot. He popped up to see what was happening. Riku was still a car's length away. He was so large he was having trouble navigating the small aisle. Ariel kept shooting, the blasts seemed to ricochet off his body. They burned his suit as they hit, but there was no flinching, no stopping, The monstrosity continued its onslaught toward them. Ariel hopped down from her perch and, turning toward J, grabbed the book from the seat and tossed it to him.

"Run, I'm right behind you."

J hesitated, but heard her yell again. She grabbed the cabin door, shutting it and stepping back, blasted the bolt holding it shut. She spun back to him, irate when she saw he didn't move.

"Run, J!"

He looked around. People were screaming and backing away from the aisle as if water was flooding in. J sprinted to the next car and waited. Riku was at the first door by now his fists pummeling the metal road block. Ariel arrived next to J and began closing the next door.

"You have the book, you have to run!" she demanded as she slammed the door shut.

"I'm not leaving you."

Ariel pointed the blaster at him, he froze. *What was she doing? Was she threatening him? He knew the book was important, but in his eyes she was more valuable.* J didn't move, unsure what to do or say in that moment.

"Down!"

J dropped on the ground and heard a blast go off. Rolling over, he saw a large shining blade slice through her blaster. She tossed it aside, her head down locked onto her target. J sat up spying a man standing in front of Ariel holding a samurai sword. He swung his blade at her again, missing. Ariel engaged her attacker, dodging a strike then landing a knee to the stomach after locking arms. She twisted the sword from his hands and slid back. The two were unarmed squaring off. J heard a rumble as Riku thumped the door again with his huge fists. Ariel advanced her strikes, blocked one after the other. A blast hit her sparring partner in the head dropping him instantly. J was leaning back on a chair, blaster in hand. Through all the commotion he had forgotten he had it.

"What took you so long?" Ariel grumbled in between breaths.

Another loud thud came from the door behind them. Ariel grabbed J's wrist and dragged him through the train, he had déjà vu momentarily. They continued amongst the screams of the other passengers to the front of the train, at each car stopping to seal the door. They reached the engine.

"What's the plan now?"

Ariel was busy surveying the room. J noticed her eyes focused on the ceiling and knew what she was thinking.

"No...no...do you realize how fast we are moving?" his voice was quick, he couldn't disagree with her thoughts fast enough.

"It's our only option," she asserted, stepping by him.

J rubbed his forehead starring at the ground. "Okay," he slid the blaster into his holster.

He took the book and shoved it into the waist of his pants, he would need both hands for what they were about to attempt. Ariel opened the last door between the engine and the car, exposing them to a gust of wind as it tore through. She went first, climbing the ladder to the top. J took his time as he stepped in between the cars. He'd need the right motivation to get him up there. He glanced back into the car, Riku was past the final block-ade and closing on him; motivation found. He scampered up the ladder joining Ariel.

The wind nearly knocked him off. Ariel was on all fours trying to fight it as she held tight to the smooth surface of the train roof. He made his way back toward her, mimicking her position on all fours. As he neared her, she stood up leaning into the wind. Reaching behind her back she pulled out a Katana blade. *She must have grabbed it earlier.*

He glanced over his shoulder. Riku's foot hit the top

of the train. Ariel slid her right leg back and raised the sword as a batter would awaiting the pitch. She adjusted her other foot. Her blonde hair unkempt, swirling around her face, she focused on the giant. J pulled out the blaster and began firing, the shots bounced off Riku. He quickly realized it was ineffective and holstered it. He raised his body upright and held his arms out, slightly leaning forward. The strong force of the wind slid him back toward Ariel. He crouched back on all fours coming to a stop just before her; it was the quickest way to get to her side.

Riku began his march toward them. J felt every step as the vibrations reverberated down the sheet metal under his hands. Ariel held her ground awaiting the battle. Riku inched closer every second, her eyes trained on the enemy, never faltering. Riku, now within reach of Ariel, lunged, grasping his hands in a hugging motion. She ducked and slid underneath him dragging the blade through his oblique. Blood flicked off the end of the blade as she finished her strike. Riku didn't flinch, simply rotated. Facing her again he charged. Again she ducked and landed a strike. The same sequence occurred and he charged her again only his reach was much lower this time. Ariel jumped, flipping over him, landing on her feet one hand stabilizing herself in the hurricane wind. She edged toward the side of the car and stood up, this time extending her front arm out palm up and rotating her back hand above her head wielding the sharp blade. She flicked her fingers toward herself. Riku didn't hesitate. He rushed at her full speed, his arms outstretched waiting for the duck or aerial summersault. Ariel spun sideways as a matador handles a bull watching Riku fly past her unable to change directions quick enough. He tumbled over the side of the train. J scrambled to the side of the roof and watched him hit a tree, breaking it like a twig, then fall to the ground. Ariel glanced back at J and pointed to the car entrance. He wasted no time climbing down the ladder and back into the car.

"You okay?" he heard as Ariel entered the car.

"Yep, you?"

He really didn't have to ask. He'd seen what she had done to Riku out there. Her movements were fluid, no hesitation. She was the warrior he had grown to know, and love. J found a seat next to a window searching around the car which was now empty. As the giant wreaked havoc during their pursuit, most people scattered and this car was no different. Ariel plopped down beside him setting the blade in the aisle.

"Don't you think you'll need that?"

"Not for the rest of this trip."

J wasn't so sure. Two villains seemed like an underestimation on the part of Takamori. Then again, TK seemed to have unlimited number of mediators. This was Earth, no robot factories, or at least ones that he knew about. Ariel checked her Datacle while the train glided gently around a bend bringing the mountain into view. It now engulfed the entire window. J stared up at it in awe. He'd never seen such a display of natural beauty in his life.

"Ten minutes," she said, resting her hand on his thigh.

J wanted to enjoy the moment, but he felt uneasy. His head was on a swivel, though he tried to hide it. Ariel leaned back onto his shoulder, which made it easier or so he thought.

"We're fine, just relax."

J figured she must have felt his head movements. He closed his eyes a moment only to see the mountain of a man Riku grabbing at him. The train's wheels screeched as it pulled into the station. Ariel had dozed off and J, not wanting to frighten her, gently nudged her. She came to cleaning her eyes with her finger, small tears had built up during her nap. As his feet hit the concrete, he studied the station. His senses were heightened; they had been since the attack.

"This way," Ariel took his hand.

She glanced at her wrist once again, her Datacle was leading them to the storage facility.

"I never asked. What did the doctor say about the Dream machine?"

"Not much. He told me that he invented it and Arcturus classified it took it and he never saw it again. He did mention Cyrellia and my father, but I didn't get many details."

"Hmm. What did he say about Cyrellia?"

"Not much about her either. Just that some people loved her and others hated her...he did mention something about seeing my father and her together, but he didn't elaborate."

Ariel examined her wrist checking the map. "Looks like it's just a few blocks."

They headed out of the main doors of the train station and toward the larger buildings in town. To J, this felt more like home, save for the large mountain casting its looming shadow down upon them. The town was small, two blocks long, only a few multistory buildings. Ariel was leading, after all, she had the Datacle. J's only device was the small simple blaster hidden under his jacket. The wind picked up, blowing items down the street. There weren't many people out, just the occasional walker. Dusk was approaching, the temperature beginning to drop. It felt chilly for spring. *Was it always this way? Or was the climate control malfunctioning?* J stayed close to Ariel as they continued their brisk walk. He kept peeking behind them, searching for something, or someone. They turned down a tight alley.

"Datacle says it's down here. Guessing it'll be like Will's door."

J's shoulders sunk, he'd hoped it would be plain as day. No tricks, no clues, no hidden doors. He should have known better. Ariel walked to the far end while he began at the street. *Maybe there will be a rag again.* But nothing was that obvious. The brick on the building was just like back in Eggerton, red, well mortared, and slightly rough. He ran his fingers along it and began walking toward Ariel, his eyes fixated at knee height. Suddenly, his fingers touched something. For a brief second he continued his walk then paused. He skipped back a few steps examining the brick. An indent of a star was ground into one of the bricks at shoulder height.

"Ariel, I think I found something."

She ran over as quick as she could.

"What is it?" she shouted out, still a few steps off.

J was pointing at the indent as she came to a stop in front of him.

"Nice."

She slid her hand inside the lapel of her kimono. J couldn't help but stare, mouth slightly open. Ariel caught him and tilted her head down looking up at him. her eyebrows pinned up.

"You know this thing doesn't have pockets. Why didn't people wear pockets in the past?"

She let out a slight growl of frustration. J chuckled mostly to himself, then took the star from her outstretched hand. He examined it in the light. It was the first time he'd really taken a good look at it. The star was simple, the points sharp. You could have tossed it in with other throwing stars and never been able to tell the difference. He reached up and placed the star in the slot; it fit. The wall began to open, exposing an elevator just like the one back in Eggerton. Ariel pushed him in, piling in behind him. She scanned the menu on the wall and pressed the only lit up button.

"DNA unidentified, please try again," a female voice chimed.

She glanced at J, then pressed it once again.

"DNA unidentified, please try again."

She rolled her eyes finishing them on J.

"Go ahead, give it a whirl," she said, exhaling the entire time.

J reached over and pressed his index finger against the glass panel.

"DNA identified. J Arcturus, alias James Campbell. Please state your name."

His eyebrows popped up into Vs.

"J...Arcturus," he stated hesitantly. He'd never used that whole name before, it had never dawned on him that Arcturus would be his last name. For some strange reason, he pictured it as his father's given name. His mind wandered still. *What was his father's first name?*

"Please look into the screen for retinal scan."

A blue light shot out of the panel. J turned to Ariel, throwing his hands out to the side palms up, his shoulders up near his ears.

"Your eye," she said, pointing at hers. "Look into the light."

She pushed him into position, the elevator beeped. She laughed, realizing he didn't know what a retina was. The blue light went away, the door to the alley shut.

"Please state destination."

They looked at each other; lab, weapons facility, storage facility, hangar. So many fancy futuristic words and locations were flying through his head. *Where were they going?*

"List options," Ariel commanded, jutting her chin out, her eyes aimed at the ceiling corner.

"Level 1 dining area, level 2 living quarters, level 3 weapons storage, level 4 maintenance equipment, level five..."

Ariel's eyes popped wide open, her head rolling vertically. J couldn't help but laugh. He understood why she was doing it, the list continued.

"Level 23 restricted, level 24 defense systems—"

"Level 23," Ariel blurted out as quickly as she could.

"Level 23 restricted, Level 5 clearance needed. Number of authorized users, 2. Would you like to continue?"

J realized they didn't have much of a choice. If the machine was going to be anywhere, it was going to be there.

"Confirm," he said, gazing at Ariel.

The elevator shot down. J felt his body go weightless momentarily. He reached for the wall, but by the time he did, the pressure came back to his legs, almost doubling.

"Level 23 restricted."

The door opened as the two of them stepped out. He heard the elevator door close behind him with the sound of steel slapping on steel. J's jaw dropped, his mouth gaping wide. The room was at least 50 feet tall, two large metal doors sat imbedded into the rock in front of them nearly as high. One small door rested closed at the bottom of the left steel wall.

CHAPTER SEVEN

J rested his hand on the glass plate exposed on the wall. A retinal scanner shined on his eye he spoke his name, once again having trouble with it. They heard steel grinding on steel, spinning gears and chains moving as the smaller door opened, exposing a hallway the same height as the main room. J stepped in first.

"Where to now?"

"Beats me. You're one of two authorized to access it."

It was dripping with sarcasm. After a moment's pause, they laughed at the same time.

J sobered up. "Should we split up? This tunnel goes on forever. I'd hate to get lost." Genuine apprehension filled his face.

"Let's stick together then. No need to rush, it's just us."

J liked the sound of that. More time alone with Ariel was always on his mind these days, not to mention running from Riku. J had enough excitement for one day. Focusing on the task at hand, finding the machine and thereby his father, J turned around to get another look at the gigantic, pitch black doors looming over the corridor like a centurion. His eyes were drawn to something on the wall to the right, a faint green glow shone out of the darkness.

"Ariel, what's that?" he pointed to the light.

"I don't know. Let's check it out," she replied, trotting toward it.

They found it to be a small video screen, Ariel touched it.

"Denied."

"This is going to get old really quick." She raised both hands, palms up, and gestured at the screen. "Can you just unlock the entire system so I can access it?"

J bit his bottom lip and approached, tapped on the screen, then held his hand there momentarily.

"Access granted, pulling up main directory," it responded.

J and Ariel leaned into the screen. Ariel tapped through several menus, disabling the security temporarily to make their movements easier. She transitioned to the main directory, a long list began near the top starting with A.

"Wow! How many classified projects did your father have?"

She spotted the "find" function near the top and tapped on it then snapped her head over to J. "Open the book."

J tugged it out of his waist, he really needed to find a better way to carry it; it was very uncomfortable and the way it bounced around made him worry that it could come loose at any moment. Thankfully that hadn't occurred. He flipped it open and unlocked it, Ariel grabbed it as soon as it accepted his fingerprint and began going through menus. He realized what she was doing as she stopped at a screen with the title "5528ME". She quickly punched it in the search function on the wall screen while handing the book back to him.

J and Ariel focused on the screen, waiting for the location.

-Vault 137

They were so close to finding the answers. Now they only needed to find vault 137. Ariel's eyes searched the endless tunnel, the smooth rock walls were rounded at the top and the floor made of metal. J thought it resembled the tunnel that led him beneath the ground and under the wall before his journey to Atlantis. J glanced back at the screen, something caught his eye. On the bottom left of the screen there was a circle with an H inside it, only the horizontal portion had two lines instead of one. He reached out to touch it, his finger hesitating just above it, then finally settled his finger onto it. The ground began to rumble, he stumbled back into the wall.

"What did you do?" Ariel cried, spinning toward him, her eyes like daggers.

She fell back toward the wall, gripping it. J continued to hold fast to the wall, his back pressed upon it. But the wall was slick, his grip ineffective as he slid around with the shaking. Ariel took up the same position, both staring at the large floor in front of them. It began to open up, large panels slid away exposing a trench. What looked like a spaceship rose up out of it. Resting on nothing, it hovered above the ground, the panels slid back into place. Ariel slapped J on the chest, he frowned over at her.

"Nice job, Doctor Jones," she grinned as the ground stopped rumbling.

J wasn't even going to ask as he watched her jog over to the ship.

"What is it?" J ran to catch up.

"It's a hover train. Now we'll find that room in no time."

They boarded the train and after requesting the vault number, the door closed as it began to move. The train zipped up to speed then decelerated nearly as quickly as it had accelerated. It reminded him of the vacuum system from sector 19, though it was much larger. They stepped off and a door the size of a normal house door greeted them, J quickly found the control panel and placed his palm over the plate. It sprang inward with a hiss as it slid away from them along the vault's interior wall. J jumped back and bumped into Ariel, he had not been expecting that. Walking through the doorway, he admired the four foot thick steel structure as it came to a stop. Inside sat a ten foot by ten foot box, similar to those in V's mother's lab. J's chin sank into his neck, his bottom lip pushed up.

"Is that it?" he asked, not moving his eyes.

"Maybe?"

As they approached it, J noticed wires and tubes attached to the ground and an average sized door on one side of the box. On the side next to the door, about a quarter of the way down, were markings that read "5528ME".

"This has to be it," Ariel perked up. "See," she pointed out the markings, reminding J that they matched the book.

J's heart started racing, he bounced slightly on his toes. He reached the door and placed his palm on the now familiar access screen. The words "access granted" displayed back at him, the door moved out of sight. J stepped in first, taking it all in. The lights flickered on. The walls were all white and in the center was a seat, the head rest tall and adorned with wires and pads.

"Where's V when you need her?" Ariel quipped.

J began to reply.

"It's rhetorical," she interrupted, snickering.

"You wanna give this baby a go?" she asked, looking directly at J.

He simply nodded.

"Have a seat. Let's get you some answers, I hope."

I hope; J thought about that saying. There were a lot of things he had hoped for, he never thought finding his father would be one of them. He thought of his hope to play baseball, his hope to run the farm, finish school, marry...he was here now. He had to find his father, he needed resolution. He didn't come this far to sit idly by. Ariel stood behind a glass panel in front of multiple screens, she tapped on one of the panels. The screen in front of J lit up, a spinning logo he'd never seen before appeared; three crossing lines all intersecting in the center placed on top of a circle. Ariel looked down at the smaller display in front of her.

"Okay. Looks like we need to hook those pads to your head."

She pressed a button and a diagram appeared of a

mannequin head with circles indicating the position of each. Ariel connected them as shown and hopped back to the control panel.

"Here's to not blowing up," she teased.

J was about to respond but his eyes became heavy as he drifted off almost instantly.

He awoke staring at his hands. No, not his hands, but he recognized them, Arcturus' hands. J settled in for the demonstration. He hoped this would be it, that this dream would have his answers. He was in a hotel room, like the Imperial Palace they'd just visited. A bed to his left, a door to his right, he glanced in both directions then headed into the bathroom. He approached the sink. Staring into the mirror at himself, he took a deep breath.

"J. I have asked so much of you, more than anyone should be asked. You have come a long way to get this message. Earth is saved, but is not without enemies. You will find many as you continue. There are a select few who have been banished by TK. They will try to take back Atlantis and restore TK's dominion over the Earth. You must stop them. You are not without help, there are Atlanteans loyal to me who favor my ideals, for all men are created equal. You will find a dossier in the files of this machine. Godspeed."

J's eyes opened, he gnashed his teeth together and let out a frustrated growl.

"You okay, J?" Brows pulled together, Ariel looked into his eyes, "I think I'm wearing off on you."

J tightened his whole upper body then began frantically peeling off the tabs on his head. Ariel gave him
some space. He finished and ran out of the box, balled
his upper body together and let out an anguished
wail, then fell to the ground. Kneeling, his hands on
his thighs, he stared at the cold smooth floor. Ariel
approached him resting a hand on his shoulder.

Eyes still downcast, he whispered softly, "More bread
crumbs."

Ariel didn't catch it. She knelt down beside him,
placed her hand on his and gently squeezed. "Did you say
bread crumbs?"

J turned his face to Ariel, his eyes welling up, though
no tears fell. "Bread crumbs. We're Hansel and Gretel
chasing bread crumbs. The witch is going to eat us!"

Ariel didn't know how to respond, she didn't understand what he had seen. She scooted closer and intertwined her fingers with his.

"Whatever it is, you have me. We can do anything
together," she gently placed her hand on his cheek, staring
directly into his eyes.

For a split second, the world faded away. He didn't
want this moment to end, she was stunning in her love
for him. But his thoughts shifted to his father, to what
he'd just learned. He stood up, clenching and unclench-
ing his hands, then started pacing. Ariel tried to grab his
hand, but he pulled it away, he needed space to work out
his frustrations. The closer he thought he was to finding his father, the farther he became. As he paced back

toward Ariel, she grabbed him, wrapping her arms around his chest. He paused almost out of shock, or as if being startled awake. She leaned in and kissed his lips, they became one. His mind cleared, his thoughts centered only on Ariel. She released the kiss and gazed up into his eyes with a smile. J couldn't control himself and smiled back, he forgot what just happened, what was said, what task lay before him.

"I don't know what you saw in there, but I'll be there for you. I will get you through anything."

J didn't question it, he believed her to his soul. She released him and walked back into the box. J stood there and took a deep breath. He wasn't sure exactly what had just happened, so many emotions flooded through his body all at once. His eyes followed Ariel back inside the box, tapping on more keys. He sauntered into the doorway.

"Dossier."

Ariel looked up from the screen. "What?"

J was focused now, his fit of weakness behind him; at least for now.

"Dossier. My father told me that there is a dossier in the computer. Seems Earth's still not safe and we need a team."

Ariel grinned back at him, "Well let's draft a team."

She began digging through menu after menu, her eyes intently focused on the screen on the panel below. J stood by her then glanced at the chair.

"Ariel?"

"Boy did your father bury that dossier. Guess he didn't want anyone to find it."

"Ariel?" he said a little louder.

She had tunnel vision, menu after menu flew by, nothing. System files, start and shut down sequences, memory files.

"Ariel!"

"I'll find it, J. If your father said it's in—"

She finally unglued her eyes from the computer. J was pointing at the chair, or rather what was beyond it. Ariel chuckled, the screen displayed four names and locations detailing down to the meter where they would be found. Ariel tapped a few buttons and uploaded it onto her Datacle.

"Seems like we have a crew to gather."

Ariel peered down at her Datacle, verifying the information loaded correctly, then called Zane.

"Hey kid. You guys find the buried treasure?"

Ariel laughed at his pirate impression, she half expected him to ask what a pirate's favorite letter was. They conferred about what happened, leaving out J's meltdown, which he appreciated, and discussed the pickup location. The storage facility had to have a hangar. The trick would be figuring out how to open the hangar doors, or so she thought. J did have the magical DNA, so she wasn't too worried. They headed to the train and boarded.

"Vault 280," Ariel stated after the synthesized voice requested the destination.

"Vault 280? I thought we were heading to the Hangar," J raised one eyebrow.

Ariel gave him a sly smile, "I saw something in the book. You'll like it."

"What is it?"

"You'll see." Her smile grew wider, eyes twinkling.

He contemplated begging, but decided to treat it more like Christmas. Over the years he had honed his patience waiting for December 25th. And while he was well out of his childhood, he enjoyed the day. It was still magical, regardless of how it had changed. J gripped the handhold and Ariel's waist, he was getting bolder with her. He waited to see if she would say something, she just leaned into him. The train zipped down the track then slowed to a stop as it had done before. It called out "Vault 280" and they stepped out onto the cold, flat featureless surface. J glanced over at Ariel, she was still grinning. It hadn't left her face since they boarded the train. She glided toward the large door, almost tugging J along. *What would make her so excited?*

They approached the massive door, Ariel couldn't get J's hand on the scanner fast enough. She tapped on a few buttons, unlocking the whole system. A multitude of thunderous clicks echoed as the gears clunked, unlocking the vault door. It slowly came alive. Ariel took J's hand and squeezed tight, she was bouncing as if she couldn't wait one more second to see what was on the other side. The door finished its movement.

"Yes!"

J smiled at her reaction. "This is going to be fun!"

CHAPTER EIGHT

J was still standing by the door, while Ariel climbed all over the object beyond. Every day since he met her, he saw and learned new things, but this one he wasn't sure of.

"It just looks like a spaceship."

Ariel ignored the comment as she continued around the ship, examining nearly every inch of it. J didn't move.

"The book? Zane? The hangar, we still need to figure out the doors."

Nothing. Ariel was in her own world; it was as if she'd found a million dollars, which for J would've been a game changer. Not getting any verbal response, he marched over to meet her near the cockpit. She was standing there with her hands on her hips, eyes alight with wonder, just staring up at it.

"Beautiful isn't it? I can't believe your father built one. I'd heard there were too many movement issues. You think it works?" Her head never moved, but he could hear the smile in her voice, the sense of adventure and challenge and outright joy at finding something she never thought to see but secretly hoped to.

"I suppose so? I still don't even know what it is. Looks like a spaceship to me, that's all."

Ariel spun around and, shaking her head, laughed at herself. In her fit of excitement, she'd forgotten the missed years, the human history he never knew. She, on the other hand, loved pop culture; it was something she studied in her spare time. Being a rebel had its perks since most of it was rewritten by TK. They had done a very thorough job of eliminating a good portion of the last few hundred years of Earth's history before the build, and this ship, or a dream of this ship was part of it.

"As soon as things settle down, you and I are going to have a history lesson, or I guess for you a future lesson," she chuckled a bit at her own joke. "This is a VF-1D Valkyrie," her eyes glowed bright as she said it.

"Nice," he faked a smile, his acting failed miserably.

Ariel didn't care, she was fascinated by it.

He walked up below the ladder she'd used to get into the cockpit, examined it as he asked, "So...what's so special about it?" The ship was small compared to many of the ships he'd flown in. A tandem cockpit sat two pilots front and back, two fins jutted out of the tail end, the cockpit was covered in glass, and large hinged wings flared out from an enormous can on each side. Ariel ignored him, or she couldn't hear him, she was heads down in the cockpit flipping switches and playing with the controls. He decided to climb up the ladder and speak with her face to face. He was unsure what response he would get, Ariel was acting like a kid at Christmas who had just opened that special toy.

"Ariel, what about Zane? Shouldn't we get to the hangar?" he asked, reaching the top step.

"I already called him, told him we found another ride. He'll wait for us there so we can figure out what to do about all of this," she glanced up at him, smiling like a

Cheshire cat.

J peered in closer, assessing the cockpit. A single seat sat in the middle, buttons and display screens all around.

A blast hit the canopy spinning away. Taken by surprise, J tumbled into Ariel's lap. She let out a groan as he smashed into her. J picked his head up as another shot hit just above them. He took a glimpse over the cockpit rail, scanning for the origin of the shots. Riku's large frame was marching toward them flanked by ten men with blasters, they continued shooting. Ariel regained her composure and madly hit switches. The screens came alive.

"Do you know how to fly this thing?"

"Nope...no time for a lesson either."

J watched as she continued wildly manipulating the sensors and controls. He heard a hum come from behind them, he could only guess it was the engines igniting.

"Get your tail back there!" she yelled, pointing to the rear seat.

The canopy began to close. Ariel pushed J to one side and tapped on three of the screens, then pushed him to the other. He climbed over her into the rear seat, dragging his body over her as she ducked to the side. His foot slipped and landed on a control screen. Laser blasts shot out of a cannon, hitting the wall in front of them. He toppled into the rear seat head first as more shots zipped over his head. Ariel was still working to get the ship running.

"Ha!" Ariel cried out. "This system is just like the

Mark IX Hawk."

If she could have seen his face it would've screamed, "I have no idea what you're talking about." Amidst the blasts, now skipping off a fully operational shield, she maneuvered the nose toward their attackers. The cannon came to life, the barrels spinning spitting out a volley of shots, decimating half of the enemy. Riku and the other half of his assault force ducked to the side. Ariel engaged the thrusters, heading toward them. She added more thrust, then noticed a new side menu on one of the screens. J had been blocking it when he fell in her lap so she hadn't noticed it before.

"Yes!" She couldn't reach the screen quick enough, her arm zipped forward, tapped the screen. The cockpit seemed to rise up into the air. J swung his head around to see if they were flying, he couldn't tell. They continued up, the cockpit seeming to fold upon itself. His seat was now on top of Ariel's and everywhere he looked screens displayed the environment around them, the glass of the canopy was opaque. He glanced down, hoping to see Ariel, but only saw more screens and the floor.

"What just happened?" J's eyes darted about, trying to make sense of what he was seeing.

"Battle droid mode!" she bellowed with maniacal laughter.

Huge mechanical arms swung in front of them. The screens made the view nearly transparent, displaying what he would have seen had nothing been there. At his feet were two pedals, between his legs a stick protruded from the floor, buttons adorning the top. To his sides were rows of physical buttons and switches. Switching his gaze to the exterior again, he spotted Riku's warriors firing at them. Instinctively he tried to duck and kicked the left pedal with his foot. The machine dipped down to the left. Not being strapped in, he hit the left wall, his hand planted on one of the screens. A beeping sound started, his eyes were drawn to the screen. He pushed his hand away, the screen read, "Mauler RÖV-20 anti-aircraft laser cannons armed."

"What are you doing back there? Get your foot off the pedal, I'm driving!" Ariel berated.

J pulled himself back into the seat, Ariel corrected his intervention, standing the craft up. He watched as she let off round after round at their attackers. Riku and his men found cover near the hangar door. Ariel advanced the mecha toward them, letting loose a barrage of laser blasts as they peeked around the corner. She continued walking the metal giant out the door into the tunnel, then turned and shot the final three, they had nowhere to run. J peered closer, his eyes scanning, leaning forward in his seat. He caught himself nearly slipping onto the pedals again.

"I don't see Riku!"

She panned the craft left and right, scanning both sides of the hallway, no sign. Suddenly, the ship lunged forward, not by Ariel or J's doing, but by a massive strike to the rear of the craft. Ariel caught the ship, stopping it as it stumbled forward. She quickly snapped the machine around, another Valkyrie stood upright facing them. A window popped up in the screen, Riku stared back.

"The book," he uttered in his low slow tone, his face determined.

The two metal machines faced off, weapons drawn, frozen. It was like the Wild West, all they needed was a tumbleweed to roll by. Ariel whistled a short tune that J had never heard and laughed to herself. J frantically searched for a seatbelt, spinning and twisting his body around. He found two shoulder straps then two more straps near his thighs. J pulled them together, clipped them into their slots as he heard Ariel's response.

"If you want it, come and get it."

She fired a cannon blast, scorching the chest of Riku's ship. It stumbled back giving them a chance to get out, Zane was coming, they'd have backup. She turned the large robotic craft's metal body and began running, thundering down on the floor beneath. J shook about as he felt vibrations from the impact reverberate up the legs into the cockpit. They stumbled sideways as they were hit again from behind, Ariel corrected and kept running.

"Figure out the weapons systems, you've locked me out. All I've got is this cannon blast," Ariel commanded.

J didn't respond, he had no idea where to even begin. His lack of knowledge with this new technology was tremendously frustrating. *At least it's in English.* He touched multiple buttons on the screens, opened more menus as Ariel continued driving the mecha toward the entrance. More false steps as the mecha wobbled from Riku's shots, they were almost there. They skidded through the doorway on one foot as Ariel twisted the mecha to the side. J was still attempting to make sense of the menus.

"Ugh! I can't find anything," he growled, waving his hands in the air.

"Look for anything that says "anti-aircraft"," she responded through tight teeth.

Blasts zipped out of her cannon, hitting Riku, knocking his mecha's shoulder back. It didn't stop his pursuit, he was nearly on top of them. Ariel braced for impact, the two metal monsters crashed into each other. Ariel leaned the mecha into Riku's as his momentum slid them back. Riku cocked back an arm and threw a punch, Ariel countered, catching it with her mecha's gigantic hand. Riku attempted again with the other arm, but was met with the same result. The two were locked, hand in hand, shoving back and forth.

"Any luck? I don't think I can hold him much longer!"

J tapped on more menus, slapped his hands over his face.

"I can't find anything."

He peered through his fingers, something caught his eye.

"What about Mauler RÖV-20 anti-aircraft laser cannons?"

"Yes, fire them now!"

J looked up for the first time since Ariel had asked

him to find the weapons. He recoiled at the sight of Riku's large mecha in front of him, shook in his chair momentarily. The huge metal robot appeared as if it were inside the cockpit with him.

Ariel was losing patience and beginning to wonder if their mecha would be able to hold out, "Hurry up back there!"

J gathered himself and saw a button labeled "launch" under the laser cannon line of text, he pushed it. Instantly he was thrown forward into his safety straps, his arms flailing. Light blinded him, as his eyes shut, everything went dark.

He blinked. Widening his eyes, J shook his head. It was dark, nearly pitch black. A small green glow filled the cockpit giving him just enough light to see in front of him. He was lying on his side, the restraint system tight. He unbuckled it, falling onto the side of the craft. Pain shot through his body, he closed his eyes again, groaned as he pushed himself up.

"Ariel?" His voice was weak, he was still stunned from what had just happened. *What did just happen?* He called for Ariel again, no response. J fumbled around the panels, nothing was on. Some of the panels crackled and sparked, creating a momentary picture of the destruction around him. He was still in the mecha but the twisted metal around him made him realize, it wasn't going to be their ride. He called for Ariel again, still nothing. *Was she okay?* He found a handle near what would have been the top of the ship. He pulled on it then was able to figure out it needed a twist. Metal grinded as the hatch flipped open. Light shined in from the tunnel, he covered his eyes, squinting as he pulled himself out. J took a deep breath as he exited, standing up he surveyed the carnage. The two mechas lay devastated about 50 yards apart. He squinted his eyes, still burning from the light. Riku's ship was a twisted ball of metal. Pieces of various shapes contoured around others creating patterns that resembled nothing like what it once was. He stared down at his pile, it appeared to be in a similar state, if not slightly more distinguishable. His head was cloudy, his knees wobbly as he made his way through the wreckage. *Ariel, crap is she okay? Where was she? Was she okay?* He rushed over to where he believed her escape hatch would be. It was open.

"Ariel," his voice quivered.

He waited a moment, nothing. He got down on his knees and crawled into the hole, he called for her again, and still nothing. His eyes adjusted to the near darkness, the seat was empty, she'd made it out. He backed out of the machine and stood up quickly, his head swinging around searching for any sign of her. Sparks kicked up from pieces of the craft with a loud crack. J nearly slipped off, but kept his balance as he moved over the curled and tangled wreckage. His head pounded as he massaged it with his hand while investigating for clues to her whereabouts. Once on the ground, he observed the main door behind Riku's mecha, maybe she'd headed out. His face tightened and his eyebrows pulled into Vs. *Why would she leave him?* J decided to head over toward the door, maybe Zane was there and she needed help getting him out. He trudged along, still holding his head. He was relieved and terrified that Ariel had gotten out.

"The book."

He knew that voice. He'd hoped Riku had fared worse than them. He spun to the sound.

"Is that all you..." his voice trailed off as the scene came into view.

Riku stood near the main door, his outstretched arm bloody, holding Ariel by the sash around her middle; her body, legs and arms dangling lifeless. J lunged forward wanting to run at him. Riku grabbed Ariel's neck with his spare hand, her head appeared as small as a grapefruit in it.

"The book," he intoned again, unremorseful.

J touched his stomach. He felt a slight sense of relief, it was still there, he had forgotten about it. The book had essentially become part of his body, he barely noticed it was there. He slid it out of his waistline and held it up.

"Trade?" He took a step forward

Riku didn't move the hand surrounding Ariel's skull, her hair dangled below. J cautiously took another step forward, his eyes fixed on the giant. Ariel meant more to him than anyone, he wouldn't jeopardize her safety for anything. Besides, they'd received the next crumb, they wouldn't need the book. Plus it was locked and only he could unlock it. Ariel began to move her hands, reaching up like small doll she grabbed onto the giant. She kicked, he squeezed, she stopped her struggle as J heard a small whimper. He continued to edge toward them. Riku set Ariel on her feet then slipped his hand to the back of her neck, his thumb and forefinger touched. She reached up, attempting to pry his fingers off her neck. J noticed her tap on her Datacle then struggled with the monstrous hand again. By now, J was within five feet of them, holding the book out in front of him with two hands as if it were a mighty shield. The big brute pointed his blaster to the book then to the ground, his grip still tight on Ariel's throat.

"No—," Ariel tried to get out, her vocal cords silenced by the massive hand.

J crept forward, bent down and placed the book on the cold steel floor, never breaking eye contact with Ariel. He stood up slowly and backed away from it. Riku's foot stomped the ground as he took a step toward J. He felt the tremors run past him as Riku continued toward the book. Ariel struggled, but was put in check by another squeeze, she relented her arms falling to her sides. J took a step forward and Riku raised his blaster, aimed at his head. He retreated a step, his hands over his head. Riku knelt down and clutched the book in the same hand as the blaster, never letting go of the blaster or Ariel. It looked like a children's book in his hand. He placed it in his waistband as J had done, then waved the pistol toward the door. J got the hint and crept toward it. He marched in front of them, turning around every few paces to see what Riku was doing behind him. Ariel's throat was still clasped by his hand and he scowled at J. They stopped at the elevator they'd come in on. The doors opened, Riku shoved J into the elevator and followed close behind with Ariel.

"Please state destination."

J glared up at Riku. As Ariel watched, J straightened up. "The Hangar," J instructed, hoping Zane would be there when they arrived.

The elevator began down. Riku pressed the blaster to J's temple, let out a growl and squeezed Ariel. She squirmed in pain.

"Where to then?" J asked, slightly lifting his shoulder.

J almost smiled waiting to see if the giant had any other words. The blaster was pressed harder into his forehead, nearly knocking him into the wall.

J took the hint, "Elevator, ground level."

The elevator slowed to a stop then ascended. J stood there eyeing Riku, the blaster sill pointing at his head. He glanced at Ariel, she was fiddling with her Datacle again. He locked in on her face. Her mouth transformed from a grim frown to a knowing smirk as the elevator stopped.

CHAPTER NINE

The door opened, night greeting them as J stepped out followed by Ariel then their captor, Riku. They'd been down there for hours, the time slipped away quicker than he'd realized. At the end of the street a parked car sat motionless, a single man inside. It was black with chrome handles, bumpers and mirrors. J could see the moonlight glinting off of it. As they approached the car, a chubby man stepped out from the far side. J realized that the steering wheel was on the wrong side. He looked at Ariel, questioning, but she was in no position to talk. The chubby man sporting a bowler hat and pencil mustache opened the passenger door smiling, his eyes so tight they resembled slits.

J reluctantly slid in, sitting on the far side. Ariel was shoved in. As she landed in the seat next to him, she rubbed her neck now free of Riku's grip. He was the next in, the car swayed, suspension straining. He sat down and the entire car bounced. His pistol fixated on Ariel, she took a deep breath and stared out the windscreen. J did the same. Two more cars, identical to the one in which they were housed, sat in front of them. Behind them another. J had noticed them as they were climbing in. The chubby man shut the front door and the engine roared to life. J wondered at Ariel's plan, she had to have one. She always had one. Riku was staring at them, his eyes never leaving their faces. The moonlight lit up the Earth as if it was dusk, Atlantis hung watching over them.

Was Zane still up there? V? The convoy motored away from town, the mountain disappearing behind them.

"Where are you taking us?" Ariel finally asked, glaring up at Riku.

J could see the bruises already forming around her neck. Riku growled in response, his eyes tightened on them. The cars moved onto a larger highway. Ariel elbowed J in the side as she slid toward him in the turn, he cried out in pain, shocked. Riku looked at him and growled again. J realized she'd done it on purpose.

"What was that for!?" he yelled, distracting their captor.

Ariel grasped the giant's wrist, twisting it. The blaster flicked up to the front seat. Riku reached for her as she ducked, kicking him in the knee. He let out a snarl, his hands clutching his knee.

"Out now, J!"

Riku grasped at the air trying to contain her as she flipped over the front seat. The chubby man swerved off the road seeing her appear next to him, his eyes widened as he attempted to regain control, tapping the breaks. J turned to Ariel and hesitated.

"Now, J. Trust me, go!"

He popped the handle, the door swung open. J stared down at the road speeding by below, cold, hard, unforgiving. He leaned out head first, one hand on each side of the doorframe, then pulled his upper body inside the vehicle leaning toward Riku. Riku turned his attention toward J and lunged at him with both arms. J darted backward, desperately trying to stay out of reach, his butt hung off the seat out into the crisp night air. His right arm latched onto the seat, his left frantically searched for a handhold until finally finding the door handle. The door swung open further and the chubby man swerved again. J's arms spread, his large wingspan stretching to capacity. He groaned as he attempted to hold on. At the same time, Ariel wrapped her sash around the giant's arms, locking them together. She was quick and had to be, he was much stronger than her. His arms now secured, he swung for Ariel missing as she ducked. She kicked the driver in the knee sliding down to the floorboards. He released the gas pedal and grabbed his knee. J realized they were slowing down and glanced behind them as the scenery began to slow.

"For the last time, go!" he heard Ariel shout from out of sight.

J closed his eyes and gave a huge kick, rocketing himself out of the vehicle. Hitting the ground, he tumbled and bounced eventually coming to a stop just off of the road. He heard the sound of skidding. The car came to a stop and Ariel appeared out the side door, her Kimono flowing in the air. Riku stepped out, his arms still tied in the sash. She turned, seeing him, sprinted toward J. Riku placed the door jamb between his arms and gave a big pull, ripping the sash like paper. He spun around and took off as well, chasing Ariel. Riku tumbled forward as he was hit from behind by a blaster shot, J bolted straight up searching for the culprit. A large ship solidified in the sky above them, more blasts fired at one of the cars, setting it ablaze. The ship continued its approach toward them, firing a barrage of blasts at the convoy. J's eyes moved to the road, men were exiting the cars to the convoy and firing back. The side ramp lowered as the rescue vessel hovered in. J scurried toward Ariel as the ship settled in only 5 yards away. Zane appeared in the door with a photoplasma anti-personnel rifle and began laying down covering fire. J had been shown one before, but had never seen one in action, the sound was deafening. He tried to cover his ears, but it was no use, the report still penetrated. Ariel hurtled the low ramp, J managed it as well but with less grace. Blasts hit the hull of the ship as the ramp closed, Zane stepped in, the door sealed shut, cloaking system engaged.

"You guys alright?" He hung his weapon on a rack near the door, the danger passed for now.

"Thanks to you and Ariel. Did you have this planned the whole time?" J asked, sucking wind.

"Not exactly," Ariel replied between breaths.

"Yeah, you were lucky I translated your gibberish. The message looked like it was from a four year old." Zane grinned, awaiting the comeback.

"Look who's talking! "Irregardless" still isn't a word, besides, you try sending a message blind while your neck's being crushed by a 500 pound gorilla." She stared back at him, straight-faced, her arms folded holding her Kimono together. It didn't last long, she broke into a mischievous grin. Zane laughed it off as he approached them.

"You didn't finally teach V how to fly, did you? How'd you get this ship to hover while you went all Rambo?"

Zane gave Ariel a chagrined smile, placing his hand on the back of his head. Rubbing his neck, he cleared his throat. "No, can you imagine that little thing flying this ship? Got a new pilot, but I think you'll want to see for yourself."

Ariel stood there a moment studying his face, her eyebrows furrowed, her nose wrinkled a bit. J was taking it all in trying to figure out where this exchange was going. He knew V and Zane, but who else was there? *Atlantis was empty, or was it?*

"Pretty slick approach, huh? Ship's on autopilot now. Everyone make it in okay?"

Ariel's ears perked up, her eyes tightened, mouth turned down. *She knew that voice but it couldn't be. He was on the Exodus.* A man stepped down off the deck onto the stairs. His hair was shoulder length, strawberry blonde. J couldn't tell his height, but he seemed fit, not Zane fit, but maybe like a quarterback. He wore a one-piece burgundy suit, what J would have described as a mechanic's suit. A gilt of light reflected off of a set of gold wings on his chest. Ariel stalked up the stairs toward him.

"Ariel...babe, glade to see you're safe," the man welcomed her, sporting a ridiculous grin.

She made it to the top, not saying a word. The guy

leaned on the edge of entranceway crossing his arms, he crossed a leg over resting it on his toe. Ariel stopped and gave him a sexy smile, he straightened up and checked her out from head to toe. She was still holding the Kimono together, but let it slip a bit. He smiled and began to lean forward, anticipating what would come next. His head snapped to the side, Ariel had open-hand slapped him. He grabbed his jaw, leaning back into the wall, his face tight with pain. Ariel didn't say a word, just stormed off toward the bridge. J gaped at Zane, his eyes wide, a look of bewilderment on his face.

"What was that about?"

Zane laughed heartily. "That's Max, one of TKs hotshot pilots. Ariel dated him, but broke it off when he chose TK over her."

"What? Why's he here?"

"Guess last minute he stayed behind. We could use a good pilot, we're short a crew at this point."

Zane had a good point. After losing Jolt, Sonya, and Gatlin, they were now down to the four of them. That would have been hard enough straightening out Earth, now they had to find a bunch of scientists. And better yet, Riku was out there. Chills shot through his body ending with the hairs on his neck, he didn't want to tangle with him again.

"So what did you guys find? Sounded like a book of some sort."

"The book!" J grabbed his belt, franticly checking his waistline. He patted himself down hoping he was wrong.

The book was gone, Riku had it. In their haste they had forgotten about it. He put both hands on his head pulling back his hairline. He closed his eyes, took a deep breath. "We left it, Riku has it."

"Riku? Who's Riku?"

"Riku's um...well...a bad guy. A monstrously huge bad guy."

J didn't know how else to explain him, he wanted the book plain and simple. He wasn't sure what he wanted with the book, but he wanted it. J explained their run-in, the first attack nearly killing Ariel. Then showing up in the storage facility. His mind wandered at this point. *How did he get in there? It was on total lockdown.* It was at this point Ariel showed up wearing a suit almost identical to Max's. J thought it must've been his, it was much too big on her. Her sleeves and pant legs were rolled up, she was still sporting quite the scowl.

Zane tried to lighten her mood, "Got tired of holding yourself together?"

Ariel just blew it off. *That's not like her, where was the zippy one line comeback?* His mind moved to the book, he didn't want to share his revelation, but figured it was now or never.

"Riku has the book."

Ariel closed her eyes and tilted her head back. "Could this day get any worse?" She sighed.

J pinched his lips together and looked at Zane for help, he shrugged his shoulders as if reading his thoughts.

"You find supplies?" Ariel broke the silence, she

needed to keep her mind occupied.

"Yep, that's where we found…" Zane caught himself, the next word out of his mouth was going to be …

"Max?" Ariel finished it for him, her nose wrinkled, her upper lip slightly curled.

J had seen a similar look before and it didn't end well for the enemy. He tried to quickly change the subject. "Got any food?"

Zane paused while Ariel continued staring at the wall. "Yep, you want some rations now or real food when we get to Atlantis?"

J didn't mind the rations, but real food sounded much more appealing. He began craving those dumplings. He passed on the rations and decided to wait it out, they'd be there in short order. Ariel sat down on one of the jump benches lining the cargo hold. J stayed next to Zane chatting a bit, but his eyes kept drifting to her. She sat legs crossed at the knee, arms folded, staring at the metal grating lining the floor. He informed Zane about the dossier and about what he saw when utilizing the dream machine. By the time Zane was all caught up, they were nearing Atlantis. Zane headed to the bridge to see if anything needed to be done to the ship prior to docking. J gingerly approached Ariel and sat down next to her. She was still in the same position, her foot kicking about at the ankle, chewing on her bottom lip, staring through the floor.

"You okay?" he asked softly, he remembered his meltdown and how good it felt to have her near. He hoped he'd be able to provide the same for her. She nodded her head slowly then took a deep breath.

"You need a Datacle right?"

J smiled searching her face, she returned it, though he could tell she was fighting through something.

"Sure do." He placed his hand on her thigh.

She relaxed her arms and her hand joined his. They sat there in silence listening to the engines change thrust, the landing gear extend, the docking sequence commence. J enjoyed her hand in his, she leaned her head onto his shoulder. J closed his eyes, exhaling deeply. The rattling of the landing sequence came to a stop, the cargo door slowly hinged down. Zane was the first to pop out of the bridge.

"Let's get you that food," he said, his eye on J.

J stood up and looked down at Ariel, "Coming?" He extended a hand out displaying a half smile.

Ariel took it and they headed onto Atlantis. Once off the craft, Zane guided them into and adjacent room where an elevator awaited. The whole walk, J's eyes explored the city, remembering some of it. In some ways, he still thought it a dream that he would wake up from at any moment, yet it persisted. At the elevator the three of them stepped in turning around as the doors began to close. Max came into view, his hand in the air, running toward them.

"Wait!" he cried.

Ariel reached up and pressed the "close doors" button, the doors shut and the elevator began to move. Zane and J looked at one another over Ariel who was leaning on the back wall, one leg kicked out the other almost in a half squat. Her arms were crossed and her upper eyelids dominated as she gazed at the door. 120 floors up they stepped off the elevator. J recognized where they were almost instantly. After a quick turn down the adjacent hallway and through another door, they entered V's lab. She was standing at a workbench playing with a device he'd never seen. Spying them, she planted it on the table and greeted them with a big smile. She ran over to Ariel, grabbing her hand.

"I need to check you out, I heard what happened."

"I'm fine. Dr. Akinosuke patched me up." Ariel's energy was coming back as she smiled back at V.

"Nonsense, he's a dream doctor. What did he patch you up with? Some ribbon and tape? You need a real checkup, come with me."

Ariel seemed to have no choice, V took her hand and towed her out of the room. J opened his mouth, but nothing came out, he wasn't sure how to react.

Zane leaned over to J. "Wanna get some grub?"

"Someone say grub? I could eat."

Max, strutted in, pushed his hair back with one hand. *Only girls have hair that long.* Something about the guy made him uneasy, but he couldn't put a finger on it quite yet. *How could Ariel like a guy like that?*

CHAPTER TEN

Zane took them up six floors to an empty dining facility, they had the run of the place. J felt guilty, like they were sneaking around someone's property, but Zane reassured him nobody was home and nobody was coming back. In the mad rush to board Exodus, plenty of food was left behind so Zane had his choice of ingredients to create culinary masterpieces. He loved to cook, it was his favorite hobby. J found it quite peculiar watching the big man strut around the kitchen in his apron, dancing to a song only he could hear, but enjoyed the show.

Zane flew around cleaning dishes while he cooked, a technique J wished his mom would've incorporated. That way he wouldn't have had so many to clean before bed. *How were they doing?* He thought of his life on the farm, how simple it was, hard work, but simple. This new life was growing on him, but it wore on him at the same time. Zane took special orders from him and Max. Max asked for a filet mignon with smashed potatoes and steamed vegetables. J requested his new favorite dish, steamed dumplings. In no time, Zane had the two plates done and one of his own, a western style skillet. The three sat down at a nearby table and began eating. J enjoyed the flavors, savoring every bite. Max concentrated on the room more than anything, he acted like he was in his own world... and the master of that world. Zane, on the other hand, devoured his plate then leaned back in his chair, instantly falling asleep waiting for the others.

"So you're Arcturus' son?" Max broke the silence.

J clenched a hand under the table, someday he hoped that everyone would just call him by his first name and leave off the Arcturus part. It was hard enough for him to get accustomed to the name "J", let alone his father's name as well. He set his fork down after swallowing.

"Yes, and you're Max from what I hear."

J studied him, one eyebrow raised. He clenched and released his jaw. He knew nothing about Max, but it seemed that he and Ariel had a past. *What did he do to deserve the greeting he witnessed?* He looked down at his plate, aggressively stabbing another dumpling with his fork.

"So, how do you know Ariel?

Max set his fork down and leaned back in his chair, a devious smirk grew out of the side of his mouth. His hands slipped over the back of his head, fingers interlocked. He kicked a foot up, resting it on his other leg then let out a long breath. His eyes flicked from his plate to a nearby window. J briefly glanced over to it, the sky glow was beginning to dim. In the distance he could see the buildings sloping up, a reminder of where he was. His attention turned back to Max still awaiting an answer.

"Childhood friends," Max stated, still gazing out the window.

J felt relieved, but only momentarily.

"We were dating," he continued. "But I had a commitment I couldn't break, she could."

J's teeth ground against each other. He firmly set

down the fork causing a metallic echo as the two surfaces collided. J's heart sped up, he could feel it pulsating through his body. The sound drew Max's attention, he noticed J's distress at the answer.

"So, how's she been? Good?"

J really didn't want to say a word. He glanced over at Zane who was still knocked out, a light snore coming from his mouth. He picked up the fork again and stabbed the last of his meal then, about to pop it in his mouth, stated, "Never better."

Max chuckled as J contentiously chewed. He turned to look out the window again. J focused his eyes on Max, studying everything about him. His burgundy flightsuit, his shoulder-length hair, the scuffed chrome boots. He had only just met the guy, but there was something about him he didn't like.

"Everyone done with their food? Looks like Zane is."

Max and J glanced at Zane, then over to the door where V was standing. Her lab coat hung past her hips emphasizing her small stature. In her right hand, she held something J couldn't quite see.

"Ariel wants us to discuss the next move. She said you found a dossier of some kind?"

J had almost forgotten the dossier. He stood up and tapped Zane on the shoulder. The big man started, his arms flailed. He gathered himself and climbed to his feet. Max laughed, following suit.

"Where to?" J asked.

"The Briefing Room," she replied, spinning around

and walking out.

J didn't know where that was, his sense of direction had never been that strong and having only been there once before made it much more difficult. He waved his arm underhanded to Zane who took the hint and led the way. They reached the room and found Ariel pulling up the dossier. She stepped back as the screen shifted in front of them, displaying what J had seen before.

-   Dr. Liliana Zabłacka Sector 9
        Block 14-Warsaw, Poland
-   Dr. Natalia Zabłacka Sector 9
        Block 14-Warsaw, Poland
-   Dr. Lucas Huergo Sector 15
        Block 6- Buenos Aires, Argentina
-   Dr. Patrick Geddes Sector 2
        Block 18-Glasgow, Scotland

J watched Ariel as she shifted her weight onto one leg, placed a hand on her hip, still eyeing the dossier on the board. Every time he saw her, his heart skipped a beat then started racing in his chest. His world narrowed until it was just the two of them and he was often caught staring. Max stepped into his line of sight, J's eyes narrowed as he shifted his view, Ariel disappearing behind Max.

Max ambled toward Ariel and the screen. "So, this is the list? What's so important about them?"

J stood there staring daggers at Max's back. Ariel glared over her shoulder, feeling Max's approach. She didn't bother to answer. Zane had found a seat on the other side of the room while V made her way to the screen as she broke the silence.

"So Arcturus told you to gather them here? Did he say why?"

Ariel turned to focus on J, her gaze passed through Max as if he were a ghost. J ran through the dream in his head. His father never disclosed why, only the need to find them to help combat a new threat.

"My father was adamant that we gain more allies, these allies because a new threat would be coming. Something about vanished TK members." He shrugged his shoulders, hands out.

"So Arcturus is alive? Where is he?" Max spun around, his mouth continued to hang open after the question.

J shook his head, but remained silent. V's eyes centered on the two of them, observing the situation.

Max's head pushed back into his traps. "So...how did he talk to you? Is he a ghost or something?"

J clenched his hands into tight fists, squeezing then releasing.

V broke J's silence for him. "Arcturus implanted memories into J's head. He has dreams of his father."

Max scrutinized V, his eyebrows dancing near the top of his head, a slight frown on his lips. His reaction ended with a long drawn out, "Okay".

V switched to Ariel, wanting to keep the conversation moving. "So who's going to get who?"

Ariel surveyed the room, finishing up with the display. Her free hand moved to her lip, tapping it. J's attention focused on her, a slight smile crossed his lips. Max stepped into view, again interrupting his thoughts.

"How about me and you go get Dr. Huergo? You've always loved South America." Max winked at Ariel.

She ignored him and kept concentrating.

He paused then cajoled, "You know we make a great team. It'll be fun, like old times."

J's mind wandered. *Old times? Fun? What did they do in the past? How close were they?* His face became hard. Max's words drifted away, the next few sentences in his mind garbled. *Had they been together long? What did he need to do about the situation?* His muscles flexed, he felt a hand on his shoulder.

"It's cold there this time of year."

V stood there smiling at him. *What just happened? What did he miss?* His eyes searched the ground his mouth half hung open, finally he focused enough to ask. His eyes locked onto V. "What's the plan?"

"You and I are going to acquire Liliana and Natalia, Zane's going after Geddes and Ariel's going to pick up Huergo. Were you not listening?"

His eyes drifted to Ariel, V's eyes followed, then she refocused back on J.

"No need to worry about him. Oh! I forgot to give you this earlier."

Her outstretched hand held a Datacle. J eyed the device, something about it was different. He grabbed it, but his focus turned again to Ariel. Max was talking to her, but he couldn't make out what was being said. He could hear his heart pumping, but as he strained to hear the conversation, only a whisper came back. The room hummed from the equipment, the screens squealed with static, the universe seemed to be telling him to give up. V tugged at his wrist, J snapped out of his trance peering back at her.

"We should go get our equipment, it's going to be cold there this time of the year."

He leaned his head closer to V. "Where are we going again?"

Her soft features hardened, brow furrowed, eyes narrowed. "I'm not saying another word until we're out of this room."

J straightened up as V led him out of the room. He swung his head back to get one last glimpse of Ariel, standing arms crossed, talking to Max. J was lost in his thoughts as he and V made their way down the corridors and took an elevator ride. He was trying to put the pieces together and getting out of the room helped, slightly. V had mentioned something as they marched and his mind snapped to his dream, his father, the dossier. *Who were those people on the list and why were they so important? What were they going to find? What was Sector 9 going to be like?* The final door opened and J told himself not to be surprised, then froze. Inside were racks of clothes, boxes of boots, stacks of weapons and other items he didn't recognize.

"It's going to be cold there, so start in aisle 9W."

J stepped in and began searching the walls for signs, there weren't any. He walked past five or six aisles then turned to ask V, she was gone.

"V?"

His hand buzzed. Looking down, he realized it was the Datacle. In his haze of thoughts, he hadn't put it on. Slipping it over his wrist, he answered and V's image appeared.

"I hear you. I'm down a couple of rows grabbing some equipment. Are you lost?"

J nodded. "Yes, I can't find any signs. You said W9?"

"9W. There aren't any signs. Use your Datacle's map feature and ask it to find 9W. Oh wait! Before you do that, you'll have to program its name. Tap the screen and press "setup"."

J did as instructed. The Datacle came to life and requested a DNA sample, he pressed his forefinger to the screen. After a series of some rather odd questions, it asked for a name. J locked up trying to think of something good, not a single name came to his head. He stared at it, his eyes wide, shaking his head. *A name, a name...Robby.* Once J input the name, the Datacle completed setup and he wasted no time testing it.

"Robby, direct me to aisle W9."

"J, I deduce that you mean aisle 9W as there is no aisle W9. You will find aisle 9W three rows over to the right and 50 yards down."

J's head pushed back, his eyes grew large at the sound

of the voice. It was British and well mannered, not at all what he'd expected. He shook it off and headed to the correct section. Amongst the hangers he found an assortment of clothes. As he began digging through them, he noticed that everything seemed familiar. Shirts, and pleated pants, shoes, cardigan sweaters, women's skirts. It all reminded him of Earth. He found a shirt and pulled it from the rack. examining it.

"You'll need a suit and I recommend a heavy wool coat and hat." V popped around the corner.

J placed the shirt back on the hanger. He thought about it a moment, he'd never worn a suit before and didn't know where to start. His turned his eyes to V who was busy slipping on a dress and quickly looked back at the rack, flipping through hangars until he got to the suits. They were made from various materials, some smooth, others a little rough. He pulled one from the rack.

"No, let's go for a three piece suit. We'll be in downtown Warsaw, want to blend in."

V approached him wearing a dull green business dress, over her arm draped a purple wool coat. She took the suit from his hand and placed it back on the rack.

"This one will look better on you," she said, handing him a dark grey suit.

J took it and held it up, trying to discern the difference between it and the suit he'd picked.

V rummaged through the rack and produced a dark grey wool trench coat. "It'll be cold there, better take this."

"Thanks, mom," J smiled. V just raised her eyebrows.

They finished getting dressed then headed down to the hangar to meet up with the rest of the crew before departure. J spotted Ariel climbing onto the ship they arrived on, Max stepped into view as he approached.

"Beauty right?" he smirked.

J had a few choice words dancing though his mind as he began to strut. He lifted his head high trying to appear larger, his arm swings exaggerated.

"She's a great ride. You'll love it," Max continued.

J's jaw tightened, his mind working overtime trying to figure out a response. It had to be good, he had to defend Ariel. Max's eyes followed the spacecraft's doorway, sliding his hand up the entranceway as he leaned on the wall.

"Her name's Omorfiá. She's a Drákon class bomber, modified of course. Nothing else like her." His smirk had now grown into a full grin.

J proceeded past him, not sparing a glance in his direction. Max watched and gave a light chuckle, tapping on the control panel to close the door behind them. J made his way to the bridge where everyone was beginning to take their seats. The bridge was set up with two seats near the front and center, one of them currently occupied by Ariel. Behind were four more seats, two facing the outer walls. Zane was sitting in one and next to him, someone he didn't recognize. J stopped momentarily as V came in behind him. The man was short, and by short he meant very short, even sitting J could tell he was small. His head was bald, his face plump, his eyes and mouth in a constant scowl. He looked like he did little exercise, his shirt was baggy, but it didn't hide that fact.

"Who's that?" he asked V as she began to walk past.

"That's Grant. It seems there are quite a few stragglers TK left behind. Guess they weren't part of the plan."

Grant, why did that name sound familiar? He made his way down toward Ariel, his tunnel vision focused on her. Grant hopped up in front of him, blocking J's path. He tensed up.

"Hey kid. Nice suit," he exclaimed.

His voice was scratchy and gruff, but a slight jovial tone came along with it at odds with his grim visage.

"Sorry about the hat issue, it was the best one I had at the time."

J's mind clicked. *Grant. He was the one who gave Ariel the hat to hide him from TK. Where's he been this whole time?* He towered over Grant, the guy couldn't have been much more than five feet tall. Grant extended a hand, he took it in return.

"No hard feelings, right kid?"

Out of the corner of his eye he saw Max glide past, taking up position next to Ariel. She glanced over as he sat down then redirected her gaze back to the screen. J's heart tightened, his shoulders sagged, mouth dropping slightly.

The ship's engines hummed to life. "Better get in our seats, this rig's freakin' fast."

Though his words made it seem like he was in a decent mood, Grant's face in no way changed from the perma-scowl. It was completely incongruous, never shifting emotion. J wanted to play with it like a puppet master to make it respond to what he was saying. J surveyed the room, spotting a seat next to V near the back of the bridge. Taking his seat, he gathered his thoughts. V would have the answers, he was sure of it.

CHAPTER ELEVEN

The ship lifted off the ground, the engines whined. J readied himself for the G forces on takeoff, his eyes drifted to Ariel.

"So why are we together? I mean why am I..." he asked.

V was digging into a small bag next to her seat. "Relax, Ariel will be fine. She's been to Argentina a few times. You're with me because you still don't know enough about our systems to go it alone. Zane can handle himself and so can Ariel. Max is just providing the ride." She handed him a blaster in a holster. "You're my escort today. I'll be the guide," she gave him a Cheshire cat grin.

He opened his coat and suit, shrugged out of them and ran the leather belt around his shoulders. While J was putting his suit jacket back on, he was momentarily pinned back as the ship took off, his arm stuck behind him, his face smacked into the headrest. He groaned slightly as the acceleration continued, then the pressure suddenly released. His body shot forward and tumbled to the floor. He heard the sound of laughter and looked up to see Ariel still smiling with her beautiful laugh. He grimaced as his eyes shifted to Max who was also laughing. J picked himself up and climbed back into the seat, crossing his arms and slouching.

"You okay? That was a good tumble. Do you need any medical attention?" V asked, standing up. J shook his head.

"Well, if you're sure you're alright, we're the first insertion. Let's head to the cargo hold and get ready."

J stood up, stared at the ground, hoping to become invisible. V headed back to the exit and he was again deep in his thoughts. A hand touched his, he almost jumped. He looked up to see Ariel, her beautiful ice blue eyes probing his.

"Be careful with V. Remember, she's a doctor not a warrior." She snickered as it rolled off her lips.

Ariel leaned in, tightening her grip on his hand and hooking her other arm around his waist. She eyed him a moment in silence then kissed him. Everything melted away as J absorbed the sensation, his body tingling.

Max's disgruntled voice broke through the haze, "15 minutes out. J should be getting ready."

Ariel stepped back and he almost felt woozy. Her eyes connected with his. "If you have any trouble, call me...maybe," she smiled, holding up the wrist sporting his Datacle to his ear.

J opened his mouth to say something, but nothing came out. He turned to head back with V, his body still buzzing. He arrived in the cargo hold to find V slipping on the large heavy wool coat, she pulled her hair out of it with both hands. She looked so young, was she going to pretend to be his sister? He didn't think she could pass as a business woman.

She noticed him enter and called him over. "Here, slide this in your ear." She held out an open hand, on top of which lay a small metallic sphere.

"What's this?"

"It's a translator, so that you'll be able to understand what people are saying. Sadly, you won't be able to talk to them though. It would take a few days to teach you."

J took the device, constantly amazed at the advancements of his new world. *Only a few days to learn an entire language. How was that possible?* He didn't ask, the answer probably too complicated, especially coming from V.

"One minute out," Max's voice rang smugly over the ship's intercom.

J thought that it sounded as if he was trying to relay the fact that he was getting rid of J and would have Ariel all to himself. He chewed on his cheek and pressed his hand against the holster. He half thought of shooting out the speaker. The Omorfiá began the docking procedure, gears whirled, hydraulics screeched, a hiss came from the bay door as it opened. V and J stepped off, turning to see the ship immediately take off.

"Why's everyone in such a hurry?"

"Since your run in with Riku, Ariel's been worried that there may be more like him. She didn't want to give them time to organize so we're gathering allies as fast as possible."

That made sense to J, but he would have liked a little more info before he was kicked out of the ship. He still didn't understand why he couldn't have gone to Argentina with her and had someone else pick up the two in Poland. She was with Max right now, his body shuddered at the thought. Something about the guy put him on edge. V reminded him that they needed to get moving and J tried to focus on their goal. *The sooner we find them, the sooner I see Ariel.* J followed, voicing to V that all of the underground tunnels looked exactly the same. For all he knew, they could've been back in sector 19 or sector 11. As they boarded the tube, his thoughts went back to his adopted parents on Earth, he hoped they were okay. Then a thought popped into his head, he'd never known anyone that was adopted. *Were his parents in on the plan with Arcturus?*

Stepping out of the transport device, V interrupted his thoughts. "Let's get topside quickly."

She grabbed his coat, tugging on it to get the fit right, and finished a button he'd missed. She patted him on the cheek like an affectionate aunt then proceeded to the elevator. He stood there a second, caught off guard by how much older she seemed to act at times, then jogged to catch up, reaching her as she stepped into the elevator. The ride up J was quiet, lost in his thoughts again. V was the same, hands in her pockets, standing as if she was a statue at the park. The doors opened and he found a similar sight to the other sectors, though instead of brick as before, the wall in front of him was made of large blocks of stone. They stepped out into the alleyway, the sound of autos bounced off his eardrums, the smell of fresh breads and fried cakes filled his nostrils. His face stung as a winter's wind rushed around his body. He shivered, clutching his torso.

"You weren't kidding. It's really cold here," he declared, teeth chattering.

V lifted her collar up around her neck. "You've been in colder."

That was true, but they'd been wearing bear fur and those fancy heated suits, not just a three piece suit and wool between his flesh and the negative temperatures. The sun was setting behind the ten story stone and brick buildings that made up Warsaw. At the end of the alley, a single building loomed over the city, as if it was keeping a watchful eye over everything in its domain. It had four small perfect rectangular pieces jutting up from the ground and a single larger piece in the center, topped with two additional layers and a massive clock imbedded in the center of the construction. J paused briefly, taking in the sight, forgetting momentarily about the cold.

"Come on. I thought you were complaining about the cold. We've gotta catch a taxi, it's quite a few blocks away. These temperatures aren't good for the human body, especially when not acclimatized to it."

J just nodded. *Acclimatized?* V's way of speaking often seemed alien to him. He was beginning to learn to just go with it. It was like trying to understand Ariel's pop culture references, only V's were very scientific. Either way, he should probably take the time to learn about his new world...once they stopped having to save it. It was cold and they needed to get out of the weather, that's all he cared about. At a brisk walk, they took off toward the main street. Cars zoomed by, horns honked, people moved quickly though the streets, shops were closing up. V waved a hand in the air as a black sedan pulled up. She reached for the door, opening it as the driver came over to help.

"Cześć," the man greeted, waiving J into the vehicle, closing the door behind him.

J looked over at V. She slid to the other side of the rear seat, legs crossed at the knee, staring straight ahead. He was about to ask her something when the driver sat down with a thud, closing his door.

V looked in the rearview mirror at the driver. "Al Jerozolimskie 45, Dziękuję."

The man rattled off something J didn't understand, then V responded with "tak."

J's eyes flicked over to the driver then her. "I thought you said I'd be able to understand the language," he whispered.

"English?" the driver perked up.

J turned to the driver, mouth half open, and stared.

"English? Are you from England?" he asked, eyes alight with interest.

"American." He turned to V, "I can understand him perfectly now. This is amazing."

"American, oh. I've never driven one before, don't get to many of you around here." His accent while speaking was clearly British.

V giggled and looked back at the driver, "That's because he's speaking English."

J raised an eyebrow at her then turned his attention

back to the driver, whose eyes switched from the road to them every few seconds. V took his arm and pushed his sleeve up exposing the Datacle. She typed a few commands on it, setting it back down in his lap, her hand still grasping the Datacle. He was still trying to figure out what she meant.

"Driver will you please say "tonight is a lovely evening" in Polish."

"Of course ma'am, tonight is a lovely," he began, then V pressed a button on the Datacle and the driver finished the sentence with the word, "cudowny."

J's eyebrows twisted up into his forehead, his eyes almost crossed. *What just happened?* V laughed as she looked back at the driver. Her laughter was infectious and he joined in. She composed herself.

"Our driver here happens to know how to speak in English. That's why you began to understand him. I forgot to turn on your translator."

She tapped his Datacle again, "It should be fixed now."

The driver chimed in again in English. He explained he loved practicing since he didn't have too many British travelers in his taxi, and J was the first American one he had ever had. The driver asked question after question, hanging on every word. In no time, they arrived at their destination. J thanked him for the fine conversation while V paid him. They stepped out into the bitter cold. The sun had set and the icy grip of night was taking hold.

J's eyes trained over the sedan as it drove away. The

large building he spotted earlier hung ominously over them, a flat area of grass and trees in between. He stared up, admiring the clock. His attention was diverted as he felt a hand grab his. Instinctively, he pulled it away, spun around.

"I don't bite. This way."

V reached over, grabbed his hand and tugged him along, leaving the looming building behind them. In front of them stood a building of stone, five stories tall. On the first story, large arched windows adorned the walls with a lighter colored stone making a sharp transition to a darker color. Upon the roof, sat a large ornate steel and glass greenhouse. V translated the sign above the door, it read "Professional School of Bioscience and Botany." V also explained what botany meant as they approached the door. J tried the handle, jiggling it.

"Locked. Any other way in?" He searched down the street, scanning over her head, hoping to see another entrance. A man studying them from the shadow of the adjacent building tossed a cigarette to the ground and stepped on it. He began to head toward them. As J scanned the building, he saw nothing to help them. Cars drove by, the wind bit his nose. V was skimming her Datacle, J caught a glimpse of her screen. It seemed there was another entrance around back.

"According to my information, there's an access door around back which I can gain entrance through."

J snickered, she sounded so formal. He responded in tone.

"Lead the way, oh enlightened one."

V tilted her head then began around the building, a beggar was sitting holding a cup out, rattling the few coins it held. They passed a couple who seemed a little tipsy and a man in a suit who appeared quite interested in them, but changed his course and crossed the street. Behind the building was a tight alleyway, the building adjacent to it was nearly as tall as the Bioscience building and had been built almost on top of it. J estimated it to be maybe four feet across. V stopped walking abruptly and J, not paying attention, bumped into her.

"Sorry," he apologized, recoiling from the contact.

V didn't say anything, but tightened her eyebrows at him. She began exploring the walls. "Should be here," she muttered, kneeling down toward the stone wall.

J began searching and found a slit just like at Will's building. He touched it, exposing a screen, then placed his hand on the glass.

"Denied," the glass shouted back.

"Good try, J, but I have to hack this one."

She pulled up the Datacle menu, a few strokes of her finger, and the wall opened revealing a stairwell. J stepped in first and began climbing up. The stairs wound around five times, leading them to a stone wall.

"Dead end." J placed both hands on the wall, tying to find another hidden panel.

V stepped around him and pressed her hand to the wall near the corner. A doorway opened up into an immense garden. J stopped, taking in the breathtaking view. They were in the conservatory he'd seen from the street. Large trees grew everywhere, flowers bloomed as if it were spring, a bee buzzed by his head causing him to duck. He peered up through the frosted glass above, the sky was clear and a few stars could be seen. The garden was dark, only a few scattered lights illuminated their view. V stepped by him, staring at her wrist. He followed as they stepped around multiple trees, shrubs, and the largest flowers he'd ever seen. They were reddish brown with white spots, had a large bowl-like center and five wide petals. He leaned down to sniff one and was immediately hit with the overwhelming need to vomit, they smelled like rotten meat. *Why would anyone grow flowers like that!?* He looked up to see that V had reached a glass wall with a door. J walked over and they stepped through it. The plants in this room he recognized. Rows of corn, wheat and sunflowers, but something was different about them. He stopped and leaned in closer to one of the ears of corn. It was huge, much bigger than anything he'd seen growing up. He spun his head around, "Hey V—." But she was already a few paces ahead. He jogged to catch up.

"Did you see the size of that corn?" he exclaimed, walking by her side.

"Yes. It was rather large for a Zea Mays. Must be something they're working on."

"Who? Lily and Natalie?"

"Liliana and Natalia. Yes, they're botanists. I imagine quite good ones if your father wanted them."

They continued walking, the greenhouse seemed to

extend forever, then came to an abrupt stop at a door made of opaque glass, light radiating from behind. J reached for the handle. Opening it, he strained his neck to see what was inside.

"Come in," a woman's voice called out.

"Yes, come in! We have some hot tea ready if you would like," another invited.

J finished pushing the door open. Two ladies sat at a small table, tea cups in their hand, a steaming kettle in the center. They were both slightly overweight, well-fed his mom would say, their faces soft and radiant. They both wore knitted sweaters, but that's where the similarities stopped. One had blonde hair, the other dark brown. They each wore a necklace, one a silver crescent-shaped moon and the other a nearly full gold moon.

"You could have just rung the bell."

"Yes, we have been expecting you, J, son of Arcturus."

J looked back at V expectantly. She'd told him that they wouldn't be able to understand him since he didn't know how to speak the language.

"Cat got you tongue?" the blonde sister quipped.

"Where are our manners? Let us introduce ourselves, we know who he is," the brunette suggested.

They stood up and walked over to J and V.

The blonde carried two cups of tea. "Here you go my dears," she handed a cup to each of them. "I am Liliana and this is my sister, Natalia."

"Arcturus told us that this day would come," Natalia added.

J took the tea from Liliana then realized what Natalia had said. His ears perked up and his head snapped back. "You spoke with my father?"

Liliana clucked her tongue, "Yes, you sound surprised to hear that dear."

"Do you know why you have come to get us?" Natalia added.

J blinked, his mind searching his memory. He hadn't been told why, only where to gather them. He finished by staring into the tea.

"We found a dossier and were instructed to bring you to Atlantis, but that was all the information we were given. Do you know more?" V filled the gap in conversation. She'd been silently reading the situation, assessing how everything was going. She was initially surprised that the sisters knew they would be coming, but realized that this was Arcturus' plan. There were always contingencies and no one person had all of the information, except for him.

Natalia started, "We know enough. There will be others to join us as we plan the future of Earth."

"We will provide the environmental oversight for her," Liliana finished.

J took a sip of tea then found a small table to set it down on. "So, should we go then?"

The sisters looked at each other then turned in unison, "Now?"

CHAPTER TWELVE

Liliana ran around packing items into a well-worn over-sized suitcase. Natalia was on the other side of the room doing the same. J watched the two women scrambling to find items that couldn't be left behind.

"We really need to get going. Any word from the others?"

V was tinkering with her Datacle, he even saw her shake it a few times.

"No. It seems I just have static. What about yours?"

"Same," he looked down at his wrist, tapping and scrolling through menus. He attempted to call Ariel and Zane again. He even went against every thread in his body and called Max.

"How much longer do you think this is going to take?" J asked no one in particular as he started to pace.

His thoughts drifted to Ariel. *Was she having the same issue? Did she find the Doctor without any trouble? Was she in trouble?* The sisters continued to toss items J had never seen before into their bags. He noticed Liliana packing a shawl and a dress. They didn't have the time or the luxury of taking their wardrobe with them. J was about to speak up when the sound of breaking glass echoed around them. All four of them froze as if playing a game. J leaned his ear toward the sound, more glass shattered, a rush of noise entered the room like the sea crashing onto the beach. Out of the corner of his eye, V pulled out a blaster. He did the same. It was warm in the apartment and he had shed the wool coat and suit jacket, the blaster was easily accessible.

Liliana gasped, clasped her right hand over her heart. "What was that?"

"Can't be good," answered Natalia, her gaze focused on the direction of the noise.

J's eyes centered on their bags then snapped up to V. "You stay here with them. I'll go check it out."

V nodded as he stepped out of the room. *What was he doing?* His arms trembled as he made his way back toward the greenhouse, his eyes flicked back and forth searching for any sign of movement. *What could have caused the crash*? He hoped it was a bird, but knew that was unlikely at night. His mind went to other possibilities as he opened the door to the arboretum. Something sharp hit his shoulder, he stumbled back in pain. His hand reached for the wound, a large metal throwing star protruded from it. Grabbing it, he yanked it out, screaming in pain then tossed it to the ground, the metal pinging as it hit the tile at his feet. His eyes shot back toward the door still clutching his shoulder. A man walked toward him, he could only see an outline. Wrapped in pitch black clothing, his body blended into the night, only his eyes flickered back. J noticed the glint of a blade catching the moonlight. The ground shook, J reached for his blaster. His fingers on the handle, he froze searching past the shadow man. The ground continued to shake. "It couldn't be," he said under his breath. Riku nudged past the smaller man who placed both hands on his sword.

Ariel wasn't here to save him this time, his knees quaked as Riku stopped in front of him. J felt the blood running down his arm from the wound, his eyes darted around.

"You're coming with us. Our master has a proposition for you," declared the man in black.

Riku grunted, stepping closer. J instinctively reacted and pulled the blaster out, pointing it at his head. Riku stopped, J's head shook from side to side. Riku's face grew wrinkles as his nose tightened, his teeth began to peek out. J held his ground. *What would Ariel do?*

He pulled the trigger, the blaster came alive, missing Riku. J jerked his hand over to the other man who was charging and landed two shots to the chest, dropping him to the ground. Riku lunged for him, but J had sensed it and ducked out of the way. He bolted through the door, slamming it behind him. The doorway behind him exploded, wood and glass shards flying everywhere. J didn't look back, he knew what he was going to see. *How did Riku find them? How did he make it to this sector?*

He ran into V in one of the halls. "Get the sisters to Atlantis! I'll draw them away and find a way to meet you there."

V's eyes widened tenfold as she let out a gasp. J ducked into a room, hearing the shots from V's blaster zipping through the air behind him. The floor trembled as J stumbled to his feet, his head darted about. The door was the only path in or out. A glass window ran along the wall nearly as tall as him. He took a shot, covering his eyes from the exploding shrapnel. The floor shook harder, Riku's steps louder. J hopped to the ledge and turned back to face the room, Riku stood in the entrance-way and took a step into the room. J glanced down behind him, his fear of heights was not going to help this situation. He peered five stories down onto the street below. He remembered their hotel run-in in Sector 7 and hoped Riku would charge him, but his steps were slow and heavy.

J looked down again, seeing a lip he didn't notice before. On the level below him was a faux balcony, it jutted out about a foot from the wall. He glanced back at Riku, still advancing. He took a shot, hitting him in the chest. Seemingly unfazed, Riku continued. J had one option, he dropped down onto his hands and knees then slipped out the window, hanging onto the ledge with both hands. He stared down, the ground seemed to climb up at him, he closed his eyes and let go. His fall never happened, Riku's large hand grabbed his arm pulling him up. J scrambled for his blaster, Riku held him up like a prize rabbit, all his teeth coming into view.

J's hand, still fumbling around, managed to pull his weapon from the holster. He got a shot off. Riku wrenched back in pain, dropping him. J sat there a moment, stunned from the fall. Riku lunged for him, but J rolled out of the way. Back on his feet, he ran out of the room, turning toward the arboretum. He knew that led out, maybe he could catch V. He sprinted, never looking back, but hearing the loud crashing and grunts coming from his pursuer. He nearly jumped down each flight of stairs, turning as quickly as possible. His hand hit the wall, opening the secret doorway, Riku's heavy steps echoed in the stairwell. J ran down the alleyway, his breath heavy, lungs struggling for air. A sedan pulled up, the passenger door swung open. The driver leaned back into his seat, retracting his arm.

"He doesn't look that friendly. Get in."

J cranked his head around just as Riku exited the building.

"I don't think he just wants a cup of tea."

"Who are you?" J spun back to the car.

"Name's Dominik. If you'd like a ride, I'd suggest getting in as I have no desire to meet your friend out there."

J hopped in, slamming the door behind him. Dominik accelerated away, J looked back at Riku as he stomped into the street.

"There will be more of them. They underestimated you, only sending two."

"Who are you?" J asked again, still catching his breath.

The man was of average build and reminded him a bit of Will. His face had well worn wrinkles around the outsides of his eyes, his hair was covered by a wool cap, but a few grey and brown hairs managed to escape it. He pulled a pack of cigarettes from a pocket, slipping one into his mouth.

He held the pack out toward J. "Want one?"

Dominik really did remind him of Will, he leaned

closer to examine the possibility.

"Will?" he asked, almost at a whisper.

The man laughed. "No, although I can understand your confusion. He's my twin brother."

J shook his head, Dominik placed the carton back in a pocket.

"Suit yourself," he said, flicking the flint on a shiny Zippo lighter.

Dominik turned down another street, zipping through the intersection.

"How did you..."

"Will called. Said you might be coming this way, so I was monitoring the tunnels. Saw you and Dr. Vesalius arrive, decided to follow in case anything peculiar happened. Looks like something did."

He adjusted the mirror as he skidded through another intersection. J spun his head to the rear spotting two cars only a few car lengths behind them.

"You're a popular fellow. Any idea what they want?"

J looked down as if searching for something in the air. *What did they want? They had the book, didn't they?* He twisted his hands around studying his palms.

"My DNA, maybe? They have the book."

Dominik's head snapped to him. His voice tense, he asked, "What book? Arcturus' journal?"

J was worried he'd let something important slip. He tried to work a way to retract it, but nothing came to mind. *How important was the book? Where was it?*

Dominik searched the mirror again. "Hold on." He

drifted the car around a corner, J felt the car's weight shift and pop up on two wheels.

He continued the slide, lining up to enter an alleyway. J gripped the seat tightly, it appeared too small for a car to fit. Into the alley they went. J's head jerked sideways as the mirror on his door snapped off. The car bounced from side to side on the cobblestone road. The sounds of scraping metal penetrated his ears. Looking back, the cars had stopped chasing them, unable to continue.

"The book, it's your father's journal?"

Dominik glanced between him and the alley several times, awaiting an answer. They popped out onto a street, nearly hitting another car. Dominik swerved then entered the correct lane, taking the first turn he could. He slowed the car down, pulling up onto a curb, placed the car in park and turned his head to J.

"Do they have Arcturus' journal?" His face was straight, his voice solid and unwavering.

"Yes," J replied, looking away out the window. "They took it from us at the facility."

"What facility?"

J didn't move his head, his eyes trained on the bakery just outside his window, fancy breads and cakes adorned the shelves on display. He remembered how simple life was back in Eggerton, that was a lifetime ago. He had to be strong, Earth counted on him, Ariel counted on him. He twisted back toward Dominik.

"In Sector 7, we found my father's journal which gave us access to his research facility. It was there Riku stole the book."

Dominik crushed his eyelids together only a slit remained. His face moved toward the street in front of them, resting motionless, thinking. J watched his breathing slow, he put a fist on his mouth resting it there a moment before turning back toward J.

"That means the Reprobi Angeli now have the book and possibly access to the lab. What did you unlock while you were there?"

J blinked rapidly as he tried to recall the numbers, levels, projects. The words didn't come so easy to him, he wished Ariel was there to explain. He placed a hand on his forehead, rubbing it between his fingers. He pointed his other hand in the air, index finger raised.

"The dream machine and a robotic spacecraft thing. Well, it was a spacecraft, then it morphed into a —"

"Did the dream machine have a dossier on it? Did it have names and locations?"

J's mind began to race, it did have names. Riku was down there, Riku was here.

"Ariel?!" he blurted out.

Dominik placed the car in gear, easing off of the curb.

"Your friends are in danger as are you. You need to get the book back. The Reprobi want Earth now that TK is gone. You are the key, they have the gateway. If they trap your friends, they'll have leverage. How many were on the list?"

"Three, well technically four, but two were here."

"The sisters," he offered, still driving. "Can you

contact your friends?"

J looked down at his Datacle. He swiped at it, rummaging through menus, then pulled up Ariel. The screen read back "unreachable". The same for Zane and V. He swiped at the name of his last resort, Max popped up.

"J, how's it going? Ready for pickup?" Max answered, chipper.

"Have you talked with any of the others?" he asked, his voice shaky.

"No, you're the first. Something wrong?"

The transmission squealed, going blank a second, then came back.

"You... ready? For pickup?"

Dominik reached over and grabbed the Datacle off his wrist. He rolled the window down, the crisp cold air engulfing them, and tossed it out the window. J's mouth dropped open, unable to speak. His eyes followed the device as it bounced on the road before coming to a stop.

"What'd you do that for?!"

"That interference, the fact that you can't reach anyone else, the man hunting you. Reprobi has control of Atlantis."

CHAPTER THIRTEEN

The door opened. Dominik threw his jacket onto a sofa, flipping a light switch as he did.

"There's deli meat in the fridge for a sandwich. I'd suggest you eat up, not sure when you'll get another chance." He popped out a cigarette, lighting it up.

"You sure you don't want one? Calms the nerves."

"My nerves are fine. Thank you though, Mr. Dominik."

"Just call me Dominik, no need for the formal stuff. Now get yourself some food, I'll be back in a moment."

J meandered over to the refrigerator and pulled open the door. A variety of wax paper rolls were stacked on top of each other. Beer bottles littered one side, a gallon of milk sat on the other. He gingerly took one of the papers, unrolling it. Pepperoni. He placed it on the table behind him and unwrapped another. It looked like turkey. He found bread and a glass for the milk then, after fixing a sandwich, sat down in the lone chair at the table. He was in a small apartment room much different than Will's place underground. He half thought he'd be talking to Sarah again and watching beautiful clouds roll by, that's how much alike Dominik and Will were. The room was plain, not a single picture or artwork hung on the walls. In the corner was a small table next to the only window overlooking the city below. They were on the fifth floor of a brick building, the exterior wall showed, while the others were plastered over. Dominik appeared from the door he'd disappeared into earlier, but he was far from empty handed.

"That's a good-looking sandwich. Went with the turkey and pepperoni, good choice."

He sat down, arms full of weapons. J recognized them, but they were covered with scorch marks and welded add-ons making them look anything but stock.

"What's all that?" he wondered aloud, mouth full of sandwich.

"Weapons," Dominik smiled and gave a slight laugh as he saw J roll his eyes. "She's wearing off on you. These are modified weapons."

J studied them closer then swallowed his bite. "Modified?"

"Yep, did it myself. I don't know if you're aware, but Atlantean weapons are strictly prohibited in some of the sectors and—"

"21, 15 18, 9 and 2." His hand rolled in a circle.

Dominik straightened up. "So, you already know that. Hmm, well, these babies can't get switched off. They operate autonomously, without Atlantis' supervision. Pretty handy in a restricted zone."

J picked up an AZAW9500, inspecting the casing and then the handle. It was a long range assault rifle like the one he'd enjoyed practicing with at Dillon's. J looked up at Dominik, assessing. He was hard to read, but seemed to know more than he was letting on.

"So how do you know all this and why are you helping me?"

Dominik walked over to the window, peering out. He paused there, momentarily silent. His arms wrapped around his back, clasping his elbows.

"I want peace. Or as close to it as we can get. No superior all-controlling government overseeing everything, restricting everything, allowing nothing. We've had that. They're gone now and the Earth is up for grabs. If the Reprobi gain power, the Earth will remain as it has been, under a tyrannical rule. Your father's plan, and all that you went through to make it come to fruition, will have been all for naught."

Dominik took a deep breath and pulled a cigarette from its package, lighting it up. He drew it in slowly then exhaled in a long steady breath.

"You see this?" he held the cigarette in his hand. "Back in the 1950's, people smoked like chimneys. By the 21st century, they were known to cause cancer and taxed like mad to eliminate them. I love to smoke and, due to Atlantean technology, I'll never get cancer. It will never kill me. We should've shared these kinds of advancements with Earth. But instead, TK treated Earthlings like cattle, grunts, robots. Anything but humans."

He turned and walked to J, placed his palms on the table, cigarette still resting between his middle and forefinger.

"I want the simple life. And I want everyone on Earth to have the most important thing they have never known given back to them." He took another puff on the cigarette, savoring the taste. "The freedom to choose."

J wracked his brain, trying to think of a plan. Every-one he knew was gone, missing. He assumed they were okay, simply out of contact. They had to be. He wasn't a tactical genius, he was a simple farm boy from Eggerton. But, Ariel would have a plan.

"Do you have a ship?" he asked, his eyes full of renewed focus.

Dominik's eyes crinkled and a slow grin spread on his face. He handed J a blaster, then pointed for him to grab a couple more. J strapped holsters to his thighs, slipped the rifle around his back. He looked like a futuristic mobster in his three piece suit. Dominik led him into the mysterious room he'd disappeared into earlier. It was actually an elevator that led down into the underground. They popped out into a large hangar housing various ships. One he recognized. In his head, he heard Ariel say, *that thing's a relic.* But, it was like an old friend. He walked over to it.

"You sure you want the Tetriack? This ship's much nicer." Dominik was pointing to a smaller, more nimble craft. J shook his head, he knew how to fly this one. He hopped into it and shifted around. It felt the way his pickup truck had those many years, like an old friend, a reliable steed. Dominik approached and hung his arms over the cockpit rail.

"You sure you want this one?"

J studied him and smiled. "Any last words of wisdom?"

Dominik didn't say anything, just slipped his hand

into the cockpit holding a data disk. J took it then glanced back at him with a puzzled look on his face. Dominik just nodded then stepped back. J placed his hand into the control cups. He was heading back home. *Wait, when did Atlantis become home?*

"DNA verified, initiating start sequence," the craft relayed.

He lifted the ship into a hover, looked back at Dominik once more, then pushed the ship forward toward the launch bay. The doors glided open as he neared. J engaged the thrusters, accelerating forward, and in no time he was zipping through the atmosphere, clouds dancing over the ship. It was peaceful as he found his way out between the plates, once more in open space. He tapped on the menus, engaging autopilot and setting the course for Atlantis. The ship adjusted course, the Moon shined back at him.

It looked similar to when he'd first hopped into a Tetriack outside the wall. Before he'd ever heard of New Atlantis, Arcturus or TK. Before he learned that he hadn't been born on Earth. Before Ariel. *That's when it became home. When he'd realized that it was Ariel's home.*

"Ariel."

He tapped the controls, disengaging the autopilot. He had to find Ariel, make sure she was safe. Flipping the ship around, now staring at Earth, he set the course for Sector 15. He hoped V was okay. She could take care of herself, he reassured himself. He was sure Zane was fine, that guy literally couldn't die. His eyes tightened when his mind shifted to Max, he let out a groan. He needed Ariel and hoped she still needed him.

Into the underbelly of the Earth the ship dove. J glanced down and saw the data disk. He lifted it up, examining it. *What's on this?* He felt silly for not asking when Dominik had handed it to him, but in that moment, his mind was fixated on finding the others. The Tetriack piloted itself toward Sector 15. J didn't know where it was, but his ship did. Within the clouds he descended, admiring the colors and the movement as he passed.

"Initiating docking sequence," the ship announced.

J was ready. He looked at the disk again then set it in a storage container on the ship. The Tetriack finished the landing sequence and came to rest. J stepped out, noticing another ship was already in the hangar. He grumbled to himself, recognizing it. He trudged toward the Omorfiá, searching for the pilot. He circled it once and found no sign of movement. Opening the cargo hatch, he was met with the same result. J grimaced as he stepped off the craft, headed toward the clothing. After finding something he thought would fit, he headed down the long hallway to the tube. He stopped in the process of boarding. He had no clue where Ariel actually was. He sat in the vessel, staring at the ceiling, then leaned back, closing his eyes. *What was he doing?* He tried to clear his mind, but the vision of Riku hoisting him up and staring through him kept popping into it. That picture alternated with several of Ariel and their time together. He took a deep breath.

Out of desperation he blurted out, "Take me to Ariel."

"Unrecognized location. Please say request again."

J placed both hands on his face in frustration, slightly covering his mouth. "Boy. Where would Ariel be?"

"Buenos Aires. Time en-route, fifteen minutes."

J peeked through his fingers watching the door close. *Buenos Aires? Why did that sound familiar?*

The tube accelerated. J threw his hands in the air, letting them fall onto his thighs with a loud slap. *Gotta start somewhere. It sounded so familiar. Was it where Ariel was going? Or was he just convincing himself it was?* The vehicle came to a stop, the door hissed as it opened. J stepped out and made his way to the elevator. Once inside, he tapped on the screen, requested the ground level. It shot up. J braced himself, it seemed a lot faster than the others. The movement came to a stop, his body lifting off the floor slightly then pressing into the tile beneath his feet. The doors opened and the sunlight hit his eyes causing him to squint and throw an arm above them. He stepped out into the blazing day, still shielding his eyes. A couple with a baby stroller walked by. The man nodded while the woman clung tight to him, her face panicked. They hastened their pace. J looked down at himself and realized his rifle was strapped to his back, holsters hung on his hips. He hadn't planned this out very well. His head snapped from side to side searching for police officers. As he scanned the environment, nothing grabbed his attention. Cars drove by, people randomly crossed the street; the only odd thing he noticed was that there were no lights to control the traffic. *It was a bustling city. Where should he go?* He tried to recall what the dossier said. He knew it was in his head, he'd seen it. He just had to remember.

His body perked up. J stood tall and smiled at himself then searched for someone to talk to. He began walking away from the elevator. Looking back, his eyes popped out of his head. He'd just exited a twenty-story tall obelisk in the center of a busy thoroughfare. The structure seemed oddly perfect, yet out of place with the surrounding hodgepodge of architectural styles, none of which were over ten stories tall. He shook his head to refocus himself and turned back to continue his walk, a few more people hurrying along at the sight of him. On the other side of the road stood a wide tower. He squinted his eyes, focusing on it as he walked. As he neared, he realized that there was a police officer inside the tower directing traffic. J spun ninety degrees, trying to play it off as if that were his plan all along. He realized that no one was really paying attention, most of the people were in their own little worlds, walking, biking, a couple riding in a horse drawn carriage. He saw a man reading the news paper up ahead and stopped next to him.

"Sir, do you know where the nearest post office is by chance?"

The man dropped the news paper and began speaking before laying eyes on him.

"I'm sorry you'll have to speak up I..."

The man took half a step back, catching himself. His mouth dropped open. His arms raised above his head, one hand grasping the newspaper tightly.

"Please. You can have whatever you want. My wallet. My jacket. Please, don't hurt me."

J's tucked his chin into his neck. *What was going on here?*

"I don't want your wallet. I want to know how to find the post office," J tried to reassure the man, leaning closer.

"I don't understand what you're saying. Please don't hurt me," his voice shook.

J froze, trying to figure out the situation. He could understand the man, but the man couldn't seem to understand him. Not wanting to frighten the man anymore, he walked away, crossing the street toward the store fronts. The cars stopped as he had seen them do for other pedestrians. He found it quite odd that everyone walked across the street as if they were invincible. Once across, he turned and headed down the street. People continued to gawk at him as he made his way. Many appeared frightened, others asked friends if that was a weapon on his back. He saw a bench up ahead and decided to have a seat and to try and figure out a plan. He was flying by the seat of his pants, making it up as he went along, but he needed to work through his problem. He needed to find a post office. Just then, he glanced up to see a mail carrier walking by. He jumped up, grabbed the carrier's arm.

"Can you take me to the post office?"

The man cringed back as if afraid for his life.

"Here take the mail, take it all."

He dropped his mail bag and slipped from J's grasp, running down the street. J breathed a heavy sigh and looked at the sky. *This is going to be impossible.*

"American?"

J snapped out of his despair and swung his head toward the voice. A young lady in her 20s stood five feet away from him. Her yellow dress glowed as the sun glimmered off it, her hair was the color of a fine chocolate, her face soft and warm, skin kissed by the sun. She stood there with her eyes raised, awaiting the answer she already knew.

"Yes," he said emphatically.

"You know if you want people to understand you, you should try addressing them in Spanish. Also, you might want to lose those..." she paused, waving her hand about. "...rockets."

J felt the shoulder strap of his rifle dig into his shoulder as if to tell him, "See? I told you." She was right, but it was too late to just set them down and leave them. Who knows what would happen then? He needed help, he hoped she was it.

"You can understand me?"

She giggled, "I'm talking to you aren't I? I know English and I know Americans. You seem lost."

Boy, was he ever. He was so relieved, it made him almost wanted to come clean with everything. Almost.

"You could say that. I'm actually trying to find someone...a friend. His name is Dr. Huergo, but I lost his address and was searching for a post office to maybe find it."

J's heart was racing, his hands trembling slightly. The young lady smiled at him.

"There's one two blocks down. I don't have anywhere to be, would you like me to come translate for you?"

J thought about it a moment. *What was the downside?*

"I'd love that, thanks."

She skipped over, taking his arm in hers. J jumped, disentangled himself.

"I won't bite," she giggled again, twining her arm with his once more. "So, where are you from in America?"

J hesitated. "Eggerton. Kinda in the middle of nowhere."

They continued toward the post office, questions shot back and forth, mostly aimed at J. He tried to keep his answers vague. They arrived in front of a four story stucco building. The young lady led him inside and they found an empty line.

"I'll go talk to them. You wait here."

J nodded to her, then appraised the room. It was fairly large, two stories tall, and along the front entrance wall were rows of empty seats. He walked over and sat down in one, slipping his rifle off his shoulder, setting it on the floor. He looked up, watched the young lady speak with the counter clerk. Her arms flew in the air dramatically as she talked, the clerk squinted, concentrating on her message then wrote something on a piece of paper and handed it to her. He then wrote something on another piece and stepped away from the desk. The young lady spun around with a huge smile and headed toward him. She held the paper up as she walked, beaming as if she had won a great prize. J stood up as she approached.

"I believe this is what you're looking for," she said, her voice as smooth as silk.

She gently grabbed his hand, he trembled slightly as she took hold. He picked up his rifle from off the floor, slinging it over one shoulder.

"Best to keep you off the streets," she eyed the rifle, then adjusted her gaze, locking eyes with him. "Follow me, I know a back way."

J had momentarily forgotten she was holding his hand until she gave a gentle tug. Her hand felt soft and warm, comforting in this strange place where no one could understand him. She led them down a few halls and out the back of the building into an alleyway.

"I'm sorry, I never caught your name. Mine's Delphina," she glanced back at him.

"J," was all he managed to get out.

"Well, J, you're in luck. We're not far from your friend. What brings you to beautiful Argentina?"

"You...you know. My friend is an engineer who is going to be building a structure for my company," he stumbled over his words.

"I see," she turned her head to the path then back to him. "Then why the weapons? Expecting a revolution?"

J realized that his lies weren't working; he was very bad at not telling the truth.

"Actually...well...no," he worked to find the right words. "There are people after me...it's complicated."

By then they'd reached the end of the alleyway and the young woman pointed across the street.

"That's the building your friend is in. Maybe you could explain it when we get there."

She leaned into him and stroked his face with her hand. "You look like a nice boy, J. I'm not sure who would be after you, but I'll help with what I can."

She squeezed his hand as they ran across the street. The building she pointed to was a hotel standing six stories tall. From pictures he remembered as a child, it looked French. The roof line was steep, windows jutted out from in between blue shingles, the exterior resembled smooth stone. He followed her into the lobby.

"He's in room 524," she said, her face as bright as when he met her not long ago.

They headed past the lobby into a stairwell. *No elevators, this is going to be fun.* He had become accustomed to lifts and stairs began to feel tasking. They stepped into the hall. J's breathing was labored, it didn't seem to affect Delphina as much.

"Almost there," she pulled him to the right.

She stopped at the door marked "524" and opened it. Light shined into the hallway. J stepped in first, his eyes squinting to adjust to the light. *Wait. How did she open the door to a room that's supposed to belong to Dr. Huergo?*

CHAPTER FOURTEEN

Delphina reached for his hand, passing him as they entered the room. He flinched at first contact, his attention drawn down to it. He shifted his eyes to her as she continued to pull him along into the room then his eyes moved up toward the window. He was about to ask about the door when he noticed a shadowy figure sitting, watching him, his features hidden as the bright sunlight shined through the glass. J's eyes began to adjust.

"J," a deep voice began. "Welcome to Buenos Aires."

J's vision cleared. Delphina tightened her grip, his eyes skated to her then squinted back to the man in the chair. He felt a tug at his rifle. The man in the seat was older, his hair pitch black. his face worn and wrinkled. His ears seemed too big for his head and his eyes too small. He wore a silk robe, yellow, embroidered with an ornate oriental dragon encircling the torso and arms.

His attention shifted back to his rifle, he pulled away as another man standing next to him tugged back.

"Best give him the rifle," Delphina smirked.

J looked at the larger man and relented. He felt his hip holsters tugged at, as the blasters were extracted. His eyes shifted to Delphina, her once empty hand now grasped his blaster.

"I'm sorry, J," she said with a devious grin. She withdrew the hand holding his, stepping back.

He tightened his jaw, balled his hands into fists. "Who are you?"

The man in the chair stood up and approached him. J's arms were suddenly grabbed and held behind him, each one by a different person.

"My name is Takamori, Tennō of the Reprobi Angeli. I believe you have already met my messenger."

The ground shook from the fall of heavy steps behind him, he knew who it was before even turning. *How did he keep finding them?* J's head spun as the hulking man stepped into view next to him.

"Riku," he muttered under his breath.

Takamori pointed to Riku, tossed the book onto the bed beside him, then turned his gaze to J. "You will unlock it now."

The two men holding him released their grip, he rubbed his biceps, pushing out the pain from their grasp. He surveyed the room. Takamori was standing a few feet in front of him, his diminutive stature made him seem like a child compared to J's tall frame, belying the power of his station. Delphina had moved next to Takamori and was now holding his arm, on his left and right were two men dressed in business suits. Riku towered over him to his right. J ran through his options in his mind, his hands free, weaponless. He remembered what Riku had done to Ariel. J's hand to hand skills were lacking, he needed a weapon. He swallowed hard then grasped for the rifle being held by the captor to his right. His efforts proved fruitless as Riku grabbed him with both hands.

Takamori shook his head. "Always making things more difficult than they have to be. You understand what we are trying to do, don't you?"

J scowled. "Same as TK."

"No, we will improve it, make it more efficient. Open up trade between Atlantis and Earth. We will create a new society better than TK could have ever hoped for. One where commerce will rule, where people will benefit from each other's successes."

"Still sounds like TK."

Takamori gave Riku a pointed look. He tightened his grip, J winced in pain.

"Very well. We will do this the easy way...for us." His eyes shifted to the table, "Take it off."

J's eyes widened. *Take it off? What did that mean?*

Riku dragged him over to the dresser and pinned his arm and face on top of it. Staring at his outstretched hand, J's eyes frantically danced around. One of the henchmen approached drawing a Katana blade from its sheath. J's eyes bulged from his head, sweat began to bead up on his forehead, his skin tingled. The man lifted the sword, preparing for the stroke.

J's mind went into survival mode. "Okay, Okay. I'll open it, I'll open it," his voice shook uncontrollably.

"Too late for that. This will be easier for both of us," Takamori stated as he turned toward J, Delphina still on his arm.

J squeezed his hand and squirmed, Riku's grip tightened around his body. J's eyes fixed on the blade as it began to descend, the stroke occurring in slow motion. J screamed, then his ears rang. The sound caused him to close his eyes. He felt glass rain down on him, Riku's grip loosened as they were thrown toward the room's entrance. A body landed on him as he slid a few feet. He opened his eyes, Delphina lay unmoving on top of him. Riku had been thrown behind him, Takamori was draped over his henchmen. A shadow cast over the scene, his eyes focused. Ariel glared down at him, disgust written all over her face. J pushed Delphina off. He felt the floor rumble and Ariel's eyes focused behind him. J pushed his head back, looking up. Riku stood there menacing, staring at Ariel, his face pure aggression.

"Get up, J. No time to play," her voice stern, shifting the knife in her hand.

J stumbled to his feet, his hands dripped with blood, his face the same. Riku rumbled behind him as he walked toward Ariel.

"The book!" he cried out, his eyes searching for it.

It was sitting on the floor next to Takamori who had awoken and was reaching for it. Ariel, catching the movement out of the corner of her eye, shifted her gaze toward the book. J tried to call out as Riku lunged for her, she slashed at his arm. She missed, his body in the air grasping for her, she spun avoiding the attack. Riku landed heavily on his feet, twisting, and swung a right hook at Ariel. She fell to the ground out of reach slinging the knife into his obliques. Riku let out a howl as he stumbled back in pain. The man with the Katana was now on his feet behind him, Takamori had reached the book and was clutching it in his arms. The other henchman gained his feet, staring at J as he backed toward the open balcony behind them. Ariel studied Riku, her attention waned as Takamori ran toward the door still clutching the book. She pulled a blade from her waist and chucked it toward him. The blade missed, sticking into the wall above.

"Ariel!" J warned as Riku swung his interlocked fists down at her. Ariel rolled, avoiding the blow then gracefully flipped to her feet. A knife came in from outside hitting one of the henchmen in the neck, dropping him instantly. The other stood his ground still holding the Katana.

"Glad to see me?" he heard a smug voice from behind them.

Max stepped in from the balcony holding a knife, blade side down in a fighting stance. He smirked at J. J grimaced, his face tightening. He turned back to Riku.

"Get to the balcony," Ariel commanded. She began to step backward toward Max.

J mirrored her. As she pulled another knife from her thigh, the man with the Katana and Riku slowly approached. J stepped over the broken glass and rubble as his feet made their way toward the steel grating of the balcony. His heel kicked a blaster, he knelt down grabbing and holstering it. He spotted his rifle at Ariel's feet.

"Ariel. The rifle, grab it."

"They don't—"

"Trust me," he said with conviction in his voice.

Ariel stopped a moment, looking as if she was going to respond. She picked up the strap with her open hand

and slipped it over a shoulder.

"You're going to have to climb," Ariel said, eyes still trained on Riku.

J looked up, a rope dangled from the roofline one story above.

"J, you first, then you Max."

"But—"

"Don't argue with me. Go."

J glanced at Max then grabbed the rope. *Just like gym class.* He took a deep breath, climbed hand over hand not once looking down. Near the top, he felt a tug on the rope. He hesitated then finished flipping over the side onto the roof. J surveyed the roofline, it was open except for the stairwell. He turned back hearing a grunt. Max had crested the wall and was standing behind him. Ariel appeared just after. Pulling the blade from her teeth, she sliced the rope.

J jogged back to Ariel. "Where to now?"

Max was wiping dust from his outfit. "I say we get to the ship. That big dude doesn't look like he should be messed with."

"Thanks Captain Obvious." Ariel slipped the knife into its sheath, J chuckled. "You shouldn't be here, let alone laughing. Where's V?" Her eyes were cold as she stared at J.

J looked down at the ground, by her tone he felt she knew the answer.

"Either of you hear from Zane?"

Neither answered. Ariel strutted past them, assessing the situation. Her head swiveling around, considering every possible solution. Then J realized something. *What about the doctor she was sent for? What happened to him?* He tightened his hands. "What about Dr—"

"Takamori has him." She didn't even let him attempt the name.

J didn't want to incur any more of her wrath, but needed more information. "How do you know that?"

Ariel grumbled, mumbling something to herself under her breath. She eyed J, about to speak when the stairwell door opened. She spun around, pulling the knife from her hip as men started to exit onto the roof. A blaster shot buzzed by her ear drilling one of the men in the chest. J stood just behind her shoulder holding the blaster with both hands. Ariel turned in surprise, "But how—"

"No time, just fire the rifle!"

The men began to scatter. J counted six, but in the frenzy of activity it could've been more. Ariel flicked the knife into the roof and flipped the rifle into shooting position like a baton, she began firing. She fell to one knee, J saw blood skip off her shoulder, tearing her shirt. It was a throwing star like he had seen before. Max grabbed J's shoulder, tugging on it. J opened fire, hitting a couple more, but they were quick and the rooftop was so open they tumbled and spun away from his shots. He glanced at Ariel, she was up on her feet, backpedaling toward them.

"Follow me," she commanded as she took off running.

J froze seeing her jump off the roof. Max tugged
harder at his shoulder then left him, sprinting toward
Ariel. J took a few more shots, stars flying at him, too
many to dodge. They hit his arm and leg. He winced as
the sharp blades pierced his skin. He turned, sprinting
to catch up to Max and then passing him. Trusting Ariel,
he blindly jumped. Midair, he glanced down. Ariel was
waiting one level lower on the adjacent building, rifle
drawn, aimed toward him. J braced for impact, his feet
hitting, the momentum causing him to roll past her. He
heard a thump behind him and pulled his head up in time
to see Max tumbling past.

Ariel began shooting toward the roofline. "We need
to get to street level. Use the stairwell."

J wasted no time heading for the door. He ripped it
open, checking over his shoulder to see Max right behind,
Ariel running toward them. Behind her, Takamori's men
were jumping from the rooftop. He stepped aside as Max
ran past, covering Ariel. He raised his blaster and fired
multiple shots. Ariel ducked, avoiding them, and slid
into the stairwell. J slammed the door shut and followed
the other two down into the building. After running
through a short hallway, they were on the street. Ariel
inspected her Datacle, then continued. He followed,
switching positions with Max, right behind her. Max
then did the same, both attempting to be near Ariel . J's
body tensed as he jockeyed for position, neither of them
paid much attention to Ariel. Suddenly, they crashed
into her, all three of them tumbling into a heap.

"What are you two doing?!"

J and Max were on top of her. J eyed Max, he returned it with a smug look.

"Seriously! What are you two doing? Get off me!"

J felt the tension in her voice. He and Max scrambled to let her up.

"There's a transport shaft a block away. Can you two keep it together that long?"

They nodded, chagrined, and followed her toward the street. J looked back several times not seeing any of their pursuers. *Must have lost them.* After a short walk along the street, they ducked into an alleyway where Ariel began searching for a door panel.

"It should be here. Start searching."

J and Max began scouring the walls for the access panel.

"Ha," Max exclaimed, the panel dropping out of the stone wall beside him.

He looked over at J with a triumphant grin, J attempted to not pay attention.

Ariel ran over and punched the codes into the display, opening the wall. The three of them stepped in and down the elevator went. After a ride in the tube, they laid eyes on the hangar. Max wasted no time pre-flighting the ship.

J turned to Ariel. "What happened?" he inched closer to her.

She stared out at the Omorfiá watching Max checking the craft's body panels.

He changed his question. "What's the story with you and Max?"

She exhaled sharply, "It's complicated. Let's focus on what just happened."

He wanted to reach for her hand, but felt the tension in the air. Instead he opened his mouth. "So what did just happen?"

Ariel, still staring at the Omorfiá, chewed on her lip. J stared at her, transfixed.

"Takamori happened." She started walking toward the ship. "What about V and the sisters? You lost them right?"

J honestly didn't know. They were alive when he left them. His distraction was the best plan he could think of. He hoped Ariel would give him some slack for not having the tactical knowledge she did.

"I don't know," he said, looking down at his feet as he shuffled along.

Ariel walked in silence the rest of the way to the ship, J took the hint and followed suit. Max finished his pre-flight and they all headed inside. Ariel stopped them inside, raising a hand. She turned around, scrutinizing each of them.

"So, what do you know?"

J started off, detailing everything he could remember about his encounter with Riku, the sisters, the Reprobi Angeli, Dominik. He cleared the air about the Atlantean weapons and why they worked in Sector 15. He thought he covered everything. Max then went over the little he knew, and it was very little. Ariel caught him staring at the ceiling more than once. She detailed what had happened after arriving in Sector 15. She followed the tracker, searching for the doctor, only to be met by Takamori's henchmen. After fighting them off, she saw J's DNA ping on her Datacle when he used the tube. She'd watched the whole exchange between he and Delphina. He sank a bit, remembering that she held his hand, he regretted the whole episode. After Ariel concluded her recap, J did his best to push them onto the next subject.

"So, where's everybody at? What are we going to do?"

Max had been quiet most of the time, his face now looked as if it carried a secret. J and Ariel watched him, waiting for something.

"Well...after dropping you off, I picked up a couple of ships inbound to Atlantis. I assume our doctors were on them."

"How do you figure?" J asked, pointing at Max. "How would you know that? Are you with Takamori?"

Max's face crinkled, he huffed. Ariel looked at him tight eyed, his mouth dropped open his head shaking side to side.

Ariel watched the two stepping toward each other, realized what was about to happen. "Boys, the enemy's out there."

They stopped, turned to her.

She rolled her hands in small circles, thinking, as her head was down gazing at the floor. She whipped her head up, snapped her fingers.

"Reprobi Angeli. Who did you say they were again, J?"

J searched her face for clues to what she was thinking. "They're a society that wants to rule Earth, like TK... Takamori is their leader."

By this time Ariel was pacing again. She began thinking out loud. "If I were going to take over Earth, I would want the systems TK had. They're in Atlantis, but I'm banished from Atlantis."

She stopped pacing and looked J dead in the eye, unflinching. "They acquired ships from the research facility."

J's head started spinning. That made sense. Riku had gotten in, they hadn't locked anything as they left in a hurry. They had the book, the dossier. Suddenly, J put a hand in the air, the other he placed on his lips. Ariel and Max froze. J bent his head toward the ship's cargo door, he heard footsteps.

CHAPTER FIFTEEN

"Your Datacle," J whispered, pulling the blaster from its holster. Ariel looked down at it, puzzled.

"They're tracking it." He inched toward the door.

Ariel un-slung her rifle. She glanced at Max, pointed to the bridge. He caught her meaning and tiptoed up to the ship's control room. Ariel stepped lightly, following J to the door. He knelt down as he arrived, peeking out, searching for the source of the noise. He glanced back at Ariel, giving her a nod. She took up position on the other side of the door. J peered out, his blaster raised. A star hit his shoulder, he dropped the blaster as Ariel found the attacker, letting two shots fly. J grabbed his shoulder, the engines hummed to life. He observed multiple enemies closing in. Stars came flying at them from all angles, J took cover just inside the ship and glanced over at Ariel. A knowing smile came over his face. Ariel's eyebrows tightened, J rolled out as the ship picked up.

"J!" Ariel screamed, reaching a hand out instinctively toward him.

J hit the ground on his feet, he didn't hesitate as he accelerated toward the Tetriack. He looked back once, seeing the Omorfiá continue its upward thrust. Ariel adjusted her sights, sniping an attacker. J kept running, sliding on one knee to the much smaller ship. His hand touched the side, opening the cockpit. J rolled over the rail as low as he could then slid his hands into the controls. The ship came alive as he rapidly began tapping menus.

"Weapons ready to engage," the ship sounded.

He picked it up while simultaneously spinning it then let loose a volley of rounds at the enemy. Four out of the five fell motionless. He watched the Omorfiá depart out the now open hangar door behind him, laid down more fire as he drifted the ship backward. Riku stepped into sight and just stared, his face tight and motionless. J spun the ship around, rocketing it into the swirling clouds. The Omorfiá was in front of him.

"Incoming message," the ship stated.

J pressed the icon in front of him.

Ariel appeared on the screen, leaning into it, her face stricken and enraged at the same time. "What were you thinking?!"

He was half-tempted to end the message, going as far as raising his arm, but realized that would only make things worse and pulled back. There were more important things right now, namely a plan. J put a hand in the air, forefinger slightly raised. "We need a plan. Atlantis or Zane?"

Ariel sat back taking a breath. She squinted her eyes, calculating, her lips twitched. J was running ideas through his own mind. Takamori had the upper hand; not only did he have the book and could track them, but for all they knew he already had Atlantis. Ariel appeared as if she was about to speak, but J interrupted, remembering something. "My father's research facility!"

Ariel's face glared back, questioning.

"There has to be something there that can help us. You remember how big it was. And you did find that ship robot thing."

"Mecha," Ariel corrected him.

"Whatever you want to call it, that doesn't matter. We need help." She opened her mouth to speak, but he interrupted again, eyes serious, "And no more splitting up."

Ariel crossed her arms, staring back at him. He made some good points. Splitting up proved to be a disaster. V was most likely captured, Zane too, for all they knew.

Then something else popped into J's mind. "Where's Grant?

"He's here, why?"

"What do you mean he's there? Why wasn't he help- ing?!" J was livid.

"Calm down, J. He fell asleep. Max had left him behind to keep the ship ready."

J couldn't believe it. *He'd been next to him the whole time?* He wanted to smack himself upside the head. No, he wanted to smack Grant. His mind went to his search in Sector 15, it all could have been avoided had Grant helped him. His face was visibly red, he tried to shake it off.

"My vote is the facility. Have Grant figure out how they're tracking our Datacles, that's how they found me. I assume that's how they found you."

Ariel looked away from the screen. J focused on her. His mind drifted, he missed her touch, her smile, the way her eyes lit up when he walked into the room. He took a deep breath, admiring her beauty, her strength. Her ice blue eyes drifted back toward him.

"Okay, J. Your plan. You know the LZ's gonna be hot."

"Hot...like warm?" he asked hesitantly.

Ariel laughed, he didn't care that it was at his expense. He'd almost forgotten how much he loved hearing that laugh.

"Meet you there," she said, still snickering, then switched off the comm.

J manually flew the Tetriack, they were still in the structure of the Earth and would arrive in Sector 7 in no time. Though they were headed back toward danger, he felt relaxed. Something about hearing her laugh again reassured him. He also enjoyed flying. While he was growing up, he thought that only birds or movie stars in far off cities could fly; he felt free. The feeling quickly dissolved. His mind shifted to his father's facility as it came into view. *Where was Arcturus during all of this?* Ariel came back onto the radio, informing him that he had to open it with his DNA which, through her coaching, he accomplished. Taking up lead this time, he entered and touched down. The Omorfiá adjusted course for landing behind him as he was crawling out of the Tetriack. He stood there admiring the sight. The ship hovered in, clouds dancing around it, the red orange glow and the ship's dark silhouette in the center, approaching. Ariel and Max stepped out, both sporting rifles and blasters. Ariel tossed one to him as they neared.

"Be ready for anything," she advised, walking past.

Max smirked as he passed, resting the rifle on his shoulder, the barrel facing the sky. J fell in behind them and they made their way toward the main elevator. Once there, Ariel noticed the system was overridden, she grumbled. "Looks like they figured out the lift, hope that's all they figured out."

She pressed the screen, switching it back to voice commands. "Elevator, what were the last five locations accessed?"

"Level 24 defensive systems, level 25 weapons storage, both accessed multiple times over the past 24 hours."

J looked at Ariel, "What about the restricted area?"

Ariel shrugged her shoulders, Max stood in the back not really understanding any of the exchange. She voiced "level 23 restricted area" and after J confirmed his identity, they headed up. The elevator let out and Ariel and J recognized the location, the wreckage was still there from their last battle. J found the directory computer and logged in.

"What are we looking for?" inquired Max, desperately trying to be part of the conversation.

J and Ariel turned around and, almost in unison, replied, "Weapons."

Max jumped back, his hands went up in front of his chest then he twisted his neck around, looking at the walls, the train, and the pile of wreckage. He began walking toward it. J and Ariel were rummaging through the menus, both with their heads down.

"Do you see anything?" J asked

"No, but then again, I'm not exactly sure what to look for."

J rested his hand on the wall leaning over the screen, Ariel was mumbling to herself as she scrolled. He watched her as she worked, her face intense. His mind shifted to Max. *What was he to her?* He glanced over at Max who was standing on top the debris with his hands on his hips, scanning the wreckage. J turned back toward Ariel, his eyes flicked about drifting to the screen.

"What's that? Wait, go back."

Ariel scrolled back a few screens. The prototype read, "J suitXDf2043". Ariel pulled up the information.

-J Suit XDf2043-Personal armor suit
-Resistance- against all current TK weapons
-Production status-tests incomplete
-Known issues-high energy drain, once shields decrease to 25%, suit becomes unstable
-Location-vault 23

"Sounds promising." Ariel nodded her head.

J smiled back then turned back to Max. He was still standing over the wreckage, looking triumphant.

"So you and him..."

Ariel let out an audible groan. J spun around to see her looking pointedly at him, one eyebrow pegged, the other tight.

"Let it go, J. Let's find that suit."

Ariel tapped the screen, turning it dark. She started toward Max, J was in trail, hopping a couple steps to catch up. Glancing down at her hand, he thought of grabbing it.

"So what did you find?" Max turned toward them.

"Some sort of armored suit. You wanna check 'em out with us? Or is the wreckage more your style?"

"Armor sounds better than this garbage," he kicked a piece off of the top of the pile.

Her lips frowned. She'd been so excited to find the mecha and it was over quicker than she'd wanted. Still, it did its job. The three of them headed to the suits' location on foot, it was only a few hundred feet away. The door labeled VAULT 23 was much smaller than the rest of the doors around it, like the size of an average house door. J scanned himself and the two foot thick door hinged open. As they stepped in, lights came on displaying two rows of suits. J walked up and touched one, they were soft with plastic plating all around them. To him, they resembled futuristic football pads. He walked along the row next to them, all were a charcoal grey in various sizes. He even found one that appeared like it would fit Zane, pulled it off its hook and held it up.

"Look! Found one my size."

Ariel glanced over and laughed. After she caught her breath, she told him to take it for when they found Zane. She sounded so confident about it, a glimmer of hope trickled through his veins. After searching the racks, each of them found a size that fit. Ariel stripped her clothes and began working on slipping on the suit. J and Max stopped what they were doing, realizing what just happened. After she finished, Max smirked at J noticing he had frozen too. J scowled back at him as Ariel turned around.

"Come on, we gotta get going. Why aren't you guys dressed?" She walked over to J, smiled knowingly up at him and patted his face, then grabbed the oversized Zane suit. "You two find one for Grant and V as well. I'm going to see if anything else will help us out."

J shook his head, trying to focus on anything but the image of her changing. He held the suit out, admiring its design. It looked sleek, new, it even smelled good. *Hope this works better than advertised.* He pulled on the new armor. Max did the same, but continued scowling at J as he did so. They searched the hooks, hunting for V and Grant-sized suits. After procuring them, they headed back to find Ariel. She was heads-down, scrolling through more menus. Her head shook every couple of seconds as she continuously dragged her finger up the screen. Finally, she found a prototype weapons store. She sent J and Max to acquire the high precision railguns. They arrived back to find Ariel leaning on the main door to the elevator, searching the ceiling.

"You boys ready?"

"Yep." J tossed a rifle to her. Max smiled and perked up an eyebrow.

In no time, they found themselves back on the

bridge of the Omorfiá, discussing the plan. Grant had been working on a device to scan Atlantis for activity by tapping into the security and monitoring system. Once they landed on Atlantis, he could hardwire it and be able to help them not only find Zane and V, but work the doors and other systems to a small extent. Ariel was concerned his hacking skills were not nearly on par with Jolt's, but his commitment was much more desirable. She recalled Atlantis' defensive systems coming online after she was saved by V, so recommended they take both ships. She knew J was comfortable in the Tetriack and she needed to be able to concentrate on gaining access without the added stress of flying at the same time. J initially objected but, realizing she had a point, relented. As he left the Omorfiá, Ariel ran after him.

"J!"

He stopped abruptly and turned. She ran into him, her signature move, and threw her arms around his neck. He stumbled back, but managed to stay upright and maintain a tight grip on her lithe body. Her face inches from his, she flushed, seeming to realize what she'd just done and how close they were. "Be careful out there."

She tried to extricate herself from his arms, but he was having none of it. It seemed like forever since he'd held her, stared into her mesmerizing ice blue eyes. He closed the distance between their lips and took hers, sweetly. As he drew back from the kiss, he slowly lowered her down. She looked up at him, suddenly shy. He smiled, "You too." Then released her walking toward his ship.

J hummed to himself as he slid a leg over the rail of
the Tetriack and looked up wistfully at the Omorfiá. He
shook his head taking a deep breath, *this was not going
to be easy,* he plopped down into the seat, his new suit
tugging and pulling at his joints the hard sides pressing
into his muscles. He'd have to get used to it. For all of
the advanced technology of Atlantis, they sure didn't put
much thought into comfort. He engaged the ship, the
propulsion system hummed. He cracked a slight smile,
he'd started to love that sound. The canopy closed above
him. Looking up, he worked the menus. It was coming
more naturally to him now. He remembered watching movies with heroes flying through space, fighting
monsters and aliens. He never thought he'd be doing
that, except the monsters and aliens bit. Well, they were
monsters, anyone who could treat other humans like they
didn't matter was definitely a monster. They could have
been labled aliens, seeing as how they hadn't been born
on Earth. They just weren't the hairy or green ones from
the movies. He looked toward the Omorfiá which was
pressing away from the cold metal floor beneath. He
thought again of his first flight to Atlantis, his father.
Where was he? That question seemed to be on repeat
in his head. Every time they embarked on a new adventure to try to make Arcturus' plans come to fruition, he
inevitably wondered why his father wasn't around to help
them. His chest tightened then he refocused on the task
at hand, guiding the craft into the red orange glow of the
wispy, swirling clouds.

He heard Ariel's voice over the ship's speakers, "Comm check."

J pressed a menu and replied, "Loud and clear."

"You follow us. If we get split up, remember the plan."

J remembered, he only hoped he wouldn't have to use it. The hairs stood up on the back of his neck, their plans never went as scheduled. *What was going to change this time?* The Omorfiá overtook him as briefed, J fell in behind, mirroring its movements, still on manual control. Max's ship wasn't as fast as his and he seemed to be taking his time navigating the bowels of the Earth. J took the opportunity to practice some maneuvers. He had no clue what they were called, but had seen them in the movies. His barrel roll needed some work, but his four point spin worked well and his lazy eights proved successful, at least in his eyes. The clouds dissipated into a clear blue sky then quickly faded to black. The stars shined brightly into his eyes and even though his life was in danger more often than not, in that moment he felt extremely blessed. *How many people get to see this view?* Nobody that he'd grown up with, for sure. He began drifting away from the Omorfiá, but quickly corrected. As he did, the Moon came into focus. His mind still couldn't comprehend the fact that the small sphere held an entire world inside of it. He'd seen it thousands of times in his life and never would have imagined such an amazing structure.

"Proximity alert. Missile lock. Impact in thirty seconds."

J woke up from his daydream. "What?" he said out loud, his voice high pitched. He was immediately thankful that Ariel wasn't with him. He tapped on the screen, his fingers fumbling through menus.

"Impact in 10 seconds," the ship called out.

His eyes searched the emptiness of space, zipping around, almost too fast to focus. He spotted it, a small light just off the nose. He pulled on the controls, his muscles tensed as he strained, attempting to avoid the collision. The craft rocked as it hit and screamed of the impact, shields were reduced by 2%. In his attempt to evade the missile, he had maneuvered the craft away from his destination. He twisted his head around, searching for the Omorfiá. His eyes picked up two lights heading toward Ariel and the others.

"Impact imminent," the craft screamed.

The ship shook all around him, he pulled on the controls and pushed the accelerator forward. The propulsion system came alive, his body pressed to the seat. He engaged overdrive, accelerating even faster, the Omorfiá growing in his canopy.

"You okay?" he screamed at the ship as he worked the comm switch.

A moment of silence came through the radio, his eyes strained as his lids narrowed. Two more explosions glowed on the Omorfiá, he added all the thrust the ship had calling out to Ariel again.

"J, we've lost half our shields. How are you holding up?" Ariel explained as the speaker crackled.

At the sound of her voice, he breathed deeply. She was okay, that's all that mattered.

"Impact in 20 seconds," the ship cried.

"Bless it!" He attempted to find the incoming round.

At the last second, his gaze picked it up. He pushed the control to the far right stop. The craft vigorously spun, the missile skipped off the hull taking minimum damage. J stopped the spin, tightening and opening his eyes wide to shake off the weird feeling in his head. He focused on the Moon as he overtook the Omorfiá.

"Change in plans, I'm going in first," he commanded.

CHAPTER SIXTEEN

J surveyed the aircraft systems, his mind running through what had just happened, the spinning, the reduction in shield degeneration. He thought he'd figured out a trick and he wanted to draw the fire, leaving the less maneuverable Omorfiá clear for entry.

"I'll take the missiles, you get that landing bay open."

"J, that's not the plan. You need—"

"No time to argue, just get that door open."

He could hear Ariel growl as she finished keying the mike. He turned his focus to the Moon, picking up more incoming ordinance as the ship continued its nonstop cries. His eyes flicked up to the shields, 60%. *Okay, not as bad as expected.* The hum of the alarm quickened, he put the ship into another spin. The missiles ricocheted off. He stopped the spin, shaking it off again, looking back at Ariel. The ship looked clean, he had become the main target. He smiled to himself, his plan was working. The ship rattled, J's hands trembled inside the control cups.

"Shields 50%," the Tetriack yelled.

J hadn't received a warning from the last blast, his eyes swung to the surface of the Moon. A glowing red light intensified in a small, dark grey crater. His ship was hit again, the shield depleting another 10%. He tried to push the accelerator forward more, but it was still maxed out. He spun the ship, his head spinning with it, but after a couple of revolutions it stabilized. He focused on the

Moon as he saw a large door opening, more shots came at him. He evaded one, the next skipped off the shields once again. The Moon approached more quickly, the black hole inside the door lit up, he centered the nose of the craft. In he went, stopping the spin. His body slumped to the side of the cockpit as he pulled back on the accelerator and let go of the controls. He closed his eyes, hoping the spinning would go away, it didn't.

"We're in," he heard over the comms, he was inextricably glad to hear her voice. He scrubbed his face with his hands. The turmoil in his inner ear was settling and, reorienting his body, he could almost sit up. His hand wobbly engaged the auto land feature then fell into his lap, his body slumped back, longing for solid ground. The ship ended its landing sequence, touching down softly on the flat steel surface. J peeled himself off the seat and slipped over the side rail of the Tetriack. He attempted to stand, but his head still felt woozy, he stabilized himself, placing his hand on the craft. He was growing quite fond of it. The sound of an elephant smacking the ground hit his ear and the Omorfiá touched down beside him. He took a step back, falling against his ship, both arms resting on it at shoulder height. Ariel stepped out first and stormed over to J who continued his pose. He aimed an index finger at her. "Hey," he said in the best suave voice he could muster.

Ariel slapped him across the cheek, his head snapping to the side. He began wiggling his jaw, his eyes half closed. He felt Ariel's hand on his chin forcing their eyes to meet.

"You stick to the plan, got it?

Before he could respond, she fisted her hand in his shirt, pulled him in, her lips meeting his. His head cleared, he stood straighter, placing his hands on her hips, pulling her in tighter. This was not the sweet kiss from earlier. She released the kiss, staring into his eyes. Hers swirled with emotion, her fear of losing him coming to the surface. J stared into their icy depths, attempting to convey the strength of his emotion for her as well, desperately needing her to know that they were partners in this, equals. He heard the clearing of a throat, they both turned their heads to see Max leaning on the Omorfiá's door.

"Can we get going now?" Max asked, his voice monotone as he tilted his head down, looking through his eyebrows.

J flexed his fingers on her hips, then released his hold. He exhaled and twisted to grab the weapons from the craft, his face still holding the smile from their kiss. Grant popped out of the ship at that moment with what looked like a white tool box in his hand.

"We ready to hack this?" he asked excitedly, face still set in its contradictory scowl.

J readied his rifle, it was quiet now, but he knew that wasn't going to last. The welcoming missile defense was an indication there would be more to come, much more. Ariel checked her Datacle and began walking toward the Omorfiá to grab her weapons. In her haste to reassure herself that J was alright and then scold him when she found out that he was, she'd left them on board. J sauntered over to Max who was still leaning on his ship. Max didn't say a word, but didn't take his eyes off J, his eyes tight, jaw clenched. J was tempted to say something, but his Earth manners were still overriding the ones he'd started to learn in his new world. Ariel appeared with her rifle slung on her back, tapping on her Datacle.

"This way boys," she directed, passing the three of them, her eyes focused on her wrist.

Their task was to install Grant's device, allowing them access to the system, and hopefully find Zane, V, and their marks. J jogged to catch up with Ariel.

"What do you know about Takamori?"

Ariel glanced at him then back at her Datacle.

"Not much. The name did ring a bell, but that was as much as I knew, aside from what you told me. I'd heard of TK members being banished...well, everyone hears if a TK member is banished. The humiliation is part of the punishment, meant to detract others from doing the same."

J pondered her words a moment. "What about Nova? You said he left the TK."

"That was different. He left on his own terms and went into hiding. The banished are sent to Earth and still live lavish lifestyles. TK dangles a carrot of redemption if their services on Earth prove to be in the interest of TK. I've never heard of anyone being reinstated though."

By this time, they'd exited the landing pad, Max and Grant were close behind. Upon entering the building, they found a multitude of elevators, J hadn't seen so many in one location before. Ariel opened one and they proceeded down, not up. J almost questioned her, but Ariel had the Datacle, his wrist was bare. Outside the elevator, they stepped into a room filled with rows of black boxes, each about six feet tall by three feet wide, and all with a plethora of blinking lights on them. J exhaled, his breath turning to mist. It was frigid, his body began to shake, his suit clung uncomfortably as he tugged at it. Ariel let out a little snicker.

"Here you go, goof," she tapped on the chest plate of his suit.

The suit felt as if it melted into his body, conforming to his muscles. He began to feel warm as it heated up around him. He inspected his arms, one at a time, twisting them to view every possible angle, then he did the same to his legs. He heard another snicker from Ariel.

"What?"

"Guess I should have given you a manual with it. Here." She pressed on his chest plate again, calling up a menu that hovered in blue in front of him. She spun herself behind him, reaching under his shoulder, she tapped on the menus. She rested her chin on his shoulder.

"So, you have heating, cooling, shields, strength boost, and it doubles as a space suit minus the helmet."

"Strength boost?" he tilted his head.

"Yep, the suit tightens or loosens with your body movements, helping to increase your strength. That uses a lot of energy, even more than the shields. Remember the warning? If the suit gets below 25%, it becomes unstable."

"Unstable?"

Ariel formed her hand in a ball in front of J's face then instantly opened it, her lips making an explosion sound. J's head flinched, the point was well taken.

"25%. Got it. Anything else?"

Grant slithered by them as they were talking, searching for the right connection for his hacking tool. J and Ariel watched.

"Not that I've found yet," she pulled her chin off his shoulder and slipped her arm out from under his.

Max was unamused at the events he just saw take place, he leaned against the door of the elevator one foot on the ground, the other leg bent with just the toe touching.

"You guys are cute," he said, looking down at his hand, then tugged at a loose cuticle. "How long's this going to take?"

Ariel approached him, her mouth open about to speak.

"Done," a voice exclaimed, standing right next to J.

He flinched, Grant had snuck up on him.

Ariel closed her mouth, spinning to Grant. "Any luck finding them?"

"Sure. They're in TK headquarters just under the top

floor." Grant pushed by, approaching the lift.

Max still stood there, leaning on the door. Grant looked up at him, then back at the other two. Unexpectedly, the elevator door popped open. Max fell back into it, landing in the arms of two mediators. Ariel and J swung their rifles up, aiming at the two metal machines.

"We only need the boy. Give him to us and we will let the others go," one of the robots bellowed.

J pulled the trigger, hitting one of the mediators in the head. Ariel reacted quickly, did the same to the other one, dropping it on top of Max. He let out a loud "oomph" as the machine crushed him. Ariel and J ran over, lifting them off of Max, who scowled at both of them. He stood up brushing himself off, Grant climbed on top of the mediators and awaited the ride. The others climbed on as well, they headed up.

"Looks like they found us," Ariel stated.

"Where did the mediators come from? Didn't they all leave with TK on Exodus?" J asked, his forehead in a knot.

"I'm guessing our new friend Takamori fired up the production plant." Ariel readied her rifle as their floor neared.

The lift stopped, opening to a scene of mediators and mayhem. Ariel took out two and J a third as they stepped into the room. Max followed behind, blaster at the ready, while Ariel and J led the way. The door across the room hissed as it opened to the hangar, two more mediators were marching around the Omorfiá. Ariel dropped prone then fired on both of them, each one dropped, rattling the ground. The four of them ran to the ship. J stopped at the door, surveying the environment, searching for movement. The ship came alive and in no time lifted off. J stepped in, closing the door behind. He made his way to the bridge, Max was busy flying the ship while Grant flicked through screens searching for information. Ariel stood behind Max, arms crossed, staring out the windscreen.

"How long until we get there?" J asked, stepping up next to Ariel.

"Five minutes," she replied, unflinching.

"Guns blazing?"

Ariel turned to him, a wicked smile on her lips, "Guns blazing."

Max maneuvered the ship into a landing pattern for TK headquarters, their large pad extending out from the main building which towered over all the rest. As it came into view, he remembered the multiple times, in multiple lives, he'd been there, or so it seemed as his mind drifted to the dreams he had. In some ways, he felt cursed. He felt like he almost knew his father, but really not at all. Ariel's eyes squinted, examining the pad.

"Something's not right," she said, pushing past Max toward the main screen, as if being closer would calm her fears.

J scanned the surface of the pad, nothing was there, it was clean, perfect for landing. Ariel stood near the screen, her hands resting on a control panel, her head on a swivel.

"Something's not right," she reiterated. "Where is everybody?" She moved back, her steps slow and calculated toward the center of the bridge. J looked back at the screen as Max continued the final approach.

"They're in there, I have DNA matches on Zane, V, Liliana, Natalia, Geddes, and Huergo. Looks like there's other movement inside as well," Grant clarified, tipping his head away from his screen.

"You know it's a trap," Max turned his head toward her.

Ariel did know that. *But what was the game plan? How were they going to trap them?* J was thinking the same thing, but he knew it was him that the Angeli Reprobi wanted.

"What about a trade?"

"What?" Ariel spun around. "With what? You? That's out of the question."

"No, I offer to open the book in exchange for the others. We could set a trap for them."

Ariel studied him, began to pace, her hand on her lips her finger sliding back and forth on them.

"Okay," she finally said. "Max, you and Grant stay in the ship. J and I will go negotiate."

"I sure hope this works," she said under her breath.

Max grimaced, but continued the touchdown. J followed Ariel as they exited the craft and headed toward the large doorway J had seen so many times before. He glanced up at the large glass wall staring down on them as they approached. The doors began to open, half a dozen mediators stepped out along with two E-Rats. J was hoping that was it. No such luck. They took a few more steps and Riku stepped into the light from the shadows, his face unchanged from the last time they'd met, the scowl tight as he sneered at them. Ariel stopped about twenty yards short of the door. J followed suit, his rifle slung on his back, his hands near the blasters. The parties eyed each other, waiting for the other to make the first move. Then J did a double take. A small man stepped out from behind Riku holding his father's Journal. Dr. Ohmura took a few steps forward, past the mediators and E-Rats.

"We want the boy," he stated, his nose crinkled.

"You can't have him, he's..." Ariel almost let slip "mine", but caught herself. "We'll unlock the journal for the safe return of our friends."

Dr. Ohmura rocked back on his heels slightly, his jaw pushing his bottom lip into a frown. He studied them a moment.

"Very well...we will do it inside," he waved for them to join him and began to turn to head inside.

"No, we will do it out here," Ariel stated firmly. "Show us our friends."

The doctor exhaled hard through his nose as he turned back, his hands wrapped around his back holding the book between them. His jaw tightened, a slight snarl escaped from the side of his mouth. He approached them. Riku took a step, but was stopped by the doctor's hand. He gently placed the journal on the ground and stepped back two steps, his face unchanged. The two E-Rats readied themselves, stepping out to a flanked position on each side of them.

"Tell your metal monstrosities to step back," Ariel commanded.

The doctor lifted a hand causing each of them to stop. J looked around, trying to see if they were missing anything. "This was a dumb idea" he said to himself, adjusting his stance. The doctor opened a palm to J, waiving him over to the book. J's eyes wandered, identifying the enemy positions. He shuffled over to the book, all eyes focused on him. His head scanned from one side to the other, he could feel the blood pumping through his arms and legs, his body tingled. He knelt down and picked up the journal, opened the cover and pressed his thumb on the plate. The TK emblem flickered then disappeared, revitalizing the unlocked menu. J sat it down on the ground backing away. The doctor was rocking heel to toe, smiling after seeing the book unlocked, he took a step forward.

"Not yet. Our friends."

Dr. Ohmura's smile waned waving toward Riku who disappeared into the building, only to reappear moments later. Behind him marched Zane, V and the others. They were all shackled, their eyes squinting in the sun like they hadn't seen light in ages. J held himself back, he wanted to run to release them. Ariel did the same as her leg drifted forward. The doctor took a step forward, then was hit in the chest with a blast, his body fell limp in front of the book. For a moment, everything froze. J's eyes flicked about, Ariel's hands tightened. It reminded him of the moment before he would steal a base during a ball game. The silence, the anticipation, then movement. Ariel tumbled forward, clutching the book in her hands, a shot rang out from the Omorfiá hitting Riku square in the chest. J flipped his rifle off his shoulder and dropped to one knee, taking out an E-Rat. He felt something hit him in the shoulder like a love tap, he twisted 90 degrees and dropped a mediator. Another love tap, this time he saw the blast hit. He smiled almost uncontrollably. He was being hit by blasts, but his suit was absorbing the shots. Ariel unholstered a blaster, firing at the other mediators and E-Rats. J turned his sights on Riku and let a volley of rounds cook off toward him, his steps steady as he marched toward the giant, fearless. Riku turned, ran into the building leaving the others outside. J and Ariel finished off the remaining enemies then ran over to release their friends.

"Man, am I glad to see you guys," Zane remarked, watching them sprint toward him.

"Leave no Zane behind," Ariel said with a big smile on her face.

She stopped in front of him and used her Datacle to unlock the cuffs. J headed straight for V, he needed to apologize for leaving her, his body felt tight as he reached her.

"I'm—"

"No worries, J. We're fine, it was a little uncomfortable, but fine. We almost made it to the ship."

J still felt bad, but didn't know what to say. Instead he smiled and gave her a big hug, he stepped back to see her smiling back at him.

"Where's Dr. Huergo?" Ariel asked, looking around at the others.

J's head began snapping around, he didn't see anyone else. Grant was certain he was there.

"Must still be inside."

J took off, sprinting toward the door. Ariel glanced at Zane.

"Crap...you get the doctors to the ship, I'm going after J."

J checked his railgun rifle, it was fully loaded. His suit read 95%, which initially surprised him. He'd taken quite a few shots. He'd need to be more careful and less superman to conserve the rest of it, he didn't want to see it malfunction. The thought of Ariel popping her hand open slipped through his mind. He rounded the door and found the massive stairwell and elevator in between. He reached the door and tapped on the screen calling the elevator up.

"Wait up you crazy person," Ariel called, out of breath, slowing her sprint to a jog.

J heard the door open behind him. As he smiled at her, Ariel's face dropped then everything went dark.

CHAPTER SEVENTEEN

The sounds of birds chirping filled his ears, the smell of fresh baked bread entered his nostrils. He opened his eyes. He sat alone at a large wooden table, a basket of dates in front of him, rice and flat breads. A dish of hummus sat next to a small, almost child-sized teacup, sugar coated the bottom as steam rose, dancing in the air. His eyes moved around the room. The walls were stucco and rough, the ground held rugs of elaborate patterns, the wooden table on the wall housed handmade trinkets and a golden oil lamp. A man with dark, rugged skin as if it was overcooked in the sun, appeared dressed in a robe.

"Do you find everything to your liking, sir?" the man asked in broken English.

"Yes. Your hospitality is unmatched," J replied.

The man nodded then headed out the door from whence he came. J took the tiny, child-sized spoon in the teacup and swirled the liquid around, dissolving the sugar. He took a sip. It was warm, almost too hot; the flavors bounced around in his mouth, the sugar tickling his tongue.

"Chai tea," he sighed with pleasure. "I have missed this."

J's mind searched for context. *What happened? He'd been waiting for Ariel, now he felt like he was in a dream. He was in a dream.* He relaxed, knowing he couldn't control it. He hoped this would help their quest or at least give him a glimpse into his father's life like the other dreams had. He stood up, placing the tea cup down, then snagged a date and popped it in his mouth. He meandered over to a wall upon which hung a painting of the Ziggurat, a huge stone structure with sloped sides and stone staircases leading to the top.

"The Prime Minister will see you now."

J turned to see the same worn man standing in the doorway, slightly bowing, his eyes never meeting J's. J proceeded to the doorway, finding himself in a large extravagant hallway. Tapestries draped along every wall, elegant wrought iron candelabras hung evenly spaced throughout, the floor was pure marble. He followed his guide past more rooms like this then into a grand hall. Wrought iron railings flowed down from a second story balcony following two sets of marble laid stairs wrapping around the edges of the room. He passed them and found himself in a lavish office, fifty feet square, a large sumptuous hand-woven rug in bright blues and yellows rested on the floor leading to a mahogany desk at the far end. A maid dusted bookshelves on one side, the other held a floor-to-ceiling window with over a dozen glass panels. The sun shone in onto the desk where a plump man sat. He had a long, straight, grey beard nearly to his belly which bounced as he stood up. His face was riddled with wrinkles, more than he'd ever seen on one face before.

"Come in, Dr. Arcturus! We are excited that you could make this visit and hope we can come to an understanding while you are here." The plump man walked over, took his hand, then pulled him in, kissing him on each cheek. J returned the greeting.

"Will you walk with me?"

It was a rhetorical question; he grabbed J's hand and gently tugged him along.

"Habibi, I understand TK is not looking favorably on the situation down here, but I assure you, it is quite under our control."

They passed through a set of double doors, J noticed that the handles were made of solid gold, the hinges and pins as well. They turned toward two other doors under the grand staircase. Two men in robes opened the great wooden assemblages, they creaked to life. The sun made him duck his head slightly and squint, the plump man continued as they sauntered into a lush garden.

"Our situation is under control. I have my men working through the issues. We do need to discuss the terms and I believe we can make a reasonable contract, for both sides."

They walked in silence past a large manmade pond full of lily pads, the frogs hopped from one to the next. He noticed goldfish nipping at the surface. Great fig trees adorned each side of the pond and a man was tending to a bed of flowers surrounding it. J's eyes danced around, admiring the lovely plants. He drew in a long breath, exhaling it slowly, still strolling with his hand intertwined with the plump little man's.

"So, what did TK have to say about our proposal?"

J looked down. He could feel his face tighten into a frown, his upper eyelids dropped. He faced the plump man.

"You know what they said, please don't push this," he implored solemnly.

The plump man huffed and almost skipped as they continued walking.

"We already export enough. We need more for us, for my people. TK has been taking more than its share over the years," his voice became louder and quickened.

J looked around at the extravagance around him as they stepped onto beautiful green sod and came to a stop before a pair of camels with saddles adorned with gold.

"I'm sorry, TK doesn't see it like that."

J felt the man's hand tighten slightly in his.

"Let's sit down and discuss the details. I know we can come to an understanding."

J swung his head indicating no, the plump man didn't see it.

"In here." The plump man showed an open hand to a smaller building. J let go of his hand and headed inside to find an indoor swimming pool nearly the size of a football field. The water was aqua blue, still and empty. To the left was a steam room and to the right several tables laden with an assortment of fruits and candies. The plump man passed him, waving at J to follow. He sat down and indicated for J to do the same, he sat across from him.

"Baklava, my second wife's recipe," he said, handing him a piece.

J raised his hand indicating no.

"You must comply with TK. They will not change

their stance."

"They must be reasonable," the plump man waved a man over toward him, unconcerned at the course of the conversation.

The man set down a heavy cloth-covered object, the table shook as it settled. The plump man motioned for J to remove the cloth. As he did, his eyes were hit with a pure yellow glimmer, the sunlight pouring in from the glass walls danced across the gold ingot. J's eyes would have popped out had he been able to control them. He abruptly replaced the cloth.

"Bribery will not change things, I'm sorry. You have children, do you not?"

The plump man tightened his eyes, puzzled at the question. He hesitated. "Yes."

"Then you know that you rule the house and no amount of begging, pleading...bribing," he looked at the object once more, "will change the rules."

"Are you calling me a child?!" The man stood up, his belly hitting the table, causing it to shake.

J's eyes drew up to him, he could feel his jaw tense. "You must comply in two hours or there will be consequences." He stood up and handed the man a piece of wrinkled parchment.

The plump man snatched it from his hand and pressed it to his face, reading it. J turned to walk back out the way he came.

"What!" he heard the man bellow.

"They can't do this! Nothing can do this, this is a

joke, a bluff. I will not comply. Do you hear me, Dr. Arcturus? You tell the…"

J continued walking, the man's rant trailing off behind him. He could feel the agony in his journey through the garden and the house, then out the front door. There, a black sedan waited. A younger gentleman in a coat and tie held open the door. J felt sweat run down his head as the sun beat down, he'd never felt heat that intense before. He nodded to the young gentleman then stepped into the car. Another man sat on the far side of the car. J recognized him as Jeffrey, the one with the glass book, his father's right hand man.

"Is he going to comply?" Jeffrey stared down at a digital display in his hands.

J didn't say a word, his gaze steady a thousand yards in front of them.

"Hmm…I often wonder what makes them defiant. Do they not believe our capabilities? Or do they honestly believe they can defy TK?"

J didn't answer, he felt the question rhetorical. The car started on its way, his unfocused gaze continued.

"Do you think if we put it into simpler terms, it might change the outcome?"

"We have. This was the last test. Now we'll be moving ahead with plan MKUltra2X,"

"Interesting. "Eradicated from the heavens" I believe was the description in that document. It sounds like something out of the Old Testament if you ask me."

"That's the way they want it, they play God. Like

Zeus in Mt. Olympus."

J closed his eyes, rubbed his forehead, then looked back out the window as they passed mud and brick stucco buildings. The car pulled up to a small structure, J stepped out, his assistant followed. The driver waved goodbye and J headed to the door, then stopped mid-stride and turned around. He looked at his assistant and pointed at the young driver, "Bring him with us."

"But...I...You know that's against TK law numbe—"

J could feel the stern look he gave the assistant. Jeffrey immediately ran over to the driver, stopping him from entering his car. All three men entered the small building, the driver wisely kept his mouth shut, his eyes down.

"TK is calling. Should I give them the order?"

J sneered, "Tell Cyrellia to give the order herself."

His assistant tapped on his wrist, the driver glanced up, his eyes turned to globes at the sight of the display projected on his wrist.

J said something in a language he didn't understand and the driver's eyes settled.

"What are you going to do with him?" the assistant asked.

"Save him. The killing stops today, my killing stops today. We'll find a new planet and rid ourselves of TK, set up a republic."

The assistant's arm buzzed, he pulled it up to read the text.

"Cyrellia gave the order. The operation will

commence in fifteen minutes."

The elevator stopped and they exited. Arcturus' assistant had to drag the driver along, his world was about to change and he didn't understand any of it. They stepped onto a ship, J headed to the bridge.

"I hear we have approximately ten minutes until the operation commences," a voice in front of him commented. The man turned his head, his jaw square, his eyes a deep blue that radiated with things no one should have to see.

"Yes, Cyrellia is impatient," he replied, his tone tight.

"Ship's ready for liftoff, sir. Recommend you take a seat."

J plunked down behind the pilot, watching the take-off sequence. The ship lifted, racing into the clouds. J crossed his arms, still watching the screen. "Pull up Sector 5."

The ship continued its assent into the heavens, the screen flashed to a bird's eye view of Sector 5. From their vantage point, it looked like a toy model of the Middle East. His eyes stayed locked on the screen, barely blinking.

"Operation is commencing in one minute," a voice intoned.

He sat there watching, unwavering. J was afraid of what he might see. Eradication, playing God, he had his ideas, but hoped they were wrong.

"Operation Nastawić commencing."

Onscreen, lines tracked from the sky to the land

below. Beautiful shades of red scattered across the coun-
tryside. More and more the heavens rained down on
the brown model, changing its color to reds and yellows,
not an inch of the sector was unaffected. The curtain of
blasts tapered off. There was no noise, nobody moved;
a slight hum from the ship's engine was the only sound
penetrating the silence. J stood up. Leaving the bridge,
he waved to his assistant as he passed. His hand was met
with a book. He looked down at it. The journal. He
stepped down a set of stairs into the cargo hold and took
up a seat next to the rear wall. He opened the book, the
familiar TK emblem swirled back at him. His thumb
pressed on the bottom right side of the screen. The first
page opened up and he quickly tapped through a few
screens. J wasn't quick enough to take it all in. The
following screen glowed back at him, the letters at the top
of the screen flashing. J read the words "Smoczy Ogień".

"Sir, we're approaching Atlantis. Touching down in
five," a man said, standing above him at the top of the
stairs. He shut the book, patting it with an open hand,
then pressed it to his chest. He gained his feet and
trudged back to the bridge.

"Cyrellia requests an audience when you arrive," his
assistant informed him, adjusting his glasses.

J felt his body tense, he would have done the same had
he been in control. Part of him hoped he would wake up
before seeing Cyrellia again.

"Very well," he replied, proceeding to his seat. "This will
have to wait." He handed the journal back to his assistant.

The craft touched down. *TK headquarters.* He wanted to rub his head, but couldn't. Mentally, his body tensed, wanting to flee, but was unable to as he wasn't in control. His assistant led the way out the craft and into the building. He quickly found himself in the familiar elevator his mind and body had ridden many times. After passing through the familiar settings, his body didn't head directly into the board room as every other time, but stopped just outside.

"Cyrellia requests your attendance in her chambers," a man walked up from behind them.

J turned with a simple nod, following the gentleman toward an ancillary elevator. He motioned for his assistant to stay. The man pressed a series of codes into the screen, accessing the very top level. He entered, leaving the gentlemen behind. *Not the top.* He thought he couldn't go higher, but he did, up to the very pinnacle of the building. As the elevator reached its peak, he noticed all four walls of the lift were made of glass. It crested the top floor, nothing but windows surrounded him. On one end sat a bed, another a metal encased fireplace, and a bath tub. The other end, a bar with marble countertops. He stepped out of the elevator and walked past the bar to the window, stared at the city below. The train slid by as a ship left a landing pad in the distance, the synthetic sun glowed down upon him.

"I don't understand why you think every time the outcome will be different." He didn't turn, he knew the voice. Even J knew the voice.

Light footsteps approached him from behind, he felt a hand sweep from one shoulder to the other, his focus remained on the city.

"It will be better this way. Your scientists are the ones who designed it, you should know better than most how efficient this will be."

He saw Cyrellia step up next to him out of the corner of his eye, gazing at the same view. She turned toward the bar.

"How was the light show," she asked, a smile in her voice.

J didn't respond for a moment. "What was it you wanted to see me about?" he asked, very curt.

"Arcturus, that's you. Always to the point." She poured wine from a red bottle into a crystal glass, swirled it as she slinked back toward him.

"I'd ask you if you'd like some, but I know you gave it up not too long ago."

"Cyrellia, what did you want to discuss with me? I have pressing matters I need to attend to."

"It can all wait, I assure you," she said with a smile.

J didn't move, he held his ground.

"Remember the last time you were up here and we opened that vintage wine?"

J's head turned.

Cyrellia's face glowed, a devious smile on her lips, her eyes heavy. "We're going to have a child."

CHAPTER EIGHTEEN

He rubbed his head, the back of his skull hurt like the dickens. He was lying on his side on a single bed in the middle of a padded white room. A single glass window hung next to the door, empty. J sat up, mumbling to himself, "Not again."

He continued to rub his head, the pain radiating from the back sliced around to his temples. He stood up and walked over to the window, his steps were labored, wobbly. The head trauma had done a number on him. He shook his head vigorously, as if trying to wake up. His gaze swung to the floor, looking intently at his toes. His legs were exposed. He ran his hands across his ribs and chest, the suit was gone. He stood there a moment searching the room for answers, none came. He'd been captured...again. This was becoming a trend, one he'd hoped he had broken. He placed a hand on the window and peered out, staring back at him was a white box like his, it had steel grating underneath and between them was a walkway. He looked up. Wires dangled, most tightly bundled, running the length of the path. *He must be in a ship.* He leaned his head against the glass, trying to see his prison better, then his eye caught movement from the box across the way. Ariel came into view, she herself was missing her suit and not wearing much. Under better circumstances, he would've enjoyed it. He waved his arms, frantically trying to get her attention. She peered over at him, placing her hand on the glass of her box.

"Are you okay?"

Ariel's eyebrows lifted, her eyes grew larger. She pointed to her ear, shaking her head. J realized she couldn't hear him. His eyes wandered about trying to figure out a way to communicate. He pointed at her then and over exaggerated the letters "OK". She nodded and pointed back at him. He rubbed his head, nodded back. J tried to figure out more signs, none of them came across very well. At one point, he was attempting to pick an invisible lock, then flying a ship, then shooting things. Ariel didn't pick up any of it. She laughed a bunch, which initially frustrated him, but enjoying her smiles, continued. His game of charades was poor, but he hoped something got through. Ariel had attempted a few, with as much luck, then a large body stepped into view blocking the whole window. J's eyes trained up, an Asian man stared down at him then reached up, pressing something on the side of his cage. The window went pitch black. His shoulders drooped, the smile he hadn't realized he'd been wearing flipped. He dragged his feet over to the bed, flopped down on it.

His mind drifted to the dream, or vision, or whatever it was. His father seemed so different from the Kontrolery, more compassionate. Cyrellia was cold and power hungry. *How could they be his parents?* He ran through more questions in his head, sometimes mouthing the words. He had come to terms, there was no way out of the ship. J bent over still seated, resting his elbows on his knees, his head propped up between his hands. The room shook gently, he continued his blank stare at the ground. The bed rocked again, J sighed, one hand slipping off his chin. His head still hurt and, having nowhere to be, he laid back down on the bed staring at the ceiling, its soft white glow illuminating the room.

He closed his eyes, the bed trembled. *Must be entering Earth's atmosphere.* He had felt the same thing many times before. The bed shook again, the vibrations of a thump pulsed through his body. Another thump and more vibrations, he tightened his eyes reopening them. His gaze darted back and forth around the room. J's arms and legs kicked out, attempting to stabilize him as another, this time audible, thump ran through his prison bed. His body flew into the ceiling. He braced himself, arms in front of his face, as he impacted the hard surface. His body was pinned to what felt like hard smooth plastic, his head began to spin. The pain from his head trauma increased. He groaned and tried to press himself away from the surface. The pressure was too great.

Then suddenly, it subsided. He tried again. He was able to stand up, his mouth hung open slightly as he looked down at the bed. His feet pulled away from the ceiling, his arms felt light, almost empty. He was weightless. J gave a kick to the ceiling, propelling himself toward the floor. He felt like his brain was going to short circuit, he didn't know which way was up, or what was happening. He'd never been weightless before. He pushed himself over to the window hoping somehow the deep black would disappear and show what had happened. He pressed his face against it, attempting to see past the black abyss. Zane's face appeared as the glass instantly turned transparent, J gasped pushing back from the window. Zane floated by, his body encased in a space-suit, his round glass helmet reflecting the sun's rays. He pressed several buttons outside the container. J floated away from the door expecting it to open.

"J, can you hear me?"

J searched the room then poked his head back near the glass. He gave Zane a thumbs up.

"You don't have to do that, just talk to me."

J's eyes slipped from right to left. "Hello?"

"Yeah, I can hear you. I'm tapped into the container's speaker system."

"Great! Can you let me out?"

"Sure, if you'd like to die."

J's head snapped back, his mouth dropping.

Zane saw the reaction and chuckled. "Don't worry, we have a plan. Just can't let you out into the void of space without protection."

J's body relaxed a bit. He looked past Zane, nothing but stars glowed behind him. He twisted his head, searching for anything to give him a frame of reference. All he saw was metal debris floating motionless. Zane's helmet reflected back an intense blue glow. A ship came into view over his head, continued past. The Omorfiá's cargo door opened, revealing the large hangar bay. As Zane turned, J could hear him speaking to someone, but not the other half of the conversation.

"Yeah, that's good...Yep, he's fine...We'll get her next. Calm down...Keep moving back."

Zane was waiving as if he was directing traffic. J assumed Max was flying and watched intently as he maneuvered the ship. He was supposed to be a great pilot, but J hadn't seen anything noteworthy as of yet. His jaw clenched and as he watched, he rubbed his fingers together. The ship closed in. He thought of catching the satellite and Earth's new heart; this seemed a lot like that, but on a smaller scale. Soon his box was inside, Zane floated next to him.

"Okay, turn it on," he heard Zane say.

Gravity suddenly returned. J wasn't ready for it, he hit the ground, crumpling into a ball. His face in the floor, he heard the door open and heavy boots hit the ground. He felt a large hand slide under his shoulder. Zane helped him to his feet.

"Better get you some clothes, it's a bit frigid out here."

J wasn't going to argue, his underwear provided little warmth as the cold air rushed into the box. He rubbed his triceps with his hands as his body shivered. He stumbled up the stairs toward the bridge, V met him along the way with a stack of burgundy cloth. He unfurled a flightsuit, Max's flightsuit. A large TK emblem was sewn onto the shoulder, his name was embroidered on the left breast, wings adorned the other. Still freezing and with no other options, he slipped it on, his hands shaking the whole time.

"Better get to the bridge. Zane's going to get Ariel

now and he'll have to decompress the cargo bay."

"Sure" J replied, his teeth chattering.

V stepped onto the bridge, J following. Max had the screen pulled up for a rear view, he was flying the ship backward. A smaller screen displayed the cargo hold, Zane became weightless then the door opened. He pushed the large white box out into space making room for Ariel's container. His eyes trained back to the large screen, another white box came into view, Max continued to close in on it.

"Let me see you," V grabbed his shoulders and pulled him down.

Her lips tightened together as she stood on her tiptoes, she popped down on her heels.

"I think it will be easier to work on a giant who's sitting. Can you grab a seat?"

"I'm fine," J remarked.

V tucked her chin, her brows popped up, she pointed to a chair. J took the hint and sulked over, plopping down. His head still did hurt, he would agree with that.

"Now let me take a look at you."

She began examining his face, eyes and throat, found the lump on his head.

"Wow, quite the contusion. You must have been hit pretty hard."

"Riku, I think," J paused then continued. "Did he catch you after I left?" He winced as she pressed on his wound.

"The giant? No it was some others. They had plenty

of weapons though."

"Swords?"

"No. I'm no weapons expert, but it looked like automatic weapons, the kind Earthlings used to fight with."

Automatic weapons? Riku's men only had swords and throwing stars. V placed a device on his head, he felt warmth then light vibrations as the pain trickled away.

"She's in," Max jumped from his seat, trotted back to the cargo bay.

J looked at V who just shook her head and smiled, he popped up and ran after Max.

"Here, take this," she said, tossing him another flight-suit.

J caught it as he spun around, not breaking stride. He entered the cargo area, Zane was already opening her door. Max had beat him there and was standing at the bottom of the stairs. J almost jumped from the top but instead raced down the stairs. Zane stepped out holding Ariel as he had done for J, Ariel stood up straight and looked around.

"What's with the welcoming party, did somebody just come home from war?"

J smiled and tossed her the clothes as she grinned at him. Max glared at him as if to say, "you spoiled my fun."

"Okay, enough of this. We have one more to get back on the bridge," Zane waved both hands up and down, palms facing them.

The three of them turned to see V standing at the top of the stairs, her face tense. "You guys better get up here," she said, playing with her hands. "You too, Zane."

J was the first one up the stairs while Ariel and Max followed. Zane's helmet let out a hiss as he tossed it aside, right behind the others. As J entered the bridge, the screen displayed a man, his chin square, his hair salt and pepper, eyes a deep shade of blue. His gaze never left the screen, staring into the Omorfiá. J continued toward the screen, standing in the center, the others stood behind him.

"Vich vun of you ess J?" the man queried, his Russian accent thick and harsh.

J's eyebrows raised, he hadn't heard such an accent before. His head swung back to the others, Max looked as confused as him, V was shaking her head. Zane hadn't arrived yet and Ariel was nowhere in sight. He figured she was climbing into the enormous flightsuit. J adjusted his stature standing more upright, his chest out. "That would be me," he said, unwavering.

The man's eyes were tense studying him. "Veery vell. You veel come vis us to Sector Tventy."

J looked over at Ariel who had just entered and was making her way to the pilot controls. He turned back to the screen, not saying a word. He squinted as he judged the man. "Who are you?" he asked, rotating his head slightly to the side exposing his ear.

"I am Admiral Titov. Vee veel board you and take you to Sector Tventy."

The picture disappeared. J stood there staring at the black screen. Ariel tapped a few keys, a ship four times the size of the anything J had ever seen stared back at them, nearly covering the screen. J looked at Ariel who was flipping through menus. "Who was that guy?"

"You heard him, Admiral Titov. You know as much as I do. Sounds Russian, not sure where they got that ship."

A spec sheet appeared on the screen. J studied it a moment, most of the data was beyond him.

"Looks like an Atlantean Leviathan class battle cruiser, but those where dismantled years ago. Zane?" Ariel switched her focus to the big guy for an answer.

He approached the controls, grinding his teeth. "You're right. They were all dismantled for parts for the Exodus." He bent closer to the screen. "Where have you been?" he continued under his breath.

J didn't know what any of that meant, but wondered aloud, "Where's Sector 20?"

"Russian block. Makes sense, at least with that heavy accent. What do they want with you?" Ariel had turned her attention back to the screen. The ship rocked, she spun around, her eyes fixed on J. "They've docked. Grab the weapons."

"Can we outrun them?" The thought of another capture made J's stomach turn. He felt lucky to have escaped the other situations, and his luck would eventually run out. Ariel jogged past him, then stopped at the door.

"Weapons, J. Grab them."

J snapped out of his daze and followed her to the

weapons lockers, Zane was already there handing out blasters when a random thought popped into his head. "What about the doctor?" His eyes fixed on Zane.

"They either have him or we'll have to come back for him. No time for that now."

The ship rocked again, metal scratched as the two ships mated, then silence. J, Ariel and the others stood weapons ready, fixated on the cargo door. J's hand shook slightly as his arm extended out, he took a slow breath trying to calm it, no luck. The sound of two slow knocks came, the steel ringing through the silent air. Zane crept over to the door lock panel then glanced at Ariel, she nodded and he tapped the icon. The door slipped open, the man they had seen on the screen stood there with a multitude of soldiers behind them. Their armament consisted of plasma rifles and cybersync blasters, items he'd seen at Dillon's facility. The man studied each of them then turned his focus back to J. He raised his hand and waved two fingers to him, indicating for him to join them. J peeked at Ariel, but didn't move.

"J, vee only neet you. Zee uzzers steey."

"Why should I? What do you want?"

Titov looked at Zane then Ariel. He turned and checked back with his soldiers then raised both arms out to his sides. "I don't zink you haf a choice."

J scanned their captors, they were outnumbered three to one and their weaponry rivaled, if not outmatched, their own. Had the prototype suit still been wrapped around him, things would be different. But in the current situation, he didn't see any other options. He dropped his hand, tossing the blaster aside. J took a step toward Titov.

"Wait," Ariel grabbed J's shoulder. She stepped in front of him. "I'm coming too."

J turned to her and scowled. As much as he wanted her by his side always, he didn't want any harm to come to Ariel. He loved her and needed her to know he would keep her safe. His father stated all of this and it was his to finish. "No, they want me," his voice stern.

Ariel tightened her grip on his shoulder. "You need me," she winked, her devious grin offered a glimmer of hope that she had a plan.

Seeing that, J relented. She'd probably find another way to follow if he didn't go with her plan now. "You have to take both of us," he stood up straight, his chest held out strong.

"Very vell."

Titov flicked a hand in the air and four of his soldiers rushed over to the two, detaining them. J's eyes drifted over to Zane, he looked like he was about to rip their heads off as he scowled. J raised a hand and nodded to him, signaling they'd be okay. He dropped his weapon, the rest of the crew followed suit. J and Ariel were ushered into the large battleship, the door closed behind them.

CHAPTER NINETEEN

The ship was incredibly huge; it felt like they walked down endless corridors and rode countless elevators to arrive at their holding cells. They were escorted into a single cell, but not a dingy, dank, dark cell like he thought it would be, it was actually quite nice. It consisted of a small room with an attached bathroom, the bed had fresh linens and one of the walls sported drawers, which J found by accident when he leaned against it. Other than the locked door, he would've thought he was in a nice hotel, albeit a cold, sterile futuristic one. Ariel was too busy fiddling with the door to notice the amenities; she was attempting everything she could think of to get it open. This proved impossible for the lack of tools and the fact that Titov had his soldiers remove her Datacle from her wrist. J sat on the bed, kicking his feet out and extending his arms backward, his shoulders slumping into his ears.

"What do you think they want with me?" J studied the tiled ceiling.

She continued playing with the control panel, a buzz came every few minutes at her vain attempt to hack the code. "Same as everybody wants, to unlock everything in Atlantis," she said, not missing a beat.

Atlantis unlocked? He was nothing but a key, a pawn. It made him think back to his life in Eggerton; there he'd been just one of the other kids. He longed for that, the obscurity, or at least, the relative anonymity. Constantly being pursued was taking a toll on him, he didn't know how much more he could bear. *Why did his father make things so complicated?* He wished he could get back to life the way it was... with one exception. He took a sideways peek at Ariel. Her compact frame radiated such confidence and strength. She stood erect and slapped the door with a growl then spun toward him and stomped into the bathroom. He heard rummaging as she bumped into the walls and tossed around items located within. She was searching for a way out, no exit existed.

"So, I thought you had a plan?" J wanted to be sure that he was loud enough that she could hear him, but that he wasn't perceived as yelling at her.

She stuck her head out of the bathroom. "I do."

J lowered his eyebrows. "What is this grand plan?"

"Well..."

"You don't have one do you?"

Ariel's lips pursed, the blood leaching out, as she stared daggers through him. Her shoulders tensed and she switched her focus back to the main door. It opened, startling her. She hopped back. Two soldiers blocked the entryway, each holding a pile of folded clothes. J stood up and shuffled over toward the door. The soldiers, not saying a word, held out the fabric to Ariel. She snatched it from them, turning her angry stare upon their presence, the door closed again. She threw the clothes on the bed.

"I suppose they want us to change." She stood facing the door, feet braced apart, hands on her hips.

J's eyes trained down the burgundy flightsuit he still

wore, he grimaced when he read the name Max upside down and decided that anything was better than what he had on. He rummaged through the pile, looking for something his size, and lifted up an off-white, button up shirt. It reminded him of some of the clothes from Earth. He slipped it on then found a pair of dark blue, almost navy, dress pants. In the pile he also found a pair of dress shoes and a thick wool coat. He chewed on his lip seeing the coat. *Sector 20 must be cold.* He was not looking forward to the bracing air of winter again. After pushing the coat aside, he saw a pile of beautiful red fabric, held it up.

"Guessin' this is for you," he held it out with a devious grin.

Ariel stopped playing with the keypad and snatched it out of his hand. "What? Are we going to a ball?" she scowled.

The last item besides shoes for her was another coat, but this one was black and made completely of fur. Ariel grumbled as she peeled herself out of the flightsuit and slipped on the dress. J's eyes fixated on the ground but...

"Can you zip this, please?"

She stood leaning on one leg, her hip kicked out with a hand planted firmly on top of it. The other held her hair away from her bare back. J swallowed then approached her, gently tugging on the zipper until it reached the top. It wasn't the first time she'd asked for help dressing, but it always felt like it. He brushed his lips across her nape.

Ariel shivered then let go of her hair and looked up at him from underneath her lashes, "Thanks."

The door opened, seemingly on command, as she finished. The same two soldiers stood there, one slipped to the side as if choreographed. Titov towered over them, his build thick and hardy.

"Goot. Zeey fit."

J was trying to read him and figure out what his game was. He was tight-lipped, not answering any questions, which was not in keeping with any of the bad guys they'd met so far. For some reason, once J started asking questions, they all started monologuing, like they couldn't wait for someone to actually listen to their crazy plans. But not Titov. He nodded to one of the soldiers then turned to walk out. The soldier motioned for them to step out and follow. They had docked in Sector 20, a new experience for J. They were not in a large hangar, the craft's size simply wouldn't allow it. Instead they rode an elevator up all the way to the surface. Ariel had seemed surprised they had such a ship. He wondered how they could have hid it from TK and what were they planning to use it for.

The elevator stopped and Titov led them out. J and Ariel held their coats while Titov wore his, a thick military style jacket, his paints the same fabric. That should've been their first clue. Black boots adorned his feet, the leather wrapping around his calves up to his knees. He marched out of the building into the bitter cold. J's fears were confirmed and it was more frigid than he could have imagined. The wind whistled as it zipped around the buildings, the snow flew at them sideways. Ariel flipped the fur hood attached to her coat over her head and threaded her arms through the sleeves, then held the neck tighter with her hands. J wished his had a hood, but then again, he had on pants. Ariel's legs were exposed to the harsh winter surrounding them, constantly blowing her dress and the coat around as they walked toward two black sedans a short distance away. The driver opened the door, motioning J and Ariel into the car. It sagged as Titov sat down beside him. J peeked out of the corner of his eye at him. He sat rigid, staring out the window, his square jaw tight, his fur hat snug on his head.

"Where are we going?" Ariel demanded.

"You veell see."

Ariel huffed and sat back into the seat, she could tell they wouldn't get anything more out of him. The car started forward and J watched the snow outside the windows to pass the time. He had no clue where they were going, how long it would take, or what was going to happen when they arrived. He could think of a few scenarios, none of them ended nicely for Ariel or him. At one point, he thought he may have fallen asleep as his head snapped up and his shoulders shivered. Outside, the snow continued obscuring the views, they seemed to be driving on country roads to the middle of nowhere. The land was barren and frozen, snow fields surrounded them. The cars abruptly squealed to a halt and J could almost make out an imposing building as he gazed past Ariel. It was about five stories tall, each corner was capped with a turret and topped with what resembled a pointy round ice cream scoop in an assortment of brilliant colors. The soldiers ushered them into the building, J was thankful to be somewhere warm, but wary as they approached the unknown. As they entered, two men took their coats, their captor giving his up as well. Titov led them through room after room of pure elegance, J's jaw hung open a he studied all of the lavish antiquities the building held. They stepped into a cathedral of a room, the ceiling multiple stories high, intricately carved wooden chairs sat around two large tables stretching the entire length of the room. They were each escorted to a seat; J's eyes grew large as he saw all of the food laid out before them. He couldn't remember how long it'd been since he last ate, but his stomach grumbled at the sight. The sweet aroma of cooked meats hit his nose, furthering his sense of hunger. He closed his eyes, reveled in the smell. After sitting down, a man came up behind him, set a glass of wine in front of him. J's head snapped over to Ariel, she clenched her jaw as a glass was placed in front of her. J surveyed the room, he counted twenty chairs at each table. They'd been seated in the middle of the table closest to the entryway, across from the open table which lay empty. Titov sat down across from them, alone.

"Eat."

A plate with a generous piece of roast and a bowl of Kasha was placed in front of each of them. Ariel took a fork and carved a piece of meat, she held it up examining it.

"Eat. Eet's not poison," Titov took a mouthful himself.

J watched Ariel slip the food into her mouth. Her shoulders relaxed, then she glanced at him with a slight smile at the edge of her mouth. J followed suit, it was the most delicious thing he could ever remember eating, though he couldn't actually remember eating anything before that moment, he was so hungry. He closed his eyes briefly as he chewed. The waiter approached with rolls adorned with butter, it reminded him of the ones his mom on Earth would make. Not a word was said as they continued eating. J observed Titov, noting that he couldn't tell whether he was enjoying the meal. J didn't touch the wine, he'd never drank alcohol before and was worried what it might do to him. Ariel took a sip, but that was all he saw her do.

J sat back stuffed, his belly tight, his eyelids heavy. Titov stood up, placed his napkin on the table. "Ten meenutes zen vee veell meet vis Prezident Novikov."

He pivoted and marched out of the room, the staff opening and closing the door. J thought it was strange, having such a lovely meal as a prisoner, though he wasn't going to complain about it. The other times he'd been captured, he was treated more poorly, albeit more briefly.

Ariel rested her head back on the chair, rolling her head toward him. "Any ideas on how to escape?"

"You're the clever one. Besides, I thought you already

had a plan."

Ariel searched the room with her eyes. It had windows at the far end from the floor to ceiling, the other walls each held two doors. J figured the one across from the windows led to the kitchen as that's where the staff came from. Titov had exited through one of the others. His eyes flicked about, trying to pick up anything else. The sun had set and the glass was nearly pitch black, the snow accumulating along the ledge. J shook his head from side to side.

Ariel grabbed his thigh and leaned in close, attempting to get his attention. "Zane has a tracker on me. If we get a chance to get outside, don't hesitate to take it."

"Outside...have you seen outside? It's freezing! We won't last ten minutes out there," his whisper was nearly a yell.

The door swung open, Titov stood with his chin held high. "Prezident Novikov veell see you now."

Four soldiers marshaled Ariel and J behind Titov as he marched them toward the large set of wooden doors. On command, they opened, revealing a sizeable office adorned with rugs from various parts of the world, tapestries from different eras, and sumptuous leather chairs and couches. At the far end, a heavy set wooden desk rested. Behind it sat an older gentlemen with his fingers intertwined, tapping his forefingers together. His hair was almost black, slicked back over his head from his receding hairline. His nose was overly large and his ears small for his head; his eyes and mouth turned down as they approached. He stood up, shuffled around the desk.

"You are J?"

J's head snapped back, his eyes widened. The man spoke perfect English, or what he thought perfect English should sound like. There was no shred of an accent. J glanced at Ariel to see if she felt the same, her reaction proved she didn't. J swung his head back to the president and nodded, pulling in his bottom lip. The president waved a man over from the corner that J hadn't noticed before. He was slender with blonde hair, about J's height, his face emaciated and boney. He peered over thick, black-rimmed glasses as he grabbed J's hand and placed it on a plate scanner. He nodded to the president then backed away.

"Do you have the book?"

J looked at Ariel. She'd had it last, but he didn't know where it went after Riku knocked him out. Ariel's eyes tightened, J slightly shook his head.

"We don't have it," Ariel said, standing strong and tall, defiant.

Novikov approached her, staring into her icy eyes. His gaze snapped over to J, reading him, his mouth in a tight frown. He walked over to J, stopped inches from his face. J inhaled the strong musky smell of cologne.

"You don't have it?" Novikov tilted his head, squinting his eyes, his fists tightened.

J pursed his lips, shaking his head.

The president shook as a snarl painted his face. "Very well." He turned to Titov. "Notify the Reprobi Angeli

Conclave, we have the key."

Almost on cue, a man came in holding a book resembling the journal, the TK emblem emblazoned on it. He walked briskly as if bringing important news, then stopped next to the president and whispered in his ear. Novikov's eyes lit up for a moment then resettled into a disgruntled stare, his mouth never altered.

"Seems you are telling the truth, the Reprobi have the journal." His eyes fixed on J. "Takamori is on his way here."

J swallowed, his skin tingled, his fingers danced as he grabbed his wrist with his other hand. The last time he'd seen Takamori didn't end well and Ariel was with him. He wished she'd stayed behind, both for her safety and his rescue. He stared straight ahead. Ariel's eyes studied Novikov, her muscles tensed, she flexed a calf as if ready to lay a kick into his head. He turned away, walking toward the door he entered.

"Ready the council room and bring the prisoners," he called as he exited.

CHAPTER TWENTY

Takamori strutted into the council room. J eyed him, remembering their last meeting. Ariel glared, her teeth clenched. They sat against the wall behind a large executive table made of rich mahogany. Four men sat, evenly spaced. Ariel only recognized Takamori and Novikov, the other two were strangers. Behind Takamori the giant body of Riku skulked. Ariel raked her hands on her thighs as Takamori flipped two fingers into the air then wiggled them toward the table. Riku produced the journal and thumped it down on the table in front of him. Takamori scowled at him. J could feel the growl come from his mouth, but there was no audible sound. Ariel tightened her grip, digging into her legs, flexing her forearms and biceps. Takamori slid his finger along the emblem on the book's cover, plotting out the insignia.

"TK is gone. The Reprobi Angeli Conclave is the future."

The men clapped and nodded to each other. J studied the two that he didn't recognize. One was a small man with very dark skin in his mid-forties; his head glistening in the light void of any hair, his mouth seemed too large for his face, and his forehead was tall. The other man's head was wrapped in fabric held up into the air as if a paper bees' nest was gently placed on it. His eyes were brown, ears small, his skin had an even tan, his thin lips pursed in a constant devious smile.

"We have the journal," Takamori crowed. "We have

the key," he motioned toward J. "Now, we will have Atlantis."

The men beamed and shook hands, congratulating each other,.

"We have been banished from our rightful place in the stars, exiled to this forsaken planet, disowned by TK. The reign of TK has ended; the reign of the Reprobi Angeli is beginning."

The men, bound with energy, stood up, applauding. Takamori pushed his hands down from the air to the table, motioning downward multiple times. The other three sat down. He looked over at Novikov and aimed an open hand at him.

"It is thanks to our colleague, Novikov, that we have the key. Let us use it."

After acknowledging the president, their eyes fixated on J. He shrank in his chair, his chin in his chest, unfocused on the ground. He glanced up, but flipped his eyes back down, he felt a tug on his shirt. J's gaze flicked upward, the Admiral stood over him, coaxing him to stand. He resisted at first, but his defiance proved ineffective as another hand grasped his shoulder, lifting him involuntarily up. Titov slid his fingers under J's arm, escorting him around the table toward Takamori. Ariel attempted to stand up, but was forced down by the guardian standing behind her. As J approached, Takamori opened the book, the spinning emblem pulled a look of disgust from his face. A man approached from the other side of the table, setting a box next to the book. He placed a hand on top, causing it to transform into what looked like a typewriter, but the slide was replaced with a glass screen. J stood next to the seated Takamori, his head turned to J, a satisfying leer swept over his face. Titov clasped J's wrist, forcing it onto the table. J tried to pull away, but his strength was overruled as his fingers were placed on the book. The screen opened, unlocking the journal as TK's emblem washed away. The man who brought the box in began typing on the contraption; as he did, a hologram rose from the center of it, rotating slowly on its axis in the center of the machine. J took a closer look; the display mirrored the journal. At the corner of the screen, J read the word "downloading".

Takamori once again eyed J then his gaze slid around the room. "Atlantis is ours."

The room erupted into cheers, fists raised into the air, one of the men clapped. Takamori again silenced the room, his face growing serious.

"What shall we do with the key now that he is of no use?"

The room remained silent for a moment, then the dark-skinned man spoke, "Euthanize him, the body we may need later."

The others agreed. Ariel attempted to stand again, but was forced down.

"Very well. Novikov, see to it that this is handled," Takamori instructed.

Novikov tilted his head, snapped his fingers and pointed to the exit. Titov tightened his grip on J and led him over to Ariel who was also forced up. They were pushed along through back corridors then into an antechamber. Titov handed J the wool coat he'd worn upon their arrival, Ariel was also given hers. Titov then took an about face and left them with the guards. The guards forced their coats on, pushed them outside into the winter storm. They marched a few dozen feet to another building, Ariel clutched the coat attempting to stay warm as the wind howled. J buttoned up his coat and slipped his hands in his pockets. He played with his fingers, wiggling them, attempting to keep them warm. Something cold and hard touched his hand; he flipped his fingers around it attempting to determine what it was, slowed his pace. The guard bumped his upper back pushing him along.

He turned. "Watch it."

The guard pressed him again, his rifle hitting J in the back, his body thrust forward again. Ariel spun around with a roundhouse kick, her foot colliding with the guard's face. He collapsed instantly. She turned her attention to the other. Pushing J, he backed off, aiming the rifle at her then back to J. She took a step forward, the guard's eyes shifted to her, adjusted his aim. She froze, her coat flowing open in the cold air. J took a step forward, his movement met by the rifle. Ariel tensed her legs, shifted her weight, about to pounce like a cat. She lunged forward, spinning around, her leg flying in the air. J's vision shifted to see her body go limp midair as a flash of light nearly blinded him. He lunged with a scream.

Voltage surged through his body as another light glowed, his muscles stopped responding. He hit the ground with a thud, sliding slightly, his eyes facing Ariel's on the ground. He couldn't move, Ariel stared at him, motionless. His eyes began to feel heavy, he drifted off thinking of her beautiful eyes.

He didn't recognize his whereabouts. From a glass window, he looked down upon Earth, the plates floated on the interwoven pillars of metal. Each plate appeared slightly different; a few were covered nearly entirely by water while others entirely by land. Clouds swept around and through them. Between the plates, the Earth's heart glowed at the center.

"It is a marvelous structure, one which brings me great joy...but I despise the inhabitants."

J knew the voice, turned to see Cyrellia standing next to him swirling a glass of wine.

"Our new program will eliminate any need to deal with those..." she tightened her lips, searching for the word. "Earthlings," she finished with hatred on her lips.

J directed his gaze back at the planet, if that's what it could be called now. He didn't know if it met with the true definition of a planet. *Could a man-made structure be given such a title?* It was once upon a time a planet, but now it was a worker colony, a space station of sorts. The people there were ignorant of what was actually happening on the Moon; their minds clouded by technology, yet given little of it.

"Let me have one last chance to negotiate with them,

they should have the choice. They are people, humans. I believe I can convince them to bend to your wishes."

"Our wishes, my dear Arcturus. I must remind you that you are part of the Kontrolery. This system was yours; it's a pity it failed. Now have some wine with me to celebrate the new order we've created. Today is a day of celebration, not grief."

J watched as a large ship crossed into view, nearly obscuring the Earth as it passed.

"I need funding for another project and for the board to approve it," he disclosed, still staring out the window.

Cyrellia crinkled her nose as she smiled, "So that's why you decided to join me tonight. And here I thought it was for my company."

"You have the council at your will. You can persuade them to approve it."

"And what is it that TK is approving...or should I say I'm approving?" Her words smooth and drawn out.

"It's a new battle class attack ship for the fleet, to ensure we have superior weaponry in the new solar system."

"Sounds like something you wouldn't need me to pull approval for. What's the catch?"

J took a long breath through his nose, his lungs expanding to capacity. "It will slow down production of Exodus and divert resources away. We'll have to find a new source of Ore, which I have found, but will add time to the final product."

Cyrellia watched him out of the corner of her eye.

She swirled her glass again, handing it to him. He took it, looking down at the dark red liquid. The aroma hit his nose. J didn't like the smell and wanted to turn away, but this wasn't his memory, it was his father's. He took a sip then looked back at Cyrellia.

"Will I get my funds?" he asked, turning his attention once again to the Earth.

Cyrellia pressed herself against him, pulling him in tight. His arm kicked out to avoid spilling the wine.

"That depends on how good you are tonight."

J's eyes popped open. He exploded into the air, his body shivered at the thought of what most likely happened next. He rubbed his arms, looking at the ground and realized he didn't know where he was. His eyes shifted around, taking in his environment. The walls were made of stone, the ground carpeted in a lush deep grey color, there was not a window in sight, but one steel door hung on the opposite wall. The others had paintings hanging on them of fields and castles. Ariel was lying on a bed behind him. He leaned over her, closed his eyes, and inhaled her unique sunflowers and ozone smell before kissing her on the cheek. She made a pleased sound in the back of her throat as her icy blue eyes cracked open, locked onto his. She grabbed his shirt and pulled him in for a quick, soft kiss, then released him. She moaned and her hands went to her head. J had noticed his hurt as well, but until then, his thoughts had kept him distracted.

"Where are we?" she asked, groggy.

"Not sure. Looks like a room in a castle or something,"

Ariel sat up, still rubbing her head. She examined her surroundings then glanced down to find herself still in the dress, she groaned under her breath. J tried to hold back a laugh at her reaction; she scowled at him, standing up.

He stood up and placed his hands on her hips, pulled her in closer. "You look beautiful. You always look beautiful."

Her expression softened, she placed her hand on his chest and gently stepped out of his arms. "Not the time, J. We need to find a way out of here. You heard what they said they were going to do to you...we're lucky they haven't done it yet."

She stared at the door, but there was no door handle, only a slot on the wall about waist high. The door was flush to the wall. She tried placing her palms on it, attempted to pull it to the side. Her hands slipped off as she tried again. J examined the ceiling, hoping to find something, maybe an exit, anything, but found nothing. It was smooth steel with only a florescent glow illuminating from the four hanging lights. Ariel gave up on the door and stood there with a forearm on her head, her hair flowing over the dress. J stopped searching, mesmerized by her every move, the red dress particularly emphasizing her femininity. His eyes noticed something on the wall. Their coats. *Why would their coats be in the room?* He dashed over to them, enthusiastically grabbing his.

"What are you doing?" Ariel walked over, trying to figure out what he seemed so excited about.

"On the way over, I felt something in my pocket. I have this weird feeling it could be something important or maybe we could use it for something."

He dug into the pocket, the first one was empty. He switched, digging into the other, his fingers felt the object once again. He pulled it out, triumphantly holding it up, then blinked several times. It looked like just a square piece of plastic, black, nearly flat like a playing card. His shoulders sank as he tossed it to the floor. Ariel watched his emotions swing from high to low in an instant. She approached the card. bending over to pick it up, J was standing with his arms crossed not paying much attention. He'd hoped it would be something useful, but instead it was just junk. J glanced at her over his shoulder.

"It's just trash," he sighed deeply.

Ariel stood up holding it in front of her face. If there ever was a definition of a Cheshire cat grin, that would've been the look she gave him. She pranced over toward the door while J watched her, puzzled. She found the slot in the wall and slipped it in then turning toward him, continuing her ridiculous grin, the door slid open gaining access to the hall beyond.

"Where did you find that?" She waved him to the door and stuck her head out, watching for movement.

"It was just there in my pocket." He was still trying to figure out what just happened.

"Grab our coats, we might need them,"

J grabbed the coats and they slipped silently down the hall. As they approached the first junction, Ariel slowed down, peeking around the corner. At the far end stood a guard next to what resembled elevator doors. She tucked her head back in, pressing a finger to her lips. J shook his head, raised his eyebrows, as if to mockingly say, "Really? I wouldn't have guessed". Her eyebrows slid down as she leaned against the wall staring back at him. She pointed the other direction as she pushed past him, heading as quick as she could without making a noise back toward their prison cell. J followed as they went past it and, finding another turn, peeked around. Dead end.

"Looks like that elevator is our only way out. Any ideas?"

J pondered the question a moment then looked at her dress and smiled, wagged his eyebrows. Ariel rolled her eyes.

"Fine." She led the way back to the elevator.

Ariel placed a fake smile on her face as she made the last turn, sauntering sexily toward the guard. J peeked around the corner, her hips swayed as she walked, her hair flowed from one side to the other. His body warmed, continuing to watch her strut toward the guard. It took longer than he thought it would for the guard to notice, the hallway was about thirty feet long and she was nearly half way there before he detected movement. The guard approached her, his rifle still slung on his shoulder. He was a foot and a half taller than her.

"Do they have a giant farm around here?" J said under his breath. Nearly all the soldiers and guards were taller than him.

The guard addressed Ariel, J only heard mumbling from his position. She shifted her arms behind her then swung around facing him. He could see the guard had handcuffs in one hand about to place them on her. She rocketed a back kick between his legs, J shuddered at the sight, almost grabbing himself. Ariel spun around with a knee to the guard's stomach then a punch to his temple, he dropped into a heap. J sprinted toward her clutching their coats in his arms. Ariel was busy taking off the rifle as he arrived.

"Remind me never to piss you off."

Ariel grinned at him and snickered, "Better not,"

They took the elevator up to the top level then navigated to a set of doors, finding a substantial garage. As they stepped into it, J saw some strange vehicles near the back wall; they resembled go-carts but had one single tank track in the back. Where the front wheels should have been, were two skis. In the center was a seat similar to a motor bike.

Ariel took off toward them. "I call the red one," she shouted, running past him.

CHAPTER TWENTY ONE

Snow flew by his eyes, bouncing off the goggles he'd found attached to the handlebars like tiny bullets off an impenetrable shield. A flash of light zipped over his head. His eyebrows lifted, he pressed the throttle with his thumb hard, his machine closing in on Ariel. She'd given him a quick lesson of the machine's operation, simple enough, he thought. Press the lever with his right thumb to go, release to stop, and steer like a bicycle. Ariel was in the lead as they raced away from the compound. The snow fell in large bits toward the ground, still swirling from the wind. Another blast flew overhead, J didn't look back for fear of falling off. He'd never ridden something so fast. And out in the open, the falling snow enhanced the feeling of speed. He knew they were being trailed; lights glowed behind them, the occasional blaster show, seemingly poorly aimed or fired as a warning, he couldn't tell. The sound of pumping pistons roared underneath him, his eyes fixated on the little red light up ahead.

The rolling hills made their ride easy, but there was nowhere to hide. Another shot drifted past him almost hitting Ariel, his eyes widened as trees magically appeared out of the blanket of falling snow. Ariel turned, barely avoiding a large pine. J mirrored her movements, slowing down. His muscles tensed, jaw tightened. He felt the blood leaving his hands from his white-knuckled grip on the controls. He continued swerving, avoiding the trees as his guide did. Where they were going he didn't know, but they had to run. His life depended on it.

Ariel took a sharp 90 degree turn, J attempted to follow, but there was something he wasn't taught in their hasty escape. To lean. He was thrown from the sled, nearly hitting a tree, his body flailing like a rag doll attempting to control the fall. He clipped a bush then plunked down into the deep snow. The sound of the machine died off. Covered in snow, he attempted to climb out. He was thankful they'd found snow gear in the garage; his head was covered in a fur-lined hat, its straps snapped under his chin. His face was the only thing exposed, growing colder from the melting snow. He wiped it away.

The sound of engines echoed in the distance, growing closer. He peeked his head above the snow, his machine lay motionless on its side twenty feet away, the light, half-covered, piercing the dark. Two round lights shined in his eyes growing larger. It was the guards they had passed on their way out of the complex, they were going to find him, he was sure of it. He hunkered down as he watched the two machines approach and come to a stop. Two men stepped into the deep snow, sinking up to their waists, their heads twisting from one side to the other. One of them pointed at his machine and said something J didn't understand then trudged toward it. The other looked right at him. J flopped down into his snowy fox hole, he turned his ear up to listen. The sound of a running engine in the distance was all he heard. He held his breath a moment, he needed to be quiet. Maybe they wouldn't see him. Darkness was his friend and he hoped it would prove to be a good friend. The sound of rustling branches bounced off his eardrum blotting out the distant sound of the engine. It was close, his body tensed, he knew the solider was right on top of him. He didn't move. Unable to hold his breath any longer, he exhaled as quietly as a mouse, closing his eyes, wishing he was a child again and could turn invisible.

A gruff voice made his eyes shoot open, the business end of a rifle was all he could see. He swallowed, looking up. Two eyes glistened in the dim light through a ski mask. The shadowy figure bobbed the rifle up, J took the hint, placing his arms in the air and standing up. His vision was drawn to the other man who was standing near J's escape machine. *Where's Ariel?* He could really use her expertise at the moment. The man spoke again, J still didn't understand, but the words felt coarse and demanding. The rifle pointed him toward their equipment. He forced his legs through the snow, which proved to be quite the challenge. Only a few steps in he found himself taking breaks. His captor would spout angry words, pushing him along, his thighs burning from the work. He trudged toward the guards' machines, glancing over at his. The other guard stood over it, his gaze focused into the woods. He was searching for any sign of Ariel, there was none. He spun around making the journey toward them, kicking his legs through the snow. The flakes had begun to taper off making the sleds' lights seem brighter,

231

their engines still gently purring. Reaching the machine, he was forced to sit as the two men chatted back and forth.

The forest lit up as though the sun had decided to stop hiding, J cupped his hand over his forehead attempting to shield his eyes. Shadows of the trees danced about as the light moved, there was no audible sound, his ears still filled with the rumble of the sleds. The two guards peered up toward the heavens, shouting at one another, their weapons aimed at the sky. One of the soldiers tumbled over the sled, the other shouted even louder. J looked down at the guard trying to figure out why he'd sudden fallen, he'd been hit with a blast. J reached for his rifle, but struggled to free it, the man's body lay on top pinning it to the machine. The other guard dropped into the snow, disappearing. J frantically worked to free the weapon from its owner. The sounds of cracking branches penetrated the night. J's hands gripped the rifle, his neck hairs stood on end. The light grew brighter, the edges of a ship came into view as it continued to descend. The rifle, now free, J pointed at the craft ready to fire. His eyes adjusting to the light, saw two figures appear as a door opened on the side of the ship. It neared the ground merely fifty feet away. J's hands trembled as he held the rifle, its stock tight to his shoulder as he watched the ship settle to the snow. One of the figures hopped into the deep powder and began fighting his way toward J.

"Put that thing down! That's some way to greet your rescue party."

J lowered the weapon. He should've recognized Zane's massive body kicking through the white fluff. J relaxed as a smile grew on his face.

"Where's Ariel?"

"I don't know, we got split up." J's mouth turned down, hoping Ariel was alright. As if on cue, the sound of a snow machine grew closer, its headlight shining toward them. Ariel stopped the machine next to them.

"You okay, J? What happened?" Her eyebrows were pinched as she spoke.

"Yeah, just took a tumble."

"Not to squash the reunion, but we're tracking more incoming. Need to get a move on," Zane said, kicking up snow as he headed back to the ship.

J studied Ariel, his body warmed and it wasn't just the snowsuit. She shut off the sled, followed Zane toward the ship. As they neared the ship, J saw V standing in the entranceway.

"You guys okay?" she asked, fiddling with a medical device.

Ariel and J both nodded as they stepped onboard, the door closed behind them. Before J had time to think, the ship rattled nearly knocking him off his feet. Ariel, V and Zane stumbled as well. Ariel took off to the bridge.

"We've got incoming. Better buckle up," the ship's internal speakers boomed Max's voice.

The craft rattled again, J fell into the wall grabbing some of the ship's contoured metal. V was nearly at the top of the stairs when another shot hit, rocking the ship once again. She fell into the railing then tumbled down. Zane caught her, lifted her in his arms. She threw hers around his neck and held on as he headed up the stairs. J gained his footing and ran to the bridge, nearly hurdling the stairwell. Once there, he threw himself into a seat. Zane arrived and set V gently down into a seat, making sure she buckled up, before sitting down himself.

"Shields 66%," Ariel yelled, pointing to the screen.

"I see it, let me do my thing," Max replied.

Onscreen, he could see the wintry forest pulling away from them as they lifted up. Max skirted the treetops as they accelerated. The snow had stopped falling, making the visibility nearly clear. The ship rattled again, whatever hit them felt heavy, powerful. Ariel spouted out the shield status, Max blew her off, focusing on piloting the ship. A separate screen showed two ships trailing them, both smaller than the Omorfiá. More missiles came inbound, Max worked the controls avoiding one of them, but the second hit the hull. The hum of the engines was smooth and the shield was holding, but for how long, J didn't know. Max flexed the ship's controls, pivoting it into a turn. Off the nose, J could see mountains coming into view surrounded by sky glow. On another occasion, the beautiful reds and pinks would have been quite the sight to see, but there were other things to focus on at the moment.

"Can't you out run them?" Ariel asked

"This is a transport ship, not a rocket," Max retorted.

Ariel pulled up a map. Just beyond the mountains,

the plate ended. "Can you take her through the canyon?"

"I don't think she'll fit and there won't be any room for error."

"I thought you were a good pilot?"

Max glanced back at her then snapped his head to the windscreen. "I'm not a good pilot. I'm the best!"

J watched Max quickly tapping on menus as he flew, the mountains grew in the windscreen. J could see the ship's aim point. A small canyon emerged. Max adjusted the power settings diverting shield energy to the propulsion system, the lights of the ship flickered. The shield menu flashed as another blast hit their ship in the rear. J held the seat's armrests tight, his pulse quickened.

"Here we go," Max said, lengthening the words out.

The ship bolted into the canyon. Ariel pulled up a screen displaying the two ships behind them. In front, the walls of the canyon flew past them, extending up hundreds of feet above them. J wanted to close his eyes, but was mesmerized by the sight. The canyon turned, the ship turned, pushing him into his seat. The g-forces intensified then were released again. Another turn as the ship rotated to stay on course. The trailing ships stayed in tight, still firing shots at them. Ariel studied the map display, they were snaking their way through the canyon and looked like they'd be nearing the edge of the plate soon.

Ariel's eyes danced around taking in all the information. She unbuckled. "Take us into the skeletal structure," she commanded, eyes fixed on Max.

"What...why?"

"Just do it. And when I tell you to, kick her into a skid."

"But—"

"Not good enough?"

Max's body tensed like a fighter about to go into the ring, he twisted his head cracking his neck. Ariel ran toward the back of the ship, reached for J on the way, not saying a word. He instinctively unbuckled right before she grabbed him, towing him along with her. *What was she up to?* She slid down the stairs into the cargo bay and ran over to the weapons storage cage. J stepped in behind her as she turned around holding a large tubular shaped item with both hands. He'd never seen the device before. It was massive and resembled a large fire extinguisher with a handle protruding from the side. Ariel tapped the side which held a small box attached to the cylinder. A holographic display appeared as she tossed it to him. He braced himself, catching it with two hands; he was surprised how light it was.

"What's this?"

"It's an ASCM 115. Just point and click."

"Am I supposed to know what that means?"

J and Ariel flew into the wall, the ship twisted into a turn, the g-forces pinning them to the wall. The ship rolled out, reducing the gravity.

J stepped forward. "Point and click?"

Ariel grabbed an identical weapon, priming it. She flipped it on her shoulder, the hologram in front of her.

"Point," she turned, looking at J with it. He stepped back. "And click," she tapped on the handle near the trigger.

J examined his weapon, finding the same layout. Ariel stepped out of the weapons cage and to the cargo door. She rested her hand on the door panel, calling up the ship's comm.

"Get to the door."

J dashed over as the craft shook again. Reaching the door and feeling the ship turn, he grabbed the door rail. His feet kicked up into the air and he resembled Superman, hanging there a moment as the ship continued its turn. His head snapped to Ariel, she was in the same position, her grip tight on the handle. The craft leveled, Ariel pulled up a screen above the door panel controls, the map she'd been studying earlier showed the ship very close to the edge of the plate.

"Get ready, J."

"For what?"

" Just fire when I tell you."

J's body trembled, he could feel his grip on the weapon handle beginning to slip. Ariel pressed the comm button.

"Skid! Now!"

The cargo door opened, the ship seemed to slide sideways, almost floating in the air. The door continued to open, J watched it descend. The two ships came into view behind them. Ariel fired, a glowing green bolt extended from the cylinder. J's eyes skipped back to the enemy ship, he aimed and pulled the trigger. The weapon came alive, his shoulder felt the warmth grow then, as the shot exited, his face was blasted with intense heat. His eyes stayed fixed on the trailing ships, his shot corkscrewed, spinning and twisting toward its target. He saw one of the ships erupt into a ball of fire then instantaneously his body became weightless. He dropped the weapon and scrambled for the handle, his fingers slipped. The ship began dropping away from him as it fell off the plate. In slow motion, he looked under the ship. The enormous wall came into view, sliding along like a black steel road. The ship twisted as it fell. J extended his arms as far as he could, attempting to grasp the handhold, his fingers just out of reach. The ship pulled up, turning toward him. He saw the flooring rapidly approach, his body bounced off it. The weapon skipped off the wall, he watched it collide with his head.

CHAPTER TWENTY TWO

J studied the skeletal structure glowing back at him from a tabletop, the white lines drawn on a blue background. They reminded him of the blueprints for his harvester, which he referenced often back on the farm. The lines contouring around in various shapes, words written and strewn about, bolts, weld spots and other connections filled the image. The table was eight feet square, he touched it, pulling back the image. The Exodus.

"And these are the final blueprints?" he asked, glancing up at a familiar face across the table.

Arcturus' assistant nodded, not looking up from his tablet.

J realized he was dreaming. He touched the screen again, dancing his fingers around as the ship grew, shrank and moved on the screen. He stopped at a section that resembled a box.

"This is where it will go?"

"Yes, sir. Everything will fit as requested with all of the necessary precautions in place. Buying silence has proven more costly than initially anticipated."

J rubbed his chin as he stared back at the plans.

"I'm sorry, sir, but it seems you have a request to attend a meeting."

He looked up, pinching his chin one last time.

"Very well." He tapped a sequence of numbers on the screen causing it to go dark.

His assistant led him out of the room, through the

building and into an elevator. The lift began moving up.

"Who called the meeting?"

"The council."

Jeffrey handed him his tablet, then adjusted his glasses. J looked down at it then over to his assistant, his eyebrows furled. "Seems it's a restricted meeting. Only the high twelve are required."

J pursed his lips as the lift came to a stop, he stepped off leaving his assistant. After a short jaunt, he walked into a room less grand than anything he would have expected from TK. He took a seat at a small square table, three chairs on each side, twelve in total, four sat empty. He surveyed the room. Five women and three men sat in various high-backed chairs. He recognized one of the men. Takamori. His attention was drawn to the door as two more men entered, one of them Novikov. Then the room stood up in unison as Cyrellia stepped in, her chin high, shoulders back, her right arm bent as if holding a purse. The door slid closed behind her and she strutted in and took the middle seat closest to the door, the other eleven joined her. She surveyed each of them. When she got to J, she drew a smirk. J felt his chest tighten.

"Do any of you know why we are here?" Cyrellia asked, her voice monotone.

The members all shook their heads no in their own way.

"It seems that some of you do not have the greater good of TK as a priority."

The room remained silent, eyes flicked about as if

absorbing more info. Cyrellia took her time letting the statement breathe, her chin still high.

"It seems that some of you have been keeping secrets. It was brought to my attention that funds have been misappropriated, misdirected...misused, if you will. For this, those of you involved will be removed from the council and banished to Earth. Cyrellia scanned the room once more awaiting a response, none came. She stood up, the door opening behind her. Two E-Rats stood side by side, peering in.

"Takamori and Novikov, you are hereby banished for crimes against TK."

She walked out, splitting the E-Rats, without saying another word, without listening to the two condemned men shouting, pleading their innocence. The E-Rats advanced, pulling them from the room. J watched, wondering if they were innocent or not. The door closed. J's body felt tense, his muscles tight, he was having trouble relaxing them. He stood up, telling the others good day, and stepped into the elevator. He reached the main floor and was greeted by his assistant.

"What was that about?"

"Seems Cyrellia is on to us. Novikov and Takamori were banished. I'm assuming that's who you laundered the credits through?"

Jeffrey fixed his glasses again, taking the tablet back from J, looking down he nodded. J began walking toward the building exit.

"I need you to send Dmitry to Earth to keep an eye

on things for me."

His assistant nodded again, walking toward the elevator. J walked outside and climbed into a transport vehicle.

"Where to sir?" the driver asked.

"Cybertronics Inc."

J awoke from the dream, blinking multiple times, his eyes attempting to adjust to the light. His vision phased out of the car to a bright white room. Feeling he was laying down, he rolled his head to the side. The room was empty. The bed he lay on was very comfortable, he contemplated staying there for awhile. No one chasing him, no one firing at him, just peace. His eyes continued to adjust and the once bright white light dimmed. He was in what looked to be a bedroom on Earth. The walls were plastered, the floor solid wood planks, there were paintings on the wall of people from long ago. But no Ariel. He wouldn't be able to keep his mind from wondering how she was and where she was and who she was with if he continued to lay there. He spun his legs around, kicking them onto the floor and sitting up. His hand rubbed his head while he closed his eyes, letting out a small groan. His nose caught a whiff of something familiar... eggs on a frying pan. His stomach rumbled at the thought. He plopped onto his feet, dragging them to the door. His whole body ached. He opened the door to a wide open living room. At one end was a kitchen, Zane at the pan flipping an omelet. In the center was a large low back sofa, Ariel was sitting in the middle of it both arms hung over the back, her feet kicked up on a stone coffee table. Max was sleeping in an oversized leather rocking chair adjacent to Ariel while Grant was playing with a holographic tablet as he paced behind them. V sat at the kitchen counter watching Zane cook. He was the first one to notice J was awake.

"Hey, you're not dead," he said with a hearty laugh.

Ariel's head snapped over her shoulder, eyes barely above the back of the sofa. V didn't hesitate to hop off the stool, hurrying to check on him.

"How's the head?"

She grabbed his shirt and pulled him down to her level, her hands all over his face, twisting his head side to side.

"I'm fine, V," he replied, mumbling through her tiny hands.

"I suppose so. You took a nasty fall, you're lucky it wasn't a concussion."

She stared at him with judging eyes.

He looked away, trying to change the subject. "How are those eggs coming, enough for me?"

Zane looked like a professional chef, all four burners going, seasonings and ingredients all over the counters. He flipped the omelet onto the plate.

"Here you go, V. Vegetarian omelet." His eyes shifted to J. "Of course I do. Pick your poison."

J hesitated, not knowing what they had, but decided he'd make it easy on Zane.

"I'll take everything you've got."

"You got it, kid."

J meandered over to the sofa where Ariel was still eyeing him. He looked past her. A two story six pane window came to a point at the top and opened up his eyes to a lush valley, mountains in the distance, bright green grass for hundreds of feet just outside.

"Where are we?" he asked, looking back to Ariel.

He half expected her to say heaven. The room was peaceful, quiet, no engines humming, no laser blasts, mediators, E-Rats, or ship guns, his mind kept going. He felt light as he continued toward the couch, plopped down bouncing Ariel up off the cushion.

"Geez, maybe you should skip breakfast."

If he didn't know her he would have taken the criticism to heart, but instead he just smiled back at her. "It's all muscle."

Ariel laughed as she readjusted in the seat, J began laughing too, it was contagious. The laughter trailed off and Ariel turned her gaze back outside, the smile still on her face. J didn't push his question again, his body became mush sinking into the seat next to her.

"It's Dr. Zwicky's retreat home. We're in Sector 4, your Earth school would have called it Switzerland."

J was enjoying the comfort of the seat too much to respond to the prodding. He instead gazed out at the snow capped mountains and kicked his feet up onto a stone. He could feel heat coming from the substantial stone fireplace to his left. The silence was interrupted by Max's mumbling as he slept.

"Omelet's up, J."

J perked up and reluctantly peeled himself off the couch, headed over for his meal. "Is it really breakfast time?"

J spun a high backed stool around then swiveled into position at the island where Zane was working. He slid the plate over to him.

"Yep, well close enough. It's about 10:38am, still morning in my book. You weren't out very long only a few hours."

It may have been only a few hours, but that sleep was welcomed and overdue. His body felt like he'd run a marathon, his legs ached, his shoulders hurt, his neck felt tight. He took a bite of the eggs, closing his eyes, enjoying the flavors. *Man Zane was a good cook.* Something kicked his mind into another file, it was like his brain wouldn't let him have peace. Parts of his dream surged back, the two exiled TK council members now their enemies. *Had his father accounted for them? What was their next move? What were they going to do? What about the dossier? Where were they?*

A finger snapped in his face.

"Hey, you okay? Kinda lost you there a moment. You want some OJ or milk?" Zane asked.

"OJ please."

J placed a forkful of eggs in his mouth then spun the chair around for a moment to look at the view. Growing up in the flat plains of Eggerton, he'd never seen real mountains, they were only in the movies, or pictures and paintings. Now they were just out the window and

245

merely a few hours ago, he almost crashed into one. His body shivered at the thought. He turned, digging his fork back into his food. Ariel bent her head over the sofa, looking upside down toward the kitchen.

"How's it going in there?"

J wasn't sure who it was directed at, he twisted the stool in a circle to see who she was looking at.

"Once J's done we should be good to get going. As much fun as this is, we need to get back to the new world order."

"Is that what they call themselves or is that a Zane concoction?"

Ariel gracefully flipped over the back of the couch, landing near J's stool. His chewing stopped.

"Stop your gawking, finish your food. You heard the man, we're waiting on you, princess."

J's head pushed back as he spun around, going to town on his omelet, the smell still engulfing his nostrils.

She took the last few steps, resting her hand on his shoulder, her lips by his ear.

"You doing okay?" she asked gently.

He almost choked on his food, the feel of her breath so close. He nodded, then swallowed.

"I am. Are you?" He twisted the stool around, eye to eye with Ariel, his hands itching to pull her in closer.

"We ready yet?" Max bellowed as he yawned. Stretching his arms over his head as he approached the kitchen.

J and Ariel glared at him.

His eyes flicked about adjusting to their new environment. "What?" he asked, realizing they were both staring at him.

Ariel looked up at him as her head tilted down. "Why don't you go fire up the Omorfiá."

"Why don't you come with me? I need some help checking the systems."

"Take Grant, he's tech savvy enough for you."

Grant stopped pacing, his arms dropped as he looked up from his tablet, his eyes big, mouth parted. "Me?"

"Yes you. Go with Max and get the ship started, the rest of us will clean up."

Ariel slid by J and started placing the ingredients back in the pantry, V tossed her empty plate in the dishwasher, while Zane worked on the counters.

J finished up as quickly as he could then helped tidy up the rest of the items. "So, where are we going?"

"Back to Atlantis. We need to ensure the members from the dossier are still safe."

"New world order," Zane piped in, smirking as he wiped down the countertop.

Ariel raised an eyebrow then continued, "Zane left them in a secure location, but it's so secure we can't get in touch with them, or that's what the hope is. Grant's been trying all morning with no luck."

"You ready big guy," V's eyes drifted to Zane.

"Yep, let's blow this popsicle stand."

J and Ariel laughed as they headed to the ship. Once outside, J stopped a moment to admire the scenery. He felt for some reason that he wouldn't ever get the chance to see it again. His body unwound as he sucked in a large breath. *It would be recycled air or what did Dillon call it? Fake air?* It didn't matter, this was real to him. Ariel stopped, realizing he wasn't moving and tugged on his hand. He huffed out a breath then allowed her to drag him into the ship.

The engines hummed as Max worked the controls. J felt like he was back in school, everyone made their way to their assigned seats. *What's the assignment today?* He strapped in, watching Max engage the engine, jumping them off the ground, the landing gear flexing inward. He could hear the engines working and, though he couldn't understand it, the ship was a marvel to him. He didn't think he'd ever get used to all the technology ...completely.

"Any luck with the comms?"

Grant was still messing with his tablet, his little fingers going a mile a minute, typing who knew what. He kept his mind engaged, managing only to shoot out a quick "No." The Omorfiá pushed forward and up, J stared at the screen, watching the blue sky fade to black.

"So what's the plan?" J asked, breaking the silence as he climbed out of the chair.

"We get back to Atlantis and make sure everyone's alright then we find Dr. Huergo. Zane, you said you think Admiral Titov picked him up?"

"It's possible that when we picked the two of you up he was in one of the boxes. We never got to him, so I assumed they picked him up."

"We don't have you in the Tetriack this time, we're

going to have to figure out another solution to get past Atlantis' guns."

Ariel held one hand on her shoulder, the other supporting her elbow, she leaned a hip out to one side then shifted back to the other. J was thinking, but nothing came to mind. They'd lucked out last time, his crazy kamikaze maneuvers paid off. Zane stood there, his bottom lip pushed out, eyebrows raised, arms crossed, he wasn't proving any help.

Max continued piloting the ship toward Atlantis. "You want me to keep heading there?"

Ariel flung her hands out to the sides and shrugged her shoulders before putting her hands on her hips. "If ya got a better idea let me know, 'cause that's all I got."

The ship flashed red letters on the screen. J had noticed Max didn't seem to like the audio system on the ship and always kept it muted. J pointed to it. "What's that mean?"

Ariel turned her head to look then ran over to Max. "Bless it! What are you doing? Are you even paying attention?"

"It just popped up, I swear!"

Max threw his hands in the air waving them about. Ariel tapped on the control console, bringing up a different view. Six fighter aircraft were nearly on top of them, Titov's battle cruiser in tow.

"They're requesting to talk on channel 28764," Grant informed them, putting down his tablet.

Ariel leaned forward on the controls. "Crap."

CHAPTER TWENTY THREE

J closed his eyes, trying to summon some special power for great ideas hidden deep inside him, nothing came. His mind was blank. Zane rubbed his chin, V studied the screen, arms crossed on the metal pedestal in front of her. Max pushed himself back in his chair, interlocking his hands together behind his head. Ariel dropped her head closing her eyes, still leaning on the controls.

"Call him up."

Grant tapped a few screen items calling up the familiar face.

"Ariel, I believe eet vas."

Ariel didn't look up, her head stayed focused on the floor.

"Ahh. I see J es vith you. Let us make zees seemple. Vee board you, vee take zee boy."

Ariel's head snapped up, clenched her jaw, her back muscles tightened.

"You know I can't let you do that. You plan on executing him."

She expeditiously tapped the controls, the call switched off, only the stars in front of them showed on the screen. She reached over Max and engaged the thrusters to 120%. The ship lurched forward knocking Zane and J off balance, they scrambled to hold onto something.

"What are you doing?" Max grabbed her hand, wrestling the control away from her. The ship rocked, the shield status displayed on the screen. Another shot hit, rocking it once more.

"You're going to overload the system! Get off."

Ariel and Max continued struggling over the controls; Ariel had her whole body weight resting in a stiff solid locked arm. Max pushed and pulled, but she wouldn't budge. He jabbed her in the oblique, hoping to knock some sense into her. She let go momentarily, but came back with a right hook. Max's head snapped to the side. Zane rushed to the fight, grasping at Ariel's waist. She landed an elbow to his nose. It began bleeding like Max's had, though he took it better. J's eyes switched to the screen, the word "Overload" flashed in big red letters on the bottom right. The ship rocked again, the shield status flashed faster gaining size to alert the crew. No one else paid it any attention as the three fought for the controls. Ariel still had the thrusters pinned full forward with her left hand and clocked Max again before he could attempt another intervention. Zane pulled her, but was struck in the kidney, taking him off guard. He winced in pain and nearly let go of her. J had seen enough and decided to help. He ran to the controls, but was conflicted as to who he should help. Max was shaking his head, wiping the blood from his nose. Zane tried to adjust his grip around Ariel's waist. The ship rattled again, the lights flickered. Then a sound filled the ship, one J had never heard before but it didn't sound good. The hum of the engines dwindled to nothing; he glanced over at the screen. "Power plant failure. Overload detected." Ariel released the controls, Zane tugged not realizing it, and flew backward with her locked in his arms. She crashed on top of him as he hit the floor, her body went limp. Everyone froze, the craft went silent. An eerie sensation filled J's body as the screen flashed "System failsafe shutdown initiated." The lights went out. J gaped at the surreal sight out the windscreen, all he could see were stars. Ariel slid off of Zane and sat, knees on her elbows, head in her hands, staring through the floor. J heard Max moan as he clutched his still bleeding nose.

Zane glared over at him, "Oh quit whining. Suck it up." He paid no attention to his own nose as blood dribbled down his chin. "Well, that could have gone better," he groaned as he propped himself up on one knee.

"Ya think?" Max griped, his voice muffled from holding his nose. "Look at my ship!"

J dropped to his knees in front of Ariel, reached down to grab her hand. "Hey," he ducked his head to get into her line of sight. "You okay?" He slipped his other hand under her chin, tilting her face up to meet his.

Her eyes moved, finding a small smile on his lips. "We gotta get you out of here."

The sound of metal scraping filled the silence, every one of them looked up to figure out where the noise was coming from. A metal ceiling floated over the windscreen continuing past them. Light strings were the next sight to appear then the movement stopped. They all watched as a hefty hangar door closed around them. The Omorfiá now rested inside Titov's battle cruiser. The sound of knocking reverberated on the walls, their heads swiveled about. J stood up, helping Ariel to her feet. Zane was already in battle mode.

"You think it's an invitation to dinner?" J winked at Ariel.

She couldn't help but return his smile. Then reality took back over and it was gone.

They slinked into the cargo bay, Ariel tapped on the screen and the door hissed open. J raised his hands over his head, over twenty fully-armed soldiers stood in ranks on the other side, weapons drawn. One of them waved the crew of the Omorfiá down the ramp. J glanced over at Ariel, her body slumped as they shuffled into the cruiser. The six of them were escorted into a sparsely decorated briefing room. A sizeable window rested across from the entrance, peering out to the stars. A table sat the length of the room, nearly three times as long as it was wide, the window and door on the longest sides. Empty seats surrounded the table. They were not forced to sit so elected to stand behind the chairs. Guards took up each of the corners, one also stood on each side of the doorway. J's body trembled, his forehead was wet with sweat. He looked over at the others. Zane stood proud, his head up, shoulders back. Grant slumped, fidgeting with his hands, but that was his usual posture. Max was still rubbing his nose while Ariel pursed her lips as she rocked on the balls of her feet, ready to spring into action. The guards stood at attention as Admiral Titov stepped in. He turned the length of the table and walked past each of them, finally coming to J at the end. He stopped, looking into his eyes.

"Zat vas a valiant attempt to escape," he continued his march. "I estimate zat you had your zrusters at 120%. A goot pilot vood know zat eet can only take zat much power for two minootes and tventy-sree seconds."

Max leaned forward, scrutinizing Ariel. Her head didn't move, her jaw clenched tighter.

Titov turned the corner, now on the other side of the table, still marching toward the middle of the window. He stopped and gazed out to the stars beyond. "Your sheep veel be alright. Zee Omorfiá, I believe you call eet."

He never turned back, still facing out into space. A smaller man entered the room and began fiddling with the controls near the door. The lights flickered off, then on again. The admiral looked over his shoulder, his square jaw tight. "Call zee prezident."

The little man pressed a series of buttons and the lights danced around. The Admiral's head still turned, his eyebrows sharpening. The window became opaque and the once beautiful star field was replaced by Novikov.

"You have the boy?"

"Yes, vee veel execute zee order on your command."

"Very well, you have your orders. Carry it out and report back to me when it is finished. I'll want a full report...in English."

Titov nodded then the picture switched off. He spun around, grabbing a chair and sat down, raised a hand. The soldiers adjusted chairs for each of them to sit across from the Admiral. J and the others were now forced into the seats. Four of the soldiers left leaving only the two by the door. Ariel's eyes scanned the room, noticing how they were standing, where their weapons were, and how confident they appeared. The one farthest from her was the weaker of the two. J, too, was searching, but his attention was drawn to the Admiral. He looked over the table at J, quiet, steady.

Ariel broke the silence. "What do you want with us? I know you plan on killing J, but what about the rest of us, huh? Are you planning on killing us too?" She stood up tossing the chair to the floor. "I won't make it easy for you. You'll have to get through me if you want him."

Her eyes were stone locked onto Titov. Without hesitation, she twisted, grabbing the rifle from the weaker guard. She flipped it, knocking him down, then she drilled the other in the knee forcing him to crouch, followed up with a knee to the head, knocking him out instantly. She clicked of the safety and pointed the rail-gun at the Admiral's head.

He smiled then let out a chuckle. "A fighter to the last...just like your mother."

Her grip tightened on the weapon. "You didn't know her...don't you dare speak of her."

J stood up, something was off, something was different. He raised his hand, placing it on top of the rifle. His eyes locked with Ariel's. She rocked on her feet, a slight shake pulsing through her body. J pressed down on the barrel, Ariel resisted, staring fiercely back into his eyes. His head bobbed up then down, his eyes fixated on hers, his eyebrows perked. "Listen to him."

Ariel relaxed her grip, lowering the weapon.

"There really is no need for the theatrics. You asked what I want. I want to give you this."

He placed Arcturus' journal on the table in front of him then slid it across. J leaned over, grabbing it before it fell off the table. They studied the Admiral who was now smiling, a hand stroked his chin. Ariel glanced at J, her eyes wet. She turned back to the Admiral.

"Why...why did you mention my mother?"

He leaned back in the chair, his hand leaving his chin. "We were in the corps together, hell of a fighter. Then we were with Arcturus together."

Ariel plopped down into the chair, dropping the weapon to the ground. Her wide eyes stared at the wooden tabletop. J dropped into a seat also. He examined the book, the TK symbol embossed on it. His head snapped up at a sudden realization. "You were in the dream weren't you?"

"I don't know about that, but I was with your father. My given name is—"

"Dmitry."

The Admiral laughed, it was deep, hearty and full of life and energy.

"Yes, yes. My name's Dmitry. Your father sent me to keep an eye on Novikov, but I don't need to tell you this because you already know your father's a smart man. Novikov was up to something, as Arcturus suspected. I was able to work my way up to Admiral and gain command of this ship. It was scheduled to be decommissioned for parts for the Exodus, but somehow it stayed off TK's radar," Dmitry winked. "Novikov had his sights set on Earth since before he was banished. Oh, you father wanted you to have this. Better take it before I forget about it." He slid a medallion across the table.

J held it up, he'd seen the symbol before, a circle with three overlapping crossing lines protruding outside of the circle. He slid it over his head, tucking it into his shirt.

"Never know what that little thing might do. Keep it safe. Now, let's get you ready for the mutiny. Time's a wastin', need to get you down to Atlantis before they build too many of those mediators. Wish they'd used up all the resources for the Exodus." He walked around the table opening the door. "Follow me. I have something you might appreciate Max."

Dmitry led them into the bowels of the battle cruiser past a dining hall, dormitories, and multiple hallways. He told them he'd give a proper tour after things settled down. J thought that sounded nice. The brief time they'd spent in the Swiss Alps made him long for peace and quiet. After the trek, they popped out into a hangar where dozens of ships sat in neat tidy rows, laid out like a game board. Most sat empty and motionless, but others had people climbing on them, some had exposed panels, and still others hovered over their platforms. On the far end was a larger ship similar to the Omorfiá. Max was in heaven ogling the ships as they passed heading toward the largest one. He couldn't contain himself and ran over to one of the smaller fighter aircraft and after circling it multiple times came to a stop placing a hand on his hip the other over his mouth. He bobbed on the balls of his feet, his hand touched the side opening the cockpit. J didn't think anyone could jump as high as he did, gliding over the rail into the seat. The others continued walking.

"No time to play Max. We've got work to do," Ariel admonished as she focused on their destination.

Max sat there a moment, a child-like grin on his face, wiggling his bottom into the seat, his shoulders shaking. J held back a laugh at the sight, continuing his walk.

As they approached the larger ship, Max came running up, his breath heavy. "A Vasilikó Árma class battle transport!" He ran past them, as if only the first to touch it would get to use it.

The ship was much larger than the Omorfiá, its rectangular shape made it seem imposing and its sheer size dwarfed all but a KracKen and the battle cruiser it rested in. J appraised it, stopping a hundred feet away. Cannons laced the outside pointing in multiple directions, the bridge could be seen at the far end, massive windows reflected the intense blue hangar lighting.

"Where are my manners? I never officially welcomed you onboard. You are on my fleet's flagship, the Parádeisos. The ship your friend is so head-over-heels for is my personal transport, the Rinókeros."

Dmitry's arm swept upwards as he spoke, like a showman announcing the main attraction. J watched as Max ran around, touching the extended landing gear, climbing up and down the extended boarding ramp, then disappearing into the ship.

"Max'll know how to fly it. I'll stay here. If you need assistance, I'll do what I can to provide it."

Ariel's weight shifted back. "I'm still a little confused. Why are you helping us and how do we know we can trust you?" She firmly placed her palm on her hip, shifting her weight away from it, her other hand raised.

"He's been with Arcturus for a long time, I'll explain on the way. See if you can find anything useful for us in here," J tossed the book to her. As she caught it, he continued with a smile, "It's Greek to me."

Ariel snickered as she slipped the book under her arm. Zane started up the ramp followed by V and Grant.

J turned toward Dmitry. "Thank you, sir."

Dmitry's square jaw smiled back as he regarded J. "Your father's a great man. If things go as planned, you'll meet him someday."

J began to speak but Ariel tugged at his arm, "Time for chat later. Like he said, we need to act fast. The longer we delay the more opposition we'll face."

J briefly stood, heavy, then let his body follow. As he crested the top of the ramp, his eyes were met with four small fighter craft. There was a hangar inside the ship... which was sitting in a hangar. J's mind was blown. At the far end, an open platform lift was raising V, Zane and Grant up to the top. His mind wandered during the walk, not noticing much more about the Rinókeros. *What more did Dmitry know about his father?* After the platform ride and another elevator, they emerged into the command section. Three tiers of seats filled the room opening to a large window screen. Just outside, the walls of the ship continued for an additional ten feet or so. Max was playing with the buttons from the pilot's chair, his arms exaggerating their movements. The screens came to life, including a hologram that covered the whole windscreen, though you could see through it. The ship's bridge overlooked the deck below, the multitude of ships looked like chess pieces ready to be played. Each ship had a glowing circle underneath, J took a few steps closer to see if it was painted on the ground. A line came out from the circle with words reading, "Vélos Type IV fighter class" underneath it read "TK 2nd squadron". J scratched his head, looking out the window. Even the soldiers walking around had the circle surrounding their feet with a label attached. Their name, rank and weapon load out was tagged on the end of the line. The circles followed each of them as they moved.

J's head snapped to Ariel, his finger pointing to the screen. Ariel was standing on the top tier peering down at the deck below, arms crossed, her hair flowed over her shoulder, her eyes glistened electric blue in the dim lighting. "What's the..." he started, holding his hands together in a circle.

Ariel smiled, realizing what he was talking about, finding his charades humorous. "Those are combat tags. Pretty useful in large battles, might come in handy someday."

J turned back, awed at the technology, then paced the tiers perusing all of the screens and buttons. He felt completely overwhelmed, not for the first time since a shiny piece of metal fell from the sky and changed his whole world. He tried to focus on their task, to find, as Zane called them, the "new world order."

"Ready to take her out, commander?" Max asked, firing up the main thruster, his words filled with sarcasm.

"Commander," Ariel rolled the title around on her tongue, a smile growing on her face. "I like the sound of that."

CHAPTER TWENTY FOUR

The Moon's size amplified in the screen, the circle around it reading "Atlantis, TK planetary headquarters." The Rinókeros moved at a steady pace, heading toward one of the bigger craters.

Max tapped a few buttons then spun his head to Ariel. "Approaching the Aitken crater. They're requesting landing codes."

"Grant, send the codes," Ariel directed as she stood tall with her hands clenched behind her back.

J observed Grant's head bobbing around, his shoulders slightly dancing.

"Landing codes input, Commander."

J couldn't tell if they were joking or if this was going to become a new thing.

"Codes confirmed, Commander," Max spouted.

J held back a laugh, it sounded like they were in a war movie. His attention moved to the screen, the Moon filled all of it now, the surface growing closer. In the center of the crater, the door opened to a familiar-looking landing access tunnel. Max piloted the ship through the shaft, the light rails pulsing blue as they continued deeper into Atlantis. J stepped up next to Ariel.

"Do we have a plan?" he asked, expecting the light-hearted answer they always gave each other.

Her face was steady, watching the light pass by. "Yes."

She let go of her wrist, swinging one hand to the controls, her other remaining pinned on her lower back.

She typed commands into a glowing typewriter, a map of the city displayed on the left portion of the screen. She continued typing and a circle appeared with a tiny image of their ship, then a dot in a hangar just ahead of the ship's course. A red line shot out, turning and twisting through different levels in the city, finally coming to rest in a small complex imbedded near the crust of the Moon.

J assessed the map then Ariel, his bottom lip jutted out as he nodded his head. "That's quite the plan, a bit different than guns blazing, running in and hoping not to die."

Ariel tilted her head, her eyes heavy, her shoulder dipped.

"Sorry, Commander." He snapped to attention, giving her a salute.

"You goof. It's easier when you have the equipment; this is some wicked awesome stuff."

J contemplated what she just said, shook his head as he filed yet another thing away, then looked back at the screen.

"So, that's where they are?"

"Yep. You take Zane and grab some weapons for us. Nothing too heavy, we need to move quick, and I'm guessing there'll be a welcoming party when we land."

She twisted toward V. "You and Grant stay here with Max. It'll be easier for the three of us to move and we need you ready in case anyone has to be patched up."

V scowled at her but it dwindled and Max just raised a hand up in acceptance. Grant's ever-present grimace didn't change, so she was unsure whether or not he was okay with staying in the ship. J grabbed Zane and they went in search of a weapons cache, found it on the fourth floor near the center of the ship. Zane rummaged through the lockers finding some smaller blasters while J assessed the rifles. He presented Zane with one he felt would work out nicely.

Zane laughed at him. "That's for crowd control. We'll need something with more..." his hand circled in the air, tightening into a fist, "oomph."

J realized he was still learning. Though some of the weapons he recognized, there were twice as many he didn't.

Zane handed him four blasters and holsters. "Pick whichever two you want, the others are for Ariel. Now let's see what you found."

He rummaged through the rifles, tossing a few aside. A couple he wavered on, but eventually decided against, then grabbed one and slung it on his shoulder. He picked up two others, handing them to J.

"If I'm not coming with you, at least take these," a small voice came from behind them.

V stood in the doorway with a pouch about the size of a basketball. She tossed it to Zane, who pressed the sides down exposing three metal paddle-shaped items.

"Medical wands?"

"Might come in handy, especially for you Zane. You tend to become a jarhead in combat and there's only so many times I can pull you back from the brink."

Zane tried to act upset, but finally relented with his hearty laugh.

V smiled back at him, slipping her hands into her pockets to keep herself from doing anything stupid.

"Well, I think we're set. Let's get to the cargo bay."

They headed through the ship into the cargo bay they'd first arrived in. Ariel appeared at nearly the same time.

"Find anything good?"

J handed her the rifle then the blasters. She examined them, strapping on the holsters and tossing the rifle on her back. J handed her the medical wand.

"Zane get one of these? God knows he'll need one." Ariel snickered and so did J.

"Ha, ha. Yep, that's me, the bullet catcher. You didn't complain when I saved your tail, how many times now?"

"Too many, big guy. Max should have us on the deck any second."

She extended her hand, displaying a tiny round sphere.

"Is that a translating unit for my ear?"

"Yep, but this one is also a comm link so we can talk to each other."

J's eyes bulged out; he bit his bottom lip as he took the device. "We're not splitting up are we?"

"If we do, it won't be intentional. But we need to be ready for contingencies. At a minimum, we'll be able to keep in touch with Max and Grant in the Rinókeros."

They felt the ship shudder as it came to rest on

the ground.

"Seems you were right, you have a welcoming party." J heard Max in his ear.

He looked at Ariel and began to repeat it, but she cut him off.

"I heard, we can all hear,"

She tossed him a Datacle. "Use the comm page to adjust who you talk to and who you can hear."

J strapped it onto his wrist, wishing he would have had time to practice with it. Zane opened the door and the ramp dropped into place, the gaping hole where it once stood now open to Atlantis. Four mediators marched toward them.

"Identification, please," one said, stomping forward.

Ariel popped it in the head with one shot, knocking it onto the ramp. The lifeless mechanism tumbled to the ground. The others paused, giving J and Zane enough time to each take out one while Ariel finished the fourth.

"Game on," grinned Zane, placing one foot on the ramp.

They trotted to the ground.

"Keep the ship locked up. We'll call for support if needed," Ariel instructed, her eyes fixed on their path.

"Roger that, Commander. We'll keep the fire stoked. Good luck."

Ariel waved them forward and they proceeded to the first of many doors then down a hall, just as the map displayed earlier.

Everything was going fine for a few moments until a

voice came over his earpiece. "So the boy has returned from the dead."

J twisted around, his shoulders shifted, he stopped mid-stride.

Ariel turned as she reached the elevator door. "J," she said in a loud whisper. "What are you doing?"

He grabbed his ear and shook it. *Maybe it was his imagination.* He shook his head, jogging to catch up. The elevator went up. The fastest way to the scientists was to catch a train, the trick would be getting it started.

The elevator sounded as it met its floor. "Level 16, Tram station #85."

"You won't escape this time. I have a special surprise for you," the voice threatened, its words slimy, the S's drawn out.

J tightened his eyes looking at Ariel, he grabbed his ear again.

Ariel noticed. "You okay?"

"Yeah just...is anyone else on this comm thing?"

"What do you mean?"

"I'm hearing something and I don't think it's one of you. Or, I hope it's not one of you."

Ariel leaned toward him, "What did it say?"

"Something about having a surprise for me."

Ariel tightened her eyes, scanning their surroundings.

"Don't worry about it for now. We need to keep the pace up."

She led them into the tram station and onto an abandoned car. Once in the engine area, she began working on restoring the power.

"You two stand guard at the door. Don't need any surprises."

"I have a surprise for you," the unknown voice said.

J spun around to Zane, "Okay, did you hear it this time?"

He shook his head. "Hear what?"

The train came alive. Zane and J looked around, stepping back as the door closed.

"Welcome to Atlantis. Enjoy the ride."

Zane looked at him, his face questioning. "I heard that. Ariel, did you hear that?"

"I sure did."

The train increased speed. J wasn't holding onto anything and began sliding, he frantically reached out for a vertical steel pole and clutched it tightly. Zane did the same. The train continued to accelerate, J looked over to Ariel who was still at the controls, one hand clutching the console, her knuckles turning white. Her free hand was tapping the console as quick as she could, her feet loosened on the floor, the car still accelerating.

"I think that's fast enough!" Zane shouted.

J's eyes drifted out the window, the buildings were whizzing by at breakneck speed and flying faster every moment. The train began rocking, a buzzing sound came from the speakers near Ariel. She let go, planting her feet firmly on the ground. She slid back, simultaneously flipping her rifle into firing position. She fired off three rounds, the controls exploding into a mess of smoke, sparks and metal debris. She snatched a post as she slid by J.

"Enjoying the ride?" the unknown voice asked.

"Not really," J answered.

Ariel and Zane looked at him in silence, they heard it too.

Ariel grabbed her ear. "Someone's tapped into our comm link."

"That's right, Ariel. Just a little trick I learned from Arcturus' journal. Quite an ingenious man he was, too bad he was so noble."

Ariel focused on the controls of the train, she aimed, firing multiple shots.

"I wouldn't waste your power cells on that. I'm controlling the train and, like I told J earlier, I have a surprise for you," the voice said, singing the last few words.

The egg shaped baseball field zipped by, making him feel woozy. J focused his eyes on the ceiling. "Who are you?"

"Katergaris, but you can call me Kat."

"What do you want?" Ariel chimed in, her head snapping about, searching for a solution to their conundrum.

"It's not so much what I want, it's what my employer wants. You know him, President Novikov."

J's mouth dropped open.

"Seems you escaped from Admiral Titov and are searching for a few Atlanteans. Ones with doctorates? He would like them. They know a great deal more about the journal. Or should I say, fill-in some of the missing pieces."

Ariel shot out one of the side windows, the wind whipped through the train as she stepped over to it. The pressure on their bodies from the initial acceleration was dwindling, the train's speed steady. It rocked every few minutes, but outside of that, the ride was smooth. She looked out the window at the buildings zipping by.

"I wouldn't try that, dear. The train's going over 600 miles per hour. Besides, you'll miss the surprise."

Ariel stepped away from the window, trudging to the controls. They sparked as dangling wires swung gently as if they were blades of grass blowing in the breeze. J let go of his handhold to follow her.

"Any ideas? Where's the actual engine to this? Can we knock that out?"

"Don't bother with that, J. Ariel knows as well as I that the engine is in every car and if you attempt to disable it while at full capacity then...well let me put it in terms you would understand, the whole train and five blocks around it would go boom."

Ariel plopped down, checking her rifle. J looked out the window, hoping something would come to him, some way to slow the train. Zane took a seat as well. Adjusting his rifle, he customized it to his hand.

J noticed, raising an eyebrow. "What was that?" he asked, dashing over and plunking his butt down next to him.

"Oh, the customize feature? Yeah, here, let me see

your rifle."

Zane took his rifle, flipped it on its side and fiddled with a red glowing display. The words "customized grip" flashed on the screen.

"Now hold it like you normally would."

J took it, placing his firing hand on the grip. The weapon contoured around his hand, it almost felt as though he was part of it. He smiled for a second then lost it, glancing over at Ariel who was gazing out the window behind them.

"Well, aren't you the good little soldiers, getting ready for battle. Hope you ate your Wheaties."

The train began to slow down. Ariel stood up, her eyes searching for their destination. She recognized the area. It'd been some time since she'd been there.

"The academy," she mumbled.

CHAPTER TWENTY FIVE

The train slowed to a stop. Ariel was the first to step out, her jaw tensed as she took the first few steps. Just outside the train, a large open courtyard stood featureless, its surface built of smooth metal ending at one of many pyramid shaped buildings a hundred yards away. Three large triangular pillars grew from the ground, one in front of each dominant building. Each structure held a symbol, one a hawk, another a lion, and the third a shark. Ariel's lips wrinkled, her nostrils flared, she took a few more steps forward.

J stepped out next to Zane. "What is this place?"

"TK Akedemia Kosmiczna, the military academy. Ariel studied here, her parents studied here, I studied here. Let's just say not the greatest of times."

J didn't need to know any more. He read Ariel's face and could see what this place did to her. He stepped forward, Zane at his side.

"Be ready for anything," Zane raised his rifle.

His normal jovial amble turned into a crouching glide, his head solid, his legs bent at the knees. His aim swung one side to the other. J attempted to imitate the walk. His thighs burned almost immediately and his head wasn't nearly as locked. Ariel had switched to a tactical walk as well, her movements graceful. J wanted to just sit down and watch, but pushed forward. Ariel threw up a clenched fist, her arm bent at the elbow. Zane and J stopped, swinging left and right. J heard a low hum, the metal ground under his feet began to vibrate.

"Run!" Ariel bolted toward one of the pillars.

A huge vehicle hovering above the ground appeared around the far building's corner. The craft had two huge cannons on the top and one on each side. It reminded J of a trackless World War I tank crossed with a spaceship, its sleek curves blending into various shapes. He didn't have time to admire it as he sprinted to catch Ariel. Zane was the easiest to catch, but then, he was the biggest. Ariel's back hit the pillar, shielding her from the tank.

J flipped in next to her. "What is that?" His words were slid in between breaths.

Zane crashed in behind him, peeking around the corner. A blast hit the pillar and an electric buzz rang through their ears. Ariel tapped on Zane's shoulder, pointing to the building. She looked at J, nodding for him to go with him.

"No point in being quiet love, I can still see you," Kat gloated in their ears.

Ariel rolled her eyes to the sky. "It's a M6A8 hover tank. Follow Zane."

Zane bolted to the door of the nearest building, J right behind him in tow. Ariel pinned herself to the side of the pillar and took a few shots at the tank, all of them skipping off. She spun around the other side, leaving her cover to join the others. The tank fired an automatic burst from one of the side guns. Ariel danced as if playing a game of aerial twister, spinning and flipping, eventually ending up next to Zane and J who were taking cover in the patio. Ariel peered up at the door, a large lion grasping the air adorned the empty space above the thirty foot tall door. Zane placed his hand on the pad.

"Denied," the red letters shouted.

"Great, now what? That tank's bearing down on us," Ariel checked her fusion cell.

J placed his hand on the sensor, a large clunk sounded and the door swung open. Zane went in first.

"Should've known. The prodigal son can get us in anywhere," Ariel shook her head, slipping in last, her chest rising and falling fast.

The room they entered was taller than the door, the structure was completely open, the walls sloping in toward the center, mirroring the outside structure. On each wall was a door with writing above it. To the right, the words read "Tactical Shoot Course." The one on the left read "Mechanized Land Course". and the one on the far end read "Hand to Hand Course".

"Which fun event would you like to try first? Ariel and Zane, this will be familiar to you. As for J, this will be a fun new experience, hopefully not your last."

Ariel growled. "Which one, Zane? I know your specialty is weapons, you want the shoot house?"

"You're going along with this? You know what's in there."

Ariel paced, placing a thumb on her forehead, she rubbed it in circles. J watched, not knowing what to say.

"Let's take the shoot house. I remember that to be easier with multiple teammates."

"Uh uh uh. Sorry, Ariel. That's against the rules of my game. Each of you has to choose one."

"What about just leaving through the front door?" J asked.

"With that tank out there? No, our chances are much better in here."

She was still pacing, her eyes wandering up the walls and onto the ceiling. She tapped on her Datacle then dipped her head, placing her hand under her ear, the radio transmitter dropped out. She held it up, examining it, then tossed it on the ground.

"J, come here. Do the same thing. I think he's using it to track us and listen to us."

She grabbed his Datacle and tapped on the screen finally pressing the extract icon. She tilted his head, holding her hand out. Zane was doing the same himself.

"We won't be able to talk to each other. What if we get split up?"

"Relax, J. You have your Datacle. We can still communicate that way, for now at least, it doesn't seem like he has access to that yet. Now, Zane take the shoot house, I'll take hand to hand. J, that means you get the mecha course."

"Mecha course? Like that giant robot thing you fought Riku in?

J's head pressed back, his eyebrows tightened together. She rested a hand on his shoulder and locked eyes. "Don't worry, J. It's just like flying. I've seen you fly, you're amazing at it."

"But what—"

"Just go in the door. There will be a mecha near the front, climb in and place your hand on the console plate. The rest will be like flying, you've done that before, you can do it again. Whatever you do, you must finish the course. You must get to the exit."

J looked down and swallowed, he had no idea what he was getting himself into, but it seemed he had no choice. He nodded moving toward the door.

"J."

He turned to see Ariel standing with a hand on her hip. "Good luck."

He watched her flip a half wave from the wrist then proceed to the door marked "Hand to Hand Course", disappearing into the room beyond. Zane did the same with the shoot house. J spun, reading the sign. "Mechanized Land Course". The letters MCL were etched into the door. He placed his hand on the plate and the door hissed open, revealing a long courtyard. The far end was nearly out of sight, merely a speck in the distance. The ground was flat, nothing but the four surrounding walls. The sound of metal squealing pierced his ears, drawing his attention to a plate rising from the ground. Underneath was a cage structure housing a large humanoid robotic structure nearly three stories tall.

He traveled over to the base of a ladder built on the outside structure. At the top, he saw an opening in the back of the machine where the shoulder blades would meet on a human. He paused after placing a hand on the first rung of the ladder, then his eyes went up. His next hand followed. He kept his eyes up, knowing the feeling he would have if he ever looked down. At the top he found a seat inside the machine almost identical to the Tetriack. Sitting down, he remembered Ariel's instructions and placed his hand on the console. The machine hummed to life, a green holographic screen flipped up, letters scrolled, obscuring his view out the cockpit. He could feel the back of the machine close up then heard the exterior structure scraping its way back into its metal home. A series of noises came from the machine ones he would have labeled as scratches and deep beeps. The mecha's speaker came to life.

"M9897Badger online."

J studied the screen then began flipping through buttons, familiarizing himself with the layout and functions.

"That wasn't very nice of you to cut me out of your conversation, I am your host for the evening."

J's body tensed hearing Kat's voice. The only comfort he could take from it was that their plan worked and he'd resorted to communicating through the mecha's speakers.

"Now the game is simple, you only need to move your Mecha to the far side and exit through the door. Good luck."

J knew there had to be more to it, that was too simple. He pressed the accelerator forward, the machine stepped forward, his seat shook as its heavy metal foot contacted the ground. He smiled, it felt liberating to control such a machine. He moved forward, the machine shaking at each step. J looked out the windscreen, suddenly the ground began to change shape, outlines of buildings rose up, most littered with blast scorches. He knew that meant one thing, enemies.

He navigated around a faux building, continuing down the corridor, making good progress. He was hoping it would only be a maze, he was good at mazes as a kid. His hopes were crushed when he saw what resembled a mirror image staring back at him from the far end of the makeshift hall. Lights flashed from the enemy mecha, then almost instantly he heard a string of loud pops come from outside the machine. The screen read "shield 99%" and a voice confirmed it. He scanned the area for cover, finding a gap in the corridor to the right. He steered the machine forward and right, dodging more rounds, being clipped by the final few. His shield still read 99%, he drew in a long breath, he was still in good shape. He tapped through the menus finding the voice command feature and switched it on.

"Voice feature active, Athena online. Would you like a demo, J?" the machine asked in a smooth feminine voice.

"No. Auto target auto rifles."

"Understand you would like to use the auto target feature. Which weapon would you like?"

A list of weapon names scrolled on the left side of the screen, none of them made sense. His eyes twitched attempting to read them, he let out a growl. "I don't know."

"State the target and I will provide suggestions."

J hesitated. *What did Ariel call it?* He ran through a list of names, ship, craft, tank, plane...Mecha.

"Mecha, the target's a mecha."

"Target mecha. Recommend Anti-Armor canons, Falcon Sidewinder missiles or Anti-Armor mines."

J searched the windscreen as he stayed behind cover, sweat dripped down his forehead, his grip tightened on the controls. "Can I engage auto fire?"

"Recommend manual fire for greater accuracy. Would you like a demo?"

Enemy incoming flashed on the bottom of the screen. J searched the screen, a loud rumble shook his machine causing him to look up. A spacecraft zipped overhead turning away from him.

"No, just engage auto fire."

"Confirm auto targeting for Anti-Armor canons."

"Yes!"

"Anti-Armor canons active, select target."

At this, a circle reticule popped up, floating in the center of the screen. He moved his hand, attempting to move the circle, the machine stepped sideways and the entire windscreen tipped up as he pulled back on the right handle. He slid the left handle right, stepping the machine right then put his head down, staring at the controls, searching for something else to move the targeting circle. The screen flashed.

"Shields 97%," Athena stated.

J looked up, the mecha was twenty yards in front of

him. It had found his position and stepped out of the corridor, firing multiple shots at him. His mecha fired back a burst of rounds, hitting the enemy. Blue light flashed as the mecha rocked. J stepped back.

"Fire Sidewinder missiles!" he leaned into the screen.

Trails of smoke came from both sides of the windscreen, a burst of reds and oranges erupted in the center of his screen. He closed his eyes from the intense light. As the blast dissipated, twisted remains collapsed into a heap on the ground. His seat rocked, the shield flashed again.

"Fighter aircraft inbound. Recommend finding cover."

J felt the mecha rock again. *Cover? Where was he going to find cover?* He thought he had cover. At his command, the ship moved forward into the corridor.

"The exit," he said to himself. "Gotta get to the exit. That's what Ariel said."

"The exit is 8.04672 kilometers due east of your current position. Would you like guidance?"

J ignored the question, advanced the thruster until it hit the forward stop. The mecha began running and after a few steps was at full speed. His seat bounced slightly, resting on a full suspension. The running felt smooth. Two aircraft flew overhead. Bearing down on him, they fired, the shields flashed. He continued as the ships disappeared behind him. The two aircraft emerged in his windscreen twisting into the sky to continue their engagement.

"Anything for those things?"

"Recommend Python missiles."

J was at the mercy of the ship's computer, he didn't have time to learn all the systems. He acknowledged.

"Python missiles online, ready to fire."

J tilted the craft up toward the sky, the aircraft were inbound. The circle swung up toward them then split into two, it flashed red letting out an audible wavering tone. The sound of a massive eruption echoed in his ears as missiles evacuated from each side of his mecha. Smoke trailed while he watched two missiles climb into the air and hit their marks, the aircraft exploded, the remnants falling from the sky, smoke trailing. He pushed forward, bringing the machine up to speed once more. A dead end came into view, he slowed and assessed his options. The left side was a longer street and the buildings had gaps appearing like alleyways of a city. In the other direction stood a dead end, he turned back to the left and engaged the thruster once more. As he moved past the first corner, a brilliant flash nearly blinded him. He felt his body pulled forward into the restraints. The sensation of spinning circulated through his ears, his eyes confirmed it as he opened them to see the ground flipping away. The mecha came to rest facedown, J could only see the steel colored ground in his face, the ship's shield warning flashed.

"Shields are down to 60%, recommend taking cover."

J grabbed his head, messaging his temple. *No kidding. Where would that be exactly?* He pulled back the controls and the mecha gained its feet. He spun as the shield sensor flashed, his rotation was uncontrolled spinning him nearly 360 degrees.

"Shields 45%, recommend taking cover."

"I got it. Take cover. Where exactly can I do that!?"

"Would you like me to calculate a route to the exit?"

"Yes, yes just get me out of here. Where's cover?"

The machine stumbled forward, hit from behind again.

"Shields 40%, route has been calculated."

J watched as a map of the complex pulled up, a red line displayed the route along with enemy locations, he almost wished he hadn't seen it. Four more aircraft circled near the exit, five more mechas were scattered throughout and the largest vehicle, resembling the tank he had seen just prior, was engaging him. J's mind attempted to gameplan the scenario. but first he had to take care of the tank. *What would Ariel do?*

"Athena, engage the tank with anything you recommend."

He flipped the machine around, eyeing the enemy. It rattled and shook as another blast exploded into him.

"Engaging target, Anti-Armor canon active."

J heard a loud rumble, watched a stream of fire come from under his belly, all of them skipping off the tank.

"Fire the missiles!" J shouted, his body tensed.

Missiles came from the sides of his ship exploding on the target.

"Recommend evasive action, incoming missiles."

J pressed the controls sliding sideways.

"Deploying flares."

Five balls of flames popped out into the air in front of him, the missiles tracked them exploding just outside. The concussion knocked J back, the mecha stumbled, catching itself.

"Recommend Plasma cannon full power,"

"Sure, do that," J said without thinking.

Anything to stop this thing. His ears heard a humming sound coming from above him, on the screen the words read "Plasma charge 68%", the numbers continuing to rise. He pressed the controls, running toward a building to the side to take cover.

"Plasma canon charged 120%. Confirm engage target?" Athena asked in her calm female voice.

"Yes, fire!"

The hum intensified then went silent, his eyes were fixated on the enemy tank. A blue bolt hit it square in the front, peeling it apart like a paper bag. Pieces erupted into the sky, others bounced on the floor skipping toward him. J sat slumped into his seat, blowing air out of his mouth. He studied the screen, the map was now small in the upper right corner. He reached up, touching it. The path looked straightforward enough. If he followed it, he would only need to engage one more mecha and two of the aircraft. He'd have to be smart not to draw unnecessary attention. The shield read "25%", an icon read "Plasma cannon - depleted", "Sidewinder missiles - 2", "Anti-Armor canons - 50%". He swallowed. Following the red line, ducking in between buildings and moving quickly through alleyways and across streets, he pressed on. A block prior to the mecha he'd planned to engage, he stopped.

"Any suggestions, Athena?"

"Two options available. Engage mecha or create a diversion to circumnavigate potential threat."

J thought the second option sounded more promising as his eyes stared through the shield status.

"How do I do that?"

"Recommend auto-piloting mecha and proceeding on foot."

"What, are you insane? I won't last a second out there!"

Athena didn't respond to his shouting. He took a deep breath, focusing. She did have a point. Not having any armor with those machines out there, it wasn't like he was fighting mediators or even the E-Rats. He Studied the map once more, there was no way around the mecha. He squinted, noticing how close the exit appeared.

"Athena, how far is the exit?"

"1267 meters."

"In yards?"

"1385.608 yards."

He did the math in his head, about thirteen football fields. That seemed long, but it was less than a mile. He weighed his options, fixated on the 25%. He remembered the suits they'd found in his father's lab, the feeling in his gut when he learned they became unstable at 25%. He decided not to tempt fate, the same number as the suit only in a mecha.

"Okay Athena, this thing's yours. Give me a diversion."

He pressed the menus, searching for the hatch controls. After flicking through more than enough and seemingly getting nowhere, he finally relented. "Athena, open the hatch."

The back of the machine opened, stale air released creating a hiss. He climbed out of his seat, peering down at the ground. His vision blurred and his stomach tightened. *Don't look down.* Doing his best to grab onto the embedded ladder rungs on the back of the machine, he made his way down. Almost on cue, as his feet hit the ground, the mecha began walking toward its target. His head swiveled around, he darted to the faux buildings nearby, pulling his wrist into view, then tapped on the Datacle displaying his present position. He sat there a moment studying it then turned to head down another street. The sound of explosions erupted in the distance, the two aircraft flew overhead, their engines roaring. Like an Olympic sprinter, he ran, the rifle slung on his back bouncing up and down. The sounds of explosions continued, the rumble of aircraft in the distance. Hugging the building like a mouse running through a pantry, he scampered across a street, then another one, turning the corner as he recalled the map. A loud boom met his ears, the sound of debris bouncing off solid walls, then suddenly silence. He froze a moment. *There goes the diversion*. Zeroing in on his wrist, he found that he was less than 100 yards from the exit once he rounded the next corner. He stayed there just long enough to catch his breath then slipped toward the final corner, peeking around it. A large platform stood at the end of the road, beyond it was a tiny door, dwarfed by the surrounding structure. His head snapped from side to side, no movement. This was his chance, he took off, his knees reaching his chest as he accelerated. His breath was heavy as he continued toward his target, his body contracted and released on command, propelling him forward. He heard metal smashing into metal behind him. He knew the sound but didn't bother to look back, it would only slow him down. A sound of rapid vibrations filled the dead air. Out of pure instinct, he dove sideways. As he slid on the cold steel floor, a trail of rounds impacted the ground where he'd been running. His head twisted around. A giant monstrosity stood a few hundred yards away, its weapons fixated on him. His heart raced, muscles tensed. He twisted his body; the door was only a dozen feet away.

He gained his feet. Lunging, his foot slipped, he fell on his face, the sound of blasters filled the air. He felt the impact of the rounds merely a few feet from him as the ground rattled beneath him. He scampered to the door, by the grace of God the shots kept missing. He pressed through the door, diving into the room, his body bouncing on the smooth ground. He dashed to the door. Closing it, he saw a puff of smoke come from the mecha missile. As he rolled away, the door shook then fell still.

J pulled himself onto the wall, his upper body leaning into in the seated position. He calmed his breathing. Staring at the ground, he pulled his head back against the wall and placed his hands on top of his head.

"Safe."

CHAPTER TWENTY SIX

"Good game, J," a scratchy voice said, filling the room.

J's arms stayed raised as half a dozen mediators aimed their weapons at him. *Where was Kat? Why could he only hear his voice?*

J stood up straight. "Where are you? What do you want?"

"To play. I like games, especially war games. But I suppose it's time to get down to business."

J shivered at the sound of the slithering voice, like a snake flicking its tongue out as he talked. His eyes darted about, attempting to find the owner of the voice.

"I've already told you that my employer requires your scientists. I would love to play more games, but I'm afraid President Novikov is growing restless. Your friends—"

Blasts came from across the room hitting the mediators, J's head snapped over. Ariel and Zane moved toward him, their rifles fixed to their cheeks.

"You were saying?" Ariel lowered her aim.

J dropped his arms, scanning the eliminated mediators. An audible growl came from above them.

"Like toys, I have many more. Eliminating these has only bought you time, but I will get what I need. I—"

The voice cut out. As Ariel reached J, he lunged forward, embracing her. She dropped he rifle to the ground and wrapped her arms around his waist. He pulled back, gazing into her icy blue eyes, her glowing face smiled back.

"Told ya you could do it. Easy right?"

"If you call that easy, I'd hate to see hard. Do you know what happened in there? There were mecha, aircraft, a city, rockets, blasters—"

She stopped his ranting with a kiss and he melted, his thoughts of death vanished, his mind was filled only with the sweet taste of her soft lips. She drew back, his eyelids fell, his arms shivered.

"Enough of that, you two. Grant bought us some time, but who knows how long we have until he gains access again."

"Grant? Is that how..."

"He hacked into the system, finally."

On cue, Ariel pulled up her wrist. Grant's image glowed on her wrist, J twisted his neck to see.

"Your tormentor's in the Aurora tower. His name's Nicholas Onecent but calls himself—"

"Katergaris, we got that. Anything that can help us?"

"The records indicate he designed and programmed all of the simulations for the Military Academy. He was terminated when his simulations killed four cadets. That's the extent of what I could find, the rest has been redacted."

Ariel peeked out of the corner of her eye, her head rotated toward Zane. "Well, do we go after him or the scientists?"

"If you're askin' me, my vote's to go after him."

"J, what about you?"

His eyes searched the ground, he picked his head up. "I'm with Zane."

"Grant, we need the quickest way to the Aurora building. Send me the specs and floor plan while you're at it. Zane, remember the instructor entrance?"

"Sure, the cadet restricted one we used anyways?"

"That's the one. Take J, I'll meet you there."

She tapped her Datacle and took off before J could even argue.

Zane checked his railgun. "Let's go, kid. She'll be alright."

J unslung his rifle and nodded, the two of them left the room and rode an elevator down through the bowels of the Academy. They passed countless empty classrooms, J could only picture what it would've been like. Filled with cadets, military instructors shouting orders and assignments? Or was it more mellow than he imagined? After another elevator ride, this time going up, they stood in front of a doorway.

Zane looked at J. "This is it. Guess we just wait."

Zane leaned against the wall, dropping his railgun to his side. It dangled by the strap while he pulled out a blaster and began spinning it like he was in a Wild West movie.

J propped himself up next to him. "So, you guys went to school here?"

"Yep, best academy around," he laughed at his own joke.

J looked at him confused, Zane noticed. "I'm

kidding, it was the only academy. Well, except for the pilot school, and you've met one of their stars."

"Max," J said under his breath.

"Yep, good old Max. For all his flaws, he is one helluva pilot."

J fidgeted with his holsters, he adjusted his feet. "So, her uncle raised her?"

"Who, Ariel? Yeah, raised her from a baby. She was always a tough one, had to keep up with the boys, a verified tomboy. But I'm not telling you anything you haven't already figured out."

"You sound like you knew her from a young age."

"As you know, you don't select your skill. You're, in a way, bred for it. TK was all about control, and that was one way they handled it. "Know your role" was taught in every school from baking to mechanics. Ariel was...is a warrior. Her uncle sent her here when she was five, most don't enroll until six, but I pulled some strings. She was ready."

"What interest did you have in her?"

Zane pointed the blaster at the wall then spun it around a finger, moving his hand sideways.

"Her uncle was my Squad Commander, TK 1st Command, 8th Brigade. Back in the day, TK didn't have control the way they do now. Lots of uprisings, some were easy to put down, others not so much. The chips fixed that, I believe you called it "getting switched off". Once they perfected that, there was no longer a need for the military, not the way we were used anyways. Saw a lot of stuff people shouldn't, her uncle got me through it. Near the end, I was sent to teach here, made sure Ariel did well, watched her from afar. Arcturus was the one who actually requested Ariel be put in the academy early, seems he planned for the two of you to meet. I didn't know it at the time, but her uncle and I were both working for him in our own way."

J continued snapping and unsnapping his holsters, Zane slipped the blaster back into its home. Scratching his chin, he looked up at the ceiling.

"What happened to her uncle?"

"He disappeared a few years ago. He was always moving from place to place. Took Ariel with him quite a bit."

J didn't respond, he unstrapped his holster one final time and pulled a blaster from it, tried to spin it like Zane.

"Oh, I wouldn't do—"

A blast rang out, hitting the wall next to J's head. Both of them froze.

"Make sure the safety's on first."

J slipped it back into the holster, not saying a word, his chin tucked into his neck, eyes as big as moons. The wall shook as he did, they looked at each other. Zane reached for the door and peeked out, his eyes were met with an enormous hovering vehicle, two auto rifles mounted on top, a reflective windscreen in the center of two cylinder-shaped body panels. He slammed the door shut. Placing his back on the wall, half-crouched.

"What?"

"It's a Typhoon combat carrier."

Zane shuffled his eyes from side to side as if reading something invisible. He checked his weapon again as if its load had changed from moments ago. J looked back toward the elevator. *Where was Ariel?* A knock came from the door. Zane backed away, placing the railgun's sights center mass on the door. J mirrored his movements, glancing over at him multiple times, uneasy. The door hissed as its locks released, J tightened the grip on his weapon, his right eye fixed through the sight. The door swung open, Ariel stood there, rifle rested on her shoulder.

"You guys want a ride."

They stood up.

"You completely freaked us out!" J strolled toward her.

Ariel grinned back.

"Where'd you find the wheels, motor pool?"

"Yep, we better get going, that M6A8 is still on the prowl out there. Took me a bit to sneak by it."

The whole front end of the typhoon opened up, J sat down next to Ariel as she took the driver's seat, Zane landed in the turret. Ariel wasted no time firing up the engines and pulling away from the building. She engaged the auto drive then called Grant.

"You have those blueprints, yet?"

"Almost, here's the route. Should get you there in about twenty minutes, provided you don't run into any trouble."

"So, more like thirty," J chimed in.

Ariel tilted her head, letting out a light chuckle. J meant it as a joke, but a serious one; nothing ever seemed to go as planned. The Typhoon sped on as Ariel and Grant talked about the route and the plans, which he was finally able to send. Max was going to meet them on the adjacent building's landing pad. The building was uncompleted; it was in the middle of a renovation when the Exodus left. Over half of it was covered in steel beams and haphazardly placed material, a veritable maze. The Typhoon pulled up under the structure, fabric hung from the open rafters, half of the bottom ten floors exposed to the outside air. J looked at the sun, remembering it was a false one. It all seemed so Earth-like, he was beginning to forget the differences between the two. The cockpit opened, J had his head on a swivel. Their ride had gone off without a hitch, he felt that was a bad sign. His neck tingled as he faced Ariel.

"I'm not feeling so great about this. Kat seemed to know our every move, but we didn't encounter any resistance on the way."

"I'm not too stoked to be here either, but we don't have a choice."

"We could just blow the building down," Zane commented.

Ariel looked as if she was contemplating the suggestion. "We don't have enough firepower, even with the Rinókeros. Besides that, we need to know he's dead or we'll be doing this again."

She started forward toward the structure, her steps soft and controlled, rifle at the ready. J followed in behind her, Zane took up the rear scanning behind them. She pushed past the hanging cloths into the shadows, a single light bar above an elevator door flickered like a distraught neon sign. J's eyes danced around, his rifle whipping about, his body on edge. Ariel opened the elevator, her hand firmly placed on the control screen. An empty elevator greeted them as the doors opened.

"Which floor please?" the elevator screamed, deafening their ears.

The three of them winced, J covered his ear with his free hand.

"So much for the element of surprise. This elevator's as decrepit as the building." Zane grumbled.

"Which floor?" J asked.

"I can help you with that. I'll even narrow it down for you."

They looked at each other as the elevator speakers continued to project Kat's voice.

"Level 11 will be your first stop."

The elevator moved up, stopping almost as quickly as it began. Ariel tapped on her Datacle. "Comms are jammed. Looks like we've got no choice but to play along."

The doors opened, the room was pitch black. Zane tapped on the rifle, bringing a light to life. Ariel did the same then helped J with his. Their lights shined into the nothingness, a hallway split off in three directions. Ariel crept forward, J peered to the left while Zane focused on the right.

"Staying together," J asserted, more as a statement than a question.

"Together. Zane, you watch our back. J, eyes front with me."

They continued down the hall, their steps quiet, their breathing calm and collected. J was concentrated on it. Something darted across the hallway, J let out a burst of fire, jumping back. Ariel grabbed his arm.

"Calm down, probably just a construction bot. I wouldn't be surprised if this place is littered with them."

J swallowed and continued, slightly behind her. Zane had glanced back for a moment during the commotion, but was now back at his post. They passed the entrance he'd seen the movement fly into, he fixed his light into the room A small four legged robot sat in the middle of the room, its round body surrounded by its legs, three black circles like eyes stared back at him. He stopped, tugging on Ariel's arm, pointing into the room.

"Like I said, just a construction bot. Need to keep moving."

The bot's top slid open, a cylinder shaped device popped up and the tip began to glow a light shade of green. He pushed Ariel to the floor as a green bolt zipped past his head. J let out a barrage of fire, this time not stopping as he lay on his side. The bot burst into flames, sparks flying everywhere.

"I got him...I got him..." he reassured himself, rolling

over toward Ariel. She was motionless, her eyes fixated down the hall.

She didn't say a word, pressing her rifle to her cheek. J followed her gaze. Over a dozen construction bots huddled in the beam of light, more could be seen just on the edges of it. Each of them popped their tops, weapons humming to life. Ariel fired, taking a few out before the return fire occurred. J stayed prone aiming at the others, he let loose. Behind him, he heard the same bots skipping around, exploding like little burning flames. J propped himself up on a knee, still picking targets and firing. The bots proved less than accurate, most slinging shots over their heads. Ariel got to her feet and started marching forward as their numbers dwindled.

"I hope you have a better view up there, because these things are multiplying like crazy!" Zane shouted.

J whipped around, he was right. More and more ran into his light, aggressively approaching. Ariel continued her march, her shots calculated, no misses as if it were a game. They approached a T-intersection. J looked left, more bots flooded the hall, to the right the path lay empty.

"He's leading us somewhere," Zane surmised.

"I realize that, but I don't think we have much of a choice right now unless you have some suggestions."

Their rifle shots continued making it hard to hear one another. J kept close to Ariel as they rounded the corner and found a doorway. Ariel pressed the pad, opening it. They wasted no time shutting the door as the bots continued parading toward them. Ariel shot the door control.

"That should hold them. We need to figure out what floor he's on."

"Do you have the blueprints?"

Ariel placed her hand on her head, then removing it, tapped on her Datacle. The blueprints glowed on her wrist, J leaned over her shoulder and studied the screen.

"J, I'll deal with this. You and Zane make sure this room's secure. Who knows what Kat has planned for us."

He rotated his rifle, sweeping the room. It was small, about twenty by twenty with a table in the center, at one time it could've been a conference room. Two other doors stood along the walls. J shined his light at one, while Zane focused his beam on the other. Ariel continued searching for a solution. Movement caught his attention as a mediator broke through the wall, J and Zane opened fire, dropping it. They held their positions, J twisted his head to look over his shoulder, his eyes locked on the gaping hole in the wall.

"Any luck?'

"Yep, I've got it. There's a climate shaft behind that wall. The next floor is completely open and a maintenance elevator is hanging outside, it's not connected to the building's network. Hopefully he hasn't tapped into it. I'm guessing—"

Blasts hit the wall above Ariel, she dropped to a knee grabbing her rifle. J and Zane fired at the mediators coming through the wall, there were at least seven.

"Good enough for me, not really in the mood to be charcoal," Zane took off toward the far wall.

Ariel followed, adjusting her weapon to join the fight. Zane concentrated his fire on the exterior wall, attempting to blast through to no avail. He dropped the rifle, letting it swing. As he ran, he pulled a square box the size of a matchbox out of his pocket. Placing it on the wall, he darted toward them. J froze, realizing what was about to happen. The wall exploded. The concussion sent everything in the room flying, J included. Ariel had the sense to duck and was still prone with her hands over her head. Zane looked like he had finished a head first slide into home plate. The mediators were strewn about, some in disarray, others attempting to climb to their feet. Sunlight illuminated the room, their eyes struggled to adjust. J shielded his as the mediators, now resembling shadows, began standing up. Two of them dropped, Ariel's aim was true.

Zane rolled over, gathering himself. "Let's get moving before this place became a mediator party." He chugged like a freight train toward their exit, jumping into the top section of the shaft. J gawked, he didn't think the big man was that nimble. Ariel shouted to J and slid to a stop as she reached the hole, she waved him on.

"Like Zane said, need to move now!"

Her voice was strong, unwavering. J hopped to his feet, dashed over. He stopped, looking down out of the hole to the city outside.

"No time for reflection, get up there."

J peered up the shaft. It was three feet deep and maybe six feet wide, the shadowy figure of Zane disappeared as light entered the shaft from above. Ariel slapped him on the back as she fired, more mediators entered the room. J half crouched then sprung like a cat into the shaft, pressing his back against one wall and his feet against the other. He shimmied up as quick as he could, his foot slipped more than once. At the top, Zane extended his hand, helping him up the final few feet. He nearly threw him out, J landed on his side with a grunt.

"Thanks," he said, groaning.

"Don't mention it. Ariel right behind you?"

On cue, her fingers clutched the top then her body appeared as if it were shot out of a cannon. She landed on her feet, adjusting her rifle in her hands. She checked her wrist. "Over there."

She pointed to the far side of the skeletal structure, the twisted exposed metal laying about, only framework remained. As J adjusted his gaze, he saw the hoist Ariel had mentioned. They headed over, Zane searched for the controls while J climbed onto the platform, it wobbled and creaked under his feet. His legs tensed up, stabilizing his movement, he clenched his teeth and breathed deep through his nose. *Don't look down.* Zane stepped on next, the haphazard makeshift lift shifted. J stumbled back, attempting to balance the platform. He slid toward Zane. Ariel hopped on, climbing to the high side bringing it down slightly. J eked back, finishing the balance game. Zane found a small control box and depressed the up button, holding his thumb in place. The lift creaked to life.

"Which floor?"

Ariel consulted the plans, her head shaking side to side. J twisted his around, the city surrounded them and open air filled his lungs.

"What about Grant, he..."

He didn't have to say another word, Ariel understood. They were outside and possibly out of range of the jamming equipment. Her head dropped, she didn't need to respond, the comms were still jammed.

"Too bad we didn't bring carrier pigeons," J said, his head sunk down into his shoulders.

Ariel snapped her head around, "What did you say?"

"Carrier pigeons. You know, birds that fly messages to people."

Ariel's face perked up, she began tapping on her Datacle. J's eyes focused on her wrist, his eyebrows squinting. He couldn't see what she was doing, just a jumble of letters and numbers filled the screen. The lift continued up past several demolished floors, elevator shafts were the only enclosures as the sun bounced through, displaying deformed metal beams.

"What's all that?"

Ariel didn't break her concentration, but let out a quick "one sec," her face intense as she diligently typed.

"Ha," she said, smiling back at him. "Thanks for your historical nonsense."

J didn't know how to take it, he blinked a few times,

raising his hands waist high. Zane shrugged his shoulders as J referenced him.

"Your comment, pigeons...While we don't have pigeons, there is an old analog data system nobody uses anymore. I figured Kat wouldn't be monitoring it. My only question is, does Grant?"

They continued up, aiming for the top floor. It only made sense for him to be on the top floor, but it was just a guess. J was ready for the ride to be over, they were fifty floors up. Forty-nine more than he wanted to be. After another twenty floors, the building began to have more skin on it. Windows adorned the now present walls, though most were shattered, the rooms beyond them empty. J glanced up, hoping to see more. What he saw wasn't expected, the lift didn't reach the top. Instead, it stopped two floors below. Zane didn't waste any time shooting out the window in front of them. They climbed over into the building while Ariel checked the blueprints.

"There are two elevator shafts and two stairwells."

"I vote stairwells," J said, his legs still shaking.

"I'm with J, guessing Kat's got control of the lifts."

Ariel nodded in agreement. Zane and J scanned the floor, rifles at the ready. It was fairly open with only a couple of walls placed sporadically inside, J recognized the sign on one of them. J smiled, it was comforting to see that even in the future they couldn't figure out a fancy way to show a stick figure walking up the stairs. His grin left him as the sound of metal crashing behind them rattled his ear. The three of them spun around, raising their rifles. A blue flash painted the windows hovering around the room like the glowing walls of a hologram, a darkened figure stood staring at them. J swallowed.

CHAPTER TWENTY SEVEN

Ariel raised her weapon, aiming at the intruder. Her smooth finger slid from the guard to the trigger, continuing through a full squeeze. Nothing. She tried again. J and Zane also attempted to fire with the same result. Ariel threw her rifle aside.

"Anti-tech field," she adjusted her stance into a fighting position.

Tossing his rifle aside, he stood tall then his body shrank, his arms out, eyes focused as a boxer eyeing an opponent. J slipped the rifle onto his back, glancing over at his clan, he mirrored their stance. His eyes adjusted to the room's lighting, staring at the enemy. Her body was similar to Ariel's, her hair short on one side and shaved on the other. Parts of her body were mechanical, a skeletal metal hand held a long steel pole. The metal shimmered from the blue glow continuing behind her.

"Tara," Ariel growled.

J raised an eyebrow. *She knew her?* He knew it wasn't the right time to ask questions so he studied their opponent, attempting to unlock her secrets himself. They held their ground as the half-machine spun the staff like a buzz saw in one hand, prowling toward them.

"J," Ariel said out of the side of her mouth. "Get to the stairs. We'll be right behind you."

"But..."

"Just get to the stairs."

J backed up a step, prompting the woman to charge.

She screamed as she bolted toward them. J's eyes popped
out, he turned and flew to the stairs. Ariel engaged their
attacker, blocking the blow. Zane stepped in swinging
a heavy fist, missing his target. He recoiled then swung
with the other hand, landing it on the girl's shoulder.
Ariel disengaged and the two of them ran to J's side.

"The stairs! Up the stairs, now!"

Seeing the intensity in her eyes, his legs propelled
him up, skipping steps as he went. The sound of a battle
erupted behind him as he climbed. Skidding around the
corner, he glanced down. Zane and Ariel and the woman
exchanging blows, Ariel slipped away climbing the stairs.
J left before she could see him, his climb paused by a
door. He threw it open, running into the next room. A
multitude of mediators spun around, J bounded to a stop
then hopped back into the stairwell. Ariel arrived at
the same moment, tossing him toward the next flight of
stairs. The fighting with Zane continued as he climbed,
defending himself against their attacker. Ariel pushed
J along. He emerged on the top floor, stumbling and
falling on his face, Ariel landing on him. Zane stepped
out next, his large hands locked onto the woman's steel
weapon, the two tugging against one another. Zane
tossed the woman across the room, sliding. He was about
to pursue her but froze, looking up. J and Ariel climbed
to their feet finding the source of his actions. Two E-Rats
flanked them and four mediators surrounded them with
weapons poised to strike. A man stepped into view in the
center of the room. The whole floor was open, chairs and

tables throughout, a bar in the corner. The man stood with his shoulders hunched into his ears, his dark black hair slicked back, a tight fitting grey jacket and pants held close to his body.

"Welcome. It's a pity you skipped some of my game," he chided, emphasizing his S's.

They all knew the voice. Kat had planned for them to have a few more tests on their way up, but their resource-fulness had provided them with an alternative.

"So, the final test then. Please relieve yourself of your weapons."

J turned to Ariel who tossed her blaster to the ground, it bounced toward their captor. J and Zane followed suit.

"What do you want?" J asked.

The man slithered toward him, his eyelids heavy.

"I've already told you, the scientists you conveniently gathered."

J stood his ground, not moving. He held his chest high, tightening his jaw, grinding his teeth.

"Playing quiet won't end well, it's not part of the game."

Kat circled him, his eyes staying on J's face. He cracked his own neck as he rounded J's shoulder.

"Let's play a game. You get to choose the competitor, your girl or that mass of a man over there."

J's head turned as Ariel glared back at the snake of a man. It seemed he didn't have any choice.

"What's the game?"

"A fight to the death."

"And what do we get out of it?"

Kat scoffed, a devious grin snarled on his face. "The winner lives, the loser dies."

J thought about his options, he looked at the ground searching for the answer, his eyes shifted around the room. His mouth dropped open, about to speak, but the building rattled, knocking him from his feet. J hit the floor, watching the others fall as well. He eyed the blaster, dashing over on his hands and knees. The building pulsed again, he raised the blaster, aiming for Kat. A blast hit his shoulder knocking him to the ground. He spun, wrenching in pain, he managed to find the culprit, one of the E-Rats. He fired back, hitting him in the chest, knocking him back. His arm throbbed, useless from the damage. The building rumbled again. Ariel blocked a kick from Tara, she pushed her leg away fixing her stance amongst the trembling building. Zane had grabbed a blaster and was shooting the mediators. He eliminated them systematically, one by one, taking a shot in the oblique another skipping off his arm.

J stood up, shooting the E-Rat again, finishing him off then searched for Kat his arm still dangling. He attempted to move it with little luck. Kat scrambled away, his gate wobbly as the building shook again. The other E-Rat aimed at J, the building dropped and the floor fell out from under them as if the legs of a table were suddenly removed. It crashed down into the floor beneath it, pulling everything down. Ariel sat up, grabbed her temple massaging it, as she recovered from

307

the fall. Pieces of the ceiling began collapsing, Ariel scanned the floor for Tara.

J peeled himself off the twisted metal floor. He spotted his rifle laying a few feet away in a pile of rubble. Behind it, he watched Kat fighting to stand up. Holding his arm, J crawled to the rifle. He picked it up with his good arm, his other hanging limp, the pain too great to move it. He targeted Kat with the weapon. Wasting no time, he let a volley of rounds fly, each of them hitting Kat in the back. Their captor crumpled into a heap. J dropped his arm, searching for Zane and Ariel. Zane had gathered himself and continued to engage the mediators.

"You okay, J...Ariel?" he shouted, scanning for more enemies.

J was alive, certainly not in the best shape, his arm burnt and not responding from the laser blast. Ariel was doing the best of the three as she crawled to her feet. The sound of a spacecraft engine hit J's ears, he turned toward the low hum. The Rinókeros hovered just outside the broken walls of the building. J smiled, temporarily forgetting about his arm.

"Grant must have gotten your message." He navigated the mess of debris toward Ariel.

She smiled back without a word.

Zane saw Kat lying in a heap. "Nice shootin', kid," he gritted. He trudged through the wreckage, holding his obliques, his face tightening at each step.

They made their way to the ship, Max had lowered the ramp perpendicular to the ship's hull making a perfect place for them to load. V stood in the door awaiting her patients. As they reached the ramp, she ran out grabbing Zane.

"What life are you on now, eight?" she admonished. "You're going to run out if you're not careful. Then where would I be?" she caught herself. "No one to doctor if that happened." Her look scolded him, but there was no anger behind it. He just smiled patiently and let her lead him away.

J watched their interaction, puzzled, then shook his head and regarded Ariel. "That stunk. Remind me never to do that again."

Ariel grinned back at him, helping him onto the ramp. She stumbled forward, shouting in pain, her back contorted. J spun around, Tara was reloading from the kick she had just landed. He checked his stance, one hand up, his other hanging near his waist, it was the best he could do. Tara's head snapped to him then she lunged, her fist swiping at his face. She landed the blow, knocking him near the side of the ship. By now, Max had begun to pull away from the unstable building. He tightened, a painful smile grabbing his face. He rolled on his side, Ariel had recouped from the blow and attacked Tara. The two exchanged punches and kicks, Ariel landed a couple knees then twisted back spinning like a ballerina. She sank back into her fighting stance, Tara charged, throwing a tight right hook. Ariel shifted her weight, grabbing Tara's hand and tossing the mechanical woman past her. Tara spun, jumping at her, both hands over her head. A red bolt hit her midair. Ariel slipped to the side as Tara bounced on the ramp, immobile. Grant came running out, his little body waddling around, a silly grin on his face.

"A Tara," he whispered reverently. "Where did you find one of those?"

His excitement was hardly contained, like a treasure hunter finding a lost city of gold. It was the most emotion J had ever seen from Grant.

"Ariel, can you bring her inside?"

Tara's lifeless body lay near the edge of the still open ramp. Ariel contemplated just nudging her off the side like a dead fish. She turned to Grant in disgust, he still glowed from his find. Her head bent down. Eyeing Tara, she took a deep breath.

"J 2.0," she groused, grabbing the wrist of the Tara.

She leaned back, tugging with everything she had, Tara's body was as heavy as J's. She grunted and groaned as she struggled to pull the lifeless body toward the ship. J couldn't help but snicker. Ariel heard him, her nose crinkled as she stared through him. He straightened up and scooted into the ship, Grant followed him in. She turned, looking again at the body.

"Grant," she grumbled to herself.

Her nose twitched, she stomped into the ship and actuated the ramp switch, it began to fold up.

"What are you doing? You'll damage her!" Grant yelled, circling like a shark.

Ariel pressed her lips together, silent, her eyebrows

in V's staring at the little man. Grant didn't say another word, staring at the ground. Tara's body began to slide into the ship, hitting the floor with a thud. Ariel, like a statue, held the button until the door hissed shut.

"There. She's in the ship."

Grant ran over and placed a sensor on her head. J had watched the whole scene unfold and, amidst the pain of his arm, found it quite humorous.

"Let's get you to the medical bay," Ariel grabbed his good hand and tugged him along.

When they arrived, Zane was asleep on one of the four tables in the room. V's eyes peeked up at them from her monitor near the wall.

"You guys need to take better care of this guy, he's not a young pup anymore."

"You tell him that," Ariel replied, leaning on the door-way.

J hopped onto an empty table, wincing as he landed. V came over and examined his arm, he flinched as she moved it, letting out a groan.

"Oh suck it up, you baby," Ariel grinned.

"Easy for you to say, your arm isn't falling off."

Ariel walked over next to V, tugging on her lab coat. "Will he live doctor?" Her acting was over-embellished, her face tight with a smile after. J scowled back at her while V examined his arm.

"He'll be alright?" Ariel looked toward Zane. "And him?"

V looked over her shoulder, slightly pulling on J's

arm, who let out a little hiss. "Yeah, he'll be fine. He needs rest though. What happened?"

"Long story, I'll fill you in once you're done with these guys. Max say where he's going?"

V pulled a gun device out of her pocket and held it in front of her face. She squinted checking the setting.

"No, I think he was waiting on you. I'll finish up with J if you want to get to the bridge. Best for him to go under, I have a lot of ligament damage I need to repair."

J looked at Ariel, then V. *Go under? Does that mean?* He felt a sharp pinch in his shoulder and a warm sensation flowed through his body, time slowed, rest sounded good, his eyes closed.

CHAPTER TWENTY EIGHT

"Sir, your meeting with the council will be starting soon. Here is the advanced read through." Arcturus' assistant handed him a tablet.

J glanced at it then slipped it under his arm. "What's on the agenda today?"

"Resource management, tonight is the vote. The scuttlebutt is that the majority favors plan B."

J felt his body sigh, he was a passenger once more. During every one of these "dreams" he hoped there'd be something, some clue, some revelation. He held his breath on this one. J, unable to control anything felt his body tense and studied the last few words as Jeffrey spoke. *Plan B? What was plan B? Or plan A for that matter?* He was in a lab of some kind, scientists with grey lab coats walked to and fro, tablets in their hands. A couple ran by attempting to catch a colleague. He followed his assistant through the halls, clean sterile walls emitting a white glow surrounded them.

The elevator dinged as the steel doors slid open, a man stepped out. "Going up Arcturus?"

He nodded, stepping in the elevator. Turning around, he focused on the door. The elevator requested their destination.

"TK council meeting?" the man asked, his voice rough like he'd engaged in one too many screaming matches.

"Yes."

The man requested the council floor, J turned and looked at him. His build was muscular like a Greek Olympian, his hair sandy blonde. He had a stout jaw line and an aquiline nose. He wore a military uniform, his chest held high, face a resting smile.

J turned his attention back to the doors. "How're your brother and niece doing, Zebulon?"

"They're good. Going to a ballgame with them this weekend. It'll be my niece's first live game."

J felt his hand slip into his pocket, his fingers fumbling with an object. He pulled it out, slipping it into Zebulon's hand. His gaze held on the doors.

"How are the battlements coming on Project Cyber-mantis?"

"Not as quickly as I'd hoped, but they'll be ready in time."

The elevator chimed as they reached his floor. J walked out, never moving his gaze. "Enjoy the game, Commander Zebulon."

His stride carried him to the boardroom, he noticed that nearly all of the seats were filled as he continued in past the mediators standing watch and took his seat. A man next to him leaned in his face like a bulldog.

"Sorry, Arcturus. It sounds like proposal A isn't going to hold up, the board's favoring proposal B."

"So I hear," he sat back in his chair.

The air was filled with chatter, much too low for him to gather anything from. He sat there staring through the wall. The room collectively stood up, as if a high ranking military officer had entered the room, J was the last one to stand. Cyrellia eyed him as she entered, her red lips sporting a devious smirk. She waved a hand, palm down, in a slow motion, the council took their seats. As she approached the table, she placed her palms on the edge, leaning over it. A small necklace dangled from her neck and the star charm sparkled in the light.

"You all know why we're here and secrets are never secret, so we know where we're going. But for the sake of tradition, formality and conformity, we will vote."

A display behind her appeared showing two boxes, one labeled proposal A the other proposal B. Each box displayed 0%. She pressed down on her hands, knuckles whitening, gazing around the table.

"Any final words before we vote?" She turned her head to J.

In response, he stood up, his hands held waist high. His shoulders twisted, facing the majority of the room. "Our current system is flawed, every system is flawed. You must ask yourself, what is better for mankind? To divide the population, to suppress the common man, to unknowingly enslave them? We have done it here, and if today we choose poorly, our new world will be exactly the same. Oppression never works, oppression always fails. We cannot control everyone, someone will turn, revolt. We must put in place systems to help mankind move forward, not repeat the past. You've read my reports, you've seen it firsthand. Remember those things when you vote today, or I warn you... there will be an uprising."

He sat down, glaring back at Cyrellia.

Her head shook as she smiled. "Lovely speech Arcturus, now it is time. Cast your vote."

At each of the seats a panel lit up with two circles, one for each proposal. The council each placed a forefinger on their choice. Instantaneously, the screen above Cyrellia changed.

She smiled, kicking her shoulders back, never taking her eyes off of J. "Proposal A it is."

His eyes flicked up to the screen, under proposal A the number read 96%. J felt his hands clench. Cyrellia spun, her dress swirling around as she made a grand exit. He waited, eyes fixated on the numbers. He could feel his breathing change, accelerate, his eyes followed each of the members as they left.

The final man to leave was the bulldog sitting next to him. "I'm sorry Arcturus, she had the council. It would be wise not to contradict."

As the elevator shot away, J held his wrist out, the Datacle came to life. "Have my transport pick me up at Pad Five. There's someone I need to see."

He turned off the call and headed out to the landing pad. The sun lit up the sky, the grand structures glistened from it. His head rotated as he stood, taking in the city, his hands clasped behind his back. A ship adjusted course, landing in front of him. He boarded the craft and was met by a younger woman in full battle gear, J recognized her as the woman who fought for Arcturus in the hangar when he was a baby...Ariel's mother.

"I hear you're going to a ball game this weekend."

"Who told you, Zebulon? Well keep your mouth shut. It's supposed to be a surprise for Dougald. So, where you headed?"

"To see an old friend, it's time to recruit."

The ship faded away as he awoke from the dream, he could move his arms once again. He clutched his injured shoulder, feeling for the damage. He rolled it around in its socket, the wounds were healed, but it was stiff and sore. He let out a groan as he flopped off the bed, catching himself with his good hand. Blinking, he straightened up, then rubbed his eyes. As he moseyed out of the medical bay, he wandered toward the bridge, not really paying attention to what he was doing. Fresh cooked food tapped into his senses and he ducked his head in to an empty kitchen, a single frying pan sat on the counter, the remnants of an omelet rested in it. *Had to be Zane, glad he's up and about.* As he drew closer to the bridge, he heard shouting, he hurried his pace to investigate. When he entered, Ariel was flailing her arms, Max leaned on the console yelling back.

"You watch too many movies. We could use the help, you've seen what we're up against. And that Riku guy, what if...No, you know what?...When we have to fight him again, wouldn't you want something that can finish him off?"

"What, you don't think I can? I'm telling you it's a bad idea, there's a reason they stopped producing them."

"You're not giving Grant enough credit. Just because

he accidentally shocked your "boyfriend" doesn't mean he's not capable."

Max's hand's air-quoted as Ariel's nose twitched and wrinkled, Max didn't stop. "You just don't want another female around," he said, grinning with a slight chuckle.

Ariel swung at him, this time he saw it coming and ducked. Zane flew in from nowhere, grabbing her before she could get in a second attack.

"Let's just calm down. We can take it to a vote when J's up, see what he thinks as well."

J cleared his throat and the three of them looked over at him like they'd seen a ghost.

"Feeling better?" a tiny voice asked from behind him.

J turned to look over his shoulder then stumbled into the wall next to him. V stood there with Grant, Tara behind them, her eyes locked onto J.

"Whoa, what's going on? That thing tried to kill us!"

"See! He gets it!"

"Grant reprogrammed Tara, I helped." V puffed up, proud of herself.

"Wait. So, that's a robot? Like a Replicant?

J continued to pin himself to the wall, his body almost merging with it. Ariel walked over as Zane released his grip.

"Tactical Autonomous Reconnaissance Android... Tara. The military used to use them, they have plenty of flaws. Zane used to have a few in his company." She turned to Max. "Why do you think this is a good idea again?"

Max peeled himself off the console. "Zane knows that with the proper programming, they can be fixed. Grant has a prototype AI he loaded in her."

"Prototype, and that's supposed to make me feel better? Those things have been known to terminate anything in their path. How's some new code going to prevent that? Machines have a tendency to malfunction. And news flash… we don't have a good track record with saboteurs."

"I can leave and find somewhere else to go. I don't want to cause any trouble." The room went silent, all eyes focused on Tara. "I don't mind. I'm glad to be alive. Thanks to Grant, all of my previous programming has been completely wiped, well, except for my combat skills. I'm afraid I might need those."

Everyone still gawked.

"Okay, so you said we needed to have J here to take a vote. He's here now."

Ariel peered around the room. "All in favor of disposing of Tara raise your hand."

Ariel shot her hand up as she spoke, nobody followed. She scowled at J and he did his best chameleon impression, his eyes peered down and right.

"Fine. If we have to keep her on board, she must be accompanied by someone at all times."

"She's not a child. It's even in her name, Autonomous. This is why people don't want to be around you, it's your way or the highway." Max stormed off.

She crossed her arms, her lips pressed tight.

J sank into himself and tried to think of what to say, the tension in the air was unbearable. "So where are we heading?"

Ariel thundered out, shouldering Tara as she went. V turned to follow. Zane rolled his shoulders, looking at J.

"Sleep well?" he chuckled.

"Yeah, but I'm guessing that's not going to be the case for the foreseeable future. What did I wake up to?"

"Ariel is afraid I'll malfunction like my predecessors. The odds of that happening are less than .001%."

Both of them turned to Tara who was still standing in the doorway. With the exception of her metal left arm, she looked like a normal, albeit well-built, female.

"And you're okay with this?"

"I am. I've known Grant a long time. His hacking skills may be lacking, but his AI programming skills..." Zane kissed his fingers, "...magnifique."

"Grant has programmed me to behave more human. V said she'll be able to fix my arm as well, making me look more human."

J studied her. She looked real. Of course, the replicants looked real too. He understood Ariel's fears, he had them himself. He'd learned to trust his crew, his new family, even Max. He felt in time he could trust...a machine. His mind shifted. "Where are we heading?

"Well, kid, we're already here. The new world order's in this bunker, we're just trying to figure out the next course of action."

J walked up to the main bridge console, in the heat of

the argument, he hadn't noticed the screen or anything about the ship. Out of the windscreen sat a sizeable hangar floor, a few people J didn't recognize walked across the deck. He peered closer, two of them were the sisters he'd found with V.

"Are they all here?"

"Sadly, no. We think Takamori has Dr. Huergo, but we can get communication with Admiral Titov."

J laughed, "Dmitry. Admiral Titov sounds so formal."

"Look who's talking, James. She really is rubbing off on you."

His face turned red, he fiddled with the controls. "What do you think we should do?"

"If you're talking about her, then keep her. If you're talking about Huergo, then we need to get back to the Parádeisos."

J had forgotten about Tara, she was still standing there watching the two of them converse. His spine tingled as he glanced over at her. He drew a deep breath. "Let's get everyone together. I'm sure once we get going, Ariel will get over the issue. I'll see if I can find Ariel and V. Can you find Grant and Max?"

"Sure, kid. Meet here?"

J nodded then began his search, he didn't know where he was going, so he wandered aimlessly around the ship. He passed through the mess hall twice and even ended up back on the bridge again eventually stumbling into the hangar. Ariel was sitting in one of the fighter craft. He approached with caution, she was staring at the controls.

He placed his hands on the rail. "Whatcha doing?"

Ariel initially didn't answer, her head still down flicking some of the panels.

J leaned in, taking a closer look. "These things sure have amazing technology. Thankfully they're ours to use."

Ariel snapped her eyes over to him. "I know what you're trying to do."

J popped his head up, a look of feigned innocence on his face. "What?"

"You guys are probably right, but we really haven't had the best luck."

J leaned further in, his arms now dangled over the side of the craft, almost touching hers.

"What do you mean? We both should have died multiple times, don't make me list them out. We had to have a little bit of luck to make it through all of that."

Ariel flicked a switch, the ship came to life, the engine hummed low. She tapped on a few buttons, pulling up menus, then pressed the kill switch. Everything shut down, the hum coming to a stop. She climbed down out of the ship.

"I still think we need to keep an eye on her, I don't trust AI."

"I don't either, but Tiki worked out. I mean, except for the biting. He was an AI, right?"

Ariel didn't say anything, but it was enough to get her to smile. J remembered their adventure with Tiki; he had no problem trusting a talking cat, which still seemed weird. Now he had to learn to trust a mechanical woman. He grabbed her hand and they made the trek to the bridge where Zane had been able to rally everyone up, including V.

"So, the Parádeisos?" Everyone nodded back at Ariel. "Okay. Grant, let's see if you can make us invisible."

CHAPTER TWENTY NINE

The Moon's Aristarchus crater appeared behind them as they exited the docking bay tunnel. Ariel stood at the helm, watching the stars ahead, concentrating on the objective. J approached her as she gazed out into the emptiness of space. His body shivered. *What an amazing view.* He stopped next to her and peeked out of the corner of his eye at Ariel, her lips soft, hair flowing, her cute little nose like a button. He smiled then peered back into the stars.

"Looks like Grant's hack job is holding up," she said.

"Looks like it."

"Or nobody's home."

She turned and walked toward Grant who was sitting a few feet away at a screen, his eyes flipping left and right, reading.

"Is Atlantis searching for us? Or are the scanners down?"

Grant continued reading as if not hearing her, Ariel knew the drill and waited a moment. She began tapping her foot while her arms crossed, she studied the ceiling.

"Yes, they are scanning. My patch is holding."

Ariel turned and walked past J, taking a position near Max. She knew that was the most she'd get out of Grant.

"How's she running?"

Max peeked up behind him then turned back to the controls.

"Good, she's running good. This ship's a beaut."

J watched the conversation closely, attempting to study them in the hopes that he'd find a clue to their past. The stars moved in the screen, a holographic ship popped up on Max's monitor.

"Looks like the Parádeisos is ready for us."

Just then the screen flashed "incoming message". Max enabled it and Dmitry gazed back at them from the deck of his ship. His posture tight, shoulders back, his square jaw held high.

"Found the scientists, I take it?"

Ariel took a step back to see the screen better, placing her body at parade rest. J hadn't seen her so...professional before, her training seemed to take over.

"Yes, Admiral, but I'm afraid we never were able to acquire Dr. Huergo. In our last meeting, I forgot to ask if you'd picked him up."

Dmitry didn't move, his posture firm. Men in the background shuffled around, tapping out commands, checking systems.

"No, we did not. That could be a problem. We can discuss it when you come aboard." He rotated his head and signaled to one of the men on the deck. "I'll have a welcome party ready for your arrival. You're cleared into hangar bay #3."

The picture dissolved from the screen leaving the stars, and now the battle cruiser, coming into view.

"Hangar #3, Max."

"I heard," Max rolled his eyes.

Ariel maintained her posture as the flagship expanded

in the screen. J adjusted his stance to look like hers, wondering if it was all that comfortable. He found his shoulders tight.

"Playing solider?" a voice behind him asked.

J jumped, spinning around, breaking out of the pose as quick as he could. Ariel turned as well her eyes judging. Zane was behind him trotting back from the galley.

"No...just...stretching."

Zane laughed placing an arm on his shoulder. "Takes some getting used to, she's done it a lot more then you. You'll pass out if you keep your knees locked like that."

J continued deflecting. "Just stretching."

Zane didn't comment again, just slid his arm off J's shoulder and strolled to a seat off to the side. He kicked his feet up onto one of the consoles. By now, Ariel had turned back to the screen while Max guided the ship to docking bay #3. As they approached, a huge door with a stenciled number 3 on it began to open. Its doors like a large mouth swallowing the ship, a squad of soldiers stood in formation near the landing pad. Max guided the ship down with precision, J didn't even notice the craft touchdown. Ariel turned, marching past the rest of the crew. Zane slid his feet off the ship to follow.

"Have you seen her like this before?" J asked as Zane approached. He fumbled with his Datacle, spinning it on his wrist.

"Not for awhile. Last time was around her uncle, but that was years ago. I chalk it up to stress...and the Admiral."

"Admiral?"

Zane pushed him along. "Cliff notes, kid. The Academy embeds things in your head which are hard to get out, certain things I'll say triggers them. It's been some time since she was around a military man."

"But you're one."

"Ariel and I both know where we stand with one another, it's not the same. Plus, do I act like the Admiral? No, I do not. I've had enough of that life."

"Then why..."

Zane shook his head and grinned. "You've got more questions than a 5-year old."

J pondered Zane's responses, sometimes he felt that Zane had his own language, code words for things. *What did he mean embedded, like chipped?* They continued walking, J remained silent, trying to sort out the answers before moving on. In no time they were in the Rinókeros' hangar bay ready to exit. Ariel had beat them there and was already walking with Dmitry, chatting. Zane had called it a debrief, the term was like so many others...new.

"Wait up guys."

Zane and J both turned to see Max trotting to catch up. J rolled his eyes back. *What did he want?*

He skidded to a stop next to them, a big smile on his face. "Thanks for waiting, not sure exactly where we're going. You guys?"

J had no clue, he would've surely gotten lost, but he had Zane with him. J stood tall raising his eyebrows. "Yep."

Zane laughed, watching the exchange. He stepped

back, waiting to see where this was going to go.

"Ready, Zane?" J tilted his head, asking him to go first.

"Oh, but I'm following you," he grinned.

J's stomach dropped. He looked back at Max who was playing with a coin, running it through his fingers, intently watching J. Zane was still smiling, trying not to laugh. He spun his head around hoping to see Ariel. The floor was nearly empty, she was gone. He swallowed then heard another voice.

"You guys know where the brief is?"

All three of them glanced back to see Grant waddling up, Tara in tow.

Zane nodded toward J. "J knows. He was about to lead us there."

J's body trembled as the four of them searched his face for answers. Max flipping the coin, Zane smiling, Grant, well, he was twitching like he usually did, and Tara had the most serious face he'd ever seen, it kind of creeped him out. He twisted around and started down the ramp, pretending to know where to go. He vaguely recalled some of the structures and doors, but as they journeyed, everything began to look the same. After ten minutes of walking, he was well and truly lost. He needed the courage to ask for help.

"Do you know where you're going?" Max asked.

This was the moment of truth, every fiber inside him said to tell the truth. But to be wrong, and to be wrong in front of Max, the Max who used to have a thing with

Ariel. That rankled. He opened his mouth. "I haven't got the slightest."

J looked at the ground like a shamed little puppy, Zane placed a hand on his shoulder and J peeked up at him, his face still in a ridiculous grin.

"I don't either."

J's jaw dropped he flailed his arms about. "What do you mean, you don't know?

Zane began to laugh. "I did know until you took us through that maze back there."

Max was laughing at the two of them, J was turning red, his eyebrows perked up.

"I know where to go" a small voice said behind him.

Everyone turned to see who it was, but only Tara stood there. *Where had the petite little voice come from?* Everyone looked puzzled, their attention drifted to Grant. He was fiddling with some device, it took him a moment to realize that everyone was staring at him.

"What?" he asked, shrugging his shoulders, still playing with his toy.

"Did you change her voice?" Zane asked.

The little man pulled the item up to his chest again, tinkering with it.

"I thought Ariel might find it less threatening. Adjusted a few more settings too."

He continued flipping the device. The other three looked back at Tara, she smiled and they snapped their heads back to Grant. Grant felt the air move his eyes fixated on his toy.

"That's one of the tweaks, hope she likes it."

"A smile?" Max asked, incredulous.

"Not just a smile, but full emotions, it's part of my new AI program. She has memories as well, you should ask her about her family sometime. All good stories. I promise."

They continued staring at Tara.

"You're making me nervous," she said. "Would you like me to take you to the debriefing room?"

J's eyes had tightened at the emotions comment. He nodded and the others followed suit, not saying a word. She continued her smile then stepped past them. J had been going in the wrong direction.

The boys stayed silent on the jaunt. J was contemplating Grant's actions. *Memories, emotions. How was that going to help?* From his experience, those things only led to bad things, in movies at least. They eventually ended up stepping into the briefing room where they'd first met with Dmitry. Ariel was deep in discussion with him and a few other members he hadn't seen before. Two other men wore uniforms nearly identical to Dmitry, but their chests had different designs on them. Ariel was leaning over the table, pointing at something on the displayed blueprints. She peeked up at him, flashing a momentary smile, then went back to work. Zane flopped into a seat across from them as did Max. Grant fastidiously settled into a seat, waving to Tara to join him. J stood, watching Dmitry and Ariel talk.

"This is where Grant tracked the transmissions when

we first arrived in Atlantis. Seems they've gone silent, though," Ariel pointed to one of the buildings on the map.

"Is that an old TK factory?" Dmitry looked over at Zane.

He walked over to get a closer look, leaning over as far as he could without toppling over. "Yep, that was a replicant factory at one time, but it's been shut down for years."

Dmitry scratched his chin, his hand then flicking the screen, searching for something. His mouth opened, about to speak, when the window behind him became opaque. A female soldier rose, standing in the bridge.

"Sir, there is a transmission coming in, requesting to talk to you. President Novikov."

Dmitry glanced over to Ariel. "Patch him in."

Dmitry spun around and stood up tall, his chest out and chin up. The image drifted in, President Novikov stood there, his eyes tight, his right cheek twitching over a sneer.

"Seems you didn't carry out the orders handed to you. The boy is still alive?"

The question was rhetorical, he could see J in the background. His eyes fixated on him then switched back to Dmitry.

"You have served me well for many years and, as luck would have it, I still need the boy. Dr. Huergo was kind enough to let us in on a little secret that your teenage friend has. Now, as a good show of faith and to prove your loyalty, you have fifteen minutes to throw his compatriots out the airlock... and I will see it live."

The Admiral stood firm, a message appearing on the bottom of the screen had his eyes shifting. "Battle Cruiser Forte inbound. Engagement zone in five minutes, requesting orders." He shifted back to the President.

"I'm afraid I can't do that, President."

On screen, President Novikov clenched his jaw, his face turning red. He was pushed aside, in his place stood Takamori.

"You had your chance. Prepare to be boarded. If you don't com—"

The Admiral leaned back, tapping the screen and turning around. The picture snapped off.

"Looks like we don't need to find them after all. Lieutenant, ready the fighters. They are not going to board this ship."

The female ran out of the room shouting orders into her Datacle.

Max jumped up. "Need another?"

Dmitry smiled, nudging his head to the door. Max ran after the Lieutenant.

Zane, still leaning on the glass table, cocked his ear to Ariel. "Whatcha say? Should we go get 'em?"

J had repositioned himself, leaning on the wall. At the suggestion, he bounced on the balls of his feet toward the table, rubbing his hands together.

"Are you crazy? You know if Takamori's there Riku is. I don't know if you remember, but he's not a pushover.

He's near invincible."

Zane looked over his shoulder, Ariel perked up. "He did bleed, he's human enough. We need to eliminate all of them if there's going to be hope for Earth. You know in your heart, that's the only way. We have to get Dr. Huergo, that's our mission."

J knew that to be true, though he attempted to convince himself there was another way. Riku nearly killed them on more than one occasion. This could be the last time. His chest tightened. He rubbed it, watching Ariel, remembering how he almost lost her after their run-in with Riku. He finally placed his hands on the screen, trying to stabilize them. They continued to shake. Dmitry tapped on the glass and a 3D rendering of a ship appeared.

"Takamori slid one by TK as well, hiding the Forte. Should've known. Luckily we're faster, albeit outgunned."

The ship's image spun slowly as the Admiral moved it around with his finger, pointing out the large plasma cannons on each side of the ship. The Forte was larger than the Parádeisos and heavily gunned, the Parádeisos had been built for speed and maneuverability. J's eyes hurt from the width they stayed as the features of the two ships were discussed. Most of it flew over his head, but bigger, faster, those were words he knew. In short, don't get caught by the Forte.

"Seems like Max wanted to play with one of your fighter toys. You got a ship we can borrow to go get the doc?" Ariel asked.

"I'll do you one better than that. You can have Zgon squad."

Ariel grinned hugely. Whatever Zgon squad was, it had to be something good to get a reaction like that from her. J was attempting to take it all in, he wondered with the new allies what part he would play.

"Zane and I will take Zgon squad to rescue the doctor, Grant you stay here with J"

Ariel didn't bother to acknowledge that Tara was even in the room.

J sat up. "What? No. I'm going."

"No, you stay here with Grant and the Admiral. Zane and I can handle it, you're too valuable."

J sat back, searching the table. He rubbed his hands on his thighs. *He was valuable? She was valuable!*

He stood up. "I'm coming with you," his voice solid.

"No," she was adamant. "You are too valuable. You will stay here."

J searched for words, his hands clenching, his eyes getting tight.

Dmitry intercepted the next exchange. "Ariel is right, you are too valuable. You should stay here and accompany me on the bridge."

J relented, ducking back into the seat. Ariel finished with a few words to Dmitry then rounded the table to exit the room. She stopped next to J, he turned away from her. He couldn't watch her leave, feeling like she still thought of him as that kid from Eggerton who didn't know anything, who couldn't be trusted to help her. He wanted her respect, wanted her to think of them as equals. He didn't want to be someone she had to protect.

She dropped her head at his rebuke, her eyebrows high over her glistening icy blue eyes. "It's for your safety."

She kissed him on the forehead then trotted out the door, Zane in tow. J balled his hand up into a fist and slammed it on the table, pain shot down his arm but he didn't flinch. She was leaving without him. He sat there grinding his teeth until Dmitry walked by.

"We will have comms with her the whole time."

He left, heading down the hall. J stood there staring out into space, the dark ominous void staring back at him, the emptiness that fills everything, yet nothing. He slid a hand through his hair, messaging his scalp. His thoughts were shortly interrupted.

"I believe we should get to the bridge," Grant said.

J looked over at him, his face still red. "Fine."

CHAPTER THIRTY

Dmitry stood at the helm, his eyes fixed on the ship exiting hanger bay #1. The craft was large enough for ten combat loaded troops, Ariel was one of them. On his way to the bridge, he'd readied the ship and Zgon squad for their departure. Now came the fun part, playing cat and mouse.

"Orders sir?" the female Lieutenant asked.

"Engage all thrusters 75% power, head for Atlantis orbit and remain out of the Forte's gun range, but don't pull away."

"Aye, Admiral."

The Lieutenant started shouting commands to the crew, typing on multiple screens near her station. Men and women went to work like an orchestra, each playing their part to execute the Admiral's orders. J sauntered up to Dmitry.

"You said we'd have comms."

The Admiral turned his head, peering out the side of his eye, chin still high. He motioned for J to have a seat off to the side, J obliged.

"Lieutenant, bring up comm and video of the Zgon Squad."

The Lieutenant wasted no time executing the order. J could see each team member's personal video, even Ariel was wearing one. He smiled, wondering what they had to do to get her to wear the headgear, then he saw the doppelganger. One of the soldiers was posing as him, using a digital facemask to hide his true identity. J found it strange to see himself on video, it was something he'd never seen before. The cameras showed the exterior of the ship as well, next to it were two fighters, one of them piloted by Max. They escorted the squad closer to the Forte.

The Lieutenant turned to Dmitry. "The Forte is hailing us. Should I put it on screen?"

Dmitry nodded.

It was Takamori, his face firm. "So, have you come to your senses? Or are we to shoot down your little ship?"

"You are most correct. We're sending a peace offering, you'll get what's coming to you."

"That is good. The boy is on the ship?"

"Yes, he is on the ship and we expect to see Dr. Huergo in the docking bay when they land. We'll exchange the doctor for the boy."

Takamori's eyes tightened, his small eyes peering through slits as if the light was too bright. He nodded then switched off the comm.

Dmitry pressed a button, transmitting to the assault team. "You guys are cleared in, but I'm not expecting the good doctor to be there as promised. Be ready for anything."

The Squad Commander acknowledged as the ship began its approach into one of the Forte's docking bays. They landed without any issues, the fighters took up position outside the ship for support. J watched the screens. By his count, there were a couple dozen mediators awaiting their arrival and the Admiral was right, no sign of anyone looking like a doctor. J held his breath as the ship's doors opened. Ariel was the first to step out, through the comms they could hear the conversation as Takamori himself appeared in front of her.

"You have the boy?"

Ariel turned her head, swinging an open palm toward the imposter, then came back to Takamori.

"Yes, but I don't see the doctor."

"Yes, well we have to verify the boy's DN—"

Suddenly, the comm cut out, the Parádeisos crew scrambled to bring it back online. A few members outside the room rushed in attempting to correct the situation. J watched, the video flickered a moment, then went dark. J stood there silent, he clenched his fists staring at the bridge door, closed his eyes. Taking a deep breath, he mentally shook himself then snuck out into the hallway unnoticed. There wasn't anyone who'd stop him in either direction. *Where's the hangar?* A hand rested on his shoulder, he jumped turning to see Tara standing beside Grant, both examining him.

"You're going after Ariel aren't you?" Tara said.

J's eyes switched between the two, his body shaking. "Yes, don't try and stop me."

He pushed her arm off his shoulder and headed down the hall.

Behind him a small voice called, "J, that's the wrong way. I'd love to help you."

J grumbled, but knew he'd have to suck up his pride.

He trudged back to the door. "Okay, which way?"

Tara grabbed his hand, it was warm and soft and for a brief second, J forgot it wasn't real. V had fixed her up, she looked and felt more human than ever. Her new personality was sweet and innocent; he was curious what she'd look like in combat. She dragged him through the ship with Grant waddling behind, finding their way down to one of the hangars. As they stepped in, they saw over a hundred fighter ships, all in rows. J ran toward a tandem craft and placed a hand on the hull, the hydraulics kicked in, lifting up the transparent canopy.

"Take Tara, she can help. I'll stay here and work on jamming their signals so you'll be able to slip by. And take this." He handed J the device he had been playing with.

"What is it?"

"No time. Now get to your girl and take care of mine. She'll explain on the way."

J thanked him, hopping into the front seat, Tara climbed in back. It felt strange to be in a ship with a machine, a replicant. He tapped the screens, closing the canopy. The engine hummed to life and he sank into the chair, sliding his hands into the controls. *I'm coming, Ariel.* The ship lifted off, the hangar doors opening on call as he slammed the thruster forward. The g-forces pinned him to the seat, the exhilarating sense of speed rushed through his body.

"Turning on cloaking now," Tara said, tapping through the menus.

Only a few hours ago she was trying to kill Ariel, now she was helping to save her. He didn't have time to worry about Tara's past. Ariel was in trouble and he could use all the help he could get.

"My systems are indicating a garbage chute located on the far aft quadrant, port side."

J's eyes twisted up, attempting to translate. "What? Is that English?"

"Yes, I believe it is proper English. Would you like me to repeat?"

J thought about it, the thruster still pegged. After a brief turn, the Forte was now dead off the nose.

"Yes, but plain English, small words," he dragged out "plain".

"Very well, I believe this may suffice. There's a tunnel on the back half of the ship on the right side."

"See how much easier that was? How do we get in?"

"Space walk."

J stared at the ship approaching. *Space walk, in space? Without a suit? Maybe she could do that, but he had no chance of survival in the cold, unforgiving, oxygen-less environment.*

"How do you suppose we accomplish that?"

"I suppose you will have to wear the emergency suit under your seat. It would have been better to have put one on before climbing into this starship."

Great, not only a high class talker, but a patronizing one at that. J felt under the seat, as he depressed a panel, a box slid out displaying a square of cloth. He lifted it up, inspecting it. The suit was solid orange except for small coiled tubes running down the sides into the neck area attached to a tiny box on the back. A zipper ran from the foot all the way to the neck. *Looks like a prison uniform.* He unzipped it, slipping it on, then realized there was no helmet. He patted his head as if one would magically appear.

"The helmet's in the floor between your feet, I'll extract it for you."

At the conclusion of her words, the floor raised up displaying a small helmet. It was egg-shaped, the front made of glass and the rear a chrome electric blue.

"I'll accept the flight controls so you can don the helmet."

J didn't respond, just slipped his hands out of the controls, clenching the helmet. Pulling it to him, he could see himself in the reflection. His hair was messy, in bad need of a cut. His eyes looked tired. And he thought life on the farm had been hard. He would've given nearly anything to get back to a lazy day in the fields. He slipped it over his head, the helmet hissed as he locked it into place. Tara actually had to walk him through the steps, he fumbled with it initially, but her guidance helped.

"How about you fly for now, you know where we're going."

Tara agreed and adjusted course, they'd be there in no time. The Forte engulfed the windscreen as they approached, still at full thrusters.

"I hope Grant can keep us hidden."

"He will, he's a great programmer. He programmed me."

Visions of the ball cap nearly frying his face off jumped into his head, he hoped she was right. The ship descended into position right under a cylinder-shaped protrusion. It was much larger than he'd anticipated, maybe twenty feet across. *What kind of garbage did they get rid of?*

"Deploying anchor."

Anchor? Aren't those for boats? Just then, a metal can shot out, snapping onto the interior of the cylinder.

"Opening canopy."

The ship hissed, his suit shouted at him. "Exterior oxygen zero. Supplemental oxygen engaged, one hour of oxygen remaining."

He shut off the menu that was blinding him. Out of the corner of his eye, Tara drifted above him into the chute.

"J, can you read me?"

"Yep, any idea how to open this tin can?"

"Once I reach the emergency controls, I'll be able to tap into the ship's system and manually override the door codes."

"Of course," he said to himself, thinking of what might be on the other side of the door. He pressed his hands onto the ship's rails and gave a strong push. Over-anticipating the amount of energy needed, he rocketed past Tara, drilling the garbage door and bounced back.

Tara grabbed his hand and tugged him into her.

"These suits are emergency only, they don't contain thrusters. I recommend you exercise more caution when operating out in space."

Tara was gazing into his eyes. Hers were full of life, the wetness made them sparkle, and her mouth still formed a small smile. She pulled his hand toward the bar she was clinging to, making him grab it as well.

"Stay here. I'll open the chute."

She pushed herself up into the chute, placing a hand on an exterior panel. Her bare hands tapped on the controls, she was fast, the codes flew by as he watched. The round hatch retracted into the side of the ship, a pile of twisted steel, cardboard and other junk floated inside, their path was blocked.

J pulled himself toward Tara. "What do we do now?"

"I'll blow the garbage. You need to take a strong hold, the pressure will be great."

J grabbed on tight with both hands, pinning himself into the metal panel of the ship. A loud roar sounded as the junk slipped by, the pressure nearly pulled him off his perch. His head swung up, the path was clear and Tara proceeded inside, waving him in. The chute went on for a hundred yards, at the end was another large hatch. Tara decoded it while closing the one they'd entered, once closed, gravity came back suddenly. J hit the ground with a thud, slamming into his hip. Tara climbed into the ship hatch as J hobbled in behind her, finding a room filled with boxes of junk and trash. A single light shined, illuminating it in a dim purple. J had trouble finding his way and bumped into several boxes along the way.

"Where to now?" he asked, knowing Tara was a walking map.

"There should be an access panel over here. I'll be able to tell you more when I download the ship's data."

J scanned the room as Tara manipulated the ship's data system, then stood silently, watching her work. It made him uneasy to be around her, she was a sort of replicant after all, though not the typical ones he'd faced. Still, Ariel distrusted her and she knew more of this world than he did. Tara tapped a final button, opening the door then turned to him with a childlike smile. J didn't return it and, after moving through the door with her, questioned it. *Was she untrustworthy or was that Ariel talking in his head?* They continued into the vast halls of the Forte, stopping at every turn to verify that the security systems were offline. Tara had hacked the system, giving her access to all of the security controls and settings. After a couple of corners, J realized he didn't even know where they were going or what the plan was.

"So, where are we going again?"

"You said we needed to get Ariel and the doctor. They're being held in the detention center on floor 18, cell block A-113. Should we go somewhere else?"

She stopped and stared at him, her eyes raised, head tilted like a cat.

J's eyes danced around. "No, no that sounds good... any enemies on the way?"

"4K."

"4K? What do you mean 4K? Four enemies?" J scrunched up his face, trying to decipher her code.

"Four-thousand."

"Four-thousand?! Four-thousand what...bad guys?"

Without flinching and almost cold she replied, "Mediators."

J believed his heart just stopped. He pressed his back against the wall, dropping his jaw, and with a sharp exhale placed his hands on his knees.

"Are you okay, J?" she asked, leaning in. "We must go quickly, there are four of them about to join us in the hall."

J collected himself and nodded. *Four-thousand. Was this ship that much larger? Had he even seen that many before?* His mind raced, attempting to contemplate what she'd said. J heard thunderous footsteps echoing from just beyond the far doorway. He felt a tug on his hand, Tara was coaxing him onward, placing a finger over her lips. She quickly placed a hand on the doorplate and flipped him inside, following closely behind, shutting the door. She pinned him to the wall, holding him up, her eyes flickering in the light as she stared back into his eyes. He was about to speak when she slapped a hand over his mouth, the footsteps thundered as they approached, stopping at the door. J placed a hand on his thigh, finding the holster. He slid his hand onto the etched handle. Tara shook her head at him, he paused, her strength was immense and his body hurt from her herculean pin. Her soft hand still held his mouth tight, the footsteps continued down the hall the opposite direction. She released him, his body thanked her as he massaged his jaw.

"What was that?"

Tara moved around the room, her motions tight as she downloaded her surroundings. "86304ECS, but data says he is more commonly referred to as Riku."

"That was Riku?"

J cringed as he placed his hand tightly on his blaster. It was at that time, he realized she didn't have one. He unstrapped his and tossed it to her.

"What's this for?" she asked, catching it.

"You don't have one, I have another. Take it."

She examined it, flipping it in her hand the way Zane did, then pointed it at him. He swallowed. *What did I just do?*

CHAPTER THIRTY ONE

J fell back against the wall, Tara still pointing the blaster directly at his head. She spun it again, grasping the handle backward and tossing it back to him.

"You keep it, I prefer hand to hand. I calculate we can make it to the detention center without an engagement."

Her voice was unwavering as if it was already a fact, her body extruded a heavy sigh as she approached him.

"The threat is gone, we must go."

"Okay."

Tara opened the door, her pace quick as they moved down the hallway. J worked hard to keep up as her mechanical body didn't need any rest, his did. After rounding 5 more corners and running through 8 rooms, he finally tugged on her shoulder. "This is a great pace and all, but I need a break."

His heart-rate peaked, his breathing labored, body slouched resting his palms on his knees.

"If we slow or stop, I'll have to recalculate our path. We may encounter trouble."

J slumped down against the wall, knees bent arms hanging over them. He almost welcomed trouble if it meant a break.

Tara stood motionless studying him. "You're right, you need a break. Your body is frail and cannot continue at this current pace."

"Thanks," he said in between breaths.

He disregarded the frail comment, had little energy

to fight it. Tara tightened up like a cat whose ears heard a mouse in the cupboard.

"We must go!"

She grabbed his dangling hand, rocketing him to his feet. "What? Wait, what? You just said we could rest."

The ship's siren sounded, a wavering tone filled the hall, lights began running from one end of the corridor to the other. J's head swiveled from one side to the next, his arms stiffened and hung tight toward the ground.

"What's going on?

"I missed a scanner and it found the ship anchored outside. They've alerted the crew that there are stowaways onboard."

J's eyes rolled in the back of his head, his mouth hung open. Just when he thought they were going to have a smooth trip for once. He caressed his blaster, pulling it from its dark sheath.

Tara started down the hall. "Two will be behind us soon, calculating a better route."

That didn't sound good, he hoped they didn't run into Riku. They rounded a corner into an empty hallway, the door at the far end sprung open, two mediators stepped toward them.

"Halt. Identify yourself."

"I thought you could—"

"I'm sorry, J. I just lost my rights, we're blind minus the map I downloaded."

J raised a blaster, letting a few shots fly.

"Okay, well...quickest route then."

He shot a few more, eliminating one. The other opened fire. Ducking, they slipped back around the corner.

J pressed his back against the wall, swiveling his head. "Well, which way?"

"I have the route but we—"

"We need to move, and fast."

Tara's head swung around. Grabbing his wrist, she pulled him down the hallway and into an expansive gym. Equipment was strewn about the two story room. It was well-lit and filled with a small number of men in shorts and tank tops. He paused a moment as they all stopped mid-exercise to gawk at him, one tossed a barbell onto the floor, J felt the vibrations in his feet. He froze, a chill running through his spine. Riku stood at the back of the room towering over the others. He stomped forward, throwing equipment aside. Forty-five pound plates flew like china dishes, J raised the blaster to aim.

"Watch out!" Tara cried.

His firing hand was hit, dislodging his weapon. One of the men had lunged forward, attacking him. His body twisted away. J glanced back, ducking the second strike, then landed a shot to the gut on his attacker. Over the crumpled body, he sighted Riku continuing toward them, grunting, his pace quickening. Tara engaged one of the other soldiers nearby, dropping him effortlessly. Spinning after a roundhouse kick to another, she ended up next to J, her hand wrapped under his armpit, her eyes fixed on his.

"Best if we run."

J didn't wait, Riku was nearly upon them. They dashed toward the door, J drawing his other blaster, firing blindly behind him. The blasts ricochet off walls, the soldiers ducked avoiding the deadly ordinance. Riku marched on unfazed. J ran at full speed, skidding into the hall, his head staring at the ground attempting to gain speed. Tara was in lead and abruptly came to a halt. Unaware, he drilled her in the back, his body bouncing off her like a new mattress. His butt hit the floor. Through her legs he saw two mediators at the end of the hallway, their weapons ready to fire.

Tara twisted her head, searching behind them. "The mediators are yours, I'll take Riku."

J's head snapped back as Tara ran past him, his eyes fixated on her stride. Riku stood at the threshold, his hands balling to fists. Tara came in with a right hook, Riku blocked it throwing one of his own. Tara flew into the wall, bounced onto the floor. Riku moved forward, his eyes focused on J.

Tara bounced to her feet. "J, go. I'll delay him as long as possible."

She threw another punch, hitting Riku in the side. He winced, but fought back blindly, his tunnel vision set on J. J turned around, the mediators were nearly on top of him. He let off a barrage of blasts, dropping them both. Looking back, Tara was still engaging Riku like a fly on a horse, landing shots then being pushed away. J climbed to his feet. Raising the blaster, he fired

a shot hitting Riku square in the chest. The scorch mark
smoked as he continued on. Tara landed a kick to his
thigh, he grabbed her leg, lifting her up. He snarled, tossing her toward J. She bounced then slid to his feet.

She pressed herself up. "Run!"

J shot again with the same result then glanced down
at Tara. *She's just a robot.* Yet, he didn't want to leave her.
She didn't need to be sacrificed for him, she seemed so
real. Riku was only a few steps away now. *If he was going
to go, he'd better do it now.* Tara ignited upward, landing
an uppercut to Riku's jaw. He stumbled back a step. Tara
wasted no time going to work on his torso, drawing Riku's
attention.

"Go now, J. I'll run out of power soon if I'm to keep
this up."

She continued her barrage of attacks, Riku blocking some and missing others. J turned and bolted down
the hall, taking out another mediator as he rounded a
corner. He ducked into a corridor, then it occurred to
him, *Where the heck was he going?* His map was getting
pummeled by Riku. Finding a nearby door, he hopped in
pressing, his back against the wall just inside. The door
closed, his movement had tripped the room's lighting
illuminating the small bedroom he now occupied. *Think.*
Pulling the blaster to his face, he saw that the power cell
read 75%. He looked at his wrist. "The Datacle." He
slapped himself in the forehead, just now remembering
it was there as if it magically appeared on his wrist. He
pulled up the menus, attempting to figure out what to do.

Calling anyone seemed out of the question for fear of the transmission becoming intercepted. There was no ship map, Tara had the only copy to his knowledge. Learning on the job was proving to be rather difficult in this environment, and stressful, to say the least. Gone were the days where things came easily to him. His mind drifted to his maintenance class, throwing answers back at Mr. MacDunna like they were simple math problems. Now he was faced with much more difficult questions, far beyond his scope. He stared at the Datacle, hoping it would shout back at him or give him some advice. It came alive with an incoming transmission from Tara.

"Are you okay, J?"

"Tara? Yeah, where are you? Where's Riku? Where do we go?"

"Slow down. I'm fine, Riku's not a problem anymore. Where are you?

J looked around, he had no clue where he was. "A bedroom, I don't know."

"Send me your location on the Datacle, I'll come and get you."

J had done this before. *Finally, something I can do.* He tapped the buttons as fast as his fingers could go, the last menu displayed the word "send". He stared at it a moment.

"You okay, J?"

"Yeah, just thinking." He pressed the final key, "message sent" displayed under the picture of Tara.

"Great, we'll be there in a moment."

The picture faded out. *At least Tara had the map, and she seemed ok.* His forehead tightened. What happened to Riku? Did she say "we"? The door opened and an arm flew in, grabbing his blaster and flipping it around, pointing it at him. Tara was at the other end, sparks danced on her right shoulder. Riku stepped in with a big grin on his face. J stared back at Tara, his face distorted.

"I'm sorry, J, but this is what my programming requires."

She waved the weapon to the door, he sulked out into the hallway dragging his feet, Riku chuckled as he passed. *Good thing Ariel's not here to see this, I'd never hear the end of it.* Tara nudged him along. He walked through the halls silently, there wasn't anything to say, she was a machine, simple as that. He marched in front of the two as they navigated the ship's inner arteries, eventually emerging into the detention center. A man stood behind a desk adorned with a set of controls. Tall, boney almost skeletal features formed his face, his sunken eyes judged J as they approached.

"Is this the one? The son of Arcturus?"

Riku nodded, pushing J toward the man who made his way around the desk. In his hand was a pistol-like device. He forced J's hand up, placing the barrel end of it on the large bone of his wrist. He tried to pull back but Riku grabbed his forearm, his hand wrapped entirely around it and squeezed. Pain shot through his arm causing him to stop the struggle. The skeletal man frowned then tapped a trigger, embedding a metal disk onto his wrist. It was smaller than a penny and the back side of it shot into his wrist fusing to the bone.

"This will make you easier to find in the future." He walked back to the controls and played with the buttons like a man on an organ, opening up a door behind him. "Did you search him?

Tara shook her head. Grabbing his shoulders, she ran her palms roughly over his body, raking it, ensuring nothing went unnoticed. Her hand hit a bulge on his right thigh, she knelt down opening the pocket. She stood up holding the device Grant had given him. The skeletal man's right eye tightened as he tilted his head.

"What is that?"

Tara held it up examining it in the light, she twisted it around. "I don't know. Takamori will want to see it."

She didn't know? He'd forgotten about it, his mind flashed back to Grant telling him that she was supposed to explain what it was. Riku released his forearms, shoving him forward. Tara walked beside him as they proceeded through the entrance. Inside, four doors hung two on each side, the first one opened revealing a small room with a bed. Riku shoved him inside while Tara watched, her face solemn, her eyes flicked about as she stood there in silence.

"Takamori will be requesting your presence within the hour."

The door closed with a hiss, J leaned forward letting his head hit the glass. He let out a big groan still leaning on the window, his eyes staring at the ground. *How did I get here? Was Ariel still alive?* Nothing was for certain. He straightened up and moved toward the bed, sitting down on it with a heavy bounce. He interlocked his hands, spinning his thumbs around themselves. *He needed to escape, but how?*

Searching for any weakness, he stood up and felt all of the walls, including the rear one which popped out a toilet. He attempted to dislodge the toilet, no luck. His attempt to kick it only managed to hurt his leg. He sat back down on the bed, placing his palms on his forehead as he leaned his elbows on his knees. The door opened, his head snapped over. Tara and Riku stood waiting. Tara marched into the cell, in her hand were metal bands, like the ones Dillon had used. She didn't speak, just slapped the restraints on. He didn't struggle, it wasn't worth the energy. Tara grabbed the link between them, standing him up. She guided him out with a nod to Riku who returned it with a sly grin.

"Stay here," she instructed J.

He obliged with a quick glance at Riku, Tara walked over to the cell across from him, opening the door.

"You stupid piece of programmable machinery! Get off me, I can get up myself!"

He knew that voice and momentarily forgot the predicament he was in. A smile grew on his face. He leaned forward, attempting to look around Riku which proved difficult. He was able to see a glimpse, it was what he'd hoped for. Ariel emerged from the small cell, arms behind her back, persuaded forward by Tara.

"I can walk on my own. No need to be so pushy."

Her eyes had been fighting with Tara, but now flipped toward J. She stepped forward trying to run to him, her attempt was foiled by Tara jerking her back, knocking her on her butt. Ariel stood up and turned around her face tight.

"If you were human, I'd call you a traitor, but you're not even worth that."

Tara didn't respond, her face blank she pushed Ariel forward. Ariel trudged along, looking back at J, her mouth cracked in a small smile. Riku pushed J forward before he could speak to Ariel, his greeting would have to wait. Riku's heavy steps vibrated the floor as they moved along. J was tempted to break the silence, but the thick breathing of the giant kept his mouth shut. He hunkered his head down, holding his shoulders up as Riku's warm breath hit the top of his head. In no time, they entered the bridge which was nearly identical to the Parádeisos, only smaller with less seats. Dead center stood Takamori, to his right Novikov flanked by E-Rats, behind them a grand windscreen full of stars and the Moon to the left. In the left corner the Parádeisos was displayed as a model, rotating 360 degrees. Stat numbers floated around it, cannon count, estimated soldiers, fighter craft, officers, it seemed they knew everything about it. A glowing red circle floated on the display indicating that the Parádeisos was still out of range. Riku shoved him forward, J almost fell on his face, stumbling. The same occurred to Ariel. Both stood a few feet in front of Takamori, his face triumphant as if he just placed his opponent in check-mate.

"You are a hard man to keep caged." He circled them once, running his eyes up and down both of them. "You also bested Katergaris...but I learned some very important knowledge from Dr. Huergo."

He waved his hand, demanding something, the doctor stepped out from behind them. J looked over to see a tan man with jet black hair, a large round nose and a small chin, his face etched with small wrinkles.

"I believe that you have a data disc which will help me acquire a great weapon. Where is it?"

J's mouth opened as he hunted for an answer, his eyes drifting from the doctor to Ariel then back to Takamori. He searched the deep vault of his mind trying to remember if he knew what Takamori was asking for. Nothing, there was nothing. His blank stare continued gazing through his captor. Takamori slammed a foot down in front of him pointing at Ariel. Tara grabbed her bindings, forcing her to her knees. Ariel grimaced as she hit the floor, her eyes throwing daggers.

"She will die if you don't tell me where it is!"

J fidgeted and began to dance on his toes, his eyes searching the ground for the answer. Then it came to him. *Maybe it was the disk that Dominik gave him.* His head shifted side to side, he almost had it. Riku moved over, placing his hand around Ariel's neck, tightening his grip. Her throat wheezed as she gasped for air.

"It's on Earth!"

357

Takamori held up a hand, he could hear Ariel's breath recovering.

"Where on Earth?"

"A hangar. It's in a ship, a Tetriack," his voice shook.

He had no clue where the ship was, the autopilot had taken him to Earth, he dug deep trying to recall. The female, the hotel, Ariel saving him in.

"Artinetineal?"

Ariel held in a laugh, she knew what he meant. But Takamori didn't. He clenched his fist, Riku tightened his grip, Ariel squirmed for air.

"Okay, okay, stop! Let her go, she knows where it is. You kill her, you won't find it."

Takamori leered at him, unamused. His hand went up stopping the chokehold, his gaze dropped to Ariel.

"So where is it?

Ariel smiled back, not saying a word, Takamori snapped his fingers. Riku released her neck, quickly grabbing both arms with his hands and stepping on her calves, he wrenched her arms up past her threshold, she screamed in pain. Takamori snapped his fingers again the tension loosened.

"Where is it?" he glanced back at J.

J held his ground, he truly didn't know the correct name of the place. The numbers floated around in his head, but he couldn't remember which one was correct.

Takamori's face wrinkled as it grew red. "I don't have the patience for this!"

He glanced at one of the men behind him, the man

unstrapped a sword, throwing it to Tara. "He doesn't need two hands, take one for me."

Tara flipped the sheath around holding it in her left hand. She popped it up with her thumb then drew it out with precision and grace. Takamori nodded to two other men, they scurried over, holding J's arms out in front of him still bound. Tara positioned herself for the strike, two hands on the Katana, she raised it over her head.

CHAPTER THIRTY TWO

J closed his eyes. *What more could he do?* He thought of his father who seemed to know everything. *Did he know this? Did he build a contingency plan for this? Who was he kidding, was his father even real or just a projection?* He gritted his teeth, hoping for as little pain as possible.

"Argentina, Sector 15, southeast quadrant, hangar 9."

J opened his eyes, his head whipping to Ariel. A tear ran down her cheek, her nose crinkled. J twisted his head over to Tara, her blade still ready to strike, her eyes fixated on her target.

"Enough, Tara."

Takamori plodded over to J, holding his head high, his slits of eyes focused on J's.

"You will take Riku and four men with these two to retrieve the disk. Bring it straight back here, understood?"

Riku bowed slightly as did Tara who then sheathed her blade. She pulled the device out of a pocket and held it up.

"What's this?" Takamori asked.

"I don't know, J was carrying it. I thought you might know, but it just looks like a paperweight to me."

Takamori took it with a small laugh followed by a much longer, evil laugh.

"A paperweight...yes a paperweight. Only a young, dumb Earthling would carry such a trivial piece as a souvenir."

He strutted to a podium and set it down.

"This will be my souvenir from the great son of Arcturus on the day I stole the Earth from him."

He laughed again gazing out into space, the Earth came into view as they rounded the Moon.

"You will be mine," he vowed, his eyes glowing maniacally, the Earth flickering on their surface.

Tara grabbed J's bindings and tugged him along.

"Don't try anything," she said as they passed Ariel.

Riku released his stance on her legs and brought her to her feet, escorting her behind the others. Four men took up position behind them, all with Katana blades and pulse rifles. J stumbled along, hoping to find a time to escape, nothing. They boarded a small craft fitting all eight of them with two seats to spare. Tara climbed into the pilot seat along with one of the other men while Riku sat across from Ariel and J. J leaned into Ariel, desperate for her touch, she leaned back.

"You okay?" he placed a hand on her thigh.

"Artinetineal?" she smirked.

"What? I couldn't remember what it was called."

Ariel continued to snicker, she looked up at Riku. "Learn how to talk yet, Andre?"

Riku's face was stone, his head rocked slightly along with the ship, he let out a small growl. Ariel smirked back at him then began searching the ship.

"Any ideas?" J asked.

"Not yet. Besides, while Zangef over here can't talk, I'm pretty sure he can still hear."

Ariel had a point, it would be pretty stupid to hatch a plan right in front of their captor. He began to survey their surroundings himself. *Doing anything now would be dumb, they were in the void of space. Once they landed, on the other hand, all bets were off.* He had to figure out a way to communicate with Ariel without Riku finding out. He tried squeezing her thigh, but that was met with a dirty look. So, he tried a few other tactics involving head nods and eye rolls, all followed with laughter. He finally gave up. Maybe Ariel had a plan, she always had a plan... almost always. J felt the ship shake as it touched down to Earth. The door opened and they found themselves staring at the Tetriack.

"Okay, J you're with me. Riku, stay here with Ariel, best if we split them up."

She shoved J forward, he stumbled toward the ship, waddling on the way. He opened the cockpit and slid his arms inside, attempting to reach the storage container. He fumbled around, unsuccessful. He slipped back down.

"Can you take these off me? I can't reach it."

Tara leaned in seemingly willing to unlock his cuffs without further explanation. J watched her unlock his bindings, she looked at him.

"J—"

He didn't waste any time and hit her in the jaw with a well placed fist, her head snapped to the side. He took off running toward Ariel, shaking his hand in pain. He had forgotten she wasn't flesh and bone and his knuckles were paying for it. Ariel, seeing the attack, tried to spin away, but was met with two of the soldiers grabbing her still bound arms. She huffed loudly as Riku grumbled. J continued his run, but felt a shock on his chest, his body convulsed mid-stride, crumpling to the ground from the stun charge shutting down his motor function. Tara approached and picked him up by the back of his shirt.

"Bring the girl, have her get the disk."

Riku grumbled, approaching Ariel, she got the hint and began walking to the Tetriack. Tara turned, dragging J along like a grocery bag, his body still limp. She lifted his body over the rail of the ship, plopping him down into the seat. J's body slumped, still unable to move. Tara grabbed his bindings, releasing them then taking his hand, placed it on the panel above the storage container. The ship came alive and ejected the drawer, J's eyes still had movement and they flicked over to the disk as Tara reached in grabbing it. She triumphantly held it up, Riku stopped a few feet away, his nose twitched as he knocked Ariel to her knees. He held out his hand requesting the device, scrutinizing Tara's actions.

She sauntered over holding the disk at eye level. "You want to give it to the boss?"

She flipped it up into the air, Riku's eyes tracked it as he reached his hand up to catch it. Tara lunged forward, drawing her razor sharp blade, executing a sweeping strike to his abdomen. His eyes popped out, pain surged through his body as she swung back the opposite direction, placing an X on his stomach. Riku stumbled back with a loud roar. Tara floated in the air, her sweeping strike spinning her onto her knees gracefully in front of Ariel, the disk held in her hand. She'd swiped it from the ground. Ariel twisted her head, slightly speechless, as Tara reached around releasing her restraints. Riku recovered from the strikes with a growl. Clutching his stomach, he snatched Tara by the arm. She sliced at his arm, the edge of the blade nearly hitting bone, Riku screamed in pain, tossing her into the Tetriack. J slowly became mobile, his extremities had feeling, his fingers began to move on command. He raised his wobbling head, peering over the rail as Ariel spun into a kick landing a blow. Riku's head snapped to the side, his arm releasing his abs, she took the opening landing two jabs. Riku swiped down with a mighty fist as Ariel rolled away. She tumbled to her feet immediately being hit with a shot from one of the men still at their delivery ship. She grabbed her arm, wincing in pain. Riku advanced, his heavy step vibrating the ground. Lifting his undamaged arm, he adjusted for the strike. It was short-lived as his back arched. Tara stood post-strike, staring at the giant. She looked past him to Ariel who hit the deck, more shots coming from the enemy ship. Tara glanced over at the soldiers, all four in a line, advancing. Two focused on Ariel the other two on her. J's arms were finally mobile, but weak. He placed his shaking hand on the ship's plate, the system menu came alive. He tapped buttons one at a time, it was all he could manage. Ariel looked up as the giant swung around, desperately attempting to hit his attacker. Tara flipped backward, a barrage of fire flying past her. Ariel came to her feet, running toward J. Riku advanced, pounding his feet, holding his wounds blood leaking through his fingers. J tapped a final button.

"Voice recognition activated, say command."

"Engage target in front," he ordered, his voice shaking.

"Confirm target."

His eyes shifted to the windscreen, each person was outlined in red a line giving each target a name. He locked onto Riku and the soldiers identifiers.

"Two, Four, Five, Six, Seven."

"Confirm Auto-rifles?"

J read the ordinance load out flashing on the bottom of the screen, he found the one he wanted. He looked, up Ariel was gone.

"Negative, Anti-Armor rockets. Fire!"

The hangar glowed white, blinding everyone. The Tetriack trembled as the rockets burst, his hearing stopped, nothing but silence as he crushed his eyelids together. His breath slowed as the ship stilled. Ears ringing, he readied himself to open his eyes. He prayed that Ariel had made it, that his desperate attack didn't prove fatal to her. He opened his eyes, white smoke swirled through the hangar, a deafening silence filled the air as the ringing stopped. He body was close to normal, but he still felt a bit drunk as he fumbled with the ship's rail. He pulled himself over it, tumbling to the ground. He groaned as he hit and immediately zeroed in on Ariel, face down, unconscious a few feet from him.

"Ariel!"

He pressed himself up, crawling to her. He placed a hand on her shoulder. His body trembled, his lip quivered when she didn't respond. He moved her hair away from her face. He beautiful skin was blacked by the battle, her hair dry, yet she still looked perfect. He nudged her once more, still nothing. On his knees, he closed his eyes.

"This is when you give sleeping beauty a kiss."

J's eyes snapped open, Ariel's one eye peeked back under a heavy eyelid. Lifting her up, he leaned in, giving her a long desperate kiss. His once tense muscles relaxed. She reached up, wrapped her arms around his neck, her lips pressed to his. His world disappeared. The troubles and strife, the challenges, all were gone. He wanted this to last forever. They released their kiss and he gazed down on her beautiful face. Ariel's icy blue eyes glowed back at his, she placed a palm on his cheek wiping a tear from his eye.

"Don't go soft on me yet, battle's not over."

Her head shifted over to their targets, J's followed, nothing remained. The hangar floor was littered with parts of the ship. J sat up to get a better look, his head hit the bottom of the Tetriack. J grunted in pain, rubbing his head.

Ariel snickered. "You can save the day, but you can't seem to save yourself."

J twisted up his lip, looking down on her. He wanted to say something witty, but nothing came to mind.

"You have the disk?"

J straightened up, smacking his head once again. Ariel just shook her head this time.

"Tara had it," he said, vigorously rubbing his head.

Ariel leaned over on one elbow, her other arm draped over her body. J wanted to freeze time and capture the picture forever.

"Well, I hope she still has it. Was that part of the plan the whole time?"

J had no idea. If it was he'd been left in the dark. He shrugged his shoulders then crouched down back on all fours, crawling out backward. After double-checking he was clear and a laugh from Ariel, he stood up helping her to her feet as well.

"What's on the disc?" she asked as they rummaged through the wreckage.

"I haven't got the slightest. Dominik gave it to me in Poland. I think that's where I was."

"Who's Dominik?"

"He picked me up and outfitted me with the weapons I had when I went looking for you in...Sector 15."

"But who was he? You had modified weapons, Sector 15 is a no weapon zone, they're disabled. Did you get any more info?"

J kept shifting through the debris. "He just said he was a caretaker, like Will. Said he was Will's twin actually. It was eerie how alike they looked."

Ariel dropped a piece of scrap she was holding. "A lot like him or exactly?"

J just realized he'd never known a twin before, matter of fact ,nobody he knew had any siblings. *Another control brought to you by TK.* He turned to answer her question.

"Exactly, but isn't that what twins are supposed to look like?"

The wreckage near his feet moved, J jumped back, nearly tripping on the debris, his hands raised. He looked down to see a leg moving under a large piece of metal.

"Ariel."

He pointed down at the wreckage then began to attempt to move it. While not necessarily heavy, it was awkward. Ariel arrived and the two of them flipped it off the body. Tara was laying on her back, her neck flickered as sparks continued to shoot out. Her whole body was scorched. J knelt down next to her, checking her head. Her eyes were shut, her legs convulsing.

"Does it have the disk?"

J pried open her hand, it was still there. He flipped it up to Ariel who caught it, holding it up into the light.

"What's on it?" she whispered.

J stood up and looked around. There were three of them and one ship, he knew from experience he and Ariel could fit, but how would they get Tara out?

"You ready to blow this popsicle stand?" Ariel asked with a smirk.

J stared back down at Tara. "How are we going to leave?"

Ariel looked at him then down at Tara, she shook her head. "No. That thing's not coming with us. It did enough already. You know me and you barely fit in that relic. No way we can fit that thing in there, too."

J fixated on Tara, he placed his hands on his hips like so many time when fixing the harvester back home.

"No...Grant wanted me to take care of her. We need to bring her back."

"Well what are we going to do, teleport her? This isn't Star Trek!"

J lifted one eyebrow. Ariel rolled her eyes. Tilting her head back, mouth open, she let out a sharp sigh. Any other time, she would have laughed at his response, but not this time. Past Ariel he saw the Tetriack, his eyes lit up.

"I have an idea."

CHAPTER THIRTY THREE

The stars grew brighter as they left Earth's atmosphere, it felt like a lifetime ago when he was in a similar situation Ariel sitting on his lap in the small spacecraft. She reluctantly let J fly at his pleadings of needing practice, they were heading to the Parádeisos to join the others. The screen lit up with a green circle, the name Parádeisos displayed underneath. Behind it, a bright Moon glowed warmly. A message popped up on screen, Ariel tapped it without hesitation. Dmitry appeared.

"Admiral," Ariel started, "we have the disk, but I'm afraid we don't have the doctor."

"That's not a priority right now. Takamori is launching fighters to intercept us. They'll be here soon. Was J able to plant the device?"

Ariel looked over her shoulder.

"What device?" J shook his head mouth half open.

Ariel turned back to Dmitry. "What device, sir?"

"Grant gave J a device, was he able to plant it in the control room?"

J remembered that Tara had the device and gave it to Takamori. *What was it?*

"Yes, it's with Takamori the last I saw. Tara gave it to him."

Grant waddled into the picture. "Is Tara with you? She has the codes to detonate the device."

"Detonate? It was a bomb? The whole time I was carrying a bomb in my pants?!"

J wondered if things would have gone differently had he know earlier. He thought about Tara capturing him. *Was that in the plans the whole time?* Ariel's fingers worked the ship's systems. J remembered Tara's selfless efforts to rescue them, he nudged her in the side.

"Tara must have had that planned the whole time," he whispered.

Ariel tightened her jaw and sat back on him, hard. He groaned.

"We have your toy, but it's not going to be transmitting any codes anytime soon."

Grant looked as though he didn't comprehend it at first, then realizing what she meant bit his bottom lip. Dmitry came back into the picture.

"We need the codes to detonate the device onboard the Forte, it's the only way to cripple the ship."

J scanned the screen, over a dozen dots appeared, more growing by the second. His chest tightened. "What are those?"

"Fighter craft from the Forte...Admiral, we'll be dropping off a package, open hangar 15. And I'm requesting support for an assault run."

The Admiral nodded, "Very well. I'll have my men standing by." He looked to the side, his body tight. "Scramble the fighters."

The picture dissolved as the Parádeisos grew in the windscreen.

"What exactly are we doing?"

"Your insistence on bringing that thing is going to pay

off. We're delivering it to Grant so he can detonate the device, but first we're going to need to save the doctor,"

Ariel grabbed J's wrists and popped them out of the controls.

"Sorry, J. Training later. It'll be quicker this way."

She pushed the thruster full forward, accelerating to top speed her target fixed off the nose, hangar bay 15. J still didn't know what they were doing so it probably was the best decision to let her fly, plus it left his hands free to rest on either side of her waist. He'd missed touching her and wasn't about to waste the opportunity. The Parádeisos loomed closer, engulfing the entire screen. The hangar bay doors opened, Ariel tapped on the screen bringing up the weapons systems. J crunched his eyes together.

"What are you doing?"

"No time to land, not with all those fighters. In an amazing stroke of luck, placing Tara in the Tetriack's bomb bay was the best thing we could've done."

J still didn't understand what was about to happen, but he trusted her, he trusted her with his life. She entered the hangar, only reducing the thrusters slightly. J tightened his grip on her waist as the interior of the ship screamed toward them. Ariel reversed the thrusters while opening the bomb bay doors. The ship reversed course leaving Tara floating in the hangar. Ariel twisted the ship around, the armada of fighters closing in. She slammed the thruster forward, the ship accelerating, her body pressed into his.

"Okay fly boy, your turn. I'll work the weapons. For what we're going to do, I'm going to be more accurate then the auto-turrets."

They exchanged controls. J left the settings alone, the course the same.

"What are we going to do exactly?"

He still hadn't received a full answer and felt it beneficial to know, under the circumstances.

"We have to engage those fighters, that ship has three times the number of the Parádeisos. We also need the doctor ,so I hope you've got your running legs on."

"But we don't even know where he is. That ship is huge."

"You leave that to me."

The Forte expanded in the screen and fighter craft were nearly in range. J felt a bead of sweat roll down his forehead as he tightened his grip on the controls, the tiny ships like a swarm of bees off the nose.

"Do your best to avoid them and target the far side of the ship."

J swallowed, twisting his head slightly. This was going to be challenging to say the least. Still, his previous experience would guide him. Ariel switched the shield to full front, diverting all the energy she could. She enabled the manual weapons, missiles, plasma balls, and a few other features he'd never seen before. When the time was right, he'd ask her about them. The first wave of ships hit firing blasts all around. J did his best to dodge them, spinning and flipping the ship, even rolling it a few times.

Ariel constantly switched weapons, firing at multiple enemies, J couldn't believe how well she could track so many targets. The Forte wasn't too far off, Ariel shouted out directions to the hangar, he adjusted accordingly, soon finding themselves on final. A message popped up, Ariel tapped it then turned her attention back to the swarm.

"Ariel, Grant says the transmitter range in Tara was damaged. We must be closer to detonate the device so I'm maneuvering the Parádeisos into position. I've shifted the ship around for a broadside attack and launched the fleet, we're taking heavy losses. We'll only get one shot at this. I suggest you fall back and help protect the ship to keep you out of the blast radius."

"Sorry, Admiral. Can't do that. We're inbound to pick up the good doctor."

Dmitry began a rebuttal, but Ariel switched off the comm. That was the Ariel he knew. J flipped the craft around, more fighters shifted to the back side of the Forte. The hangar bay was still open, its doors beginning to close.

"Better hurry!"

"Gonna need some help, the thruster is pegged!"

Ariel frantically tapped the menus while still warding off attackers. She diverted nearly all the shields to the thrusters, J felt a kick in the pants. The doors continued on their path. He steadied his course, his tunnel vision locked onto the opening, the attacking ships fading away. The Tetriack zipped into the hangar, sparks flew as the edge of the ship hit the hangar door. Ariel kicked out the landing gear and opened fire on the few mediators standing on the landing pad. J planted the craft hard onto the surface, the ship shaking from the impact. Without hesitation, Ariel opened the canopy and, hopping out, ran toward the exit. J followed as quickly as he could, only then realizing that they were unarmed. *This whole play it by ear stuff sure had its disadvantages.* They managed to make it clean to the exit and slipped into the hallway behind.

"Where to now?"

Ariel read the hallway signs, her eyes scanning about. She pointed as she ran down the empty hall. J hoped this would continue as the ship's lights flickered and a siren screamed. He trailed Ariel on their journey through the ship's arteries, passing multiple rooms not seeing a soul or mediator. Ariel stopped at an elevator door, planting her hand on the control.

"Detention center should be up a few floors."

The elevator door opened, a mediator stood menacing, raising its weapon. "Halt. Ident—"

J threw his body at the machine, pinning it to the back wall, his hand dislodging the weapon. He pressed himself off it, falling back toward the weapon. The mediator lunged for him, but found Ariel's foot instead. J rounded up the blaster, firing two shots into the enemy's chest. The mediator fell into a heap on the floor. Ariel looked over at him nodding, her bottom lip pressed to the top.

"Any plans on getting out of here? That ship's not going to hold three of us."

Ariel commanded the elevator to go to the detention center.

Leaning back against the wall, she replied, "Should be ships big enough for the three of us in one of the hangars. We'll worry about that once we get Dr. Huergo."

The doors opened into the detention center, the same boney man still behind the controls, his hands working the screens. His eyes flicked up, spotting them. J took a pot shot at him, hitting the console, the man ducked. The lights turned red and a new siren blared out.

"He must have hit an emergency switch. We have to move fast."

Ariel ran toward the console, jumping over it, slapping the panic button, shutting the sound off. The boney man cowered next to the controls.

Ariel's eyes fixed onto his. "Where's Dr. Huergo?"

"You don't have the clearance for that information."

J rounded the corner his blaster trained on the man, he shot his leg.

"That clearance enough for you?" J asked.

He raised the blaster, his target now the man's head. The man shook as his eyes snapped from J to Ariel. "He's on the bridge, he's on the bridge," his voice cracked.

Ariel slapped her face with both hands, pulling them down to her chin, let out a groan. She bent down, grabbing the man's collar, pulling him to his feet. Her eyes intense glaring into his. "Take us there."

The man nodded his head like a bobble head.

They escorted the boney man to the elevator, he remained silent, only giving quick responses to any questions asked. J kept the weapon in his back as they navigated the ship with him in the lead. They managed to walk by mediators without trouble, having a prisoner was proving useful. The last elevator they rode opened to the bridge, they hadn't discussed a plan. Old Ariel was back. J pushed the boney man forward onto the bridge and scanned the room. Only two guards with weapons stood between them and the doctor, the rest were technicians manipulating the controls of the ship. Outside the screen, tiny explosions popped up like fireworks on the 4th of July. The Parádeisos was being overtaken, the ship turned allowing the Forte to come alongside of it. Fighter aircraft zipped around, J stopped focusing on the screen, looking for the doctor. He found him standing next to Takamori and Novikov, the three were discussing something.

"Halt!" One of the guards had finally noticed them.

J and Ariel stopped. Takamori and the others turned to investigate the commotion. Ariel dropped down, sweeping her leg under the guard's feet, his arms flailing in the air as he smacked the ground. She rolled over, disarming him on the way, aiming the business end of her newly acquired weapon at Takamori. At the same time, J shoved the skeletal man forward, turning his sights on the other guard, his shots eliminating the threat. Their prisoner scampered away, J let him go, focusing on the three up front. Takamori stood proud, studying the intruders.

He smiled. "You brought us the disk, how convenient." He took a step forward.

"Not another step," Ariel commanded. "What are you doing with Dr. Huergo?"

Takamori glanced over at him, interlocking his fingers.

"He has decided to join us. It seems what we can offer is very, how do you say it? Lucrative."

J glanced at Ariel, questioning. He didn't know anything about the doctor except that his father had sent him to find the man. *How could he be persuaded to join the Reprobi Angeli?*

"What did you offer him?" J questioned.

"A third control of the Earth and a better control system than you could offer him."

He examined the doctor's face, it told a different story.

Ariel noticed too. "You're lying."

Takamori laughed, taking a few steps toward them. J and Ariel tightened the grip on their weapons.

"It doesn't matter if he has done it willingly or not. He is going to help us and that disk of yours is the key."

"What's on the disk?" J asked, lifting the blaster.

Takamori laughed again, then with a tight devious smile. "You haven't checked? You father was a very smart man, do you think he would keep everything in one journal? The journal is but a portion of his knowledge. That disk is another. Now give it to me."

J shook his head as Takamori stepped closer.

"You don't understand the secrets we can unlock with it, wha—"

J let a blast go, drilling Takamori in the shoulder. He stumbled back clutching it in pain.

"Don't come any closer." J waved his empty hand, inviting the doctor. "Dr. Huergo, let's go." His gaze adjusted to Takamori, "You don't move another muscle."

J was calling the shots. He had the weapon, he had the disk, he was done playing games and being the pawn. They needed to leave before the device was detonated. In the screen, the Parádeisos was within target range, Dr. Huergo took a step forward then froze. Ariel looked back, inside the elevator two mediators with weapons drawn aimed at J and stood poised to strike.

"Tell your metal toys to let us by or J will blast you again," Ariel shouted, her rifle aimed at one of them.

Takamori snarled signaling for the mediators to part, Dr. Huergo jogged to the elevator, nodding at J as he passed. Ariel fell in behind him while J kept the blaster tight on Takamori's head. He stepped in as Ariel hit the switch, the doors closed, Takamori began shouting orders. The elevator started down.

"You know they're going to lock down the ship," the doctor said.

Ariel was busy scrutinizing the elevator, it stopped abruptly, nearly knocking the three of them to the floor. J and the doctor placed a hand on the wall to stabilize themselves; Ariel maintained her balance without any support.

She hopped over to the control panel. "I might be able to override this, or perhaps you could do the honors Dr. Huergo?"

The doctor slid his hand through his hair, pulling his forehead back, studying the system.

"It's been a long time since I programmed anything like an elevator."

The elevator began back up.

"Well it better come back fast, like riding a bike."

They all knew what would present itself if the elevator reached its starting point. Ariel backed into the corner of the elevator, her sights locked onto the door. J did the same, they wouldn't last long if more enemies had arrived on the bridge. Dr. Huergo tapped the keys, punching multiple buttons, slow at first but then quicker. Ariel smiled and J sensed it, too. It was coming back to him. The elevator stopped, opening the doors to the bridge. The two of them opened fire as the first enemy appeared, the door closed, a couple rounds ricocheting back into the elevator. J and Ariel ducked. The lift descended and the doctor fell to the ground. Ariel dropped her rifle, rushing over to him. She rolled him over, his chest bleeding as he held it.

"Bless it! You have any medical supplies?"

J padded himself down as if he might, he already knew the answer, nothing. All he felt was the disk. J crawled over, the doctor's eyes were heavy.

"J...J, your father was a great man, you must know this."

J nodded as he attempted to put pressure on the wound, Ariel's hands were doing the same.

"The disk...the disk contains a message from him with instructions on how to find him."

J leaned in close doing his best to stop the bleeding, the doctor's breath was short, his eyes nearly closed.

"You must stop Takamori...free Earth...and find your father. He will..."

The tension in Dr. Huergo's body eased, his breath gone. Ariel sat back as the elevator stopped, grabbed her rifle. J was still holding the doctor, hoping he would finish his thought. Ariel stood up.

"I'm sorry, J. He's gone. If you don't get on your feet, we'll never find your father. There isn't a lot of time or else we won't have a ship to get to either."

She was right, the Parádeisos was out-gunned and if it came to a showdown, the Forte being more heavily armed, would obliterate Dmitry and his friends. He snatched the rifle from the floor, the doors now open.

"You're right, it's time to find a ride."

Ariel smiled back at him. J took a deep breath look-ing out into the hall, a sign stared back at him.

> Hangar #6
> Emergency pods
> Dinning hall
> Cabins 239-255

Each of labels pointed in a different direction, J

opened his mouth.

Ariel cut him off. "We're going to the hangar, end of story." She started running in that direction, brooking no arguments.

J agreed, though something told him that the escape pods could prove the easier route. Never the less, he sprinted to catch up to Ariel. The two of them ran through a maze of corridors eventually ending up in an enormous hangar. J gazed down onto the metal floor, not a single ship remained.

"Great. Now what're we gonna do?" He threw his arms up in the air, his hands landing on his head. His rifle swayed over his shoulder.

A shot whizzed over his head, he turned to see multiple mediators advancing on them. Ariel slapped the door control, closing it as she fired two shots, hoping to disable the controls. She nudged J forward onto the hangar floor.

"We gotta keep moving."

"But where to? The ships are gone. I had a feeling we should've taken the escape pods."

Ariel glared at him her hard look softened as her gaze moved past him.

"What?"

She ran by him, grabbing his hand, her soft small hand caressing his. Inside, he smiled. There was no time for enjoyment, they needed to find some way to escape. Right now it felt as if it would take a miracle to save them. Ariel tugged him along then released him to gain

382

more speed. She sped toward the ten story hangar doors, still closed, not allowing anything in or out. The ship shook from a great blast, knocking both of them to the floor.

Ariel pushed herself up. "Must be the Parádeisos engaging, we don't have much time."

She stumbled over, grabbing him again as the ship rattled a second time, each time feeling like an earthquake under his feet. J searched up ahead, a symbol of a space helmet was etched in blue above a smaller door on the edge of the platform. Shots began skipping off the floor around them, J twisted his head around to see multiple mediators and what looked like two E-Rats running toward them. He dug deep, sprinting as hard as he could, his breath labored. Ariel was keeping pace, she was fast, much quicker than he would have imagined in the state they were both in. She was working overtime as well. They met the wall, Ariel punching in codes to hack the door. J spun around, taking a knee to steady his shots. He fired, taking down the closest two, the others continued their advance.

"Better hurry up, they're coming."

"Not helping, J," she fired back. "Aha!"

The door opened and she hopped in. J inched back, still firing at the mediators, they were getting closer and their aim better. One glanced off his shoulder causing him to slouch momentarily. He fought through the pain, firing back then felt Ariel's hand pull him in and shut the door behind him. He investigated the room to figure out what could have caused Ariel to choose to come here. It was filled with space suits along with large backpacks.

"You planning on doing a moonlit space walk?"

She tossed a suit to him. "Yep, and you're my date."

She was already nearly undressed. J froze. One of these days they'd talk about her propensity for shucking off her clothes at inopportune times. He shook his head, snapping back to reality. The sound of banging came from the door, and ship rattled again. J's legs became wobbly, attempting to maintain his footing. He glanced over to Ariel who was now slipping on a half square, half rounded backpack.

"What's that?" J continued working as fast as he could, fumbling with the suit, his shoulder shooting pain down his arm and chest.

"It's our spaceship."

J raised an eyebrow.

"Just put one on."

She slid a backpack over to him then attached a helmet to her suit. J finished the suit, the banging intensifying at the door. The pack was much lighter than it appeared, he slipped it on connecting four of the five straps, two on each side. He slapped on a helmet, the menu appearing, and disabled it as he'd done before. The door shook again, he turned to Ariel.

"You missed one," she trotted over to him, bent down and reached between his legs. His face flushed bright red. "Crap."

J's eyes flicked side to side then down. "What?"

"Open the emergency comm channel."

She snatched the dangling strap, pulling it through his legs to the front and attaching it to the other four.

J repeated the words, as he finished, audio came ringing into his ears.

"If you can hear this, we'll be detonating in one minute. Our ship can't take much more damage, the casualties are too heavy. God bless."

It was the Admiral speaking, he must've been transmitting in the blind, hoping they'd hear him. *Would've been nice to have known that sooner, not that it would've done much good.* The voice switched to a woman's, counting down from 59. The door burst open, Ariel pushed him aside, picking up her rifle as she fired at the incoming horde. The first mediator dropped into a heap the second stumbling over him.

"Find the control panel!"

"Fifty seconds until detonation."

J was laying on his back like a turtle, his arms and legs kicking in the air. He pulled himself to one side, rolling over, his rifle was laying a foot away. He dashed to it. Gaining a knee, he let a barrage of fire go, dropping the next mediator. He advanced on the door.

"Forty Seconds."

"I'll take the door, you get the controls."

Ariel didn't question, it made sense. She knew what she planned and target practice didn't require much thought. Her head swung around searching the walls, in her haste to find the suits, she had forgotten to identify the panel. She looked past J who was still advancing toward the door, large pack and all. Behind him, on the wall, was the control panel. She huffed as she bolted for the controls, sliding to a stop beside him their packs bouncing off each other.

"Twenty-five seconds."

J stumbled forward, throwing his aim off. One of the bolts danced around the room, nearly hitting them. He steadied himself as an E-Rat stepped through the threshold.

"Twenty seconds."

"Whatever you're going to do, do it fast!"

Ariel hit the final button of the sequence, the E-Rat disappeared. J felt the suction coming from the door and scrambled to hold onto something, his hands slapping at every surface around. Ariel attempted to grab a handle on the wall, her fingers slipping off the edge. Her body careened into J's and they bounced around like ping pong balls slipping out the small door.

"Fifteen seconds."

CHAPTER THIRTY FOUR

The hangar floor appeared then the stars swam in J's vision as he spun uncontrollably in zero G. His head was becoming dizzy, he closed his eyes, attempting to remove the sensation from his body.

"Tell the suit to stabilize," he heard Ariel say.

"Stabilize, suit."

He opened his eyes as the sound of hissing surrounded him, the spinning stopped, the stars became fixed. Lights flashed in front of him, fighters flew around, blasts and missiles zipped by, his mind blocked out all sound. The two battleships came into view, each one with gigantic tubular metal protrusions recessed into the ship's hull, firing large blasts individually. Both ships were slugging it out while fighters engaged all around. Ariel was between the ships and him, they'd been thrown out the far side of the Forte away from the battle. The whole scene played out like a movie as he floated there, weightless.

"One second, Detonation."

Suddenly, the Forte shuddered then glowed as the bridge exploded into a ball of flame. Metal tumbled into space, the ship's cannons fell silent. J floated quietly, contemplating what just happened. Takamori, Novikov gone, they had to be, they were on the bridge. His shoulders sagged as he watched the fighters disengage, Dmitry must've recalled them and the ones from the Forte floated motionless. He smiled, gazing at Ariel floating only a few feet away, the threat was neutralized. His visor flashed a message, "incoming transmission". He accepted to see Dmitry smiling back at him.

"You two ready to come aboard?"

J didn't respond, just pressed his head back drawing in a deep breath.

"Max will be with you shortly. How's your oxygen?"

He read the screen, the oxygen level stated 95%.

"95."

"96," Ariel said, right after. If he'd seen her face, it would've had a devious grin attached to it.

"Good, that should hold you until Max arrives. Nice job you two, Admiral Titov out."

J floated in his suit, the view serene, the stars, the ships, the debris floating in slow motion. Zero gravity felt amazing, something he was still unused to. A smile came to his face realizing what they'd just done. The Reprobi Angeli were vanquished, the disk was secure and most importantly, Ariel was with him.

"You okay over there?" Ariel asked, firing her thrusters to float toward him.

"How do I control this thing?"

"Your thumbs. Feel for the pads inside your gloves."

J wiggled his thumbs, the pads touching a small dome inside. He lightly pressed the one on his right hand and the pack spun, he let go and the suit stabilized like a rock. He played with the other hand, flipping himself backward. He stopped as the Moon came into view.

Ariel stopped next to him. "Whatcha looking at?

He turned to gaze into her beautiful ice blue eyes. "Something I only thought existed in a dream, a movie, a fantasy. Yet, it's all too real."

His stare drifted to infinity as he was lost in his thoughts. *What was on the disk? What was the next task? Would he ever meet his father as Dr. Huergo said?* So many questions overwhelmed him, his smile dwindled. Ariel mirrored his position gazing at the Moon.

"Must be quite a sight, never seeing something like this before. Thinking the Moon was solid, only a lifeless rock no man ever touched. Not a place run by corrupt, mind-bending bureaucrats. Those days are over, because of you. J."

She grabbed his hand as the ship came into view.

"Heard you guys needed a ride."

At this point, even Max's voice sounded great. Floating in space was an experience, but he wanted solid ground, he wanted peace. Max slid the ship in next to them, opening the cargo bay, loading them both in. Ariel and J braced themselves as the door shut, awaiting gravity to return. Once it did, they removed their helmets. Ariel snatched his suit by the chest with both hands, pulling him in for a kiss. J melted, embracing her back. She leaned back, her icy blue eyes flickering in the light.

"We did it, J. We did it."

She smiled, showing all her teeth. J returned it, he felt so happy in that moment. His body tingled, he pulled in a long breath, holding it a minute before exhaling. His adrenaline was dissolving, his shoulder began to pulse and pain radiated outwards. He clutched it with his hand.

"You alright?" Ariel asked, her eyes big. She unzipped his suit, pulling it over his shoulder. She nudged him down into one of the seats.

"You need medical attention, I'll get the first aid kit."

Ariel returned with the medical wand and began treating his wound.

"If you wannna do this again, I say we get another set of those invincible suits."

"Why, you like feeling like Iron Man?"

J tilted his head like a golden retriever. Ariel laughed, she still enjoyed puzzling him.

"Like I said before, when things cool down, we're going to have a long history lesson."

The ship's speakers turned on. "On final approach, might want to take your seats."

Ariel spun into the seat next to him holding his hand. The ship came to rest, the cargo bay door descending into a ramp. They peeked outside. Admiral Titov, Grant and about a dozen soldiers stood awaiting their arrival. J peeled himself out of the seat, following Ariel of out the ship.

"There are the heroes!"

The men and women behind the Admiral clapped and cheered, J forced a smile. He'd never become comfortable with the accolades after a win, this felt the same yet on a grander scale, something he thought he would have felt in college, or if lucky the pros, this pushed all of that to the curb.

"You have the disk?" Dmitry asked.

J dug into his suit. Finding the pocket he'd placed it in, he pulled it into view. Dmitry smiled back, giving him a slight nod. V tightened her gaze on J then came running up.

"Let me see that," she said, pulling him down to her level. "You need to have that fixed up. Used a medical wand I imagine."

J peeked over to Ariel who was laughing at the sight. J attempted to pull away but V held strong.

"Shall we find out what's on that disk?" Dmitry asked, interrupting the examination.

V spun around, standing tall. "Not until I patch him up. He's a wreck and needs some rest."

Dmitry laughed, looking down at the tiny doctor. "Very well, we've waited this long, I'm sure we can wait a few more hours."

J handed him the disk as V dragged him toward the medical bay. Ariel marched along behind them, quickening her pace to catch up.

"We'll get this prepped for when you're ready, J."

Dmitry's voice trailed off as the three of them walked out of earshot. Ariel was walking beside them now, she studied V. "What's going on V? You know J isn't that hurt."

V looked behind them, then to each side. "I just don't trust Dmitry. Something seems off and his crew is a little suspect as well."

"Why do you say that?" J asked.

"Just seems like too good of timing that he helped you escape, aided us in taking down the Reprobi Angeli. I get a weird feeling around him."

They continued their walk, reaching the medical facility.

"I haven't noticed anything strange," Ariel said.

"Me either," J added.

V shook her head, opening the medical door. "Why don't you sleep on it. Dmitry seemed very eager to see what's on the disk, maybe you should view it first. I don't know, but you do need me to fix that shoulder of yours. Those medical wands aren't the most efficient and leave much to be desired."

J agreed that he could use the sleep, his body was worn not only from the wound, but everything else. V took him into a surgical room and prepped him for a minor surgery. She informed him she could operate while he was awake, but insisted on putting him to sleep. His body would recuperate quicker that way. After some convincing he relented, as Ariel thought they could all use some rest. J laid on the table as the sleep agent was administered, his body softened as he fell asleep.

His eyes opened to a picturesque view of a beach, waves crashing on the sand. Birds flew overhead, the sun warmed his face. His hand held a drink, he took a sip, a prisoner to his movements.

"Arcturus, imagine this being ours, with a family."

J knew that voice, but it was softer than he remembered it, more loving. His head turned to the right, Cyrellia came into view staring off into the beach.

"You know it would be for the betterment of the people, one union, one set, one family ruling all."

"You ask for a dictatorship. We were built on democracy, that would be a monarchy. You think one family would always hold the people's welfare above all else? You are sadly mistaken."

"Arcturus, dear, you are the most intelligent man on the council, the most influential besides myself. It only makes sense that we could rule better together, without dealing with the democracy. You have to know it slows down progress."

"I'm sorry, I've made up my mind, Cyrellia. Though you carry my child, I will not marry you. I know your motives and they are not for family. I will stay true to the council and obey the collective's rules, but I will not set up a monarchy."

Cyrellia touched the air, the beach faded away leaving behind her penthouse atop the TK building. She tightened her jaw. "Very well, then the baby will die."

J woke up, rubbing his eyes. His body felt like new, but his mind was terrified. He sat up, adjusting to his surroundings.

"Wow, what was that?" he said out loud to himself.

He hopped off the bed, exiting the recovery room. Ariel was knocked out on a sofa bed in the next room. He bent down to give her a kiss on the forehead, her eyes fluttered awake. She breathed in deeply.

"Oh, you're awake. Did I fall asleep?"

He nodded as she sat up stretching.

"How're you feeling?"

J rubbed his shoulder rolling his arm around in the socket. "I feel good, that sleep was what I needed. Could've done without the dream though."

V walked in as Ariel was about to ask about it.

"J, good timing. I was coming to check on you. Dmitry wanted to know how much longer until you'd be able to unlock the disk."

Now fully awake, J was eager to see what was on it as well. They headed to the briefing room. Dmitry thought it best to show the contents in a smaller setting and there was no opposition. When they arrived, Dmitry was already there along with his two guards.

"Welcome. Sleep well I trust? V is the best doctor Atlantis has to offer."

J shuffled in, searching for his friends. "Yes, it was good...where's everyone else?"

"This is it. I wanted to have it a small group. None of us know what's on the disk, the information could be sensitive."

J didn't like that idea. His friends had given so much for him, now he was to shut them out? He weighed his options, quickly coming to a conclusion. "I want them here, Zane, Grant," he hesitated. "Max."

Dmitry crunched his nose up then released it. "Very well. I don't have a choice in the matter it seems."

He waved to one of the guards to go fetch the others.

J took a seat across the table while V and Ariel joined him. He looked out at the Earth floating in the window amongst the stars, still in disbelief like a child who only recently found out there was no Santa. They all remained silent, awaiting the others. J continued to gaze out the window, the others straggled in, first Zane then Max. J almost regretted asking for him as he strutted in taking a seat next to Ariel. Grant came in last with Tara behind him, Ariel made a face at her as she rounded the table taking a seat.

"Good. We're all here. Now, shall we get started?"

J nodded his head, the two guards shut the door standing on each side.

"Are they staying in here?"

Dmitry raised his eyebrows then nodded to the door, the guards left, shutting it behind them.

"Ready now?"

J nodded as Dmitry's fingers danced on the table, opening up multiple menus. The screen behind him became opaque. Tapping a final button, the screen read "DNA and face recognition required." Dmitry pointed to a shape of a hand glowing on the table, J reached up and planted his palm on it. He looked down at a picture of himself below, a horizontal line zipped down it.

"Scan complete. Welcome, J. Files unlocked, welcome video activated."

They all waited in anticipation, J leaned into the table as far as he could awaiting something on the screen. Arcturus appeared. He was older than in the dreams, and memories. He wore a beard, salt and peppered, his clothing was that of a deep red robe laced with gold accents. In the background was a simple room with a table and chair pushed against the wall.

"J, I know you want answers and I wish I could answer them right now. But I promise that I'll deliver them to you soon. First, there is another task I have for you. On this disk is a list of items you'll need. In order to keep them safe, I've placed them in various locations throughout Earth, away from TK's eyes. I pray they'll all be there when you receive this message. Every one of the items must be collected in order to continue your journey. After you collect the items and implement the steps I've provided, you'll be ready to travel to Acadia and remove Cyrellia from power. You must stop her from destroying another planet. I will meet you there."

The video cut out. He snapped his head over to Ariel, confused and conflicted. Ready to lash out, when she opened her mouth.

"I think we're about to build an army."

END OF BOOK TWO

FLAT EARTH SERIES

If you enjoy sci-fi action adventure and want to see what happens next with J and Ariel, stay tuned for book three of my Flat Earth Series. If you would like to be notified when the next book launches, sign up for my mailing list.

or visit my website at:

www.g11wingedhussar.com

or E-mail me at:

g11wingedhussar@gmail.com

I would love to hear from you and don't forget to leave a review!

ACADIA

FLAT EARTH BOOK THREE

BRENT GOLEMBIEWSKI

About the Author:

Brent Golembiewski is a U. S. Air Force veteran with 20+ years of service. He started his career as an enlisted troop, working as an Electronic Warfare Technician, and completed it as an officer, never working a day as a Helicopter Evaluator Pilot, flying the mighty UH-1N "Huey". After retiring from the USAF, he began Valkyrie Air, providing aircraft charter operations for people who find value in time. He met the love of his life in the second-worst place he'd ever been stationed and she's still on active duty. Together they have two boys (the terrible Ts) a giant Yeti, a miniature ThunderCat and one old caricature of a dog that will never die.

For more information and to subscribe visit
www.g11wingedhussar.com

Made in the USA
Columbia, SC
18 December 2020

28706689R00250